THE WISDOM OF DISHONOR

THE CULT OF ANICK

Book Two

L.E. Brooks

Blueflight Press, LLC

2024

The Wisdom of Dishonor
The Cult of Anick: Book Two

This is a work of fiction. Names, characters, places, organizations, events, and incidents are either the product of the author's imagination or are used fictitiously. Any resemblance to actual persons, living or dead, events, or locales is entirely coincidental.

Text copyright © 2024 by L. E. Brooks

All rights reserved.

No part of this book may be reproduced, stored in a retrieval system, or transmitted in any form or by any means, electronic, mechanical, photocopying, recording, or otherwise, without the express written permission of the copyright owner except for the use of quotations in a book review.

Published by Blueflight Press LLC, PO Box 652, Bettendorf, IA 52722.

www.blueflightpress.com

Cover design by Rebecca Frank

Book design and interior illustrations by Leo Hartas

ISBN: 978-1-962922-03-6 (paperback)

ISBN: 978-1-962922-04-3 (ebook)

ISBN: 978-1-962922-05-0 (audiobook)

For Elsie—wherever you are.

Beware!

This novel contains:

- An open-door sex scene. This is an *adult* fantasy novel with a romance. If you didn't catch that after the first book, then I'm not sure what to tell you. Spice rating: 3/5.

- Mention of sexual assault (off page) and moments of dubious consent (on page).

- Copious swearing. I don't know who needs to hear this, but the author is not their characters. I honestly have very little control over what these weirdos say.

- Have you ever found a typo in a novel and wished you could report it? Now you can! This novel is professionally edited in the same manner as any traditionally published novel. However, we all know that sometimes errors still make it through. Please feel free to email any typos you find to lebrooks@brooksbooks.net. Thank you.

- A black-and-white map. A color map, glossary, magical system index, and more fun stuff can be found at www.brooksbooks.net or scan this QR code:

IRONWOOD FOREST
Noble River
OXEN FIELDS
GROVES FARM
Neesee River
Caravan Trail
THE WALL
AETOS PALACE
GREY DISTRICT (Wall Slums)
NEESEE
GROVES TRADERS
EBOROS ESTATE
Bridgestone
BAY of MARCH
CENTRAL DISTRICT
WEST BRIDGE
EAST BRIDGE
Mines
GALE RIDGE MOUNTAINS
DOWNTOWN NEESEE
RIVER DISTRICT
Neesee River
SCHOOL of NOBLE ARTS (SONA)
Caravan Trail
Meriweather Sea
SEAL BEACH
THE RHOYA
Standing Bridgestone
AARON'S COTTAGE
O'FELD COMMERCIAL DOCKS
Caravan Trail
Jarring Weed Grove
O'FELD FARM
OARDOO FIELDS
O'FELD HOMESTEAD
Bridgestone
Priscilla Bay
MOORE FARM
VILLAGE of SEAGRAL
Shadow Caves
MERIMO ISLAND
The Province of SOUTHERN GALE
N
W
E
S

Chapter One

In the queen's garden, there is a key that opens up our destiny.
Covered in mud and blood, it pleads the wisdom of dishonor.
It helps you face your enemy and searches out what seems empty,
But if you wait, and don't misread, you may avoid a slaughter.
It dreams of time beyond the trees and sounds the call to mutiny
Because it cannot help but lead the horses to the water.
For though we may not all agree, our hearts are longing to be free
And so, we'll follow, fight, and bleed until death weighs upon her.
Then through the rubble and debris, the saplings grow in twos and threes
From stone to stone, their shade of creed expanding ever broader.
And so, my dragon, use the key; and in time, I'll have with me
The only thing I'll ever need, my husband, son, and daughter.

—*The Crystal Key*

In the bright glare of morning, I rode Fantasma bareback, flying down the grassy trail away from the stables and toward the bridgestone. The wind whipped my face like a solid mass, stinging my cheeks and tugging at my hair as I hunched over, riding low against her dapple-gray coat.

In the waking world, Fantasma hated having her mane pulled and would toss her head repeatedly if I tried, but in my dreams, she and I were one. I squeezed my legs together and gripped her silvery mane to steady myself.

The ride shouldn't have taken more than a few minutes, yet even as the trees were a blur of brown and green, we didn't progress. Frustrated, I glanced down to see that the ground wasn't even moving. Somehow, we simultaneously galloped and were also frozen in place.

When I raised my eyes again, Fantasma had disappeared. I stood on the trail alone, baking under a sun that felt more like LA in the summer than my beloved redwoods.

Through the trees, just ahead, I could make out the carved *X* of the bridgestone. A man with sandy blond hair and a red beard knelt atop the large flat rock, carving with a chisel and hammer.

He caught my eye, then smiled and raised his hand in greeting. His face was open and warm, and I thought, *There's my friend. I need to hurry.*

I tried to walk, but my feet sank into the ground like I'd stepped into wet cement. Glancing down, I realized it *was* cement, and now I'd sunk down to my ankles. I swung my arms, which only threw me off-balance. Though I called for help as I fell, the bridgestone was now farther away and my friend couldn't hear me. He knelt again, chipping away at his task, my existence forgotten.

I sank to my waist, and my attempts to lift myself up resulted in my hands becoming stuck as well. Though I wasn't deep enough yet, a chalky flavor filled my mouth, my brain's interpretation of what cement must taste like. As it sucked me under, a deep growl vibrated through my body, a sound that came from behind me.

THE WISDOM OF DISHONOR

In the time it took to look over my shoulder, day became night. A white wolf towered over my sunken form, its eyes glowing bright red in the dark. He directed his wrath at a man who floated beside me, just above the ground and unaffected by the trap I'd fallen into. I tilted my chin up to see the face of the ghost giant. He grew as I sank, his features remaining out of focus as he rose upward toward dark clouds in an even darker sky.

Bert, I thought. *No, that's not his real name.*

The man spoke, but I couldn't understand him because I now had cement in my ears. All that was left above the ground were my eyes, staring up, up, up. I couldn't breathe, but I was unafraid. Somewhere in my mind, I knew this couldn't be real, but I also knew that it was important. The ghost giant wanted to tell me something.

What's Bert saying? I closed my eyes before the ground swallowed me. *He's calling my name.*

"Lee," a deep voice whispered. Aaron gently shook me awake.

"Hmm?" I opened my eyes to bright morning light shining down through the oculus. Blinking at the unwelcome glare, a dull throb settled behind my eyes and sank into my head. I was still dead tired, having only slept a few hours, and couldn't help but squeeze my eyes closed again. The blanket became a soft shield against the world as I yanked it over my head and tucked my face down into the pillow.

"We have to get going," Aaron said, shaking the bed as he scooted toward me. He pulled me against his warm body, then tugged the blanket down to kiss the back of my neck. I groaned in pleasure at the heat of his mouth against my skin. He chuckled, probably because he knew exactly what his kiss did to me. This is how our mornings always started on the days when Aaron was home.

Home.

It was no wonder I'd settled in. I had loved Jorin's farmhouse from the beginning. It was elegant yet efficient, with two stories, a cellar, and a hidden attic containing Aaron's bedroom. Every inch of it was handcrafted and lovingly maintained. From the transformed wooden floor to the spiraling dome roof, a lot of thought and effort had gone into its creation.

Transformation, Aaron had explained, wasn't just a magic trick. It required raw materials and meticulous planning, not to mention an artistic eye. Aaron's grandfather had possessed that talent in spades. He'd been a master artisan in the Woodworkers Guild, using a brightly colored veneer to create the illusion of jarring weed hanging down around the domed ceiling. The flowering trees burst with fuchsia while a crimson dragon peered down from the canopy. At the peak of the dome, a piece of clear glass was set into a circle of marble, an oculus, which let light into the room.

I felt at home there, and I could see myself staying with Aaron indefinitely, following the same routine every morning that we'd had for the last two months. He would wake me up with his too-hot kiss, make tea, then leave me to pore through books and practice my fragmentation techniques.

Later, he would teach me one of Aunt Clare's recipes, which he said I picked up surprisingly quickly. Or I would work in the garden while he took the skiff out fishing, sometimes taking Ward with him, though not without calling him either a "dumbass" or a "smartass" at least once, his two favorite Earth insults.

It had been a beautiful little life.

Now, Ward, my best and oldest friend, was missing, and there were people in the room with us, hiding just as we were from Seleca and her Ministry cronies.

"Are they still on the rug?" I mumbled.

"Mmhmm," he answered, then I felt his teeth on my skin, nipping at my neck, then my shoulder. His broad hand massaged my other shoulder, then trailed down my spine, a wordless invitation.

"You better stop that before it's too late," I whispered. He groaned quietly, pulled away, and sat up. I was glad one of us had some restraint.

I rolled toward Aaron and sat up next to him. He planted another kiss on my temple and then got out of bed, straightening his tunic. I took the hand he extended to me and stood to survey the room.

Ellis still slept in Ward's cushioned reading chair, his head lobbed to one side, and his legs draped awkwardly over the chair's other arm. He'd probably wake up in pain from how he'd slept.

Markus was on the braided rug next to the chair, face down and snoring. He shared a blanket with Falon, whose long, slender frame was curled on his side, one arm folded beneath his head. His eyes were open and averted, but he raised them to meet mine. When he saw me staring at him, his lips parted, and he looked quickly away again.

What am I going to do about this guy?

Falon hadn't been able to take his eyes off me since I'd saved his brother's life. Perhaps that was what prompted his interest. Or maybe, as I later discovered, it was because Falon was a minor pariah within his own family and saw me as a kindred spirit. I'm sure the fact that women were scarce in his life didn't help either.

Whatever the cause, his interest presented a potential problem since he had Transmutation, a reservoir with the unfortunate side effect of hypersexuality.

Over the course of the last two months, I'd made my way through nearly every banned book in Aaron's library and had read that fragment use always had unintended consequences. Sometimes, like with my increased lifespan, the side effects were beneficial. Often, they were not.

Evocation, for example, lets the fragmentor create fire but causes an unnatural increase in body temperature and makes it difficult to control emotions, especially anger. I had seen this in Aaron more than once, and it still made me nervous.

Falon and Markus both had Transmutation, a fragment that lets the user turn one substance into another, but which shortens lifespan and magnifies the sex drive. If I was right about Falon's crush on me, then I needed to be more careful about public displays of affection. In fact, given the extreme sexual repression that this world suffered, that was probably a good policy in general.

We'd gotten to know the men a little better the previous night and had started using the word "crew" when referring to them, a word borrowed from Fitch and Shane, who lived aboard fish-herding ships. I wasn't convinced, however, that the crew's deference to Aaron would extend to me.

This was a world where women were often unsafe, even in their own homes, and the previous day's confrontation with Axel had taught me that I was vulnerable despite my multiple reservoirs.

Axel, a high-ranking magister in the Ministry, had attacked the house during a torrential downpour, and one of his minions had kidnapped Ward, my best friend. It didn't matter that I had so many reservoirs. If Aaron hadn't been there, I'd probably be sitting next to Ward in a cage somewhere.

I shuffled over to the counter where I'd laid out the clothes that had gotten wet during our stormy confrontation. A brown tunic taken from Jorin's closet and hemmed to my diminutive stature lay next to the red tank top and blue leggings I'd brought with me from Earth. The tunic, made of a light linen material, was dry, but my Earth clothes were still soaked from wearing them in the downpour.

The brown tunic wasn't the warmest option for traveling but would at least be comfortable, though I was hesitant to wear men's garb in front of all these strangers. The last thing I needed was to showcase how bizarre I was, but there was nothing to be done about it. It was cold outside. I couldn't wear wet clothes.

I repacked my bag, leaving the tunic out and rolling the wet clothing tightly to minimize getting other items in the bag wet. Next, I packed a book about bridges that Aaron had recommended as well as one on Conjuration, the spirit fragment.

An hour later, after a light breakfast of a warmed grain cereal called goshe, we were all ready to go. Shane and Fitch both offered to carry my pack for me, but I declined, not wanting to appear weak.

I did accept the men's offer to help with sailing, however. As members of the Fish-herders Guild, one of the only guilds that didn't require a greater reservoir, Shane and Fitch would be able to help us sail Jorin's boat up the coast to Neesee.

I wanted to teleport there, of course, but I didn't know exactly how it worked yet, and I was deathly afraid of accidentally sending us out into space. Given the very real risk, we trudged out into the cold to travel the hard way, Fitch leading while Aaron brought up the rear.

It had stopped snowing, but the beach was draped in bridal white, only turning to gray where the waves gulped at the sand. My heart fluttered for a second as I peered out at the ocean, squinting into the early morning light that slanted across the water from a west-rising sun. The Meriweather Monster, or Merimo, as Aaron and his family called him, was nowhere to be seen, and I sensed no resonance.

Maybe we can take the boat out to see Merimo after we've saved our friends, I thought as we hiked out to the dock.

"Oh, is that all you're doing now?" Spirit asked.

I jumped in surprise, then scanned my surroundings guiltily. Spirit had silently appeared directly behind the group, a habit that, as a ghost, she found very amusing.

"I thought you were planning to save the world? Now you're just gonna take your friends on a fishing trip, then head home?"

"I don't know," I said, shrugging. I knew Spirit was just teasing, but she was still right. We were there for more than just sightseeing.

Aaron glanced over his shoulder toward the sound of Spirit's voice, then stopped short. I backtracked to stand beside him. "You can see her now, can't you?" I asked. Aaron didn't answer but gawked, wide-eyed.

Spirit grinned, her white-blond hair and whiter teeth practically glowing in the dim light. She wore a deep red gown that hugged her ample curves and stood out starkly against the pale landscape. It stretched out behind her, floating atop the snow. She was stunning, as always, and Aaron ogled her just a little too hard. Not that I needed to worry about him leaving me for a ghost, but he was not *not* staring at her breasts.

I narrowed my eyes, then walked in between the two, facing Aaron and blocking his view of the crimson goddess.

"Um, excuse me, *beloved*? I asked you a question. Were you planning to answer, or should I just ask Spirit to tell me what you're thinking right now?"

Spirit giggled, and a cough came from one of the men. Aaron blinked a few times but still didn't respond.

"You can't," I said.

"Can't what?" he asked absently.

"Touch her."

The crew erupted in muted snickers. Aaron grimaced, turning toward the beach to cut through the group, the back of his neck flushed red as he stalked away from me.

"I didn't even tell her that!" Spirit called after him, laughing so hard that she snorted. I think I liked it better when Aaron couldn't see her.

We trekked the rest of the way through the pine and deciduous trees that surrounded the house, then walked toward the beach. The air was frigid, wet, and smelled of the dark brown seaweed that lined the beach.

Perched atop a sand dune and surrounded by pale driftwood and tufts of scrub grass, lay a truck-sized boulder marked with a large *X*. They called this the "sight boulder," as they used it mainly to sit upon when looking out to sea. Neither Aaron nor I had ever witnessed the bridgestone being used for Teleportation, but the marking was unmistakable.

My thoughts drifted to the strange dream. Who was the man carving the markings into the stone? His smile had been warm and welcoming, like a friend who'd been waiting for me to arrive.

Thick fog obscured our view down the beach or out to sea, and the waves sounded like a hundred freight trains all headed for a single destination. There was another sound, too, a new, resonant *ding* that pulsed out of the fog.

"Wait," Aaron called, waving the crew behind the cover of the sight boulder. He scaled the log to the top and rested on his stomach, waiting. The sound became louder until I could make out the ringing of a bell. Impatient, I scaled the log and lay down next to him.

"What is it?" I asked.

"A sailboat coming up from the south," he whispered. "Spirit, can you go see who it is?"

Spirit blinked out, then returned to the top of the boulder, causing Aaron to nearly fall off the side when she appeared next to him. It was still creepy to see her move like that, especially when she giggled while doing it.

"Two men," she said. "One older and one younger, and a woman who is very pregnant."

"Does the older man have burn scars on his hands and arms?" Aaron asked.

"Yes," Spirit said.

Aaron stood. "It's Jorin," he said, frowning. "He must have Terik and Farrah with him. Let's go wait for them at the dock."

Aaron had probably frowned because the couple didn't have permission from the Ministry to have children. I had no idea what would happen if someone found out.

We descended the log, Aaron leading. He instructed the men to stay back to avoid startling his family, but I went along.

The dark gray sand was perfectly even, pressed flat by the tide and subsequently undisturbed. Aaron supported my elbow as we walked across the soft sand, leaving behind a trail of wet footprints. I didn't actually need help with a little thing I like to call *walking*, but if I'm being honest, I liked how he took care of me. Though the feminist in me wanted to shout from the rooftops that I could handle wet sand without needing a fainting couch, I had to concede that I liked leaning on his strength.

What worried me was what might happen if that strength suddenly vanished. As devoted as Aaron seemed, I had known that same care and attention once before, and it had been shockingly easy for that person, Drew, to walk away. I hadn't even thought about committing myself to anyone since then. I never thought I would meet someone that might be worth the risk.

I wondered idly what Drew had done when I'd disappeared into the woods. The vindictive part of me, Evilina, smirked at the thought that she might be crying somewhere over me.

Aaron squeezed my hand, and I looked up to his ice-blue eyes staring at me. He always seemed to know when I was trapped in my thoughts.

"What are you thinking about?" he asked.

"The people I left behind," I answered. It was more or less true.

"What about them?"

I shrugged. "From their point of view, I disappeared without a trace. I'm sure they're worried about me."

Aaron nodded. "I get it, but that's not a problem you can solve right now. You'll read the bridge book on our way to Neesee. We'll get back to our families as soon as possible afterward. That is, if you don't get seasick. Have you ever sailed before?"

I shook my head. "Not really. I've taken a ferry, but I've never really traveled by boat."

"And did you get sick on the ferry?"

The taut line of my mouth must have been answer enough because Aaron chuckled. Yes, I had gotten very sick indeed. This would not be a pleasant journey.

It was a few minutes before the sailboat came into view. A bright swirl of orange and green on the mainsail cut through the fog as an outline of the hull appeared. An enormously tall man waved from the deck, and Aaron returned the wave, a rare grin spreading across his face. Another man, bulkier than the one I presumed to be Jorin, hunched beside him like a gargoyle.

As the sailboat drew closer to the dock, Jorin dropped the mainsail in a beautifully organized fold of heavy canvas. I wondered how he would manage to bring in the boat given the rough waters, but Jorin made it appear effortless. He used the waves to slip in smoothly behind the rocky outcropping that jutted from the beach at an angle, protecting the dock from the harsher waves.

"Ho there, Aaron!" Jorin bellowed as the boat approached. He was nearly bald, with only a wisp of steel-gray hair at the base of his head. He smiled broadly with two missing teeth, one on the top right and one on the bottom left, giving him the air of a human jack-o'-lantern. The rest of his teeth were crooked and yellow, and his face was beardless and deeply lined.

"I wondered if ya would be here," Jorin called from the boat. "I'm glad to see ya safe, nephew."

Jorin's accent was slightly different from Aaron's. He spoke more slowly with a little bit of a drawl, having traveled with the Caravan Traders from a province beyond the Gale Ridge Mountains. Though not an official guild, the Caravan Traders were powerful in their own right. As a youth, Jorin had worked as their scribe; a position Aaron had once hoped to attain prior to becoming an unemployable outlaw.

Jorin fit the sailboat snugly against the dock, using a long wooden rod to prevent the boat from smacking the dock as it came in. The rod had a hook on the end that he then used to pull in the boat the rest of the way. The other man, Terik, I presumed, assisted Jorin using his own hooked rod, then tossed a rope to Aaron, who tied the boat securely.

Terik vaguely resembled Aaron, though he appeared a few years older with brown eyes and paler skin. He was less handsome, too, with a long, beardless face and a weak chin. The deep scowl he wore didn't help either. He glared at Aaron, then eyed me, unconsciously twisting a silver cuff bracelet with a large, lime-green gemstone set into the band.

I tried to withhold judgment about his sour demeanor, suspecting that he wasn't pleased Aaron had brought a stranger to witness his illegally pregnant wife exiting the boat. Standing back from the reunion, I waited for Aaron to introduce me.

Jorin threw Aaron a second rope to secure, then disembarked, hopping easily across the gap between boat and dock. He embraced Aaron with a chuckle before he caught sight of me. The arms wrapped around Aaron's back were covered in horrific scars that disappeared under the sleeves of his tunic.

Aaron said something that I couldn't hear over the wind and waves, but which made Jorin's eyebrows climb his forehead. A smile grew on his face, then he strode toward me with Aaron on his heels.

Jorin's long legs covered the distance a little faster than I would have liked. After more than two months of waiting and worrying over his safety, a surge of irrational anxiety hit me over the head. Until that second, I hadn't considered that this was the man who took care of Aaron after his family abandoned him. It was the next best thing to meeting the parents.

I wore Jorin's own mud-brown tunic, sheared off roughly at the hem, with my blue windbreaker on top and ill-fitting leather leggings that I'd made myself. I looked ridiculous. I hadn't even properly brushed my hair or teeth since I'd arrived.

Dear lord, what was I thinking? I should have stayed with the crew. God, I hope he doesn't recognize his own tunic. A flush crept up my neck while Spirit giggled somewhere behind me.

Shut up, I thought. She laughed harder. I smiled through my annoyance as Jorin approached.

"Avelina Silva?" Jorin asked, grinning down at me with his comically bad teeth. He gave my clothing a once-over but didn't seem fazed. He really did seem like a jolly, nice man.

"Please, call me Lina," I said, craning my neck to peer up at him. He had to be eight feet tall. He was literally the tallest person I'd ever met—even taller than Ward. "And you're the famous Jorin that Aaron's been talking about all summer."

Yes, good start, I thought to myself. *Be flattering, but not too flattering. Don't overdo it. Don't underdo it. Shit! Stop overanalyzing and just be cool!*

I smiled as pleasantly as I could while Spirit continued to laugh behind me. Aaron gave me the *look* and then stretched his neck to peer quizzically at Spirit from around Jorin's tall body.

"It's very nice to meet you," I squeaked.

"Likewise, young lady," Jorin said. He probably guessed why I was nervous. I wasn't sure exactly how much he knew about Violet Atticus's predictions, but I was fairly certain that he knew, at the very least, that Aaron had been waiting around for someone for several years.

What if I don't live up to the hype?

Aaron's hand came to his mouth as he cleared his throat, then his thoughts came to me through Spirit. *Relax,* he thought. *You're doing fine.*

"Hey, Punkymidge," Terik said from down the dock. "You finally found someone small enough for you. Did you get her a high chair for the dining table?"

Punkymidge?

Aaron shrugged, rolling his eyes. *Nickname,* he thought to me through Spirit. *It's a small, annoying bug that harasses the oardoo.*

I turned back to the newcomer, narrowing my eyes. *I guess Terik is an asshole, huh? That's unfortunate. On the other hand, now I don't have to feel bad that we stole all his clothes.*

Spirit must have relayed my thoughts back to Aaron because he huffed out what sounded like a suppressed laugh. Jorin made a displeased sound, then he and Aaron turned to face Terik, who held the arm of the most beautiful woman I'd ever seen.

Farrah, I thought. *Now, here is someone who absolutely lives up to the hype.*

She looked like she was about a thousand months pregnant with octuplets and yet was somehow still way out of my league. Her enormous green eyes and full pink lips brought to mind a mythical goddess with the kind of beauty that penetrates your thoughts and lingers there uninvited. Yet, that wasn't what was so striking about her.

I could *feel* her. She exuded tranquility to the degree that everything seemed to stop when she approached. It felt like I'd established a Connection link to her through the air, sending me just one message: *Peace. All will be well.*

What is this? I wondered, in awe of her sheer force of presence. I recalled Aaron saying Farrah had greater Production, a fragment that helps things grow and flourish. But I felt nothing like that from Jorin, and he also had a Production reservoir.

Farrah has greater Production and lesser Projection, Aaron thought to me through Spirit. *She's not doing it on purpose—those two reservoirs just interact like that naturally.*

Wow, I thought. *What must it be like to go through life with such intense natural charisma? I could have used that in school.*

Terik escorted Farrah up the dock toward us, her cheeks flushed with the effort of moving her over-encumbered body. The breeze swept her ebony locks out to the side, like the wind itself wanted to steal her away. We all seemed to be rendered speechless by her calming energy, a phenomenon that could have made her famous on Earth as a natural "it girl."

As they drew closer, a realization struck me like a ton of bricks. Growing up, I'd always had a hard time making friends. My parents had insisted that it wasn't my fault, and that people just didn't understand me. In truth, I hadn't believed them, but had they been right all along? Perhaps *my* combination of reservoirs was the opposite of Farrah's, like *anti*charisma, making people wonder what the hell was wrong with me. Hell, it made me wonder the same thing.

Spirit quieted at the sight of Farrah, leaving us in silence other than the crashing waves beyond the rocky outcrop.

She's married, Lina. Quit staring.

You first, I responded, glancing down at Farrah's hand. A silver cuff bracelet on her left wrist matched the one that Terik wore on his right, but neither wore rings.

Aaron stared at Farrah for a before tearing his eyes away. I recalled the night we arrived at the farmhouse, when Aaron had given me a strange look while describing Farrah. I'd thought he was afraid I would be jealous of his description of her beauty, but now it seemed there was more to it.

My guess was that Farrah was a source of tension between the two cousins. I wondered if she'd married her second choice. I felt a knot developing in my stomach as I realized that Aaron's attractiveness was much more in alignment with Farrah's than my own.

Oh god, am I Aaron's second choice?

"No," Aaron said, glancing at me, then he turned back to Terik, who had a decidedly smug expression on his face, "but it appears you two are about to need a couple of high chairs yourself."

Oh right, the high chair comment. He's not even talking to me.

Aaron's eyes shifted to Farrah, then back down. "Hello, Farrah. You look well."

"Ha," Farrah responded. Her voice was deeper than I was used to in a woman, yet breathy and musical. "That's very charming, as I'm currently pretending to be a house." Farrah turned her lovely gaze back to me, and my emotions flitted between jealousy and desire. "And who is this?"

"This is Avelina Silva, of course," Jorin said, turning back to me. "The long-awaited Lina."

"Ah, the dog girl," Terik said.

I narrowed my eyes. "I guess so," I murmured, staring the man down.

Aaron had had enough. He positioned himself between me and Terik, taking my shoulders and physically turning me around to face away from his family. I didn't resist when he directed me to walk up the dock, keeping his arm around me.

"Can you be civil, please?" Farrah whispered.

"Listen to your bondmate, Terik," Jorin said loudly. "She's always been smarter than ya." Jorin walked on Aaron's other side. "Lina, please excuse my son. He's on edge, seeing as how he's about to become a father."

"It's all right," I said. "My presence is a bit of an unwelcome surprise, I imagine."

"About that," Aaron interjected. "Jorin, before we get too far, there are five more men up by the sight boulder."

"What?" Terik hissed. "You brought strangers here? Rhoya, Aaron! You always know the exact way to ruin everything."

Aaron ignored him. "Magister Axel attacked us last night." Jorin turned to Aaron, clearly alarmed but not nearly as shocked as I would have expected. "He brought six men with him," Aaron continued, "all in a Projection trance. He meant to kill me, burn the house down, and take Lina."

Jorin nodded, as if he'd expected as much. "What happened?"

Aaron paused, then said, "Axel is dead—or *was* dead. I'm not sure if he still is. Seleca showed up and collected his body. She might be able to bring him back."

Jorin closed his eyes, bringing his hand to his forehead. Terik and Farrah gaped at Aaron, dumbfounded.

"Bring him back?" Terik said. "Great goddess, that's—"

"Then what?" Jorin asked, interrupting. "What happened with the men?"

"Lina freed them from the Projection trance," Aaron said, "and healed them. They were nearly starved to death."

The group studied me, perhaps reassessing.

"That's impossible," Terik said. "You're mistaken. Only the projector can release a thrall."

"Not anymore," I said simply. "And they took my friend, Ward, as well as a couple others. I mean to rescue them."

"You're a healer?" Farrah asked.

I nodded reluctantly, not wanting to elaborate. The word "healer" had the connotation of prostitute in Neesee, and the last thing I wanted was Aaron's family thinking I turned tricks on the side. Not that I personally judged sex workers, but in Neesee, they were treated as state property.

"She has several greater and lesser reservoirs, actually," Aaron said, hugging me around the shoulders. "Protection, Connection, Absorption, and a few others."

"Oh, dear," Farrah said. "That's quite a combination. I thought you couldn't combine Protection and Absorption." Her eyes bounced from me to Aaron, then she seemed to notice something about him because she frowned. Dropping her gaze, she cradled her swollen belly under her arms.

The sky darkened, and thunder rumbled somewhere in the distance.

"Uh-oh," Spirit mumbled. *Uh... Lina? I may have messed something up.* She switched to internal communication so Aaron wouldn't hear her.

Aaron still had his arm around me, and I leaned into him. Ya know, because it was cold, not to make sure that everyone knew what our situation was. That would be petty and hypocritical.

What? I asked irritably.

I don't know how to tell you this, she answered. *Uh, did you notice Farrah and Terik's matching cuff bracelets?*

Yeah, what about them?

Well, Farrah just noticed Aaron wearing a bracelet, too, and she didn't show it, but she was pretty shocked.

Why? I asked, a sinking feeling building in my chest.

Well, Spirit thought to me, *on Monash, I guess they don't wear wedding rings. They sort of wear bracelets instead.*

Oh, I thought, then I lowered my eyes to Aaron's wrist. He wore the bracelet I'd given him the first week I'd arrived on Monash, the one Spirit had crafted with fire agate and aquamarine to help him control his reservoirs. It wasn't a cuff bracelet, but it was close.

Oh crap.

Chapter Two

Every dragon was a brilliant shock of color. Indeed, that is why a group of dragons is called a shock, but among all dragonkind, there was none more beautiful than she.

One of the primary reasons greater producers make such great farmers is that the weather seems to mysteriously give their crops exactly what they need. Unless, of course, that farmer is pregnant, in which case the weather goes batshit crazy.

By the time we got to the house, grapefruit-sized balls of ice hailed down from an angry sky. Farrah wasn't just upset. She was upset and wildly uncomfortable. Though we probably had reason for a rivalry, I felt so bad for her that I resolved to help however I could. I had, on occasion, taken care of pregnant horses, and she was almost as big as one. That's not fat-shaming but a literal fact.

The hasty walk from the boat to the house took a toll on the poor woman, and she collapsed onto Ward's favorite green couch the minute we stepped inside. Aaron relit the hearth using Evocation, prompting Terik to sit in a cushioned chair next to it to warm his feet. Jorin stood in the open doorway staring at the sky until it was safe to go outside again, then headed back out to attend to some unnamed duty.

"Farrah, can I get you some tea?" I asked. Over the last two months, herbal tea had taken the place of coffee. I was finally used to it, not that I wouldn't hunt down a cup of coffee the moment I had access again.

"That sounds like a dream, Lina, thank you. Is there peppermint?"

"There is," I said.

"That sounds good," Terik said. "I think I'll have some too."

"Oh, sorry," I said with a saccharine-sweet tone. "I only have enough for Farrah. What a shame." I headed to fetch the tea from a ceramic jar on the other side of the great room. Aaron followed me, chuckling under his breath.

As we walked away, Terik whispered something. Farrah answered, very much *not* in a whisper, "Well you should have thought of that before you called her a dog. I wouldn't serve you either."

The crew settled themselves at the giant table, waiting to hear the new plan now that Aaron's family had unexpectedly arrived. They chatted among themselves, avoiding the people whose house they'd inadvertently invaded.

"Gentlemen," Aaron said to them. "Don't get too comfortable. We depart for Neesee as soon as Jorin gets the boat squared away."

"Is there enough room for all of us aboard?" Ellis asked.

"It will be tight, and we may have to remove ballast, but it should be okay. There's a four-bunk cabin on board."

Aaron continued speaking with the men while I found the jar of loose peppermint tea, of which there was plenty. I stuffed some into the pot strainer with water, as Aaron had taught me, then carried the pot over to the hearth and hung it on the hook. Terik left the house to go help Jorin, so I sat down on the couch next to Farrah.

"So, Farrah, how are you surviving your pregnancy torture?" I asked. Farrah huffed a husky, melodious laugh, and I smiled at her.

"It's the pits," she said, stretching her back with a groan. "I can't wait for it to be over, but I'm scared too. I was supposed to be a twin, but the healer was delayed and my mother and brother both died during the birth."

I let that information bomb sit for a moment. "You're having twins?" I asked gently.

Farrah gave me a wan smile, then nodded.

"And you can't go to a healer because . . ." *Because it's an illegal pregnancy.*

Farrah's smile faded, then she looked down at her belly, her shoulders sagging. She was right to be scared. Childbirth in a world of no hospitals would be difficult enough, but twins? Without a healer to keep everyone alive, it could be deadly.

I paused, taking a breath. "I may be able to help you, if you want me to."

"How?"

Aaron was deep in conversation with Fitch, who was quickly becoming his friend and advisor. He glanced at me, smiled, then went back to his conversation. He appeared relaxed in a way I had never seen, like a weight had been lifted. His family was safe for now. I couldn't simply stand aside and let something bad happen to Farrah and her babies.

"Well, birthing twins will be difficult," I said, "but I can help you through labor using Protection. Or, if I can figure out how to use it, I can send you over to Earth using Teleportation. You could go to a hospital, where people go when they're sick or giving birth. They can help you there."

Farrah stared at me, not speaking for a moment. "It's true then," she whispered.

"What is?" I asked.

"You're the one Aunt Vi told us about. You are the one from over *there* who is supposed to change the future."

"I'm not sure what that means," I grumbled, the weight of the world unexpectedly settling on my chest. "If Violet saw what would happen, then how is that a change?"

Farrah sighed heavily. "I'm going to tell you something now, Lina," she said, lowering the volume of her voice so I could barely hear her. I leaned in. "I need you to listen carefully. When Violet left, she entrusted me with a message to give to you. I never told anyone because she asked me not to. This is for you alone, okay? You must promise not to tell Aaron."

"What is it?"

"The last part of the poem."

"There's another part?" I asked incredulously. Violet, Aaron's mother, had written a book containing a poem that was meant to act as a message to us. We'd used it to make a few key decisions, like staying in the house when it had been empty and freeing the enthralled men who were to become our crew members. Overall, however, the poem had seemed to me like an annoying waste of time that could have been replaced by two seconds of straightforward communication.

"Sort of," Farrah said. "It's more like a separate riddle, but I need your promise first. You can't tell anyone about this."

I cringed at the demand. How could I promise that? I had recently vowed to be more deserving of Aaron's trust after an awkward incident involving Ward and myself in a bed. I mean, it was completely innocent except for the part where I tried to hide it from Aaron, but it was a breach of trust nonetheless, and I had pledged to do better. Now here I was, already keeping secrets.

Why do you hate me, universe? I sighed. "Okay."

"Promise," she insisted, her expression serious.

"I promise," I said, returning her penetrating gaze with some difficulty. It was all I could do not to lower my eyes to her perfect rosebud mouth. *Sheesh. Get it together, Silva.*

"Because if you break your promise, I think bad things will happen."

"Okay, Farrah. I get it," I said, not quite concealing my annoyance. "I'll keep my promise. I swear."

She released a breath, then turned her eyes up to the ceiling as if to recall something she had memorized a long time ago. "Okay, here it is," she said, clearing her throat. "Once she knew, time split in two. One path left, straight toward death. One path right, chasing life. Though both are true, right's up to you. For right to be, use the key. Before the fire burns any higher."

You know, sometimes I think Seleca had a point when she complained about Violet's book. I would be giving the woman a resounding one-star review when I got back to Earth. I groaned in frustration as Farrah quietly laughed, her face lit up with a cheerful grin. The woman was so gorgeous it made my eyes hurt.

"She said you'd react like that."

"Oh? Did she tell you what her annoying little riddle meant?" I asked.

"Not exactly, but it has something to do with Anick. That much I know."

"Okay," I said. "Let me get the tea, then tell it to me again."

For the next several minutes, we drank peppermint tea and went over the riddle. After a few repetitions, I had it memorized.

"Once she knew," I said. "Seleca, maybe? As in, once she knew about my Protection?"

"Or maybe once she figured out how to use Precognition," Farrah suggested, "since it goes on to talk about time splitting in two, as in two possible outcomes for the future."

"That makes sense," I said. Farrah was smart, and she'd had years to think about what the riddle meant. I was lucky to have her here. Maybe that was the point. We could help each other.

"The middle part seems obvious. Choose the right future or die," I said bluntly.

"Yes, but is the 'straight toward death' part for you or for all of us?" Farrah asked.

"Damn. Another good point," I responded. "Okay, but how do I know how to go the right way? The riddle doesn't seem to answer that question, except to say that I need to use the key, whatever that is. I thought I *was* the key. Maybe I'm wrong about the whole interpretation of the original poem."

"Or maybe there's more than one key," Farrah said. "Just like there's more than one future."

I shook my head and ran a hand down my face. "Why did it have to be a riddle?"

"You know what's good about riddles?" Farrah asked. "They're easy to remember. She gave me that thing to memorize when I was ten. She probably just didn't want me to forget it."

"I can't do this," I whispered, covering my eyes with one hand. *Why me? I'm not smart enough to save the world.*

"She said you'd do that too," Farrah said softly. "I know you can do this because you've already done it. If you hadn't, then Violet wouldn't have seen it. You *can* do this."

A twinge of guilt nagged at me. Farrah was so uncomfortable and yet she was the one reassuring me. *No reason to be jealous*, I thought. *None at all.* I sighed again. *I'll work on it.*

"Thanks," I said. "You remind me of my friend, Spirit."

Farrah's leaf-green eyes crinkled at the corners. "Will you do me a favor?"

I nodded. "What?"

"Will you connect with my babies?"

"Oh, of course! I'd love to." I held my hand out, and she took it without hesitation. She had long, elegant fingers that were soft and warm. A frisson ran through me at the contact, and it occurred to me that her reservoirs were having a greater effect on me than I realized. I had to fight the urge to bow and kiss her hand as if she were the pope.

Resist, I ordered myself. *You're a damned grown-up.*

I closed my eyes determinedly, then delved into her as gently as I could manage. She had no Protection, but she had another form of resistance I hadn't encountered yet. It was more like a callus than a wall, like a toughened exterior developed from years of friction. She centered herself, taking a breath in and out before letting me in.

To feel another's emotions through Connection is a bit like diving deep into your own feelings. I'm often so preoccupied with events as they happen that I don't stop to analyze how I feel about them. I might get the vague notion that I'm uncomfortable with something, but until I put the brakes on to think about it, it's easy for me to put aside my feelings to deal with another day.

When I reached out to Farrah through Connection, it was like unexpectedly realizing that I was terrified about something and had been in denial. Her description of herself as scared was a vast understatement.

Suppressing a shudder as unanticipated anxiety coursed through me, I visualized the babies within her womb and reached out for them. The first one, a boy, was healthy. I smiled when I sensed him, still small enough to hold in one hand, and with a heartbeat nearly twice as fast as Farrah's.

Is that normal?

I thought back and recalled having learned something to that effect in one of my college science classes. The second baby, a healthy girl, also had that same strong, unusually quick heart rate. They were both asleep, but when I connected with them, they woke, opened their eyes, and stretched.

Farrah winced. "Oh," she said, running a hand over the side of her belly.

"I'm sorry. I woke them up. They're both small but healthy and . . . wait a second," I said, feeling a pulsing vibration. I sank deeper, examining the movement of the babies and trying to distinguish their individual bodies. *One, two . . . three. Damn.*

The third was smaller than the others, and barely moving. His heart rate was slower, too, though not as slow as Farrah's. I wasn't sure, but he seemed *too* sleepy, like he wanted to wake up but couldn't.

"What is it?" Farrah asked, sensing something was wrong.

"There's a third," I said.

Her eyes widened, then squeezed shut. "Oh goddess," she said.

"Farrah," I said. "He's . . . I'm not sure. I don't have any experience with this, but it seems like he's not doing well."

"He?" she said, smiling a little. "Can you help him?"

"I'm honestly not sure," I said. "I've never healed through a substrate, if that's what you'd call one body around another. Maybe it would be best to wait until you're in labor. I have no idea how Protection might disrupt your pregnancy." *Of course*, I thought, *it might be too late by then, but what if I accidentally start her labor?* "Maybe you should talk to Terik about it. He hates me enough already."

"He doesn't hate you," Farrah said. "He's just... Terik. He's perpetually cantankerous, but he's harmless until someone threatens me—then he is a force. He always protected me at SONA." She smiled, remembering. "He's rough around the edges, but he's a good man."

"I'll take your word for it," I said.

Jorin and Terik came in the front door, and I turned to them. Terik rolled his eyes at me, then noticed me holding his wife's hand. He looked questioningly at Farrah, who let go of me but didn't show any outward sign of embarrassment.

"You'll be with me then?" Farrah asked.

I nodded. "Yes. We'll help each other."

"Okay," Farrah said, her eyes locked onto mine. "We'll help each other."

Chapter Three

*L*ord Otterhai, the eldest among the shock, was the only dragon who used his great wings to swim instead of fly, and there, within the deepest currents, swam a dragon of dazzling blue. His scales matched the azure sky so precisely as to give the impression that the sky itself whirled and spun within the river.

As it turns out, I'm bad at boats. I had wanted to read in the cabin and hang out with Farrah, but, as I feared, I couldn't stop vomiting. Jorin sent me "aft and leeward" (i.e., downwind) so as not to unintentionally involve anyone else in my lovely retching. Aaron attempted to attend to me, but Evilina told him to leave me the hell alone so I could puke in blessed solitude.

The water was rough, though it was less so once we sailed farther away from the beach. Luckily, we had five men with extensive sailing experience. We had one woman with sailing experience as well, but she was busy growing far too many babies at once.

After several hours of torture, I finally figured out if I pushed my shield out just far enough to surround my head, my nausea lessened dramatically. I had no idea if vomit would be netted within the shield, but the relief from seasickness was worth the risk. I was tempted to go back into the cabin at that point but was afraid that walking would renew my nausea. Instead, I clung to the railing at the stern just behind a strapped-down barrel of fresh water.

It was a mystery how Jorin knew where to go. He didn't appear to have a compass, and the fog was so thick out on the water that there was no way he could navigate by sight. That's why I was shocked and terrified when, sometime around sunset, we hit something. Or, rather, something hit us.

Jorin called out to the men, but I couldn't make out what he said. I released the shield around my head to get a better sense of what was going on and was assaulted by a profound resonance that practically vibrated me right off the deck.

It was kind of like turning your car on when you'd left your radio's volume on maximum the previous night. It scared the hell out of me and was physically painful, producing a throbbing that started in my chest, then shot like lightning through my stomach and down to my tailbone. My knees buckled, and I clutched the railing, hoping it would steady my mind as well as my body. It didn't help, but then the resonance lessened, like whatever it was had passed or had swum away.

Merimo, I thought. *The Meriweather Monster.*

The boat rocked, and my nausea returned.

"Lee!" Aaron called. "Are you all right?"

"More or less," I called back to him. "What was that? I could feel it!"

"Me too," Aaron said, walking toward me from the helm.

"That was just Merimo," Jorin offered. "Don't ya worry, he won't—"

Something touched my leg, and I looked down to see that a tentacle had slipped over top of the railing and wrapped itself around my ankle. In the space of a heartbeat, it advanced around my leg enough times to reach my thigh and wrenched my lower half up and over the side of the boat.

I hung on with all my meager Earthly strength, barely maintaining my grip while the boat rocked violently. Then whatever trick he'd used to mask his resonance dropped and the vibration flared again, pounding in my heart and ears.

In retrospect, I probably could have done a few things to defend myself, like push my shield back out, or use Evocation to burn the creature. Unfortunately, I was so shocked at its sudden appearance that I did the most unhelpful thing imaginable. I screamed, of course. That's what I do.

"Lee!" Aaron bellowed.

"Help me!" I shrieked.

I managed to hang onto the railing with my arms through the first tug, but the thing was massive and much stronger than me. It pried my arms loose on its second attempt, just as Aaron reached me. The warmth of his fingers grazing mine without holding fast was like a cruel joke, but even worse was the look of horror that overtook his face as I flew away from him into the cold fog. Voice quavering, he shouted my name one more time before I hit the black water.

The shock of cold got my brain working again, and I put my hand to my chest to summon a shield. A tentacle attached to my wrist, yanking it away from my heart, but I completed the initial sphere, and from there I fed Protection into it with my mind. I pressed the shield out desperately, my heart hammering in my chest, but was met with unexpected resistance. I couldn't even push it out enough to wrap around my head.

Panicking, the terrible realization hit me that air passes through a shield, but water doesn't. Even if I could lift the water away with my mind while fighting the vacuum it created within the shield, I'd still suffocate. If I had raised my shield before being submerged, I might have had a chance. As it was, my fight was over before it had begun.

The monster wrapped another tentacle around my waist and pulled me deeper, farther from the surface, and the light flew away from me, dimming to nothing. I lifted my hand and sent Connection into the creature, praying that I could convince the thing to let me go, but nothing happened. Merimo wasn't just protected, he was as protected as I was.

I recognized it now—the impenetrable shield, the overpowering resonance. He was an ascendant of Protection, like me, but how could that be? An animal couldn't possibly know to go on a bridge to Earth and then return on another Earth bridge in order to ascend, could he? Unless he was . . .

A man. You're a man.

Merimo stilled, loosening his grip, not that it mattered. I was out of air, my vision rapidly narrowing. It would be seconds before I lost consciousness. There was no way I'd get my shield up in time to push him off, figure out which way the surface was, and swim there.

Spirit! I called. *Spirit, help me!*

I'm here, Lina, she thought to me. I couldn't see her in the black water, but I felt her presence more clearly than ever. It was almost like I could smell her. I wondered if that was because I was about to join her in death. *I'll guide Aaron to you!* Her presence retreated and did not return, but I didn't call her back again. It was useless. Merimo still towed me through the water and even if Aaron could somehow get to me, he'd probably just drown right beside me. I would see Spirit soon enough.

A strange calmness washed over me once I accepted that it was futile to attempt escape. Time slowed, and I observed my situation as if from the outside. My whole body shivered violently in the ice-cold water. I relaxed, letting the tremors have their way with me. Seawater had gotten into my nose and the back of my throat. It tasted salty and a little sweet, not entirely unpleasant except for the growing burning in my sinuses.

Above the surface, a rich and vibrant sunset had swathed the sky in red, orange and purple, but ensnared beneath the waves, the darkness murdered both my hope and my sight. I closed my useless eyes and concentrated on my sense of touch. Merimo's tentacle was smooth and spongy. He'd finally stopped swimming and simply held me, turning me this way and that like a child examining a new toy.

I knew I couldn't do this, I thought, letting him examine me without struggling. I could feel him listening to me too. *Farrah was wrong. Violet Atticus was wrong. Spirit was wrong. I'm sorry, everyone. I tried, but I'm not who you thought I was.*

My thoughts turned to Aaron and to my parents, to Spirit, and to my dear friend Ward. *I didn't even get a chance to say goodbye. Maybe I'll meet Ward on the other side. We could go over the bridge together. That sounds nice. I hope I can say goodbye to Aaron before I go.*

A man's voice spoke softly in my mind. It was surprisingly gentle, almost reverent, but with growing anxiety. *Who are you?*

There was no time to respond. Flashing lights invaded my vision beneath my eyelids. Water filled my lungs, burning like fire. I coughed, but it didn't help. I let the dark and cold overtake me, keeping Aaron's face in my mind, then drifted peacefully into the abyss.

Chapter Four

"*What troubles you, Otterhai?" Linorra asked. "What could make a great and powerful dragon so sorrowful?"*

Otterhai beheld Linorra with covetous eyes, as she was the first human he'd seen in many years—and the only one to ever ask him such a thoughtful question.

I dreamed of Aaron. We were in our bed, cocooned under a soft blanket that smelled of peppermint and musk. His heat seeped into me. I was safe with him. He loved me, and he made love to me as he desperately pushed Protection. God, it was strong tonight.

My own moan woke me up, then I coughed, hacking up seawater. Groggy and confused, my eyes opened to complete darkness, but relief flooded me when I felt Aaron's heated body wrapped around mine. His beard tickled my cheek as he panted, pushing Protection as well as heat into me as I shivered violently. He stank of seaweed, but that was forgivable under the circumstances.

I lifted my chin to kiss him, and he hesitated, then obliged. The kiss was tentative at first, then he sank into it, becoming almost frantic. He pushed Protection even harder, and I released another loud shuddering moan.

Then, like always, I took my turn, sending Protection back into him. His defenses were so strong that we hadn't even connected yet.

"Let me in," I whispered. He took a breath then released it, lowering his mental defenses. I drew him on top of me, spreading my legs to wrap around him as I directed waves of healing fragment through his body.

He grunted, a little laugh escaping his lips. We connected instantly, and a flutter of relief surged out of him like an energetic sigh. He sucked my bottom lip into his mouth, then rocked his hips forward as if his growing erection could puncture right through my clothing.

My wet clothing. Wait...

I reached out around us, my mind clearing. Cold, wet sand. Yanking my face back to peer at him, faint aqua light emanated from my skin into deep cobalt-blue eyes; the face of a man I didn't recognize. A very *naked* man.

My heart leapt into my throat as I released a rasping cry. I shoved him away to get up and run, not bothering to look back.

"Ugh," the man sputtered indignantly from behind me, likely due to the sand I kicked into his face as I fled into the dark.

True night had fallen while I'd been unconscious, and I stumbled over a driftwood log on the shadowed beach. Still slightly dizzy from my ordeal in the water, my clumsy tumble was mercifully cushioned by the sand. The seawater was mostly expelled before I woke up, but each inhalation of moist, salty air felt raw and heavy, burning my chest as I forced air through my injured lungs.

Ignore it and keep going, I thought, jumping back up to run again.

"I'm sorry!" the man yelled after me, his voice growing more distant. "I thought you were someone else!"

I was a hundred yards away when I finally looked back. Only Heshia, the white, delicately ringed moon, hung in the sky, but there was just enough light for me to make out the outline of a man sitting on the beach, his head bowed. I stood there staring, poised to run again, but his dejected vibe made me pause. He seemed . . . *broken*. That was the only word for it.

This is crazy. He almost drowned me. Then he pressed his naked body against mine while I was unconscious.

I backed away, preparing to run again, but something stopped me. Yes, he had pressed his body against mine, but was it to heal and warm me up when he realized he'd attacked the wrong person? Who had he wanted to kill? That kiss had been desperate, and the subsequent relief palpable. It didn't seem like something a monster would feel. It just felt human. And fucking sad.

I squatted to see if sand worked as a Connection substrate, then reached out for the man through the sand and found him. Surprisingly, he was still open to me. He was frustrated and lonely, grieving even. *So much grief*, I thought, remembering the day I arrived. This world was full of that unwelcome emotion.

I can feel you, too, ya know.

I jerked back, startled. The strange man had just pushed his own Connection fragment through the sand, and his voice had been loud in my mind. He was *much* stronger than me. I wondered, if I stood up, if he could connect right through the air.

I should just run away, I thought. *Shouldn't I?* I stood up and called to Spirit.

Lina! Spirit exclaimed. *Thank god you're okay.*

Yes, I thought to her, my emotions a jumble. *Merimo is a man! He almost drowned me, but then he saved me. Then he kissed me! Or maybe I kissed him, but it was an accident. I was only semiconscious and mistook him for Aaron. He says he thought I was someone else too. Can you go tell Aaron that I'm okay? Then come back. Don't tell him about the kiss, though. Shit.*

Okay, she thought to me. *Calm down. I'll be right back.*

I bent down to dig my trembling fingers into the cold, wet sand again, reaching out for Merimo. Though it felt like pushing a boulder up a hill, I managed to find him and connect from my end.

You tried to kill me, I accused.

A heartbeat of surprise passed before he answered. *I'm sorry. You remind me a lot of someone who very much deserves to drown. That's why I hauled you off the boat. After I realized you weren't her, I saved you. You're welcome.*

I raised my eyebrows. *I need to thank you for fixing your own screwup? What are you, new?*

He laughed. It was the short, gruff laugh of someone who hadn't done it in a while.

I stood up again, uncertain. Merimo, or whatever his name was, didn't have the same tall body type as the rest of Monash. He seemed more like a regular Earth man, though it was hard to tell with him sitting in the dark and at a distance.

I'm sorry about the kiss, too, he thought. I jumped in surprise again, then inspected my feet, which were still in my soggy shoes, and not touching the sand.

Why, yes, you can *connect through the air*, I thought with a mix of awe and irritation. *That's just great.*

You must have made the same mistake I did, he thought, his amusement unmistakable. *Who did you think I was?*

I didn't answer, and worried that he could pry the information out of my brain if he wanted to. His skill with Connection was clearly superior to mine. I was a child playing the recorder while he was Beethoven playing his *Moonlight* Sonata, conveying rhythm, tone, and feeling.

Please, come sit, he implored me, emotion infused into his thoughts. *I'm not going to attack you again. Or kiss you. Unless you want me to.* The music of his telepathic message drew me in like a siren lures a wayward ship.

"I'm back, Lina," Spirit said, interrupting the spell. I turned to her, shaking myself a little. "Aaron's elated that you're okay. After you went into the water, he jumped in but couldn't find you. He almost drowned himself, but Fitch dragged him out. He was shaking when I got to him. I've never seen him in that state."

"There's no dock here," I said, silently fuming at her words. I hadn't considered that Aaron might be in danger. Merimo was damned lucky nothing permanent had happened to Aaron or he'd have gotten to experience the land version of a piranha attack. "Please tell them to wait offshore and let me know when they get close, would you?" Spirit nodded and disappeared.

I observed the man for a moment, still sitting down the beach with his bare ass in the sand. He had let me go when I ran, hadn't he? And he didn't appear to be overly interested in me anymore. It felt relatively safe. I sighed, then raised my shield to walk toward him.

"So, you're a man, not a monster. Does Jorin know this?" I asked.

"I'm both, actually," he said, one side of his mouth ticking up. "And Jorin knows a great many things he doesn't tell anyone. Who were you talking to just now?"

I hesitated, digging the toes of my shoes into the sand as if I might run again. A gust of cold, seaweed-scented wind blew my hair over my shoulder, and I hugged myself against the chill.

"Come now, Schatzi, I answered your question," Merimo said. "Answer at least one of mine."

Did he just call me a tchotchke? I paused. "A friend," I said flatly. "Could you see her?"

THE WISDOM OF DISHONOR

He smiled, a muted laugh barely escaping his throat, then shook his head. I wasn't sure if his answer was no or if he shook his head in amazement. "You have Conjuration," he said. "A rare gift." He stared at me, waiting for my response, but I gave him none. His eyes were shadowed and missing that catlike glow to which I'd grown accustomed.

"I'm sorry I hurt you," he said, giving up on my response. "It won't happen again, I swear." He paused to regard me, then he said, "Your eyes are like mine."

I kept my silence but sat on the sand a few feet away from him, hugging my knees and shivering. Merimo nodded in approval, then leaned forward to touch the sand in front of him. He piled it into a mound and dug his fingers into it. After a moment, the sand sparked and popped, then the entire mound blurred, finally bursting into a flaming campfire.

I leaned back reflexively, throwing my hands up to protect my eyes from the sudden heat and brightness, then I turned to him with wide eyes. He'd transmuted the sand into something resembling wood, then lit it on fire, all in one quick move. It was astounding.

He saw my expression and laughed again, evidently remembering how to do it as the sound had gained a rich warmth that made me want to grin back at him. I resisted, recalling the way his thoughts had nearly hypnotized me. This man was charming. *Too* charming for someone who'd almost just murdered me and then shrugged it off as a silly mistake.

The fire reflected off sandy blond hair, a red beard, and piercing cobalt-blue eyes. With a jolt, I realized I recognized him. He was the man from my dream, the one I'd somehow known as a friend and who'd crouched over the bridgestone with a hammer and chisel.

Holy crap. A deep sense of déjà vu swept over me as my whole body went rigid with surprise. I gawked, my mouth hanging open as he stared back, his eyes searching.

"Do you know me?" he asked.

I shook my head, uncertain if it was a lie or not. I recognized him, but I didn't know him. "I don't believe we've met."

He smirked, turning his eyes back to the fire. "Not in this life, anyway."

I frowned, unsure if his comment was serious. "Well," I said, "this is the only life I remember, and I don't believe in reincarnation."

The man laughed, shaking his head, a response that should have irritated me but felt comforting instead. He was familiar somehow, and yet I was convinced I'd never laid eyes on him.

On a whim, I brought my shield down to hold my hands up to the fire, but our shared resonance hit me again like a clangorous bell. Based on what I felt in that resonance, he had every single one of the reservoirs I had, except Conjuration. It was almost like I could sense the fragmental energy bouncing between us, as if drawn to us both and uncertain of which reservoir to fill. That was what had drawn me out to sea that day on the sight boulder near Jorin's farmhouse.

"You feel it, don't you?" he asked. "That's the resonance of another ascendant. I haven't felt it myself in quite some time." He turned his face back to the fire. "I could help you get the rest of them, if you like. To make up for my . . . mistake." Though he didn't move his hands, I heard the implied air quotes.

I remained silent, mostly because I didn't know what to say. One minute he was attacking me, the next minute he acted like we were old friends and nothing out of the ordinary had happened. I wasn't sure what to make of him. He was amiable now, but I didn't trust him enough to give him any real information. So what if he'd been my friend in a dream? That didn't mean anything, did it?

Also, *what the hell*? I didn't have Precognition. How could I have dreamed of someone before meeting them? I couldn't, that's what. The whole thing was as fishy as he smelled.

"Please, what shall I call you?" he asked. "Say *something*. I'm dying over here."

I tore my eyes away from him and scanned the sea for a boat. I could feel myself being sucked in by his charisma and wasn't entirely certain that I objected to it. "My friends call me Lina," I said.

"Lina," he repeated, rolling the name around in his mouth.

"You have all the reservoirs I have except one?" I asked.

"Yes," he said. "All except Conjuration. I have no ability there, though I would love to hear about it. Over dinner, perhaps?" he suggested. "I promise to be fully clothed, if you prefer."

I suppressed a laugh. Oh, he really was smooth. He had literally tried to kill me—and would have succeeded if not for his own intervention—then he sort of tricked me into making out with him, and now he sat there in the nude, covered in dirt and sand, smelling like seaweed, and still somehow made me want to say yes.

Seriously, what in the hell is happening? Wait, maybe he has Production and Projection, like Farrah. That would explain his charisma.

Spirit appeared in front of us, and I flinched in surprise, glancing up. "They're here," she announced, watching Merimo with an expression of distaste. "They saw the fire."

"Okay. Thanks, Spirit," I said out loud, then I asked privately, *Why the face?*

He wants something from you, she thought to me.

What?

I... don't know. He's blocking me now.

I gaped at Merimo. He stared back, a barely restrained smirk on his face. "I can teach you to block, too, if you let me," he said.

Smug bastard. Spirit and I traded a look of mutual understanding, the sort you can only share with someone who knows you well.

Aaron won't like it, we both thought.

I know, but I do need someone to teach me. I think he made that fire using Transmutation and Evocation. He says he can help me get other reservoirs. Maybe he'd just give them to me.

Yeah, I'm sure he'd be more than happy to give *it to you*, Spirit thought, rolling her eyes.

I sighed at her double entendre. *Actually, I don't think sex is required. I think it's the intimacy part that does it, like when I got into Ward's mind. Real affection has to be present, not just body parts.*

Whatever. Do you want to have hot and dirty "affection" with this man? It wouldn't take much to get him on board.

I won't.

That wasn't a no, Spirit thought back, mocking the phrase I always used on Aaron.

I shrugged. *He's not using Projection on me, is he?*

As a ghost, Spirit couldn't sense resonance, but she had the ability to see fragments that were in use. She shook her head at my question.

Merimo tilted his head like a dog, as if listening to something fascinating. I wondered if he could hear me talking to Spirit.

"Can you take me out to the boat?" I asked, perturbed at the thought of him hearing my private thoughts.

"Yes, of course," he said. "I can even keep you from getting wet, if you prefer."

"I'm already wet," I said. Merimo nodded, holding my eyes. *What the hell did I just say?*

"And then?" he asked, his eyes crinkling at the corners. "Will you come to dinner?"

"I have some friends to save from an evil queen, Merimo," I said.

He nodded. "I know. And then?" he asked again.

Man, he was persistent. And how did he know I had people to save? Had he stolen it out of my brain?

"I'll pay," he added before I could get further into that line of thought. "Spain is lovely this time of year."

My lips parted at his comment. *Spain.* The word was a reverent whisper in my mind. My father was from Málaga, a province on the southern coast of Spain. He'd taken me there once to meet the rest of the family, and it had been a magical experience.

If Merimo could teleport me back to Earth, then maybe he could teach me to use the reservoir that I'd absorbed from Axel the previous day. Guilt nagged at me, but the truth was that I wanted to say yes. This unclothed weirdo not only had crazy charisma but also knowledge and experience that I desperately needed to acquire.

But what about Aaron? We'd only been together for two months. Under ordinary circumstances that would hardly be enough to promise a commitment. But circumstances had been extraordinary, hadn't they? He'd called me his beloved and risked his life for me.

But shouldn't I figure out what I want before I make promises I can't keep? I closed my eyes, reflecting. I was still hesitant, but I owed Aaron honesty at the very least. *God, I really am a hypocrite, aren't I?*

I stared at the sea but saw very little through the dark and fog. The ocean was a symphony of waves crashing onto the beach while the wind blew, unobstructed, over the sand and water. A faint, rhythmic dinging cut through the white noise, calling to me.

"Maybe," I said finally. "I need to think about it, but one dinner probably can't hurt."

I stood, and Merimo stood next to me, smiling. He was only a couple inches taller than me, which was shorter than I'd imagined when he was on top of me earlier. I wondered if he might be making himself smaller for my benefit, like I might be more comfortable with someone less imposing. That idea might have worked better if he weren't stark naked.

"Will you help me save my friend?" I asked, forcing myself not to gawk at his body.

"Possibly. Why don't we talk about it on the boat?"

"That might be awkward in your current state. Any chance you could create clothes out of thin air?"

Merimo chuckled. "Yes, of course." He did something with his fingers, then I saw clothing shaping itself around him. It was essentially a pirate costume with black knee breeches and a puffy white shirt. A wide red leather belt wrapped around his hips, a sheathed cutlass hanging from the side. He even wore a black tricorn hat with a feather à la Captain Hook. He had a sense of humor, at least.

"What, no eye patch?" I asked, which made him laugh. "I thought you had to transmute in stages to make metal," I said, scrutinizing his sword.

"You do. But I do it so fast that you can't tell."

Of course you do.

"They're getting impatient," Spirit chimed in, sounding annoyed. "Aaron is threatening to jump in and swim to the beach."

"Tell him we're on our way, Spirit," I said, then I turned to Merimo. "Aren't we?"

He held out his hand to me. "We are."

I only hesitated for a moment, then accepted, noting that his hand was hot, like Aaron's. As we approached the waves, Merimo let go of my hand and knelt, digging his hands into the sand again.

The sand sparked and popped again before I saw what appeared to be a wooden dinghy forming. The sand fell away, making it seem as if the boat had been buried all along. Merimo shook the extra sand loose, then slid the boat into the water.

"Ready?" he asked, turning back to offer me a hand into the boat. He smiled, his face alive with the dancing light of the fire. Then his smile faltered as he stared past me into the deep woods that lay just beyond the beach.

"Lina," he said urgently, "get in the boat. Quickly!"

I glanced back toward the trees, sensing nothing, then I took Merimo's offered hand and stepped into the boat, choosing the bench facing the beach.

"What is it?" I asked, my eyes focused on the woods.

"Mountain bear," he said, pushing the boat farther into the water. He jumped in with me and then produced oars seemingly out of nowhere. They promptly attached themselves to the boat so he could start rowing vigorously on both sides.

We were twenty yards out when the bear stepped out of the trees and onto the beach. It was shaggy with a wide head like a grizzly bear, except it was blue black and twice the size of an elephant. It definitely could have swallowed me whole. The bear's eyes fixed on us, the hair along its spine standing up between the shoulders.

"That bear is too big," I squeaked.

"And it swims like a fish," Merimo added.

The bear lumbered down to our campfire, stomping around in an agitated dance as I watched, my heart racing. I called to Spirit and asked her to get the men ready to heave us into the sailboat to depart as soon as possible, but something told me that it wouldn't be soon enough.

Just as we disappeared into the fog, the flames flickered and went out, lowering a suffocating curtain of darkness. The ocean and beach were transformed into a pitch-black void that made me envy Heshia in her empty but illuminated orbit around the planet. I might as well have been wearing a blindfold for all I could see.

The wet air clung to my skin and invaded my lungs with each breath, pressing down on me and reminding me of my most recent dip into the ocean.

"You're okay," Spirit cooed. "You're not drowning. Slow, deep breaths. Everything will be fine. Aaron's only a few hundred yards away. We'll get there." Her voice soothed me, even knowing that her promises were empty. She couldn't possibly know if we'd make it to the boat before the bear swam to us.

After a tense moment, I relaxed but continued to stare, hoping in vain to get some clue as to the bear's movements. I couldn't even see Merimo, let alone the insanely big predator that, I assumed, wanted to eat us.

A *splash* made me jolt in my seat.

"Uh-oh," Merimo said. "We'll never make it. Here, take the oars."

"Excuse me?" I spluttered. "Are you crazy?"

"Quite," he said flippantly, "but take them anyway and keep rowing!"

He shoved the oars blindly into my hands and stood, causing the boat to wobble unexpectedly. My heart lurched as I attempted to steady myself with my hands full. Merimo sucked in an audible breath, then a faint golden glow appeared, lighting up the boat. I recognized the color of Transformation emanating from Merimo's body. It grew in intensity until it was so bright that it shone right through his clothes. It was gloriously beautiful.

He clearly knew it, too, as he stared down at me with an expression of joyful exhilaration. I remembered the feeling and smiled back at him despite myself. He unsheathed his cutlass and dropped it into the bottom of the boat with a *clank*, then he plucked off his feathered hat and flicked it onto my head as if it were a ring toss.

"Ah," he said, grinning. "It suits you."

With that, he jumped into the water, allowing blackness to envelop me once again. I wondered idly if he was showing off or if this was just a normal day for him. I wouldn't stick around to find out. I wasn't nearly as strong and efficient as he had been, but I rowed blindly with everything I had.

"Spirit, am I still going in the right direction?"

"Yes, you're almost there. Keep going, Lina," she said. She was in the boat with me now. "God, that bear can really swim!"

"Not helping!" I rasped.

"Sorry," she said. "You're doing fine. Keep going."

"What is Merimo *doing*?" I asked, already breathing hard. Two months of not running had taken its toll on my endurance.

"He transformed into that red megalodon thing," she said. "*He's* hunting the *bear*. He uses Transmutation and Transformation at the same time to appropriate the water and increase his own body mass, and I think he's using echolocation. It's extraordinary, not that he needs any encouragement. The man is a great mound of arrogance. You know that, right?"

"Rowing here!" I panted. I was pretty sure I had already pulled a muscle in my back. I mean, it would heal itself the moment I stopped rowing, but still. It hurt a little bit. "How much farther?"

"At this speed, I'd guess five minutes."

"Five minutes?!" I screeched. "Can't they come toward me?"

"No, I don't think so. Jorin says his Production reservoir lets him sense the land, and he can't come any closer without the risk of grounding the boat."

I released a string of swear words, gasping between each one.

Something splashed off to my right, like an animal treading water. I froze. It sounded close, but I couldn't see a damned thing.

"Turn the back of the boat to your left, Lina!" Spirit said. "Paddle with only the right oar for a stroke and then keep going. It will take you away from the bear."

I did as she said. My legs, arms, and back burned with the effort, but my adrenaline kicked in, and I rowed with everything I had, clenching my teeth and involuntarily grunting with each stroke.

Then something bumped the boat and I let out an instinctive shriek. If it didn't know I was there before, it did now.

A second passed in stunned silence before something pressed down on the opposite end of the boat, causing my side to lift into the air. I screeched as I was thrown forward into the other bench.

Though I was blind, I had the presence of mind to cling to the bench to keep from falling right into what I assumed was the bear's waiting maw. The oars weren't so lucky. They disappeared as if they'd been sucked onto a bridge, without even the courtesy of a *clank* to indicate if they'd landed in the boat or water.

Somewhere in the distance Aaron bellowed my name, and I briefly considered jumping into the water. Maybe if the bear thought I was in the boat, it might mess around with it long enough for me to swim toward the sound of Aaron's voice.

I didn't get to think for long. A deep, rumbling growl, so low as to be nearly inaudible, vibrated through me, followed by a surprised yelp of pain. Suddenly, the weight was released from the front of the boat, tossing me to the bottom of the now water-logged vessel as it plopped back down.

Panicked, I forced my shaking hands to blindly feel around for the oars, not remotely convinced they were still in the boat with me. But that search party was promptly canceled when the bear made another noise, one so loud that it could hardly be labeled as such. It was more of a sonic assault.

The best way I can describe it is to compare it to a fighter jet doing a fly-by right over your head. Though low-pitched, it was literally stunning in its volume, shaking both the boat and me.

My hands flew to my ears, which didn't help in the slightest. The sound did not end until the bear ran out of breath, then it breathed deep and made the sound again, even louder this time but directed away from me, seemingly down into the water.

Terrified, I tried to bring a shield up, but the bear made the sound a third time and directed it squarely at my head. It stunned me senseless, and I collapsed down into the boat, slicing my hand on Merimo's stupid, useless sword. I hardly noticed.

I covered my ears the best I could, drawing Merimo's hat down hard around my head. My brain vibrated as hard as the boat had, and I experienced an excruciating pain in my temples that quickly became all-consuming. By the fourth sonic assault, I lost my hearing as well as any hope of escape. I was deaf as well as blind, and everything was pain. I think I cried, but that could have been the blood dripping from my eyes.

Just before I lost consciousness, I thought, *I'm sorry, Aaron. I should've kept running.*

Chapter Five

*S*yndeth had always been different from the rest of his shock, but never had he been so scorned.

"I am an outcast," he said mournfully.

"Oh, Syndeth," Linorra cried. "If you are an outcast, then so shall I be. If we must be alone, then let us be alone together."

I was blind and deaf, but I felt hands on me, hauling me into the sailboat. I lay on the deck for a few minutes, drifting in and out of consciousness. Then I was in Aaron's arms. For real this time.

I didn't need to see, hear, or even smell him to know that it was he who held me—a little too tightly, as always. I don't know how I ever mistook Merimo for Aaron. Nobody holds me like he does. Nobody.

Lee! I'm here, Aaron thought to me.

Aaron, I thought, crying. *I'm sorry. I'm sorry. I'm sorry.* I repeated it like a mantra, the words steadying my mind so that I could endure the burning in my eyes and ears. Finally, I managed to think, *Please don't let go of me.*

Never, he thought to me soothingly. I could tell my thoughts confused him, but I couldn't explain it. I was afraid if I tried, he would let go. I clung to him, weeping, shaking so hard I thought I would vibrate right out of his grasp. He shook too.

It took several minutes before I healed enough for my senses to return. Smell came back first. Aaron smelled like himself, and also like the sea. He was soaking wet, but I buried my face in his chest anyway, inhaling him. The scent of the ocean on his clothing evoked the smell of seaweed, reminding me of my interaction with Merimo.

Idiot! How could I have thought he was Aaron?

My vision came back next. Just light and shadows at first, then blurry images. I lifted my chin to squint at Aaron's face as he dragged me onto his lap. A nearby oil lantern illuminated the deck and, little by little, his face came into focus. His was the only one I wanted to see.

"Aaron," I whispered. My voice sounded muffled to me, as if I were underwater.

He gazed down at me, then lifted his bare hand and wiped blood away from my eyes and nose. His jaw was clenched, and his red-rimmed eyes were watery as if fighting back tears, though that could have been the seawater.

After a second, I guess he decided he didn't care about the blood. He drew my face toward his and kissed me harder than he should have.

We stayed there, locked in that embrace, for several moments, until the sounds around me came into focus. Jorin shouted instructions over a cacophony of wind and waves. I could barely understand what he said, but it sounded frightened. Shane ran past, practically jumping over us, but the sailboat lurched, throwing him to the deck.

Oh god, I thought. *Is it still out there?*

Don't worry, we'll get away. Just stay here with me. Aaron wouldn't take no for an answer, and I didn't want him to. His heat was my refuge from the terror all around us.

The boat rocked again, but this time it was the sails catching the wind, causing Aaron and me to topple over sideways. From behind us, somewhere in the darkness, the bear yelped in pain again. Shriller and more sustained than the last time, I imagined the sound to be the result of Merimo attacking from below.

I threw up a shield as fast as I could in anticipation of the bear's dangerous bawl. The sound came, but I got my shield around our heads before it could incapacitate us. The rest of the crew weren't as lucky. They clapped their hands over their ears, ducking their heads. Jorin fell to a knee, but he kept one hand on the wheel.

"Aaron, we have to help them!" I cried, trying to get up.

"No," he said, holding on too tightly for me to move, "we're heading away at a good clip. A few more seconds and we'll be too far away for it to do anything. Just stay here with me."

His words gave me permission to relinquish responsibility for the shit show I'd helped create. I stopped struggling and rested back on the hard deck where I'd fallen, but I had to clench my teeth against the throbbing in my skull. I'd lost Merimo's hat somewhere, I noticed.

After several minutes, when no second bawl came from the bear, I released my shield and turned my attention to Aaron. He trembled, repeatedly alternating between inspecting various parts of me—my face, my back, my hands and arms—and tight hugs where he buried his nose in my neck. It was as if he had to reassure himself over and over that I was still there.

"Spirit said you jumped in after me," I said, intending to distract him.

"I did. Twice."

"Twice?"

"Yes. They held me back at first, but when I heard your scream, I—" He choked up, his eyes glistening. My heart ached for him as he reverted back to another tight hug.

He really does love me, I thought, realizing that I hadn't entirely believed it. *What is wrong with me? Aaron jumps into freezing black water to save me from monsters—plural—while I'm thinking about my prospects with another man. Why?*

After a moment, Aaron composed himself and said, "I thought I'd lost you. *Again*. What is it with you and death? It follows you around."

I sighed, pushing down my own self-recrimination. "It always has, even before I died that first time back on Earth. I've never been afraid of it. When I believed I would drown,

I accepted death. I regretted all the missed goodbyes, but I wasn't scared. There's a bridge on the other side, Aaron. Spirit says she's seen it."

"Where does it go?" he asked.

I shrugged. "Not even she knows the answer to that."

Aaron remained silent for a moment before he asked, "Did you think of me?"

"Of course," I whispered, knowing what he really wanted to know. "You were one of the goodbyes I hadn't gotten to say. The most important one."

Aaron laughed bitterly, which surprised me, then he sat up. I had expected him to kiss me, not laugh in my face.

"What's funny?" I asked irritably.

He shook his head. "You," he said. "You think I'm the one who can't trust, but you're just as bad."

"What do you mean?"

"What do I mean? Tell me what you were sorry about, Lee," he said, the accusation ringing clear in his voice. "You said it repeatedly when we got back to the ship. I want to know why."

I gaped at him, speechless. "I . . ." I couldn't bring myself to finish, so I sat up next to him instead, giving myself time to think of an answer that wasn't a lie but that wouldn't make him hate me.

Aaron took my face between his large hands. *Lee*, he thought. *Trust in me. Be honest with me. I won't let go until you tell me to. I promise.*

"I . . ." I said, then thought, *I thought he was you.*

Who? Aaron asked.

Merimo. He's not a monster. He's a man; although, he says he's both and I'm beginning to understand why. He's powerful.

Aaron lowered his eyes as I explained, nodding, then slid his hands from my face to my shoulders. His firm grip grounded me and gave me something to concentrate on so that I wouldn't float away on a wave of anxiety. His expression sobered, taking on the faraway look he sometimes got when he tried to work logically through a problem.

Jorin told me about Merimo while we waited for you on the boat, he thought. *He's a highly skilled fragmentor, very old, with multiple reservoirs. When did you think he was me?*

Reluctantly, I explained why Merimo attacked me, and why he stopped. I confessed to what happened when I woke up, what Merimo had offered, and where he wanted to take me. I admitted what my answer had been and why. Then I described the fire on the beach and what Spirit said about Merimo wanting something from me.

Aaron's face darkened when I got to that part, but he didn't interrupt and, as promised, he didn't let go. He only hugged me as I recounted my experience in the rowboat, how Merimo abandoned me to go hunt the bear, but how it got to me anyway.

As life-changing as the last two months have been, I explained, *it isn't enough time for me to know whether or not I should pledge my life to you. I'm not saying that I don't want you. I do, but the thought of bonding to you after so short a time makes my insides twist. If I had known what the bracelets meant, I never would have given you one. And yet, when I thought I would die, all I wanted was you. I hate it that Farrah seems to be secretly in love with you. I know it makes me a hypocrite, but I couldn't stand it if I were your second choice.*

I expelled a long breath that came out almost as a moan. When I finished, we sat there in silence for a moment before Aaron finally said, "Thank you." He took a deep breath in and out, as if preparing himself for something painful, then gently pressed me away so that he could look into my eyes as he responded.

I do have a history with Farrah, but I always thought of her as a little sister. When we met at SONA, I was fourteen and she was eleven. I protected her during her first two years there. That school is dangerous for girls, and many disappear without finishing. When I escaped SONA and ran for my life, Terik assumed the job of protecting her, but when Axel attempted to bond her against her will, she asked me to bond her first.

He stopped, searching my face for my reaction. *I was tempted, I admit. She is calm and makes the people around her calm. I like that, as you know, but after thinking about it, I refused. My life since leaving SONA was too dangerous. She was . . . distraught when she was forced to go to Terik. Terik hates me for it, not only because he was her second choice but because he says I abandoned her, which I suppose is true. But he was the right choice for her in the end because he loves her the way I love you.*

Aaron paused, letting the last part sink in. The message was clear. He wasn't afraid to say it outright. Not like me.

You will always be my first choice, Lee. Always, whether you choose me or not. I knew it the moment I met you. I wanted to bond you that first night, before we even connected. He took my face in his hands again, gazing into my eyes. *Two months may not be a long time, but it feels like I've been waiting for you my whole life. If you want to go with Merimo, then go. I will agonize over it, but I'll wait, because even if we both end up with other people, you will be the one my soul longs for.*

By that point, Aaron had already saved me three or four times, but this was the first time I truly grasped the depth of his bravery. He was willing to give me raw honesty while I could barely even admit my feelings to myself.

Before you choose, though, he continued, *you should understand something. Everyone in this province knows not to start a fire on the beach this time of year. The bears and dragons come down from the mountains to hunt the seals that migrate through these waters. When the dragons find them, they cough up a molten chunk that, when it strikes down the seals, produces an odor like smoke and rotten fish. The bears track that smokey scent for miles such that even a small fire will attract them.*

I gaped at Aaron as it dawned on me what he was trying to say. *Merimo did it on purpose.*

Aaron smiled grimly, nodding, then sat back a little, letting his hands fall to mine. He'd always been unusually perceptive, intuiting when I needed the space to process difficult news.

I groaned, embarrassed that I had been taken in so easily. Before Merimo blocked her, Spirit had said he wanted something from me. Had he really put my life in danger just to show off? If so, then maybe he really was a monster.

Aaron's pale eyes flared incandescent as they pierced the barrier I'd unintentionally thrown up between us. *I figured you didn't know what the bracelet meant, Lee, but you already gave it to me and I'm keeping it. I'm going to get you one in Neesee, and when you're ready, you can put it on.* He drew me closer, gently brushing his lips to mine. *Don't make me wait too long.*

I nodded, my chest squeezing at his implied message: he wouldn't wait forever. My nausea flared again, and I couldn't tell if it was the seasickness returning or the pressure of making a big decision. I exhaled and leaned into him as he wrapped his arms around me. His warmth and acceptance were enough for now.

There's one more thing, he thought.

What? I asked.

THE WISDOM OF DISHONOR

Aaron paused, then thought, *Just because death follows you doesn't mean you have to let it catch you. I know you were drowning, but you gave up too fast. I need you to fight a little harder to stay with me, Lee. I can only save you so many times.*

Okay, I thought, closing my eyes. *I'll try.* Then, after a second, I said out loud, "That last one wasn't my fault, though. A bear basically melted my brain. I pulled a muscle trying to get back. It kind of hurt a little bit."

Aaron chuckled at my weak attempt to lighten the mood. "You did fine. You got far enough for me to reach you, anyway. There isn't much you can do when a mountain bear projects at you like that. It's extraordinary that you survived the first one in such close proximity, let alone four times."

"It directed the third one right at my head," I said. "I'm going to kill Merimo, if he ever shows his face again."

"I'll make it up to you," Merimo said from behind me. I jerked in surprise, then shifted so I could glare at him. He appeared out of nowhere, like a light had flicked on, only now revealing his presence. I seriously needed someone to teach me that trick.

I stood slowly and carefully but still wobbled, my stomach turning at the movement. Aaron rose to steady me, but I felt unexpectedly ill.

"Did you light that fire purposely to attract a bear?" I asked bluntly, fighting back the nausea.

"Of course not," Merimo chided. His absurd pirate costume was crisp and dry, but somehow his hair and beard dripped with both seawater and what I could only assume was bear blood. I narrowed my eyes, wondering if the display was for show. "I lit the fire because you were shivering. I wanted to *help* you. I'm sorry. *Again.* Let me make it up to you. I'll help you rescue everyone from the 'evil queen' and then take you to Spain for some chorizo and patatas bravas."

Spain, I repeated the word in my mind again, reveling in the feeling of safety it imparted. My dad was from Spain. I imagined meeting him there and falling into the safety of one of his tight hugs, the type that enveloped both my mother and me. The thought sent a spark of hope and warmth into my chest that I couldn't deny.

Merimo smiled at me mischievously, then he raised his eyes to Aaron with an expression of casual, unconcerned challenge. Aaron was likely stronger than Merimo, but for all I knew, Merimo could call a ten-ton anvil into being right above Aaron's head and squash him like a cartoon villain. There was no way Aaron could take him in a fight.

Unfortunately, despite what he'd said about respecting my choice, Aaron would never back down in a direct confrontation. He stepped in front of me to confront the monster-man.

"You've put Lina's life in danger twice now, *Gerhelm*," Aaron murmured. "There will not be a third time."

Gerhelm?

Merimo's smile faltered as he eyed Jorin, who stood stalwartly at the boat's raised helm. Noticing Merimo's expression, Jorin simply shrugged, then focused his attention out over the water, dismissing our conversation entirely.

Merimo stepped to the side to address me directly. "Does this man speak for you?" Merimo asked, gesturing to Aaron.

"*For* me? Yes," I said. "*Instead* of me? No. As far as I am aware, he hasn't almost killed me twice in as many hours, so I would say that makes him much more *for* me than you are."

Merimo snorted derisively. "I see," he said. His gaze shifted to Aaron and then back to me, his expression now conflicted. *One dinner. That's all I'm asking*, he thought to me. *I am for you, Lina, believe me.* His telepathic sending wasn't just words but included a memory of our make-out session. The thought of it sent an involuntary thrill through me that his eyes told me he felt.

The nausea vibrated in my stomach like a bomb about to explode, and I couldn't hold it in anymore. I tripped over myself to get to the railing and puked my guts out right in front of two men who were competing for my affection. Aaron followed me to hold my hair back.

"Well, at least we know she prefers Earth men," Merimo said as I finished retching. I wiped my mouth on my sleeve, then turned to lean against the railing.

"What?" Aaron asked, scoffing at the implication. He glanced at Merimo over his shoulder while he helped steady me.

"Earth men," Merimo repeated, his tone clearly taunting. "You're from Earth, Aaron, like me. Didn't you know? You were born in Seattle, a city close to where Lina came from, if I remember correctly. Your mother brought you here using your father's Teleportation when you were just a babe." Merimo coolly regarded Jorin, who glared back at the man, his brow furrowed and his mouth forming a taut line.

Merimo shrugged, mimicking Jorin's earlier dismissal, then walked over to the opposite boat railing. As he turned, he said, "I'm gonna go find my hat, Schatzi. I'll meet you at the docks." Then he jumped overboard.

There was no splash.

I stared at Aaron, my eyes wide, but his attention was fixed on Jorin.

Oh, no, I thought. *Is that what Violet meant when she wrote "Time for Jo?" As in, time for Jorin to finally tell Aaron the truth.*

"Now, Aaron," Jorin said, lifting one palm as if afraid Aaron would charge him like a bull. "There's no reason to get upset."

"No reason to get upset?" Aaron demanded in his quiet, dangerous voice—the one he'd used on Axel just before he'd kicked in all his minions' teeth. Every one of those former minions must have remembered it because they all simultaneously had somewhere else to be. Even Terik retreated to the cabin, looking as shocked as Aaron.

"Aaron, I couldn't tell ya till it was time," Jorin said. "I promised your mother."

"Oh, well, I'm glad to know that you had a good reason for a *lifetime* of lies!" The familiar whistle of stones heating up on Aaron's bracelet pierced the air followed by a loud *pop!* as one of them exploded. The heat coming from Aaron was so extreme I had to take several steps toward the stern of the boat.

"Aaron, please. I *couldn't* tell ya," Jorin stubbornly insisted. The old man was brave, I'd give him that. I was skeptical of his intelligence, but he certainly had courage. "We're all counting on ya for this. Every one of us. Terik, Farrah, her babies, everyone in Neesee, everyone on this world, and on Lina's world, even. Lina's family, your parents, your sister, and her kiddos. We're all counting on the two of y'all." He pointed two gnarled fingers at us.

"My sister and her kiddos," Aaron muttered. "How would you know that my sister has children, Uncle?"

Jorin's face flushed, and he broke eye contact. "Your father comes back twice a year to bring me supplies and to check on ya," he admitted, shaking his head.

Aaron balled his hands into fists before turning away to grasp the wooden railing where I'd been standing a few moments prior. It practically disintegrated in his hands. The droplets of water that clung to the wood instantly vaporized along with chunks of railing, which released a blast of steam and wood smoke right into my face. I yelped, falling backward onto my butt.

"Lee!" Aaron shouted, rushing to my side. He examined my face, which stung fiercely. "Goddess, I burned you. I'm sorry," he said, choking up again.

"It's all right," I said, taking his hand from the tender flesh of my cheek. "I'll be fine."

My injury had distracted him for a moment, and his heat had dwindled almost back to his norm, but his expression was tortured. I got to my feet and hugged him gently while he remained kneeling beside me, burying his face in my chest. His body shuddered with silent sobs that could not be contained.

He was strong, but he wasn't unbreakable. I didn't need him to be, though. At least not all the time. I held him while the ship rocked us both into a trance, my heart beating in time to the breathy gusts of wind and the lapping of the waves against the ship's hull.

The deck was an ice box, but with Aaron's body flush against mine, I could never be cold. He pulled his face away to gaze at me with red-rimmed eyes that reflected the dying light of the ship lantern. I used my shirt to wipe his face, then I bent down and pressed my cheek against his forehead.

I'm here, I thought.

He hugged me tightly, thinking, *You're the only one I can trust.*

I didn't necessarily agree, but I couldn't blame him for feeling betrayed. If he was truly from Earth, then his family had not only abandoned him but had also brought him to Monash for that specific purpose. The thought of it was so messed up that I literally couldn't believe it.

I must be missing something.

Jorin quietly watched our interaction with a strained expression. We locked eyes for a moment before his face relaxed into neutrality and he turned back to the wheel without comment, gripping it with white knuckles.

Aaron took a ragged breath in and out, then he got to his feet. "We need to plan for our arrival," he muttered, avoiding Jorin's inscrutable gaze. "I'll go talk to the crew." He stalked toward the cabin door, which Terik had wisely shut at the beginning of the confrontation.

Once Aaron disappeared inside, I approached Jorin. His eyes were sunken, and the wrinkles on his face were so deep that he reminded me of my mother's old shar-pei, Molly. His gray, wispy hair floated around the base of his head, flapping in the breeze. He met my gaze briefly before fixing his attention beyond the bow.

"Jorin, what would have happened if you had told him the truth?"

The weather-beaten man inhaled, then exhaled a heavy breath, shaking his head. He wiped the back of one hand across his brow. "Vi saw many paths, young lady. Many paths, and she planned for this one. She didn't tell me everything that might go wrong." He took another breath, then groaned low in his chest. "I argued with her, ya know. I didn't want to do it this way. But she was dead set on it. She said that going the right way would be hard and that ya needed my help. I trust her, and so should you."

"The right way," I repeated, nodding. *One path right, chasing life.* "How long until we arrive?" I asked, wondering if the words were a coincidence.

"A couple hours if the wind holds. Y'all need to stay out of sight while we dock, ya hear?" I nodded. "Good, now go take care of my nephew. He needs ya. We all do. I'm glad you're here, Miss Lina."

Jorin peered out over the water, his eyes scanning the dark horizon. He seemed to have aged since I met him just that morning. My eyes dropped to the wicked scars that started at his fingers, snaked up his wrists, and disappeared under his tunic. It appeared as if strips of flesh had peeled away, then scarred in ragged lines. I wondered if he'd gotten those when Clare died. She'd been an untrained transmuter and had accidentally caused a fatal explosion. Had he tried to save her?

Jorin had clearly been through a lot but had taken Aaron in and treated him like a son. I couldn't believe he'd want to hurt him. At the very least, Jorin seemed conflicted. He'd confessed to arguing with Violet and had appeared decidedly guilty when Aaron discovered his secret. He'd probably agonized over it for years.

The sound of Fitch's and Shane's hesitant footsteps as they returned from the bow of the boat snapped me out of my reverie. I turned and walked to the cabin feeling uncertain. Jorin seemed like a good man. I hoped that Aaron would forgive him, but it wasn't my place to meddle in Aaron's family affairs.

Before heading into the cabin, I peeked back at Jorin one more time. If Merimo or Gerhelm—or whatever the hell his name was—knew Jorin, then he might have learned from him where Aaron had been born, but how did he know where I was from? He'd claimed to have mistaken me for someone else and asked me what my name was, which implied that he didn't know me. I hadn't told him where I was from when we spoke on the beach. Either Merimo was lying about knowing who I was, or he'd gotten his information some other way.

Jorin's sharp eyes met mine, but he looked quickly away again.

Time for Jo indeed. I had a feeling Aaron's origin story wasn't the only thing Jorin kept hidden. I'd get to the bottom of this mystery, but not yet. I was dead tired, and the seasickness was steadily creeping back.

I turned to the cabin door and pushed a shield out around my head again. It never ceased to amaze me when the fragment colors popped into view to silently swirl inside a shield, but they were especially striking in the dark. They didn't cast light around them when circling within a shield, but they, themselves, glowed like sparks.

I smiled, then stumbled when the boat swayed to the side followed by a heave up toward the sky. I seized the cabin door handle to steady myself, then closed my eyes, waiting for the seasickness to recede as Jorin barked orders to Fitch and Shane.

It was getting late, and I had only slept a few hours the previous night. The exhaustion of frantically rowing that boat to escape the bear now hit me like a ton of bricks, and if I didn't lie down soon, I was going to fall down. My limbs felt heavy and sluggish, and my back and abs ached like I'd had the most intense workout of my life.

I dragged myself into the cabin and released my shield to crawl into a narrow spot next to Aaron. Lying on my side to face him, my back was to Terik and Farrah, who were on the bunk opposite us. I felt Farrah's eyes on us as Aaron kissed my forehead, then wrapped his arms around me. Surrounded by his warmth and scent, even seasickness couldn't touch me.

I closed my eyes, running through everything that had happened that day, starting with Falon's longing gaze from the floor of Aaron's bedroom and ending with the comfort of Aaron's embrace. Learning I was immortal had been a total mind fuck. In truth, I wouldn't come to believe it for many years, despite what happened next.

Chapter Six

Linorra and Syndeth accepted Otterhai's offer of aid. They knew that without his great power and knowledge, they may never recover the key.

Syndeth, who was among the cleverest of dragons, asked, "And what do you wish in return?"

Otterhai, a sad smile upon his silvery-blue face, replied, "I will help you find what you have lost if you will do the same for me."

When I felt the boat change direction, my eyes snapped open. It felt like only moments had passed, but Aaron was no longer next to me. Farrah snored from the opposite bunk, and I turned to glance at her only to notice Falon's scrutiny from the bunk above. He'd been watching me sleep.

"I think we're here," he said, breaking the awkward silence.

"Oh," I said stupidly. I was conflicted as to whether I should be flattered by his attention or creeped out. Falon was a handsome guy, if young. He had the same coloring as the rest of the crew, with pale skin and black hair, but his eyes were a more striking hazel than the rich brown of the others. They were eyes that could draw you in.

I averted my gaze to roll over and peer through a porthole on my side of the cabin. I was surprised to find that the fog had cleared and the lights of the Neesee docks cut through the night, reaching out for us.

I stumbled from the bunk to poke my head out the cabin door, hesitant to venture all the way out. The air was frigid, but the lesser Evocation I'd gained from Aaron made it bearable.

Aaron had once shown me a map of Southern Gale, the province that stretched from the peninsula south of Jorin's and Humboldt Moore's farms, to the Ironwood Forest in the north, with its hundreds of thousands of acres of impenetrable timberland. Neesee, the capital of Southern Gale and home to the Ministry headquarters, sat on the southern edge of the silvery-white ironwoods and about a hundred and twenty-five miles north of Jorin's farm.

Between the farm and Neesee, a wide river flowed down from the Gale Ridge Mountains in the east to empty into the Meriweather Sea. This protected the southern farms from unscrupulous Neesians, but limited land travel to one meandering path across the Groves farm bridges, too far northeast for practical use. So, Jorin shipped his crop yields to the city by boat and had been leasing the same boat slip for twenty years.

To get there, we had to pass the Bay of March, the protected water around which the city had sprouted, so we could turn back and head downwind through the inlet and into the bay itself. Jorin had wanted me to wait in the cabin, but I was too fascinated by how the men handled the boat, taking one sail down at the stern as we turned downwind and then bringing a different, more billowy sail up at the bow.

Just as the new sail was raised, the wind unexpectedly picked up, lurching the boat forward and throwing me to the deck outside the cabin. My empty stomach threatened to escape through my throat and abandon ship.

"Reef the jib!" Jorin yelled at the men, who scrambled to pull ropes. The sail somehow curled in on itself to become smaller, presumably to slow down the boat so we didn't sail into the bay too swiftly. The boat, which had tipped forward slightly, righted itself and stabilized, letting me stand back up.

Jorin then barked other commands, using the word "Rhoya" several times, which I'd come to learn was a religious term on Monash. It referred to the redwood trees, which were considered sacred by the Ministry, but it was also sometimes a curse, sort of like

"Jesus." It made me laugh every time someone angrily shouted "tree" like it was a great blasphemy.

I chuckled, then cowered away from Jorin's impatient glare, sneaking back into the cabin to track our progress through the porthole.

Dozens of large oil lanterns backed by mirrors illuminated the docks, one at the end of each dock and several more hoisted up on poles. It was just after midnight when we arrived, yet the docks teemed with activity that could be seen from miles away. There were boats everywhere with impossibly tall, black-haired men unloading boxes and baskets into handcarts.

The docks were full, with many more ships anchored in the bay itself, their ship lanterns tiny dots in the night. Jorin's regular slip, large enough to accommodate a ship three times the size of our sailboat, welcomed us like an old friend.

Terik and Jorin moored us before hurrying off to their usual inn of choice, the Shipstone, to ensure that our delayed arrival hadn't caused their room to be given away. Falon and Markus, claiming they were eager to get off the boat and stretch their land legs, had gone with them. The rest of us waited in the dark, cramped cabin.

I was exhausted and still queasy, but I felt worlds better with the boat docked, so I pulled out *Beginning Bridges*, the Teleportation textbook, and read with my flashlight.

The twelve worlds are divided into four triads. With the exception of Killmount, the theoretical Conjuration planet, a greater teleporter may open a bridge to any world within their current triad by directing Teleportation fragment into a *resonance article* from that world (see *Bridgestones and Other Resonance Articles*, p. 20).

Though a resonance article may be used by any fragmentor to store excess fragmental energy, these items are of particular use to teleporters as they allow the intentional direction of a bridge. Without a resonance article, there is no known way to predict where a bridge will lead.

When used to open a bridge, a resonance article is typically called a *skipstone*; a misnomer, as these resonance articles are often not made of stone at all, except in the case of rare gems and, of course, bridgestones.

A living skipstone, such as a plant, is the most commonly used item, and will take the teleporter directly to the place from which the skipstone was collected or grown. The most reliable of these is one's own body (see *You Are a Resonance Article*, p. 23), which will direct the bridge to a point between where the teleporter was conceived and born.

This presents a problem when that point is an unsafe location, such as deep space. However, this issue may be corrected by ensuring all teleporters are born in close proximity with a bridgestone, as these stones naturally magnify resonance.

It was quite a coincidence that the bridgestone near my parents' stables connected to the one at the base of the Gale Ridge Mountains, so close to Aaron's hidden cottage. But *was* it a coincidence?

Probably not, I thought. *Nothing seems to be.* I closed the book, yearning to lie down and go to sleep.

"I wish I could have gone to the inn," I said. It was just down the street from the docks and close to the stand that Jorin used for selling oardoo feathers.

"I'm glad those boys left," Farrah whispered to me. "Falon spent the entire time pretending not to stare at me, and Markus didn't bother pretending. They need to get themselves bonded."

"Can't really blame them," I said, glancing around. The ship cabin had barely enough room for us all to squeeze in. Fitch sat on the floor between the bunks, taking up the entire space while Ellis and Shane chatted quietly from the top bunks. Aaron's soft snore on the bottom bunk across from where Farrah and I lounged gave me a funny warm feeling in my chest. Who knew snoring could be so cute?

Farrah's quiet laugh made me think she watched him as well, but when I glanced up, she was giving me an odd look.

"What?" I asked.

She pressed her mouth into a line, not quite hiding her smirk. "You don't know, do you?"

"Know what?"

"Markus and Falon's father, Regalinius, competed with Magister Axel to bond me after his wife died. That melonbelly would have been far better than Axel, but still, I didn't want that life. Their dispute gave me time to come to Terik. If Jorin hadn't helped us get permission to bond, I might be Markus and Falon's stepmother right now."

"Oh," I said. "That's awkward. I hope they weren't rude to you." I couldn't reveal the fact that the Eboros brothers both had Transmutation, which has the side effect of amplifying the sex drive. For them to have a stunning woman like Farrah as a stepmother, who was only a few years older . . . well, the thought made me laugh, though I knew it shouldn't.

"What's funny?" Farrah asked.

A quick knock on the cabin door saved me from having to explain that particular kink. Fitch stood up and cracked it open to peer outside. His huge body blocked the entire doorway.

"May I speak with Lina?" a man asked.

Merimo.

I didn't like the way my pulse quickened at the sound of his voice. I couldn't stop thinking about how I'd dreamed of him *before* meeting him. Though I knew he was dangerous and powerful, he was intriguing, as well.

Fitch glanced back at Aaron, who'd awakened at Merimo's knock and now sat at the side of the bunk. Clearly Fitch expected him to decide if I was allowed to speak with our visitor. I bristled when Aaron stood to confront the man.

"Aaron, please," I hissed, slipping between him and Fitch. Aaron looked like he might argue, but he sat down again, and Fitch sat next to him so I could pass. I stood in the open doorway, not wanting to go all the way out.

"It's all right," Merimo said. "I'm veiled. No one can see me except you. If you take my hand, I'll veil you as well. Please, I need to talk to you." He held his hand out to me. He had a pleasant expression on his face but was all business. He wore what appeared to be a regular Monashi belted tunic now, in gray, with black pants and knee-high leather boots. He completed the ensemble with his ridiculous pirate hat, but the feather was missing.

I peeked over my shoulder in much the same way Fitch had done, but Aaron stared at the ground with a decidedly neutral expression.

"I'll be right back," I said.

Aaron's ice-blue eyes flicked to mine as he nodded, then turned away. I sighed before taking Merimo's hand, closing the door behind me. Men's muffled voices escaped from the cabin, but I decided to ignore them.

"What is it?" I asked coldly.

"I did some investigating while I waited for you to arrive," he answered, seemingly oblivious to my tone. "I couldn't find your friend, Ward, but the other one, Cobb, is in Axel's holding cell. The younger girl was already delivered to the Rhoyal Healers Guild."

"You found all that out already? How long have you been waiting for us?"

Merimo grinned. "I was joking about finding my hat, Lina. I actually just dropped myself onto a bridge and came directly here."

"Oh, I see. So, you just instigated a major emotional crisis and then performed a little comedy. That makes perfect sense."

"I'm sorry—"

"Yeah, I'm hearing a lot of that from you, *Gerhelm*," I said, raising my voice. "Your many apologies sound empty to me. Thank you for the information, but I can't imagine spending any more time with someone who thinks hurting people is funny." I turned away from him, but Merimo didn't let go of my hand.

"Lina, wait. I haven't told you what you need to know yet," he said. I didn't jerk my hand away, but I didn't turn back to him either. I simply listened.

Merimo exhaled loudly in frustration, then steadied his breath. "Look. My understanding is that it's relatively easy to call a spirit back if they haven't crossed the death bridge yet, but if they have, then it's nearly impossible. There are only two times per year that it can be done, and the next one is at the fall equinox."

"When is that?"

"Tomorrow night. Or, rather, early the next morning, around one a.m. Every year, there is a Harvest Festival before the equinox. The festivities start in the early afternoon and run into the wee hours. It's a big celebration, a bit like America's Thanksgiving mixed with Mardi Gras. There is a town feast, with cider and music. Men come in from all around the world and get very drunk."

I sighed. "Do you have a point?" I asked, though I was curious how he knew about American traditions.

Merimo paused, then said, "Lina, please. I'm sorry. I got carried away, but you must understand. People like us aren't just rare, we're . . . virtually nonexistent." As Merimo's frustration escalated, a minor German accent broke through what I had previously thought to be a standard American accent.

"What do you mean?" I asked.

"You have Absorption and Protection *together*. That's not supposed to be possible. The two are true opposites. Some reservoirs repel each other, but those are the only two that do it so strongly that they can't mix. Do you understand? If someone has one, they *never* have the other. But somehow, impossibly, we do, and it gives us the ability to absorb life from the world around us and use it to heal ourselves. From anything. Including aging."

He let that sink in a moment, and I turned back to see his face overcome by raw emotion. "I have been searching for someone like you for nearly two thousand years." He squeezed my hand hard now, pleading.

"Two *thousand*?"

"Yes," he said. "I've spent a lot of time tracking rare reservoirs, but Protection is the only one that doesn't run in families. You and I have all the time in the world. But Aaron . . . if he ascends his Protection, he could live four hundred years, but he will die, in time. We will not."

My breath caught in my throat. He was right about one thing. This was exactly what I needed to know. Merimo gazed into my eyes, drawing me close to him and into a deep Connection link.

Let me show you, he thought.

In the space of an instant, he opened himself wide to me. His life, his memories, the people he loved and lost, his triumphs, failures, joy, and despair all soaked into me like water seeping into dry sand. I gasped at the flood of memories and emotions and felt him steady me as I swayed to one side. It was like having an instantaneous recovery from amnesia. I didn't see every single memory, but I saw more than enough. I saw *him* as he was: beautiful, deeply troubled, and utterly alone.

He was born in Germany and spent his first few decades fighting against the expansion of the Roman Empire. Eventually, people noticed that he didn't age normally and made various attempts to murder him. One day, he decided to let them.

He faked his own death—an activity that would become one of his favorite games—then traveled to Norway, and later Russia, where he spent several centuries. At that time, he only had greater Protection and lesser Absorption along with lesser Transformation. He didn't know any of that, though, or even understand his own extended life. He spent more than two centuries searching for others like himself and honing his ability to heal and make a shield.

One day he traveled south to Madrid, where he came across a bridgestone. He felt the stone's Transformation resonance, but he didn't understand what it meant since he couldn't yet use his own lesser Transformation.

After marking the stone with a large *X*, he visited it hundreds of times over the course of a decade before he finally witnessed a spontaneous bridge occurrence. In a moment of pure recklessness, he jumped onto the bridge, which brought him to Monash. He ascended his Protection on that bridge in what he remembered as the most shocking experience of his life. Though he later learned there were more painful ascensions, nothing prepares you for that first time.

On Monash, he met a woman, Yuha, who taught him about reservoirs. She had greater Connection and lesser Protection and Production. Together they traveled to eleven of the twelve worlds, acquiring new reservoirs along the way. He loved her, and despite his increasingly desperate attempts to keep her with him, she died at the age of four hundred and eighteen.

Afterward, Merimo spent almost three hundred years as a giant blue octopus, never coming to the surface. He thought he would get over her, but he couldn't, and eventually he attempted what he had only pretended to do back in his homeland. He tried to take his own life, but no matter what he did, his Protection and Absorption worked together to regenerate any damage.

Merimo wasn't just alone. He was trapped in eternal solitary confinement. Some years, he would find something to distract himself from the torture of it, but he'd spent the last quarter century transforming his brain into that of an uncomprehending marine animal so he could be numb to it. That's what he'd been doing when he found me.

It had taken a few moments for him to pick through the resonances and recognize that I had both Protection and Absorption. He'd held me underwater for nearly thirty minutes while he transformed back into his natural human form. To him, bumping into another immortal had been like discovering the Ark of the Covenant in his own basement. A true, precious treasure. He'd been astounded and elated to the point of madness.

Then, I'd kissed him.

I was out of my mind, Lina, he thought. *I'm sorry. I regret my actions, but you were never in any danger. For better or worse, you are immortal, like me.*

I don't understand, I thought. *If I can't die, then how did I get Conjuration? And why do we have both Protection and Absorption?*

He shook his head. *I can't answer that. What I do know is that I have to leave you here. If I interfere, then Violet's plans will fall apart.*

"How do you know about Violet's plans?" I blurted.

Merimo looked down with a pained expression. "Things are not always as they seem," he said, then he glanced at the cabin door. "Sometimes, people you've trusted your whole life turn out to be liars. And other times, people you barely know turn out to be the only ones you can trust."

"Your cryptic messages are exceedingly unhelpful," I complained. "I thought you were here to support me. Now what do I do?"

"I am supporting you, Schatzi. Listen, Ward has escaped."

My eyes widened and a bursting joy threatened to knock me over. *Escaped? Yes! My boy is all grown up! But he was hurt when I saw him last. I must have given him Protection, after all.* My hands came to my mouth, and I squealed in excitement. "Where is he?" I asked. "What happened?"

Merimo relaxed, smiling at my reaction. "He reportedly overpowered Cobb and fled into the city, but Seleca has men searching for him, and they seem optimistic about finding him."

"Why do you say that?"

"There's been an announcement that everyone must attend a ceremony after the Harvest Festival tomorrow. It's being held at one in the morning."

"The equinox," I said.

Merimo nodded. "If that's when they plan to resurrect Anick, then they must think they can recapture Ward by then. If you want to find him, going to that ceremony is probably your best chance. Perhaps you won't even have to do anything. You could just hide and watch from the rooftops. Either way, I will see you afterward and take you to dinner. As friends. I am *for* you, Lina, I promise."

He watched me, clutching my hand, and through Connection, I knew that he was thinking about our kiss on the beach again—that it had been the first time he'd felt relief since his wife died more than a millennium ago.

"I'm not her," I said.

"Of course you aren't. I'm not asking you to be. No one could ever replace her." Merimo's cobalt-blue eyes glistened as he dropped them. He ground his teeth together and swallowed before refocusing on me. She'd been dead a thousand years, and he still missed her desperately. At that realization, all remnants of my anger deserted me.

My dad used to say that I was too forgiving, while my mom said I wasn't forgiving enough. I guess the true answer depends on where you're standing. When it comes down to it, I simply have a soft spot for lonely people because I've experienced it so much myself. Maybe Merimo knew that about me and took advantage. Then again, maybe he didn't.

Spirit's observation about him wanting me had been a vast understatement. He didn't just want me. He needed me, in any form that I was willing to give him.

"Friends," I said.

Merimo nodded, exhaling a long breath. "Friends," he repeated, then he coaxed me into a gentle, tentative hug. I relaxed and let him hug me, resting my head on his shoulder. He didn't smell like seaweed anymore but like something I couldn't quite pinpoint. Cinnamon and something else. Myrrh, maybe. I liked it.

"Before I go," he said, talking into my hair, "can I do something for you?"

"What?" I asked.

"You can't walk around Neesee in those clothes. As your friend, I should tell you that you look ridiculous."

"That's rich coming from you." I laughed, leaning back so I could gawk at his hat. "But even if I agreed with that argument, women's clothing feels like it's made out of steel wool."

"May I?" he asked, pointing at my clothes.

I nodded, though I was hesitant to give him permission to remove my clothes. He reached up to my shoulder and grabbed a bit of my tunic. The clothing immediately felt slippery on my body, like it had been transformed into water. I held my hands in front of me in case I ended up naked and needed to quickly cover myself.

It wasn't necessary. The fabric vibrated and heated up, then it stretched and grew in volume. The tunic, which had been loose, cinched in at my waist and became rather snug in the bodice, though it covered me all the way to a high neck. The bottom tripled in volume to become a heavy skirt while the color faded from brown to a lighter cream color, a subtle aquamarine and leafy green brocade stitched throughout. It was elegant and surprisingly comfortable as it stretched and moved with me.

"Wow," I said. "Not exactly Xena: Warrior Princess, but it'll do."

"The heavy skirt releases if you need to run. Just tug here, and it will come loose." He showed me a piece of fabric hidden on the right side. "And here," he said, pointing out a hidden compartment, "is a pocket where you can keep your weapons. There's a built-in sheath right here." He lifted a flap of fabric to reveal the top of a leather sheath just big enough to hide a large dagger.

"Pockets!" I exclaimed. Apparently, it doesn't take much to make me happy. "That is exactly what women's clothing is always missing."

"I know," he said, a smile tugging at one corner of his mouth. "It has always been that way."

"The question is," I said, rubbing my hands together like the villain I was, "what shall I put in this magical pocket?"

"Ah," he said, his eyes sweeping over his work, "that is the limit of my help, I'm afraid. Though, if I may say so, I've done a wonderful job. You look lovely."

I smiled at him. "Thank you, Merimo."

He nodded in acknowledgment of my gratitude. "Call me Zig."

"Zig?" I asked. "Not Gerhelm?"

He shrugged. "Gerhelm Meriweather is a pen name. I have a lot of those."

"Zig," I repeated. "Thank you."

"You're most welcome," he said. He seemed like he wanted to say something else, but then he withered a little. "Good luck, Lina. I'll see you on the other side."

With that, he let me go and disappeared entirely from view, though I could hear his steps on the deck as I backed up to the cabin door.

"Bye, Zig," I said.

I turned and opened the door, then held it open to air out the dirty sock smell that smacked me in the face. I hadn't noticed it before, and it kicked my nausea into overdrive. It was deeply unfair that I had to be seasick while the boat wasn't even sailing.

Snoring resounded from the top bunks, but Aaron's reflective eyes shone out of the darkness, and I smiled at him. After a minute, I closed the cabin door, stepped over Fitch, who was fast asleep and taking up the entire walkway, and slipped onto the bottom bunk next to Aaron. It was small for a Monashi bed, just big enough for me to squeeze in if I lay on my side.

The air was moist and chilly, so Aaron dragged the covers up over us as I snuggled into the crook of his arm, then intertwined my fingers with his, connecting. He speculated as to how I'd managed to change and where I had gotten such an extravagant gown. Then he wondered how difficult it would be to take off me. I grinned at him, thinking about my interaction with Merimo.

Not Merimo, I thought to myself. *Zig. My ancient friend, Zig.*

"I think the word you're searching for is 'classic,'" Spirit whispered, making me jump. She had communicated in a way that I'd heard with my ears rather than with my mind, which meant Aaron had also heard her. We both surveyed the cabin, but she was nowhere to be seen.

"Spirit?"

"I'm here, Lina."

I wanted to ask why I couldn't see her, but I had an even more important question on my mind. "Zig said Ward escaped—is that true?"

"Yes! He's hiding out at his boyfriend's house."

"His what? Since when does he have a boyfriend?" I stared at Aaron, gauging his response to this news. His mouth tugged up ever so slightly at the corner, an expression that made me feel all warm and tingly inside.

"He doesn't, really," Spirit responded, "but the sparks are clearly flying. The guy's name is Benz, and he's Ward's former roommate from SONA. They were basically kids the last time they saw each other. Ward managed to ask around and find him, then he just showed up on the poor guy's doorstep. His shiny new Protection reservoir has made him bold. Oh, and Ward heard me speak too."

"What?!" Spirit was full of shocking news today. "How?"

"I think it had something to do with you transferring pieces of your reservoirs to him. His soul looks different now. Brighter, or like the color is different."

"Souls have a color?"

"No, not really. It's hard to explain. It's more like a flavor. That's it. His soul *tastes* different now."

"You're making fun of me, aren't you?"

Spirit giggled, making me wish I could see her face. "Forget it," she said. "Just do what you came in here to do."

"What do you mean?" I asked, then stopped, realizing that I knew exactly what she meant because she had stolen the thought from my own head.

Aaron tensed, then finally met my eyes, his focused concentration piercing. I had come to a decision, and he knew it. The temperature in the cabin shot up, making the air unbearably hot and stuffy. I kicked a leg out from under the bunk blanket and took a deep breath in and out.

I'll put it on, I thought to him.

What?

Your bracelet. When you get it for me, I'll put it on.

Aaron blinked in surprise. *Lee, you can take your time.* He'd expected me to announce I was going off with Merimo.

I don't need time, I insisted. *I've decided. Just like you, I think I knew the day I met you, when you walked toward me with those weird dragon-skin boots and your terrifying scowl. Even when you pointed your tiny crossbow at my face, I knew you wouldn't hurt me. I followed you home like a lost puppy. I'm not an inherently trusting person, Aaron. Yet I trusted you. I love you, and I don't want to waste one minute of our time together. So, get me my cuff bracelet. I'll put it on.*

Aaron searched my face, his disbelief still plainly written across his features, then released a deep sigh that sent a thrill of excitement down my spine.

I love you too, he thought, squeezing his eyes shut against the emotions that threatened to overtake him. To relieve the pressure, he heaved me toward him for a kiss that was probably inappropriate in a room full of people. He came to the same conclusion and leaned back, then decided it was too dark in the room to matter and attacked my lips again. I laughed into his mouth.

"I'll get it tomorrow," he whispered, elation spilling out of him like a storm cloud finally releasing its burden. "We'll be spoiled for choice, believe me. Tomorrow is the Harvest Festival. The streets will be filled with vendors. I love this time of year."

A whole slew of visions and fantasies swirled between us, each of us adding our own ideas. I thought of how surprised my parents would be and wondered if there was enough room to build a house on their property. Then we imagined two homes, one on Earth and one on Monash. When I showed him how pregnancy worked where I was from, however, we were back to just Earth, and then he was mentally designing a tree house in the backyard.

I returned his grin but let go of his hand, carefully severing our link. I'd have to explain the difference in our lifespans at some point, but I didn't want to ruin the moment by dwelling on our inevitable parting.

Oh my god. I'm engaged, I thought to myself. *Is that what I just did? Yeah, I guess it is. I'm engaged. Whoa. I wish my mom were here.*

Having to experience this monumental moment without my parents sent a pang of regret through me, like I had lost something dear that I could never get back. I couldn't even call them to tell them. My mind swam, and I began to feel a little lightheaded. This wasn't at all how I imagined this moment would go. None of what was happening felt like it could be real and instead felt like an all-consuming delusion.

What if this really is a delusion and I'm in a psychiatric hospital somewhere?

Calm down. This is real, Spirit thought to me.

But what if it isn't? You could be a delusion, too, Spirit.

Take a breath. Everything is okay. You love Aaron. He's your Mr. Right. I see that now, but I still want you to be careful.

Why?

Well, Spirit thought, her voice fading to a whisper, *he may be Mr. Right, but that doesn't make him Mr. Perfect. As you go along, you'll find things out about him that will make you want to run in the other direction. Don't.*

Spirit, what is wrong with your voice? And why can't I see you? She didn't respond. *Spirit?*

Chapter Seven

"*This inn provides no dragon's den as do others of a more sensible nature,*" commented Syndeth, "*but I will never be too far away for you to call me. Our bond will alert me if you are in need.*"

Linorra knew this to be true, as she remembered that when she lay, mortally wounded, within the witch's cottage, she had heard her trembling heart call to his.

Terik yanked the door open without knocking and bellowed in a voice deeper and gruffer than Aaron's, "Well, we've lost them." He glared at me and Aaron accusingly.

Fitch sat bolt upright at the sudden noise, and Shane did the same only to crack his head on the overhead and nearly fall off the top bunk.

"Who?" Aaron asked.

"Those Eboros boys. That arrogant ass, Markus, took one look at the inn and decided he'd rather go back to daddy's estate. Falon tried to talk him out of it, but Markus wouldn't be persuaded, so the boy had to follow him. They're probably on their way to announce our presence as we speak."

"We'll need to go after them," I said, "but before we do, there's something else." Everyone turned to me with an expression that made me think they were surprised I'd spoken at all. I rolled my eyes. I would have to fix that expectation somehow.

I swung my legs over the side of the bunk into the space that Fitch had vacated, then I stood up to address the room. They all stared at my new dress as if I had performed some kind of magic trick.

"Merimo paid me a visit, and he had some information," I said, ignoring their confused expressions. I told them what Zig had told me about Ward, Cobb, and the girl, revealing nothing about our immortality discussion. Neither did I tell them his real name, though I had already informed Aaron.

"We heard about the ceremony," Jorin said, squeezing in behind Terik. "I thought some lordling must be bonding another unfortunate girl, but then they announced that the ceremony wouldn't be until the wee hours of the morning and that attendance was mandatory. Very unusual."

"We need to go after Cobb tonight," Fitch said, watching me. "Before it's too late." He waited for my agreement since I was the only one who could release Cobb from her Projection trance. Cobb, who Spirit had discovered was a woman posing as a man, was in serious danger. It was a wonder that she hadn't already been exposed.

"If we do that, we'll alert them to our presence prior to finding Ward," I said, ignoring Fitch's simmering frustration. I understood his fear and admired his commitment to his sister, but we needed to be strategic about this rescue attempt or it wouldn't work.

"If the Holy—" Shane began, then corrected himself. "If *Seleca* has Precognition now, then won't they know we're here anyway?"

"Not necessarily," Aaron answered. "Precognition is so difficult to control that it's almost useless to someone without experience."

"Not to mention the debilitating headaches that make ya not want to even try," added Jorin.

"That too," agreed Aaron, though he didn't meet Jorin's gaze. Given his history of abandonment, I questioned whether Aaron would ever forgive his betrayal.

"We should wait until the ceremony," I said, "get Ward if he's there, then go after Cobb. The girl who went to the Rhoyal Healers Guild will have to wait until we have the means to rescue the entire compound."

I made eye contact with Ellis, thinking of his daughter. Only he and I knew of her, and I imagined it should stay that way. I also guessed that he wasn't leaving this city without her, which meant we'd also have to rescue her mother, at the very least.

I then looked to Aaron to confirm. When he nodded, I felt absurdly grateful that he'd supported me in front of the crew. Even if I were a man, I'd still probably need his support to exert any influence, but the fact that I was a woman made it indispensable. I was dead in the water without it.

"We'll go to the Eboros estate first," Aaron said. "We need to contain that problem before we do anything else."

"Do we know where their estate is located?" I asked.

"Everyone does," Shane said. "Regalinius Eboros has the largest property in Neesee. It has a view of the bay with a private dock, not too far from here."

"They have a lot to lose by helping us," Terik commented.

"That's true," I said, glancing at Aaron. "They also have a lot to lose by *not* helping us."

Aaron met my gaze, then bit one side of his bottom lip. He and I were the only ones who knew the Eboros family secret. If anyone found out about their Transmutation reservoirs, they could lose everything they had. "You two should go back to the inn," he said, turning back to Terik. "Act like nothing out of the ordinary is happening. Sell your oardoo feathers tomorrow as planned, then come back to the boat and wait for us in case we need to escape quickly."

"We're supposed to go to the ceremony," Terik said. "Jorin is well known in this town. If he doesn't show, people will notice and come hunting. They'll check the boat first."

"Something bad is going to happen tomorrow night," I said, considering Farrah. She cradled her enormous belly again, looking truly sick. "If Jorin must go, then so be it, but Farrah, at the very least, should stay in the cabin and hide. In fact, everyone who won't be missed should stay here."

"I'm going," Fitch said. "If Axel is back from the dead, he'll bring Cobb with him to the ceremony. If my brother is there, then I need to be there." Shane nodded emphatically, eyeing my dress again.

"I'm going too," Ellis said. "You have a lot of people to save. We need to keep you alive." He said it casually, like he was adding items to a grocery list and didn't care if I lived as long as I accomplished my task.

I shivered involuntarily, not because I was afraid of dying but because I doubted the world would thank me later for releasing Ellis from his Projection trance. A well of darkness simmered beneath his mask of calm, as if hatred had grown inside him during the years he'd been imprisoned within his own body. Little by little, like water through cracks in a levee, that trickle of dark energy would wear away at his facade until the whole thing came crashing down.

Somewhere inside me, Evilina smiled.

"Fine," I said, "but you have to let me work. No interfering for the sake of my safety. I'm not as fragile as you may think."

I was uncertain if Zig was right about me being invulnerable. I must have died at least once if I had Conjuration, and I'd witnessed my own body trying to die again when I'd allowed my spirit to wander out of it that day in the oardoo fields. But Zig had supposedly kept me under water for a half hour, and I had survived. If these men accompanied me as my bodyguards, then I could be putting them in danger for no reason at all.

Aaron nodded. "All right," he said. "Let's get going."

We all shuffled out of the cabin. Aaron and I left our packs, which had been stuffed into a locked storage bin outside the cabin. I said goodbye to Farrah, who seemed distressed that I was leaving her, but I promised to be there when she needed me. Then, we headed out for the Eboros estate.

As it was the middle of the night, early morning really, the docks were quiet, but there were still some stragglers loading the last of their wares onto handcarts to be dragged out to wherever they'd be sold. Some of the carts were painted a golden color and marked with a *V*. It reminded me of Axel's golden cloak.

"What is that?" I asked Aaron, pointing to the symbol.

"That's the symbol of the Ministry," Aaron said. "Transformation is the fifth fragment of the Noble Six. It's supposed to symbolize Eve's rise to divinity. All merchants trading in this area owe one-fifth of their wares as tribute to the Goddess."

"Oh, I see," I said. "I guess in Neesee taxes are even more certain than death." Aaron nodded, a little frown on his face. He likely had no idea what I was talking about, as usual. He took up position on my left, giving me his right hand to hold. Shane walked on the other side of me, while Ellis and Fitch walked in front of us.

The streets were gray and smooth like a modern asphalt street on Earth. I guessed they were the work of Transformation, but as they didn't need to accommodate vehicles, all the roads were narrow, occasionally opening to a wide courtyard with gazebos and landscaped gardens.

I had imagined Neesee to be a sleepy little preindustrial town, but this was not the case. Neesee was huge, with gray and brown buildings up to six stories tall. The buildings had trees grown directly into them, like they'd used living wood as framing, then built the rest with stone transformed to perfectly match the frame.

It had the appearance of a contemporary European city, except greener, with oil lanterns instead of electricity. The street was lined with shops and cafés, all still open and busy. The heady aroma of grilled meat and baking bread saturated the air, along with a mix of spices that I couldn't quite identify, something like onion or garlic, with a heavy herb like sage. It made both my eyes and my mouth water.

For the first time since I'd arrived, music rang out clear and jubilant, a mix of string and wind instruments playing energetically in a nonstandard scale while men sang loudly, half yelling, half laughing. I didn't see many women among them.

"They're having fun," I noted.

"They are," Aaron said. "It's the only time of year that they're allowed to openly celebrate."

"What are they celebrating?" I asked.

"The Ascension," he said. "The Ministry teaches that on the fall equinox, the Holy Mother, Eve, received the last reservoir of the Noble Six and became the Ascended Mother. Her mortal body was burned away, purified, and she was transformed into an ever-youthful goddess. She never leaves her palace, and she rules all Monash from her throne of Rhoya, which bend to her will."

"In other words, she killed her last victim, absorbed his reservoir, enthralled everyone around her, and forced healers to extend her life," I said.

"Shh, keep your voice down," Aaron said. "You'll start a riot." Then he said, as an aside, "But yes. That's the gist of it."

"The day is coming when I won't need to keep my voice down," I said.

"Quite possibly," Aaron agreed, "but that day has not yet come."

I shrugged. "Maybe tomorrow. How long is our walk?"

"The docks are surrounded by a high wall, so we'll have to exit on the street side, then snake back around toward the bay. From there, we'll walk along Bayshore Boulevard. The Eboros estate entrance is on that road, and the house itself is set back on a hill overlooking the water. It's maybe fifteen minutes total."

"Probably longer for a silken goat like you," Fitch commented.

Aaron laughed, and he wasn't the only one. Evidently, it was common to call a child or a smaller female a silken goat as the animals were comparatively tiny and beautiful but also twitchy and rather useless for anything except growing silky white hair that could be transformed into fine clothing. Aaron had already called me that once himself. Clearly, the silken goat comparison wasn't going away anytime soon.

"You are all so hilarious," I said dryly. "Why don't you come to Earth and see how many people call you a giraffe. Then we'll see how funny it is."

"What's a giraffe?" Shane asked.

"It's an absurdly tall animal with a long, skinny neck and a long, skinny tongue. They're big and awkward and completely adorable."

"So, you think I'm adorable?" Shane asked, grinning down at me. I wasn't certain, but it seemed like Shane had already put on some weight. Maybe it was just because he had rehydrated, but he appeared much healthier, handsome even. Another twenty pounds and he'd be downright pretty. He noticed me studying him, and his grin widened. "Do you want to see my tongue?" he asked.

"That will be enough of that," Aaron interjected. He pulled me toward him a little. *Watch out for that one*, he thought to me irritably. *He just made a pass at you right in front of me. The men here are starved for affection, so I'm not surprised he's testing how serious we are. That will stop when you put the bonding cuff on.*

I squeezed his hand. *You have nothing to worry about*, I thought. I found Shane's minor attention amusing, but the last thing I wanted to do was encourage Aaron's jealousy. *I made my decision. You're mine for the next four hundred years.*

Four hundred? Aaron laughed. He thought I was kidding, but when he didn't sense any telepathic teasing from me, he stared at me hard. *You're not joking.*

I shook my head. *Aaron, you're the one who told me that healing extends your lifespan and that Seleca is more than a hundred years old.*

Yes, but they're—

Goddesses? I finished. *No, they aren't. Merimo said that his wife lived for four hundred years, and I suspect that you will too. Are you sure you still want to bond with me? That's quite a long commitment.*

His brow furrowed, and he looked down at his boots. I stopped in my tracks, staring at him. I hadn't considered that his answer might actually be no. He barely noticed when my hand separated from his.

Shane glanced back at us, then called to the others to stop. Ellis and Fitch, who had come to a decorative stone wall separating the street from the Bay of March, turned back as well, confusion written all over their faces. They were all staring when another wave of nausea rolled over me. With my hand over my mouth, I searched wildly for a place to throw up and spotted the wall.

Perfect.

A moment later, I was draped over it to once again puke my guts out in front of two men who competed for my affection. Well, dry heave, really. And it wasn't really a competition unless you count the race to see who could get away from me the fastest.

I'm not even on the boat anymore. What the ... hang on.

Shit.

When was my last period?

I hadn't had one since I left Earth, but the IUD does that. I wasn't one of the lucky ones who stopped having periods altogether, but they were irregular and light, coming every two to three months. I stared up at the sky, racking my brain.

It's been longer than that, I thought, *but that doesn't mean anything. Could my IUD have gotten damaged during my accident? Or ... what if the IUD doesn't work due to Aaron's reservoirs?*

I tried to recall any warnings given to me way back when I'd gotten the IUD nine years before, but I doubted there had been anything about superspecial fire sperm.

Wait ... nine years? Wasn't my brand of IUD supposed to expire after eight years? Or is this like when juice expires, but you can still drink it?

I stared at the dark sky again, thinking furiously. My heart suddenly pounded out of control as sweat beaded on my forehead despite the cold.

God? I know I said I don't believe in you, and that's still mostly true, but I just want you to know that if you're taking revenge by surprise-pregnancy-troping me, I'm going to fly up there and fucking de-grace you.

But this wasn't an act of some angry deity, I knew. This was all me. I hadn't even checked to see if my stupid IUD string was intact before I started having hot sex with a man I'd known for five minutes.

What in the hell is wrong with me? I covered my face with my hands, a common habit during my daily episodes of self-loathing. There was no one to blame but myself. And Aaron, I supposed. *Yeah, let's blame Aaron. I like this plan.*

I peeked back to see Aaron still preoccupied with our previous conversation, a deep line between his brows. *He's already overprotective enough. How will he behave if I really am pregnant?*

I turned back to the bay, my mind desperately trying to make sense of my new reality. The lighted docks we'd walked from were visible from this vantage point, but clouds had blown in to block out any light from Heshia or the stars. The ship lanterns out in the water were the only constellation, tiny specks of life floating in an endless void. I wondered how many of those lights would be snuffed out should Anick return.

Specks of light, like this baby who's connected to me by a—

Inspiration knocked me over the head. I'd connected with Farrah's babies, hadn't I? Maybe I could do that with my own. I'd never tried to connect with *myself* because, ya know, that's stupid, but it might work the same. Hesitantly, I laid my trembling hands on my belly and searched for signs of life.

After a moment, I found it—a teeny, tiny heartbeat, nearly twice as fast as my own. A little girl with resonances so faint that I hadn't noticed them . . . *Oh my god. She has multiple reservoirs and—*I sucked in a breath—*both Protection and Absorption. She has both, like me. And Evocation.*

Like her daddy.

My heart squeezed, and a sudden and fierce wave of protectiveness like nothing I'd ever felt overcame me. *She's both of us*, I thought. *But Zig said Protection doesn't run in families.* As if that argument could make it not true.

I flinched when Aaron's hand landed on my shoulder. I hadn't heard him come up behind me.

"Lee, I'm sorry," he said. "I didn't mean to upset you. It's late and I was just surprised, but this changes nothing." Then he saw my face. "What's wrong?"

I hesitated to turn toward him, debating how to break the news. Or *if* I should break the news.

I didn't want to be deceitful, but I worried about what Aaron's reaction might be right before we confronted a possible enemy. What if he got angry with me for getting pregnant after I'd sworn up and down that it was impossible? What if he thought I was trying to trap him?

What if he decided this mission was too dangerous for a pregnant woman and called the whole thing off? Ward's fate hung in the balance, not to mention Cobb's. If my surprise pregnancy affected *me* this much, then it might affect Aaron even more since his Evocation made emotional control so difficult for him. But . . . I had promised to be honest with him.

And I will, I told myself. *I'll tell him at some quiet moment in a way that will make it special. Not right before we ambush the most powerful man in Neesee. That is not the time for a gender reveal party.*

"I'm fine," I said, wiping my mouth on my sleeve to hide the drool that had been the only product of my nausea, then smiled weakly. "I just thought you'd changed your mind. So, we're all right?"

Aaron smiled warmly at me, taking my face in his hands. "We're better than all right, Lee," he said. "Rhoya! Sometimes I miss you even when you're standing right next to me. I'll take every moment I can get with you, whether it's a hundred years or a million. I'd bond you to me right now just to get one extra minute."

He pulled my face to his, gazing into my eyes. His were a crystal-clear blue that I swore let me see right into his soul, a sight even more beautiful than his perfect face. Both were far too good for me. "Forever wouldn't be enough," he whispered.

His kiss told me that he meant every word.

Chapter Eight

*L*inorra held her sword out in front of her. She would not fail this time. "Stay behind me, Syndeth," she said. "I will protect you."

"We're here," Ellis said, pointing. "There's that pretentious durrite gate."

The gate was set into a high stone wall covered in vines sprouting white, pink, and purple flowers that looked and smelled like wisteria. The gate itself was enormous, reaching several feet above the tallest of our group and wide enough for a semi to drive through, but it had a delicate design with vines and a variety of flowers that I didn't recognize.

This was the first time I fully appreciated the beauty of durrite and could understand its value. It was black, like wrought iron, but it had a silky texture that gleamed with an iridescent golden sheen. The gate was clearly an elaborate display of wealth.

"Goddess, that gate is worth more than our boat," Shane murmured. Fitch grunted in what I assumed was agreement.

Oil lanterns burned on either side of the gate, and two more cast light through the gate from the other side. We skulked in the shadows a few dozen yards away.

"How do we get through?" I murmured. "Do we walk right in? Or does someone need to scale the wall?"

"None of the gates are locked, but I guarantee that they have armed guards," Ellis said. "We should do this the polite way."

"Oh, I don't know," I mused. "There's really no polite way to march into someone's house uninvited, is there? I think I'm just going to walk right in with my shield up."

Aaron glanced at me, then closed his eyes for a second and nodded. "Here, Fitch, take this," he said, handing the massive man his crossbow. Even without the weapon, Fitch was an intimidating hulk, but he took it without comment, following Aaron's lead like they'd worked together for years.

"Follow us up the path," Aaron continued, "then stand at the front door to guard our retreat. If anyone causes trouble, Shane is to come warn us while Fitch holds them off. Ellis, you come with us within the shield and guard our backs if we take it down. Do you still have the other crossbow?"

Ellis nodded, pulling the small one-handed crossbow he'd used to kill Axel out of a deep pocket of his tunic.

"All right," Aaron said. "Spirit, are you there?"

For a moment, nothing happened, and I wondered if I needed to be worried. I hadn't seen her since she'd talked to us in the boat cabin without appearing. Could something hurt a ghost? Spirit had mentioned being bound at one point, but I had never followed up with her to get the details.

"I'm here," Spirit said finally, letting me breathe. She materialized beside Aaron but appeared more transparent than usual.

What is going on with you? I asked privately. *Are you secretly in trouble?*

Apparently, you're the one who's secretly in "trouble," she quipped, inspecting my belly, then staring at me with raised eyebrows.

I jerked in surprise. I hadn't sensed her presence for a while, and I hadn't actively been thinking about the baby when she arrived. How had she known that I was pregnant let alone that I planned to keep it a secret from Aaron? I would have asked, but I didn't want to take the chance that Aaron might accidentally hear our telepathic conversation.

Nice deflection, I thought, darting a furtive glance at Aaron. *And I'm not ready for that discussion yet.*

Same, girl. Same. Let's just get through this confrontation. Then we can worry about catching up on girl talk.

Fine, but I'm not letting this go. I was planning on sharing my news with you, but it doesn't seem like you can say the same. Spirit glanced at me guiltily, then directed her attention to Aaron.

"Spirit, stay with us too," Aaron said. "Keep a silent communication open between me and Lina and tell us if anyone around us might be a problem."

"Roger that," Spirit responded in an echoey voice.

"I need a weapon too," I said. Aaron gave me the *look*. I sighed. "Aaron, you have, like, ten knives on you. I'm only asking for one."

"Here," Ellis said, holding out Axel's dagger. "You can borrow this."

"Thank you, *Ellis*," I said pointedly to Aaron. "I'll take good care of it."

Aaron now directed his disapproval at Ellis, whose detached countenance left no question about how many fucks he had to give. I slid the dagger into my dress's built-in sheath, listening to the satisfying *shwip* as it slid in. It fit like a glove.

I brought up my shield, taking Ellis and Aaron by their hands to bring them in with me. Fitch opened the gate and slipped in, holding the gate open as we entered as quickly as possible. Fitch then softly closed the gate and fell in behind Shane as he followed us up the paved garden path.

The walkway was edged with the same flowers depicted on the gate. They were a burst of bright orange, like overgrown tiger lilies but fluffier, and issuing a powerful citrus scent. Behind the flowers, boxwoods rose above our heads, occasionally narrowing and arching fully over the path to create a tunneled bottleneck. It felt like it was designed to both impress and create a series of defensible positions, passable only by a maze of side paths.

"Halt!" a deep voice barked. I hate it when I'm right.

An armed guard who'd been posted just beyond the first bottleneck stalked down the path toward us, a crossbow held at the ready. He wore two pieces of armor, a vest, and a little skirt that hung to his knees over black pants. Both were made of golden-black durrite and almost as intricate as the gate. "No soliciting here," he said. "Please exit the property."

"We're not soliciting," I said in a voice that I hoped sounded both bored and annoyed. "Markinius and Falondeitric are expecting us. Please tell them we've arrived."

"If you're expected, then why are you shielded?" the guard asked, keeping his weapon trained on us. I wondered how expensive intelligent guards were.

"In case any of the help makes a stupid mistake. It is late, after all. Go tell them that the healer is here, or I'll turn around and go back to the guildhalls. I don't care which—I'll be sending a bill either way."

I was only guessing, but it seemed reasonable that a family this wealthy could afford to have high-end healers sent to them for a night of pleasure, especially during a time of approved revelry. It also made sense that a guard or two would accompany such a valuable pet to see them safely returned to their kennel.

"You're a healer?" he asked, peering skeptically at my comparatively tiny body, then back up at the men. "Where is your reflector?"

I rolled my eyes to mask my befuddlement and give myself time to think. "On a floor somewhere in a puddle of his own vomit, I suspect."

The guard snorted. "Again?"

I smiled, genuinely pleased with the kismet of my random response.

"Stay here, please." The guard gave me a final lingering once-over—for what purpose I didn't want to know—then he turned and strode back up the garden path.

As soon as the guard was out of sight, Aaron pulled me forward. "Come on," he said. "This is not a good place to be caught in a fight."

We walked another few minutes before the path opened to a manicured garden surrounding a manor house. The gardens were luxurious, draped in purple and orange flowers that bloomed despite the cool, damp weather. Oil lanterns, encased in ornate stained glass, shed a rainbow of flickering light over the property. Even at night, the garden was spectacular.

"Wow," I said. "I'd bond a melonbelly for this garden too."

Shane snickered in his pleasantly high voice, but Aaron gave me the *look* again. "I'm only joking," I said, squeezing his hand. *Mostly.*

"Beltran Cole's work," Fitch commented.

"Who?" I asked.

"Farrah's father," Shane supplied. "He's the only greater producer in Neesee, now that Irish Eboros is gone."

"Irish?" I asked.

"Falon and Markus's mother," Aaron said. "This garden was her masterpiece, but she died unexpectedly when they were kids. Beltran took over after her death."

Oh, poor Falon and Markus.

"And he charges obscene fees for his work in private gardens," Ellis added. "This is just another extravagant display of wealth. Axel has one just like it." Ellis's hand trembled in mine. I glanced up to see him grinding his teeth.

"Hey," I murmured, squeezing his hand. "If that bastard is alive again, I'll personally hold him down while you beat the shit out of him."

"I don't want to beat him," Ellis replied calmly. "I want to castrate him, then carve out his heart." The words were cold, calculated, and completely serious.

I knew I shouldn't encourage his thirst for revenge, but I couldn't help myself. I felt his dark side calling to mine, yearning for companionship. "Only if I get to carve out his tongue," I said.

Ellis relaxed a little, like my acceptance of his darkness was a relief, or maybe it let him accept it as well. He opened his mouth to speak but paused when he noticed Aaron following our conversation.

"One thing at a time," Aaron said and gently but decisively tugged me behind him toward the house.

It was much like the other buildings I'd seen in Neesee, except with more trees woven into the structure and elegant arched windows and doorways. The house was tall, maybe five stories, with redwood trees extending through the roof, planted in the middle of the house itself. This family literally lived within a grove of trees.

"Magnificent," I breathed, feeling an uncomfortable jealousy with which I was all too familiar.

They got all this through Transmutation, Spirit thought to me confidentially. *You could get that reservoir too.*

Maybe, but I don't see myself getting it from the Eboros family without giving Aaron a stroke. I'd have to steal it from someone.

The image of Axel gushing blood like a geyser from a hole in his chest invaded my mind. I didn't regret the decision to let him die so that I could take his Teleportation, but the gruesome memory was one I could do without. *Would I literally kill to live in a place like this?* My thoughts turned to Seleca. *Perhaps not, but I would take it as a side benefit if I was already killing someone who needed killing.*

A warning bell went off in my mind as I recognized that I had gone from mourning my innocence over Axel's body to calculating the benefits of a planned murder. It had taken one day for that to happen. *Get a grip, Silva*, I chided myself.

"Hold here," Aaron said, scanning the area, *and concentrate on our task*. Aaron sure got bossy when he was on a mission. It was necessary, I conceded, but it was still annoying.

Three guards patrolled the property within view. One within the gardens, one at the front door, and one on the roof of the house, all wearing the same two-piece durrite armor. The one in the garden made his way warily toward us.

"Shane and Fitch, file in behind our shield and cover the path," Aaron ordered. The instructions sounded completely natural coming from him, as if he'd been commanding military units for years.

The front door slammed open, revealing Falon in the entryway, breathing hard. He surveyed the scene and then jogged toward us, making his way down a few steps and onto the garden path. His long legs moved fast, and he intercepted the guard just as he reached us.

"It's all right," he said quickly. "No need to get excited. They're with me." Falon scooted past the guard, positioning himself between us and the armed man, though his slender body wouldn't have been much cover. Suddenly, the term "sapling" made a lot of sense.

"Falon," I said. "I thought we had an understanding." I looked past him to the guard, who had stopped, but still watched us intently, his crossbow in hand. Evidently, Falon's word alone wasn't enough to let us go about our business.

"We did," Falon said, staring at my dress. His gaze lingered a little too long over my body for comfort before his eyes flicked to mine. "We do. You can put your shield down."

I hesitated, unconsciously placing a hand on my belly, then glanced at Aaron, who shook his head. "The boss says no," I said, shrugging.

Falon gave Aaron side-eye, then sagged, lowering his gaze to the ground. "That's fine. Maybe later. Follow me, please." He turned to escort us back toward the house.

We all trailed closely behind, Aaron still leading while Fitch and Shane brought up the rear. We made our way up the steps and under the covered entryway, then through a massive front door, also made entirely of durrite. I had a feeling the door was reinforced and had a secret way of being locked. There was no way a house like this would remain unlocked for anyone to walk into freely.

The inside of the house was not what I expected. I thought it would be like a typical wealthy home, with lush furnishings, thick carpets, and lots of hardwood, but instead it was like walking into a greenhouse. The entire front of the home was an atrium, open to the roof, five stories above, giving it an airy, outdoor feel. Yet it was somehow warm and humid, with plants everywhere and four enormous redwood trees growing through the middle of the space.

It was hard to tell with the night sky, but I thought the roof might be glass, and small lanterns lit a spiral staircase that wound all the way up to the ceiling. The underside of the spiral burst with flowers and fruiting vines, creating a hanging garden for the level below. I had not eaten since breakfast, and my mouth watered at the sight of dozens of colorful fruits.

Another guard stood at the bottom of the stairs, and one at the top. I wondered if he would shoot me if I ate some grapes.

"Do you always have this many guards, Falon?" I asked.

"No. We used to have only two, but Father hired more when my brother and I were taken. Markus says he's going overboard, but I agree with my father for once. I'm afraid that they'll try again."

"They?" I asked.

Falon acknowledged my question with a nod but didn't elaborate. "Come on, they're back in the library."

"Okay," I said, as if a library were a totally normal thing to have in your house.

At a gesture from Aaron, Fitch and Shane stayed behind to watch the front door while we followed Falon. He led us out of the atrium through an archway created entirely of tree roots and down a dimly lit hallway with a few closed doors. At the end of the hallway, a staircase led up and to the left while an open door to the right spilled flickering light, the sound of a crackling fire, and the aroma of grilled meat.

Jesus, I'm hungry, I thought, then pushed the feeling away when it made me think of "eating for two."

The guard we'd encountered on the path stepped through the doorway, gave Falon a flat stare, then scowled at me. I supposed he'd figured out I had manipulated him, but it was too late to do anything about it. He held his crossbow at the ready but pointed at the ground. I smiled at him as sweetly as I could, but it didn't make a dent in his annoyed glare. After a moment, he looked away, dismissing me outright.

"Leave your weapons here and take your shield down," he said to Aaron. "The healer may enter, but all guards must stay out here."

I clenched my teeth, then turned to Aaron. *If you grab him, I can incapacitate him.*

Aaron shook his head again. "We'll take the shield down and leave the weapons out here with him," he said, pointing to Ellis, "but I go where she goes."

I held my breath as the guard turned to someone in the room whom I couldn't see. After a moment, his scowl deepened, then he pivoted back and nodded to Aaron. I knew I should be relieved that he ignored me, and by extension, my baby, but it rankled that I could be disregarded so easily. I felt my face flush as I turned to Aaron.

Release the shield, Mr. Bossman, sir?

Go ahead, smartass.

You love my smart ass, I responded, rolling my eyes as I let down our defenses. I half expected the guard to attack us the moment I did, but nothing happened, so I let go of Ellis's clammy hand.

Ready?

I guess, I thought. *Let's get this nonsense over with.*

Aaron led me into a room lined with shelf after shelf of leather-bound books. Cushioned chairs were tucked into private alcoves with oil lanterns just waiting to be lit.

Ward would have loved this room, I thought.

The only light came from a fireplace positioned opposite the door. I spotted Markus there, standing stiffly next to a high-backed seat that was turned away from me, toward the fire. He'd changed clothes and his hair was damp, brushed, and tied at the nape of his neck. He avoided my glare as we entered, fixing his eyes upon the man in the chair, who I assumed to be Regalinius.

Aaron paused just inside the door, taking in the room as I had, then guided me farther into the room until we stood next to the fire, facing Regalinius, who regarded me with a bored expression. His spindly legs were propped on an ottoman piled with decorative pillows as he drank from a steaming cup that smelled of jarring weed.

"Father," Falon said, coming in behind us, "this is Avelina Silva, of Earth, and Aaron Atticus, of the O'Feld—"

"Yes, yes," Regalinius interrupted. "I've been expecting you. Please excuse me if I don't get up. It's been a long night." He handed his cup to Markus, who set it on a table that had been well within his father's reach. The table had a plate of fresh fruit arranged with flatbread and another piled with shaved meat.

Regalinius Eboros was a bit like his house in that he was not exactly what I expected. I'd imagined a serious power player with a hardened exterior; the sort of man who could build an empire, then go toe to toe with Magister Axel and come out on top. What I got was an older, wearier version of Markus, whose belly was too large to see his own toes let alone set them against someone else's. He had black hair and brown eyes, typical of Neesee, but instead of pale skin, his round cheeks and bulbous nose were ruddy and flecked with tiny broken blood vessels.

"I'm sorry that you're so stressed," I said, masking my sarcasm as I stared at the food. I risked a glance back at Falon, who watched me intently. "I imagine having your sons kidnapped and enslaved would be rather harrowing. How happy you must be to have them home."

"Yes, yes," Regalinius repeated, appearing not at all happy. "Markus has informed me that you played a small part in that. I suppose I owe you something for the favor, even if it was at an unreasonable hour. Is that why you're here?"

I double-blinked, biting back a response about how next time I'd be sure to wait until a more convenient hour to save his kids' lives. "Not exactly," I muttered. A peek at my watch showed it was two in the morning—late, but not so late that the townspeople were finished partying. I raised my eyes to Markus, who didn't meet them but who at least had the decency to look embarrassed.

A glimpse of Aaron's furious eyes told me I needed to take control of this situation before he did or else I'd be scraping charred asshole out of an overpriced chair. I spotted a wooden bench I might be able to lift, walked brazenly over to it, dragged it to His Highness's table, and helped my freaking self.

"Got anything to drink?" I asked.

A snort-cough came from the hall. I glanced up to see the guard standing frozen in the doorway doing a passable impression of Edvard Munch's *The Scream*, while Ellis stood behind him, eyes slightly crinkled at the corners.

Only Evilina could make that man laugh, Spirit commented.

I bit my lip and turned to find Regalinius's face even more pink than before. I knew I should play his game and attempt diplomacy so that I could later exploit his influence during my campaign against the Ministry. But at that exact moment, I was on the shaky side of hangry. If I didn't eat soon, baby girl Atticus was going to burst out of my belly and kill me like that one dude from *Alien*.

"Look, Reggie," I started, popping a grapelike fruit into my mouth.

For a moment, I forgot what I was about to say. I had never tasted fruit with such vivid flavor. It was like a superpotent strawberry and a randy apricot got together and had a magical grape baby. My brain stuttered as my salivary glands contracted like they were orgasming, but I resisted stuffing my face and instead swallowed the gush of saliva that filled my mouth so I could finish my thought.

"We both know I saved Markus's life outright after his skull was crushed. I also saved *both* of your sons from thralldom. Then, to be a good *friend*"—I eyed Markus, who still didn't meet my gaze—"I returned them to Neesee free of charge. So, you're going to listen to what I have to say."

Regalinius narrowed his eyes as I leaned forward, lowering my voice. "I know how you got your pretentious front gate and your comfortable chair and this . . . mind-blowing fruit. Jesus Christ." I grabbed a handful of the not-grapes and stuffed them in my pocket for later. Pockets are the best. "I know your precious family secret."

Regalinius's face shifted from outrage to incredulity, then he scowled up at Markus. A savvy poker player he was not. I suppose if you have unlimited money, you don't have to be. Falon retreated to a chair on the other side of the room and out of his father's line of sight.

So, they didn't tell him everything, I thought, glancing at Aaron. His face remained neutral, but he was nervous.

Careful, he thought to me through Spirit. *Don't back him into a corner.*

I nodded. "So, I'm here to make you an offer. You keep out of my business, and I'll keep out of yours. I wish you no harm. My efforts might even help you if all goes well."

"Help me?" Regalinius sneered. "What could you possibly have to offer me? My son tells me that the Holy Daughter has defeated you at every turn."

He opened his mouth to continue, but my laugh interrupted him. "Holy Daughter? Is that a joke? Seleca is no more *holy* than the seawater I spewed over the side of the boat earlier today. She's a monster. And I'm going to slay her."

With that, I stuffed a piece of flatbread into my mouth, chewing vigorously. Regalinius's dark brown eyes dropped to my lips, prompting me to lift my hand to cover my uncivilized chewing. As I swallowed, he raised his gaze to mine again, his expression now very serious.

"Close the door, Markus," he murmured.

Markus hesitated, finally meeting my eyes, then traded a look with his brother that could've held a lifetime of family secrets. Finally, he sauntered to the door and closed it, shutting out Ellis and the guard.

"You can't kill the Holy Daughter. She's the offspring of a goddess," he said, though I could tell he was interested.

"False," I said. "She is no more divine than you or I. She has absorbed every reservoir available and uses the Rhoyal Healers Guild to extend her life. She kills or enslaves everyone who opposes her and burns their houses down. But she is not protected. If I can get to her, I can kill her. Once that happens, your family business will no longer require secrecy. You will be free to do what you will, openly, and without shame or deceit. I will give this to you, and all I need in return is for you to stand aside. If Psycho Seleca defeats us at the next turn, as you say, then you lose nothing."

I had not yet openly stated which secret I was talking about, but it was clear from the way he leaned forward, nodding, that we were on the same page.

"Let's assume for the moment that I accept your offer," Regalinius said. "The most I could do would be to not volunteer information. If anyone in the Ministry comes here asking direct questions, I will not lie to protect you. My family comes first."

"Yes, yes," I said, knowing full well that what he really wanted to avoid risking was himself. I flashed my best fake smile at him and grabbed a ribbon of shaved meat with my bare hand. I was going for antisex appeal right then, so I just tore into it with my teeth like a stick of beef jerky.

Apparently, that was the wrong approach with Regalinius because he leaned back in his chair, then licked his lips as his brown eyes flicked over my body. "Of course, ever since Irish died, this family has felt empty in many ways."

For fuck's sake. I stood abruptly, the scrape of my chair not quite covering a groan from both Falon and Markus. "I'm very sorry to hear that, Reggie," I said. "Maybe you could meet someone at the wedding." I leaned over and grabbed a whole stack of flatbread, intending to stuff those into my pocket as well, then walked to stand beside Aaron.

"Wedding? What is that?" Regalinius asked. His eyes narrowed, then flicked to Aaron, who seemed just as bewildered as he did.

"Where I come from, we have a bonding ceremony called a wedding. It's a huge celebration."

"I see," Regalinius said, his eyebrows squeezing together. I couldn't tell if his confusion stemmed from my sudden engagement announcement or the idea of celebrating a bonding. It didn't seem like that worked out very well for women in this world. "And who, may I ask, has earned the privilege of bonding you?"

"I have," Aaron said, using his low, dangerous voice again.

It baffled me as to why that quiet little voice revved my engine, but I smiled at Aaron, thinking about the last time we'd made love. We'd been on his bed the night before he left on his last walkabout. *God, was that only a few days ago?* I'd been resting next to him while he read, listening to the rain tap on the oculus, and I'd leaned over to kiss his bare shoulder.

I reached up to touch that same spot now, sending him that memory and meeting his pale eyes. Though his expression didn't change, a burst of heat erupted from his body, engulfing me. We had rarely gone this long without making love since we'd met. I supposed we'd have to wait a little longer.

Do I need to be here for this? Spirit asked, pulling me back to the present moment.

"It was a pleasure to meet you, Reggie," I said, sighing, then I glanced back at the men. I had been distracted by Aaron for a moment and hadn't noticed them reacting to my display of affection. I had thought it subtle, but I guess not—not to transmuters, anyway. I should have remembered my lesson from that morning. Of course, I wouldn't be Avelina Silva if I didn't make the same dumbass mistake over and over again.

Regalinius and Markus both stared at me hard—Regalinius at my chest and Markus at my face. They both clenched their jaws as if resisting the urge to jump up and fight. A shockingly massive erection pressed against Markus's tunic, which he made no effort whatsoever to hide.

He blinked twice when he noticed my line of sight, then for the first time since I'd met him, he smiled, an expression that sent a confusing thrill through me. Out of nowhere, my vision narrowed, and I imagined myself bent over a thick, oardoo-feather mattress with Markus behind me, one hand pulling up my skirt and the other hand digging fingers into my hip.

I shook my head to dispel the image—or maybe hallucination was a better description—but it stuck in my mind like that stupid "Oscar Mayer Wiener" jingle from the 1960s. The comparison was weirdly appropriate.

Markus leaned over me, molding his body against mine to latch his mouth onto that spot between my neck and shoulder. I knew I should hate it, but I didn't. His scent enveloped me, a mixture of clay and that citrusy fragrance from his mother's garden. I didn't struggle against him. On the contrary. When his hand slid forward from my hip to rest between my legs, I lifted one knee onto the bed to give him better access.

"He's projecting," Spirit announced aloud. "Put your shield up."

The bread I'd been holding dropped to the floor as Aaron yanked me behind him, physically shaking me out of my trancelike state. Shaken from how easily he'd captured my mind, I ignored Spirit's suggestion and pulled out Axel's dagger. I didn't point it at Markus so much as show it to him.

Though I was now aware of Markus's intentions and could resist his influence to a degree, I still couldn't dispel the pornographic image that had already seeped into my mind. Heat pooled between my legs as Markus's penetrating gaze devoured me.

"Markus," I said, trembling from the effort of keeping him out of my head, "do you remember what happened to the last man who tried to take me against my will? You of all people should know how evil it is to project yourself onto others."

Before I could get further into that line of reasoning, an embroidered pillow with ridiculous golden tassels flew across the library and hit Markus in the face. The vision immediately vanished. The pillow ricocheted off Markus toward his father, who, in a display of unexpected deftness, caught the pillow and laid it over his own lap.

"Seriously, Markus, is there no limit?" Falon spat. Markus's smile dissolved as he turned a murderous glare on his brother, who had emerged from his nook to stand at Aaron's side.

"I didn't trap her. I only showed her what her options are. She is too valuable a female to bond to a—"

"Markus, leave us," Regalinius said, interrupting his son. Markus didn't move. He continued to stare daggers at Falon, who stood his ground calmly, channeling Aaron.

"Markus!" Regalinius barked. "Leave. Now."

Markus dragged his eyes away from his brother, then stomped toward the door, capturing my gaze as he did. One corner of his mouth turned up as he passed, showing not an ounce of remorse. I remembered what Farrah had said on the boat and had a new insight into her struggles. I was glad Markus was leaving and wondered if he remembered Seleca forcing her thumb into his skull. I hoped so, for his own sake as much as mine.

After Markus stormed through the door, the guard poked his head in and saw my dagger. He darted into the room and raised his crossbow at Aaron, who still stood in front of me. Falon noticed and stepped around us, placing himself in the line of fire once again.

How are these two even brothers?

Regalinius sighed and rolled his eyes. "Stand down, Brick," he said, then he finally rose from the chair and physically ushered the guard out of the room. He closed the door again and turned around, pensive.

"Please excuse my son's behavior, Avelina. He is under a lot of pressure right now and is eager to bond a woman."

"I'm done making excuses for selfish men," I said seriously. "There is nothing more precious to me than my freedom, and that is impossible when I need the constant attendance of one man to protect me from another. Perhaps Markus should look to Falon as an example."

To my horror, Regalinius scoffed. "Falon takes after his mother," he said, eyeing the boy. "And I know exactly what it's like to require a constant guard. You don't have a monopoly on that experience."

Oh, you poor beleaguered rich man. I feel so sorry for you.

As a side note, this was the moment I realized that I did, in fact, have it in me to steal a man's reservoir for no other reason other than that I despised him.

"Then you should understand why I'm doing what I'm doing," I said, holding my temper. "Eve, the *not*-goddess, and her crazy daughter are the cause of this, are they not? Wasn't it Seleca who abducted your precious sons? Let me work, and you will reap the rewards. That means keeping our presence here to yourself. Do we have a deal?"

Regalinius hesitated, studying Axel's dagger. I slipped it back into the built-in sheath within my magical pocket, then held up my hands, palms out, as a sign that I meant him no harm. It was a lie.

Before he could answer, there was a pounding on the door. Regalinius jumped out of its way as it swung open to reveal Shane.

"We have a problem," he said. "Rhoyal guards in the front garden. They're questioning the guard posted there, and I saw him pointing at the house."

"Well," Regalinius said, "it appears that our deal is a moot point. It was a pleasure to meet you, Avelina Silva. Brick, with me, please." With that, Regalinius turned and stalked out of the room and down the hallway with the guard on his heels. He did not command Falon to follow.

So much for family first, I thought.

Shane looked to Aaron for instructions. "Go tell Fitch not to engage. Watch the front door. If they come inside, retreat here to us." Shane nodded and took off down the hallway.

"If you can make a bridge, Lee, now's the time," Aaron said to me. "Otherwise, we're going to have to find a rear exit."

"I can show you the back way out," Falon said.

"Let me try the bridge first," I said.

I turned away from the men, toward the empty library, and took a deep calming breath. I placed my left hand over the top of my stomach and stretched my right arm out in front of me, as I had learned from the bridge book.

The left receives. The right gives.

I reached for my newly acquired Teleportation reservoir, which hovered there within my solar plexus, and pulled that fragment out, using my own body as a skipstone.

I still wasn't clear on exactly what that meant. I just hoped, since I didn't have any plants or dirt on me, that using my own body would automatically take us back to where I was born. But nothing about opening a bridge is automatic. It was like trying to suck a milkshake through one of those tiny red coffee straws.

I sagged, useless.

"You have to think about something that makes you feel confident," Falon said, coming up beside me. "The first time is the most difficult because it's hard to be confident about something you've never done."

"How would you know, Falon?" I asked.

"I have lesser Teleportation," he answered. "I can't make a bridge, but I had to study it anyway, in case I get the chance to ascend my other reservoir."

"That would raise your Teleportation," I said. I stared up at Falon, analyzing the possibilities. If I could coax Falon into the fold and help him to become more influential within his family, then he might be of serious use in the future. It was cold and calculating but necessary. And it could only help him, right?

"Help me learn Teleportation," I said, "and I will take you to ascend your Transmutation reservoir. I will never do that for Markus, though. He can't be trusted like you can, Falon."

Falon flushed, dropping his gaze. "He's not as bad as he seems," he said.

"I'll take your word for it," I said, not wanting to argue. It was obvious to me that anyone who engaged in mind-rape was exactly as bad as they seemed. "Teach me and come with us," I said. "You have integrity and courage. You are exactly the kind of man we need with us."

Laying it on a little thick, aren't you? Aaron thought to me irritably.

I haven't said a single thing that isn't true, I responded, not looking in Aaron's direction.

You're manipulating him.

Maybe, I thought, *but I also won't leave him behind like his father just did. What is Falon thinking, Spirit?*

He's crushing on you hard, she said. *He wants to come, but he doesn't want to do it just because he wants to be near you. He's analyzing his own reasoning.*

Smart kid, Aaron thought.

Shut up, I thought back.

Yelling echoed down the hallway, then footsteps. "Fitch and Shane are running toward us," Ellis said from the open doorway.

"Last chance to run," Aaron said.

"I'll come," Falon said.

I grinned up at him, and I could practically feel Falon's heart rate increase. I turned toward the empty space in the room again and assumed the position.

"All right," Falon said, stepping so close behind me that I felt his warm breath on the back of my neck. "Think of a time when someone you admire praised you. Remember the feeling you got from that praise, the pride that swells in your chest and in your belly. Instead of concentrating on pulling out your Teleportation fragment, pull out that feeling. Let it run into your reservoir through your left arm, filling it before you release through your right."

"Okay," I said, concentrating. I took another deep breath and thought of my father.

My dad grew up on a horse farm in southern Spain. He comes from a long, proud line of horse breeders, and he was the one who purchased and trained Fantasma, my dapple-gray Andalusian.

When I was in high school, before we had Fantasma, I used to compete in dressage with my father's bay horse, Bucky Baby. We weren't very good. The truth is that I didn't really like it. I always preferred to just ride the trails, wild and free, but I wanted to spend time with my dad. He helped me train because he had a passion for horses. Even though he knew that I wasn't that into it, he still came to every one of my shows and cheered me on.

When I was a senior in high school, I won second place in the junior championship, and my dad was over the moon. It was my last show, and he took it as a personal triumph, calling it *un final espectacular*. It made me laugh every time he said it because it was so ridiculous and adorable. He was so proud.

As I stood there, facing that empty space with my arm stretched out like a lunatic, I held his beaming face in my mind. I thought about what it felt like to receive his praise, his faith, his love, and his unreasonable enthusiasm for my meager accomplishments. He was a great man, and I was proud to be his daughter.

That's what I pulled out, letting the emotion fill my body. Similar to when Transformation made me feel indestructible, I leaned into that feeling of confidence and, possibly for the first time ever, I let myself feel worthy of praise.

Who knew self-esteem could be so powerful? Teleportation fragment practically flew out of me, invisible until it coalesced in a bright golden sphere.

The bridge opened, releasing a windstorm-like rumbling that somehow barely made my skirt billow. Fitch and Shane stomped into the room, slamming the door closed behind them.

"I'll hold it!" Aaron yelled over the noise. "Everyone jump on the bridge! Hurry!" Ellis ran for it and disappeared, followed by Fitch and Shane. Then Falon turned to me, grinning wide. I smiled back at him, genuinely happy and grateful for his help. He grabbed the two plates of food, hugged them to his chest, and serenely stepped onto the bridge.

There was a banging on the door, which Aaron was leaning against, holding it closed. "Your turn!" he yelled.

"No, Aaron," I said. "We go together." I held out my hand to him.

Aaron nodded. "All right. One, two, three!" He ran for me, grabbing my hand, and we jumped toward the bridge together. Just as we did, three men in golden armor burst into the room, Seleca on their heels. I barely had time to register her existence before something punched me in the side of my head and everything went black.

Chapter Nine

"*Well, what do we have here?*" *a familiar voice said.* "*I believe I have arrived just in time once again.*" *Linorra forced her eyes open and saw the witch gazing down upon her with a bemused expression.*

I die a lot. It's kind of a problem. I mean, I miss things when I black out. I've since discovered that I can die and not come back for days, but that's another story. This is the story of how I learned my "classic" friend Zig was right on the money.

When I woke up, I was having a really bad hair day. I don't want to sound ungrateful. Yes, I know. I got shot in the head and didn't die. Everyone witnessed a true miracle. Yay me. But my goddamn hair, though! I mean, my brain grew back, as did my skull and the various accoutrements, but the hair didn't grow back right away. It was like someone pranked me, shaving an irregular splotch on both sides of my head right down to the fragging scalp.

I heard crying, and I thought it might be mine. But no, I was mostly just pissed off. My next guess was Aaron. It was a rage cry—half sobbing, half growling—and very manly, or so he later claimed. I also heard what I thought was Ellis wailing in the background. He had ascended his Transformation reservoir without Protection and was in more danger than I was. I had forgotten all about that.

I jerked, realizing that I needed to heal him before it was too late.

"Lee!" Aaron cried. "Lee, oh goddess. You're alive." He was squeezing the daylights out of me.

"Aaron, let go of me, dammit. I need to help Ellis!"

Aaron released me, gaping. I was drenched in my own blood, and so was he. I twisted around, searching for Ellis, while everyone stared at me like they'd seen a ghost. Actually, I've seen a ghost or two, and the crew were far more surprised than that. They were stupefied. Every one of them.

"Hey, *idiots*, someone tell me where Ellis is. Ward is going to be pissed if I get his brother killed."

"Over here," Falon called. He had Ellis in his arms, cradling him like a big bloody baby. His skin looked like it had been turned inside out. I remembered the excruciating pain of my own ascension and gasped.

"Ellis!" I crawled over to him and grabbed his hand, pushing both Connection and Protection into him.

I was almost too late. The blood in Ellis's entire body had become sticky, clogging his circulation. Every one of his organs was damaged. The blood vessels feeding his heart had become sluggish as well, and he was in the middle of a massive heart attack. Every nerve ending in his body screamed with pain.

I tried not to be as aggressive as I'd been the first time, but my haste made that difficult. The moment Protection rushed into his body, his wailing ceased. His eyes rolled back in his head, then closed. His mouth dropped open, and he nearly bucked out of Falon's arms.

Unlike me, Falon is strong and easily held on to him, which allowed me to hold on too, but when Ellis realized he couldn't pull away, he clutched my hand tightly. A *crack* split the air just as lightning shot up my wrist. Still, I didn't let go.

Watching someone being healed in public is always awkward, but this was especially true on Monash, where people considered healing to be akin to prostitution. It was dark where we landed, which offered some privacy, but Shane and Fitch stood together a little way off, chatting quietly with their backs turned. Falon, by contrast, watched me work, not even pretending to be embarrassed.

It might have been unpleasantly intimate had Aaron not also knelt closely beside me, poised, I was certain, to intervene. It was damned lucky that Ellis wasn't attracted to me, or else we would have had his moans of pleasure to add to the awkward moment.

Through Connection, I felt Ellis's pain dull to a throb while a rush of narcotic euphoria overtook his senses. Though I knew he objected strongly to forced physical contact, even of this variety, I could tell he preferred this over the pain. Within a minute, sensation vanished entirely within his body, and he went limp, unconscious. I withdrew Protection but remained connected to him, hunting for anything that I may have missed. Even asleep, he didn't let go of my hand.

"Ellis," I said, shaking him gently. "Wake up. It's over, buddy. You made it." Ellis opened his eyes and regarded me dully. "Congratulations. You survived ascension."

"Ascension?" he mumbled.

"Yes. I'm sorry I didn't think to warn you." I hadn't anticipated what would happen because I'd been too busy thinking about how I could benefit from manipulating the people around me. What a fantastic friend I turned out to be. "I have no excuse. I'm so sorry."

Ellis sat up and glanced around, clocking every person he saw around him. Despite the healing, his dark brown eyes were still glassy and bloodshot, his skin ashen. I got the impression that I'd healed him mere moments before death. He still clutched my hand like it was the only thing keeping him alive. I let him, ignoring the pain while pushing Protection into the extremity.

At least his hair's okay, I thought, touching one of the bald spots on my head with my free hand.

Fucking. Seleca.

The was officially her new name. I had never truly hated someone in my life. Even my attitude regarding Mousehead had just been fleeting anger turned begrudged sympathy. But I *hated* Seleca with every fiber of my being.

I mean, she shot me right in the head with my own father's Glock. The bullet hit me just above my right ear and passed all the way through and out the other side, leaving two giant, gaping, bloody holes. You could have passed a baseball bat through that thing.

Okay, that might be an exaggeration, but it was big and messy and terrifying to all who witnessed it. That's what they say, anyway. I don't remember because I missed it, dammit.

I tugged my aching hand gingerly out of Ellis's grasp. *My poor battered body.* With a start, I realized that I hadn't checked the rest of my body for wounds.

The baby.

How could she not have been the *first* thing I'd thought of? In a panic, I brought my uninjured hand to my belly to search for her. In an instant, her Protection resonance floated out to me lazily, as if to purposely calm my skittering heart. I closed my eyes and steadied my breathing as my heart slowed to a normal pace.

In. Out. Everything is fine. She's immortal, like me. She can't die. I don't have to have a meltdown. But . . . didn't Seleca know I was immortal? Could she have been going after the baby?

I clenched my broken hand into a tight fist, pushing Protection into it vigorously while imagining that the popping noise it made was Seleca's nose breaking. "I am going to kill that bitch," I growled.

Falon snorted. I opened my eyes to see him staring at me with a bemused expression.

"Sorry," he said. "You're just really scary right now." Having released Ellis, he picked a piece of flatbread off the ground and blew it off, tearing away the parts covered in dirt and blood. After a moment, he sighed and then discarded the bread on top of all the other food he'd dropped, which had attracted a substantial number of flies. He got to his feet to shuffle over to Fitch and Shane, who observed me warily.

I smirked at Falon's retreating form. Though I sincerely hoped that I was "scary" enough to have killed his crush, I was really starting to like that guy.

"Where are we?" Ellis asked.

"Earth, I hope," I answered, peering at Aaron.

He shrugged, then rose to his feet, leaning over to lift me up by my hips. I shook my hand out just as the last of the pain receded, but it still tingled like it had fallen asleep. Before I could do anything else, Aaron pulled me into a tight hug, connecting.

I was certain you were dead this time, he thought. *I can't understand how you healed from that.* He squeezed my body so hard it hurt, but I knew he needed to feel me against him, alive and well. He thought he'd lost me and had literally cried over my supposed dead body.

A wave of guilt swept over me that he didn't yet know I was pregnant. I had wanted the reveal moment to be perfect, but was that even possible? Not likely, given the sort of life we lived. In fact, this blood-soaked moment was a better representation of our time together than any other. I sighed, resigned to my fate. Now was as good a time as any. Except never, maybe. Never is a fantastic time to do things you don't want to do.

Aaron, I have something to tell you.

His eyes were red-rimmed and puffy, but he had reclaimed his stoic expression. *Merimo explained to me that there's something about having both Protection and Absorption that not only extends my life, but also makes me... immortal. I will never die, no matter how badly I get hurt. Someday, when the Earth blows up, I'll be floating around in the vacuum of space.*

Except... I thought.

Except what? he asked, his intense gaze zeroing in on my face, then falling to my hand, which still rested on my belly. And, of course, Aaron being his brilliant self, he instantly knew.

Except I won't be floating out there alone, I thought, smiling weakly.

Aaron stilled, his eyes going wide. *You're pregnant?* he asked, staring into my eyes again. I couldn't tell exactly what I saw in his gaze, but it could have been a thousand emotions warring for dominance. He rested his hand on top of mine, his focus dropping into the middle distance as I guided him to the baby's resonance through our Connection link.

Um, yeah. Surpriiiiise. It's a girl.

Evocation, he noted, his eyebrows squeezing together.

Yes, among others. I'm so sorry, Aaron. I should have been more careful, but the birth control I have—or thought I had—is usually foolproof. I don't know what happened.

Aaron lifted his free hand to cover his mouth, then he closed his eyes, his face contorting into something like pain as he pulled away from me to turn around. My chest ached at the sight of him turning his back on me.

He's upset. He didn't want this. He'll think I was trying to trap him. He's going to back out now.

I anxiously studied the crew, who all stood a distance away. I wasn't ready to share this news with anyone else yet, especially if I was about to become a single mom.

Aaron whirled to face me again, his face bright red and his body radiating an intense heat that I knew to be rage. Instinctively, I stepped back, but he reached for me, pulling me back to reconnect. *How long have you known, Lee?*

There was no way out of this conversation. I couldn't pull away, but I also couldn't look him in the eye. I lowered my chin to stare at my feet. What did it matter when I found out? It's not like I could have made it untrue if I'd found out sooner.

I figured it out a few minutes before we walked into the Eboros estate.

Why didn't you tell me right away?

My eyes flicked up to his. *Oh.*

I hesitated, not wanting to dig myself a deeper hole, but it's much harder to stop your thoughts than it is to stop talking. I felt my brain pulling toward an answer, but I redirected it toward the one I had used to convince myself.

Because I wanted you to be able to focus on our task without getting distracted. That could have put us all in danger, especially you. You're not quite as bulletproof as I am.

And now you're lying, he thought furiously. His lips pulled back from his teeth in a snarl, then he raised a thick finger to stab the air in front of my face. *You didn't want to tell me because you knew I wouldn't want you going into the Eboros house while you were pregnant. Isn't that right?*

I stared at his angry gesticulation, then his expression, completely at a loss. He wasn't upset that I was pregnant. He was angry I hadn't told him right away. Why did that fact seem so much shittier coming from him?

Yes, I thought defensively, *but that wasn't the only reason. I was worried about you, and I knew that I'd be fine no matter what.*

And what about the baby? Did you worry about her? Did you stop for even one second to think maybe there are more important things than pretending to be some mythical warrior princess?

Whoa, I thought, throwing one hand up to protect my face from his dagger finger. *You did* not *just bring Xena into this.*

That's when a thought crystalized—one I had not previously let myself acknowledge. Back when I'd first met Aaron, he'd accidentally used Protection to slice through my Connection link, severing the link and causing it to snap back at me. It's a dangerous move that could have seriously hurt me if I hadn't had Protection myself. I didn't think he'd ever do it again, but I had stiffened nonetheless, bracing myself for the pain. Maybe I hadn't just been afraid *for* Aaron but afraid *of* Aaron.

But there was nothing to be afraid of, was there? He was angry, sure, but he wasn't going to hurt me. Why had I thought he would? Why had I assumed he would bolt the second things got hard? He wasn't going to cry over me one minute and then drop me the next. That didn't even make sense. I shook my head, resolving to revisit this self-reflection later, when Aaron wasn't in my head.

The baby has Protection and Absorption, I thought. *She's immortal, like me. She and I were safer than you were.*

He blinked at that information, but it didn't slow him down for long. *Rhoya, Lee! You only believe that because that goddessforsaken Meriweather* monster *told you so, but you don't know that for certain, which is why you panicked over the baby's safety when you woke up.*

I froze. He was right. I had done that.

You should have told me the moment you knew, he continued, *so that we could discuss it and make that decision* together. *Instead, you went rogue without even considering that I might have a right to weigh in.*

A right? Are you kidding me? I'm sorry, Aaron, but I don't need your permission to go places. Just because I agreed to bond to you does not *mean that I* belong *to you.*

That's exactly what it means, Lee. You said it yourself, remember? You're mine for the next four hundred years.

I scoffed. *No, I said* you were *mine.*

That's the same thing, dumbass.

I snorted at his use of the Earth insult, then I ran one hand down my face. I should never have taught him that word.

Fine. I'm sorry, Aaron. I'm sorry I didn't tell you. I should have. I know that.

And I did. I had let my fear of rejection, not to mention my fear of commitment, get the better of me. Again. Maybe at some distant point in the future, like in three hundred and ninety-nine years or so, I'd stop waiting for the other shoe to drop.

Aaron sighed, then wrapped his arms around me, pulling me into his chest and resting his chin on my head. *I would never hurt you on purpose*, he thought, letting me know that he had heard my little moment of introspection. *And I won't leave you every time you do something stupid, but I reserve the right to be angry. There's nothing I can do about that. I just wish you trusted me to take care of you.*

I tried not to send my next thought—that I didn't need anyone to take care of me because I would never die—but it came through anyway. We would never agree on that point. It wasn't in my nature to let someone boss me around, and it wasn't in Aaron's nature to stop trying. Was this going to be a deal-breaker? I pushed the thought away, throwing it into the slush pile of things to deal with later if there was time. Which, with any luck, there wouldn't be.

Obviously, he came to the same conclusion, opting to change the subject. *If you can't die, then how did you get Conjuration?*

I shook my head. *I don't know. It's a mystery.* One that I didn't really give a crap about solving right then.

I pulled away from Aaron, scanning the shadows that surrounded us. I had used my own body as a skipstone, and I hadn't known exactly what to expect, but I was positive that I'd been born in Eureka, so we should have ended up somewhere close to there.

What I saw dashed any hope of that. It was nighttime, but I could see that we were in a glade of some sort, surrounded by manicured grass, palm trees, and plants with great big waxy leaves. The chorus of insects was deafening, as were the growing swarm of flies attacking Falon's spilled food. I batted one away from my face, then wiped away the sweat that streamed from my forehead into my eyes.

"What the hell?" I spluttered, spinning slowly to get my bearings. I'd left my stupid pack with the GPS in it on the boat, but I was sure this wasn't Northern California. This place was tropical. The temperature was far too warm and humid, and there was no fog anywhere. I didn't see a redwood tree or anything remotely like one. Had my parents conceived me while on vacation?

"Heads up!" Fitch called, and I turned toward the sound of heavy footsteps. If I wasn't mistaken, that was the clopping of horse hoofs.

"Lina," a woman called.

Holy crap. That sounds like— "Mom?"

"Lina!" she yelled again frantically. A slender woman ran through the dark glade toward us.

"Mom!" I yelled, jogging toward her. It really was her. Behind her stood two horses with another rider—my dad. A small LED lantern shone on his ecstatic expression.

In that moment, I was overwhelmed by the release of a burden I'd been carrying since the moment *Fucking* Seleca stole me away from my safe, cozy reality. Even before I knew I was immortal, I hadn't cared much about dying on some alien planet, but I had been deeply afraid I would never see my parents again. I had not let myself recognize it until that moment, but now that they were in front of me, an overpowering grief from what *might* have been reared its ugly head and squirted right out of my eyeballs.

"Mom," I whimpered, tears streaming down my face. She reached me and took me in her arms, hugging me tightly. Well, tightly for an Earth woman. I could still breathe. She smelled like lavender, horses, and *home*. My father wasn't far behind. He ran up, dropped his lantern on the ground, and wrapped his arms around both of us.

"Lina, thanks to God you made it," Dad said in his perfect accent. "Thanks to God."

I let them hug me, but something wasn't right. I pulled back and stared at them, my heart hammering in my chest while a sliver of dread crept down my spine.

Aaron picked up the lantern and held it up so we could see one another, revealing that my parents both had my blood all over them from the hug. But that wasn't it.

"What do you mean, *made it*?" I asked. I glanced back and forth between them a couple times before my brain weeded out my distracting emotions enough for the truth bomb to explode all over me.

Both my parents resonated with Protection and Connection strongly enough to indicate they were ascendants of both reservoirs. My stunned gaze settled on my mother's face. Her expression was a lot like Jorin's had been on the boat yesterday. "What does he mean, Mom?"

"Now, Lina. Don't get upset."

I stepped back from her to get a better view. Her voice didn't sound normal. She had an unfamiliar accent that sounded like some version of British English. I held up one palm to her and reached the other out for Aaron. He took my hand, connecting.

Are you certain this is them? he thought to me. *They could be transformers.*

You're right, I thought, scrutinizing my mother again. "What present did you give me on my sixteenth birthday?"

She rolled her eyes, then gave my dad a look that clearly said *I told you so*. She turned back to me and said, "A key. I left it on the bridgestone for you."

"The bridgestone," I repeated, mimicking her strange accent. My eyes bounced between her and my dad, my vision narrowing as my mind struggled to wrap itself around the only possible explanation.

My parents are both ascendants of not one but two reservoirs. My father expected me to return. My mother knows about bridgestones, and she has a fragging accent.

I thought furiously, performing mental gymnastics to come up with some reason for how this could all be true and not be a betrayal worse than Jorin's. I came up empty, and Zig's words came back to haunt me as a red-hot rage erupted at the base of my spine, flushing up my neck and cheeks like a geyser.

Sometimes, people you've trusted your whole life turn out to be liars. And other times, people you barely know turn out to be the only ones you can trust.

"This can't be happening," I whispered. Aaron tightened his grip on me to prevent me from falling over. A bead of sweat dripped down my forehead, and I wiped it away with trembling hands.

"Lina." Mom stepped toward me, but I backed away, my palm still held up to her.

"You knew what would happen that night," I said, tears streaming down my face. "You *sent* me into danger. You put that stupid, useless survival kit in my pack because you *knew*."

"And your toothbrush," my mother protested, her head tilted to one side. Was she really confused as to why I might be upset?

"But no fucking toothpaste!" I screamed. It was an irrational complaint, I knew, but I was too livid to care. I turned away from them, letting Aaron envelop me in his arms. He knew all too well what I was going through.

"I'm sorry, Lina," Mom said, though her voice was more stubborn than apologetic. "It was the only way. If I had thought for a minute that you might actually get hurt, then I never would have—"

"She shot me in the head, Mom," I insisted, but the fight drained out of me with each word. I was so exhausted. A moment of stunned silence surrounded us as I buried my head in Aaron's firm chest, inhaling the scent that was just *him*. His warm hand glided up and down my back as I willed myself to stop crying.

Other than my parents, I'd never allowed myself to depend on another person like this. Not really. I'd always treated what looked like solid ground as if it were wet cement; like if I dared to trust anyone, I'd end up sinking while everyone who claimed to care about me stood around watching. I thought about my dream from a couple nights ago and wondered if it had been a warning of some kind.

"But you didn't die," Mom said softly. "You will never die. That is why it has to be you. You are the only one who can stop it. If you don't, then you will get to watch the rest of us be slaughtered."

"She'll probably get to see that anyway," Dad mumbled. My mother shushed him.

I didn't bother asking what they needed me to prevent from happening. I didn't care. I felt like a child discovering that Santa wasn't real, only instead of Santa, it was my parents. I had thought my concept of reality had been shattered when I was sucked into that first portal to Monash, but that was nothing compared to this. How could I ever trust anyone again?

I leaned more heavily into Aaron. *You're the only one I can trust.*

"Where are we?" I asked, my voice muffled by Aaron's clothing.

My mother took a breath in and out and then she thought to me, *Hartha, dear. You're finally home.*

Chapter Ten

"*Who would have guessed that a witch could be so ordinary?*"

I didn't want to believe it, but you can't argue with results. I had used my own body as a skipstone, and it had brought me to Hartha. Minh, to be precise, the capital of the Hartha-a-Minh province, and the largest city on the planet. Outside of a multigenerational literary conspiracy, I couldn't imagine how I could follow the instructions of the bridge book and be transported anywhere other than home. There was no denying it. I was not Avelina Silva, of Earth. I was Avelina Silva, of Hartha.

I swore under my breath as we followed my parents along the mulched path toward their house. *This whole time. My parents knew where I was this* whole *time.* Not only that, but my mother had confirmed in her little "Surprise! You're an alien!" revelation that she could connect through the air, which definitely made her an ascendant connector. I growled, my frustration bubbling back up.

Aaron chuckled, squeezing my hand a little.

What? I snapped.

Oh, nothing, he answered. *It's just that you and I have more in common than we thought.*

I nodded. *It sucks.*

Yes, he agreed. *However, viewing it from this side does give me some perspective. Your parents clearly love you a great deal. I can't imagine that they would have done this unless they felt they absolutely had to.*

I gave him my best death glare, refusing to concede the point.

I'm not saying it was the right choice, he added hastily, *just that they thought it was.*

My death glare collapsed into a frown. *Does this mean that you forgive your own parents? And Jorin?*

He shrugged. *I don't know how to forgive them, but I can try to let go of my anger. At least one good thing came from their lies.* He pulled me toward him, slipping his arm around me, then he leaned down and kissed me right on one of my bald spots. His lips felt strange on skin that didn't usually receive direct touch. I jerked my head away at the unexpected sensation, which made him realize what he'd done, and he broke up laughing.

Jesus Christ. I can't catch a break.

Embarrassing as my hair debacle was—hairmageddon, if you will—his unguarded laughter made me feel instantly better, like maybe everything would be okay. My parents glanced over their shoulders at him, gave each other a knowing look, and turned forward again.

I groaned. "My hair will grow back. Probably. In the meantime, I can shave the sides and spike it up into a mohawk. It'll be a great wedding style. Very traditional. You and I can get matching eyebrow piercings and facial tattoos."

My parents both twisted in their saddles to stare at me, their eyes wide. My mother's hand came to her mouth. "What?" she exclaimed.

Oh, right. "You're not invited," I said sourly. I meant it too. I had no idea who these people were, and I wasn't inviting strangers to my wedding. For all I knew, they weren't even my real parents. Come to think of it, I didn't even look like them.

Wait...

"Lina!" Mom yelled, preventing me from traveling too far down that line of thinking. "You're getting married? But you've only been gone two months." She must have heard herself because she promptly course-corrected. "But that's wonderful!" She turned forward again and clasped her hands together. She may have been wringing them, but it was hard to tell from behind.

What is wrong with her? I wondered. *Other than her stupid accent?*

I had rarely heard my mother speak this many words together at one time. I guess that probably becomes a lifelong habit when you have telepathy and are trying to avoid accidentally speaking in the wrong accent. For twenty-six goddamn years.

"I said you're not invited," I repeated. She ignored me.

"We're almost there," Dad said. At least he sounded the same. "See the light? That's her house."

"*Her* house?" I asked, looking toward the light. It appeared to be a modern Earth home with electricity, though I couldn't see much. *Please let there be toothpaste.*

"Your grandmother's house," Mom clarified. "I better go warn her that there's a group. She'll want to feed you all." She reached down and placed her hand on Gem's flank, and the horse jumped into a slow canter.

"That sounds promising," mumbled Fitch.

"Goddess, I'm hungry," Shane agreed.

The rest of the crew all echoed that sentiment. I glanced back to see Falon staring down at the ground, chagrined.

"I still have a handful of ambrosia grapes," I said, holding out a few for the crew, who fell on them like rabid beasts.

"Ambrosia grapes?" Falon asked.

"Yeah, it's just like a fruit from Earth called a grape, but it tastes like nothing I've ever had before."

"My mother cultivated these," Falon commented, taking his own grape. "They're called *pips*. Highly valued as gifts, but my father mostly keeps them for himself. He gave a cutting to Beltran Cole once in lieu of payment and thought he'd cheated the man. Now

Beltran makes a killing selling them at market." He considered the fruit in his hand, a sad smile on his youthful face. "Markus and I used to steal them off the vine when we were kids, till he decided he was too mature for my childish games." His eyes flicked to mine briefly as I turned to face forward again.

Despite my negative interaction with Markus, and Reggie's hasty departure without a second thought for Falon's well-being, I didn't wish either of them ill. I would hate to be the cause of permanent damage to Falon's family. I hoped Psycho Snow White—or *Fucking* Seleca, as I now thought of her—didn't think they were in collusion with us. On the other hand, would it matter if she did? She might punish them anyway, just for the fun of it.

Spirit, I called, thinking I'd send her back to the Eboros estate for information. She didn't come. *Spirit!* A whisper so soft I thought it might be my imagination swept past me like air in a drafty room. It sounded like Spirit, but it was incomprehensible.

Aaron shot me a worried look that matched my sentiments exactly. *She's been fading for the last day*, he thought.

I know. Any ideas as to why?

He shrugged. *I barely got to see her at all before she disappeared. Maybe it has something to do with too many people seeing her?*

I don't know, I thought, shaking my head. *It makes no sense. I should have asked her about it while I had the chance. Spirit, my friend, please be okay.*

The slap of a porch door snapped my attention back ahead of us. We'd reached the house, and my mother had come through a door and down a few steps to intercept us, followed by her gray-haired doppelgänger.

My grandmother was an elegant woman, just a hair shorter than my mother. I could see their resemblance clearly, with the same slender build and dark, caramel-colored skin. She had a different nose, though, sort of long and hooked. She held one long, steel-gray braid in her hand, pulling and twisting it absently, the only sign that she was anything other than placidly calm.

She looked oddly familiar, but that could've been the family resemblance. I narrowed my eyes, trying to figure out where I might have seen her before. I couldn't think of anything, and the constant buzzing of flies made me give up trying. I slapped one that landed on my face.

Beside me, Aaron visibly stiffened.

What is it? I asked.

Aaron stared for another moment, then thought, *She has Evocation. Lesser only, but it's there.*

I focused on the woman, but my Evocation reservoir was meager, and I couldn't pick out the resonance over the energetic hum of her Connection reservoir. *I think she's an ascendant connector too.*

"Lina," my mother said, using her formal voice, "meet your grandmother, Linorra Dragonrider of the Rhoyal Dragonrider line, first cousin to Queen Harthar-a-Dragona, first in line to the throne of Harthar-a-Minh."

Um . . . what? I glanced over at Aaron, who had his hand over his mouth, wrinkles gathering at the corners of his pale eyes.

"Oh, Gigi, you're scaring the poor girl," the woman said. Her accent matched my mother's. "Just call me Gran, dear. I can't tell you how pleased I am to see you again. You were barely a toddler when you left this house."

"Was I?" I asked, fanning another fly away from my face.

"Indeed," she said, then she turned to Aaron. "And this handsome bloke is Aaron if I'm not mistaken. The infamous Dragon."

Infamous?

Aaron's brows pulled together, looking at me like I could explain it to him. I shrugged. *If the shoe fits.*

"Yes, come in, all of you. I've got Delya inside setting out food. You are all welcome." My grandmother took in my bloody clothing, then turned away without comment.

We followed her into the house, which was blessedly cool and insect-free. The light we'd seen was the back-door light, just off the kitchen. We traipsed through, the Monash men all squinting against the bright electric lights and ducking under ceiling fans, wonder written all over their faces. I predicted a long night of explaining the concept of electricity to them. Wrongly, most likely.

The kitchen was modern, with electric appliances and butcher-block countertops. The wall plugs were a little different, probably a different voltage, but otherwise just like home. I watched Aaron's eyes bounce from item to item in amazement.

What is that? he asked.

That's a stove. You use it to cook food instead of a hearth.

What is that?

That, thank all that is holy, is a coffee maker. My universe brightened a little, and I glanced at my watch. It was three in the morning, California time. I doubted that was the right time for this location, but coffee would still have to wait until after a good night's sleep.

We settled at a large dining table in the room adjacent to the kitchen. The table was long and low with bench seating, built for people my size. The crew all appeared as if they'd been relegated to the children's table with their knees hitting the underside. They didn't seem to care, though. As soon as they saw food, nothing else mattered.

Delya, a plump woman with pale skin and auburn hair, turned out to be Gran's housekeeper. She'd set out meat and cheeses, cut fruit, and bread. The crew devoured everything that appeared before Mom and Dad showed them the guest rooms. Evidently, Gran's house was the occasional lodging for a Rhoyal delegation, whatever that was, so there were several guest quarters, each with its own en suite bathroom. The luxury of it felt like waking up from a nightmare.

My father agreed to orient the crew to their accommodations, and my mother found clothes for both me and Aaron that weren't covered in blood. She tried to talk to me again, but I wasn't ready. I didn't know if I'd ever be ready. For now, and maybe forever, my parents were on the outside of my castle walls, across a shark-infested moat.

I shut the door to our bedroom in her face, walking straight to the bathroom. I finally brushed my teeth properly and took a shower. While I was luxuriating under the hot water, I checked for my IUD string, something I hadn't done in more than a year. Lo and behold, I had lost my IUD entirely somewhere along the way.

I tried to imagine at what point that might have occurred and guessed that it may have been while I was unconscious in the hospital, before I'd ever set foot on Monash. Could the IUD have been dislodged during my riding accident and the hospital staff had to remove it? It was impossible to say, but one would think they would've told me something like that.

I showed Aaron how to turn on the shower, put on the muumuu-style dress my mother gave me, then collapsed onto the memory foam mattress with a deep sigh. As I lay there waiting for him, it occurred to me that Mom had known exactly when we would be out in the glade. How was that possible? By the time Aaron walked out of the bathroom in his newly acquired clothes, I had concluded that there was really only one answer. Violet Atticus. I had some questions for that sneaky bitch.

I sat bolt upright.

"What is it?" Aaron asked.

"I might know where your mom is," I said. "Or at least where she was."

Aaron sat down on the bed next to me. "Where?"

"Eureka," I said, and face-palmed. I couldn't believe I hadn't seen it before. "Freaking Marti!"

No wonder Marti had such a well-developed mom voice. She was *Aaron's* mom. I was sure of it. She'd manipulated me into hanging out with Drew instead of Spirit that day because she knew I would never take Drew back. She'd been the one to remind me to pack Rogue's leash, "just in case," knowing that I would grab it on my way out. It was so obvious now that I'd put the pieces together that I felt like an idiot.

I filled Aaron in on the details as we snuggled into bed together, telling him about Marti and Milo—his parents—and how in love they were. I marveled at the thorough job Violet had done in tricking me, how she must have managed to accomplish full-body Transformation and learn passable Spanish in order to become Marti.

It had been an elaborate hoax. I didn't know who the twins were, but they must have been in on it. Violet had managed to get close to me and guide me to where she had wanted me to be. She had been in collusion with my parents the whole time, which made me want to scream.

Then, as if that weren't bad enough, a thought hit me like a sledgehammer, one I knew I shouldn't dive into yet because I couldn't afford to fall apart. I had always thought Marti was my first real friend. She was the first person to take an interest and coax me to lower my guard. And it had all been fake. It had been a manipulation intended to accomplish a goal that didn't necessarily include my personal well-being.

She wasn't my friend. She never has been. She was just using me.

No matter how old you get, the things that hurt you when you were a child can rush back in a flash and shove a knife right in your chest, cutting you just as deeply as they did the first time. An immense sorrow welled up in me, threatening to spill out. I had so much trouble making friends when I was a kid. I thought I had finally figured it out by my early twenties. But I hadn't. None of it was real.

I squeezed my eyes shut and turned on my side, away from Aaron, not wanting to cry on him *again*. He had his own problems. I couldn't expect him to keep taking care of me. *And why would he even want to?* I shook my head, trying to push that evil thought away.

Because he loves you, stupid. At that moment, I wanted to give up, but I couldn't deny that Aaron had proved that multiple times. I hoped I wasn't wrong about him the way I seemed to be about everyone else in my life. I didn't think I could handle one more betrayal.

"I can't believe this," I said, a silent tear running sideways down my face. "Just when I think I know what's going on, I find out someone else has tricked me. And they let Spirit die, and the twins. I don't understand how they could do that."

"They might not have known," Aaron said, wrapping his arms around me. He wasn't fooled by my attempt to turn away and handle my own grief. "Precognition is never exact. It's more like rolling a ball downhill. You kind of know where it's going, but it can bounce unexpectedly and veer off course. That's why your mother didn't know about our bonding. She probably doesn't know that you're pregnant either." At that, Aaron's hand drifted down to rest possessively on my belly. I set both of mine over top of it.

"I hope that's true. I don't think I could forgive my parents for letting people die when they could have done something about it." *Yes,* I realized, *that's the crux of it. They didn't just lie to me and send me into danger. They got Spirit killed. Spirit, my person, whom I resonate with like she's my bridgestone.*

Aaron kissed the back of my head. I sighed and then turned back to face him again, letting him pull me in tighter. This discussion would have to wait until morning. I was exhausted.

Aaron wiped the tears off my cheek and kissed the spot where they had been, then he continued down to my mouth, then my neck. His lips brushed down my throat, then back up to that sensitive spot behind my ear. He stroked my back, lifting my shirt up as his fingers trailed up my spine.

On the other hand...

I rolled to my back and Aaron shifted with me, settling himself on top of me. It had only been a few days since we'd made love, but it felt like a lifetime. So much had happened since then. My world had turned upside down like an open purse, and everything I thought was mine had spilled out. Now I had to decide what I was going to put back in.

This, I thought, wrapping my legs around him. *I want this inside.*

Aaron heard my thoughts and groaned, separating from me long enough to yank off the fresh clothing he'd just put on—black pants and a white T-shirt that actually fit him and had come from god knows where. I did the same, my body so hungry for his that I

THE WISDOM OF DISHONOR

ripped the dress trying to get it off. By the time we came back together, Aaron was fully erect and adjusting himself to get the right angle.

I'm not convinced what we did really counts as lovemaking. It was more akin to starving people inhaling an unexpected meal before someone stole it away. He crushed his mouth to mine and pushed into me without preamble, pushing Protection at the same time to start the first cycle of fragmentation. Warmth spread over my body like a shiver, then morphed into exquisite pleasure that made me gasp.

This isn't going to take long, I thought, then I pushed Protection back into him to complete the cycle. He moaned loudly. Too loudly.

"Shh." I laughed, but my heart wasn't in it. There is nothing hotter in the universe than that sound coming out of Aaron's mouth.

For a disconcerting moment, my thoughts flicked to Falon and how he'd gazed at me that morning we all woke up in the same room. It was jealousy, I realized now. I wondered how close his room was to ours and if I'd be treated to that same expression in the morning, or if a bloody hole in the head coupled with insane behavior really was enough to kill his crush. And why did I even care? The thought flew out of my brain the second Aaron started the next cycle, pushing Protection into me and eliciting my own loud moan.

During our time together, Aaron and I had learned to better control fragmentation during sex, making it more restrained and measured. We learned to draw it out to a slow burn that lasted for an hour or more instead of a blazing inferno that left us wasted and spent in minutes.

This was *not* an example of that.

We lasted only two more complete cycles before Aaron's thrusting became desperate and it was all I could do to hold on.

"I love you, Lee," he whispered. "I love you so much." His body shuddered as he pushed Protection into me one final time.

I released the tenuous hold I had on my own body's responses and let his Protection fragment pull me over the edge with him. It was perfect timing, which wasn't unusual for us, but it meant something different now that I'd agreed to bond to him. Now that we were going to be a family. This thing between us was fierce and true. Permanent.

My center used to be Silverstone Stables, my parents' home, but that was over now. This was my new center.

Aaron slid off me, panting, and then shifted on his side to spoon me, his hand once again reaching around to rest protectively over baby Christine.

Christine. That's her name.

I didn't know where the name came from, but I knew it was right, almost like she'd already been named, and I'd recognized it rather than created it. It had been floating around in my mind like a word on the tip of your tongue. It had been there, but I hadn't been able to wrench it out of my memory. But now that I had it in the front of my consciousness, I knew it would stick.

Christine, Aaron echoed, letting the name bounce around in his head for a moment. *That sounds right.*

We drifted like that, Aaron's solid body a gravitational weight pulling me out of any bitter thoughts and back to safety.

"Promise me something," he whispered, his voice groggy.

"Hm?"

"If you ever decide this isn't what you want, you'll talk to me first. Don't just disappear. I couldn't take that. It would kill me."

"Why would I do that?" I scoffed. "Don't be ridiculous."

"Just promise me," he insisted.

This is my home now, I thought, *wherever he is. As long as I have him, I can handle my parents and freaking Marti and everything else. This is all the family I need.* I took a slow, sleepy breath in and sighed it out.

"I promise."

Chapter Eleven

*L*inorra's experience away from home had taught her to consider any information given to her as mere rumor until proven otherwise.

"How would a regular human man have the knowledge to cure my queen mother when you do not?" she asked the witch, then she wondered why she had not thought to ask this sooner.

The witch cackled merrily, her eyes dancing with mirth. "That, my dear, is a fine question. I am delighted to see you are not just a girl after all, but a woman, and a clever one at that."

I awoke to the smell of baking bread and coffee. In other words, heaven. The aroma attracted the crew as well. We all dragged ourselves back to the table, looking groggy but human again.

By the time we settled in to eat, it was noon, Minh time. My grandmother's estate was located just inland of Minh, a city that sprawled out along the southern coast of the main continent. It was home to a working farm employing hundreds of people, and as a result, there was a steady supply of fresh food.

Fluffy bread, something resembling sausage, and pale green hard-boiled eggs that tasted like chicken eggs except half the size, covered Gran's dining table. The crew was reluctant to try the eggs, but as a fan of Dr. Seuss, I dove right in and showed them the error of their ways. They soon devoured everything in sight, including a waxy cheese that I wasn't convinced was food.

I sat quietly with my cup of coffee, observing as Aaron discussed the day's plans with Fitch. Aaron watched me, too, but didn't include me in the conversation even though they seemed to be discussing the rescue of Fitch's "brother." I didn't need to be involved in every discussion, but it irked me that if this were the army, Aaron would be the general and Fitch the lieutenant general. I, on the other hand, was more like the mascot. I guess that would make me Luigi Francisco Seal. Or maybe the US Army's mule—I'm sure Aaron would have said that made more sense if he knew what a mule was.

My grandmother sat down next to me at the end of the long picnic-style table. Again, I got the strange feeling that I knew her from somewhere. The scent of lemon wafted off her, as if she had just been cleaning dishes or scrubbing the floor. Something about that scent tried to trigger a memory, but I couldn't quite get there.

"He loves you," she said, watching the men. Gran's voice was soft and high-pitched, almost childlike. I hoped she hadn't heard us the night before.

"Yes," I agreed, "but he doesn't know how to treat me like an equal. He will need to learn."

My grandmother snorted. "He already knows you're indestructible, and yet he carries on like he has to take care of you, which isn't always a bad thing. Never assume that you can change a man. Assume instead that you can't change a damned thing and decide whether you can live with him the way he is."

I shrugged, smiling a little. "Probably." I did like how he took care of me at times, but other times I wanted to throttle him.

Gran smirked. "I married your grandfather after knowing him for less than a month. It was arranged, though. That is how they did things in the Rhoyal line back then. Your mother was the first to do it her own way. Gigi married an Earth man from an unknown lineage, but he was a powerful healer. They came to live here with me a few years after your grandfather passed and stayed until you came along. He's a charming man, your father."

I nodded but didn't comment. Everyone always thought my father was charming, but I was still angry and didn't want to think about my parents.

"Your grandfather, though, now he was an amazing man. Still is, in some ways."

I stared at her, confused. Then I got it. "Can you see him?"

Gran smiled, nodding her head. "He isn't here all the time, but he comes when I call."

"Why can't I see him?" I asked.

"He's not here right now, but also, it doesn't work like that. Maybe you could see every ghost if you ascended Conjuration, but that world has never been found."

"Huh. So, you can only see certain ghosts?" I asked.

"Yes, only those you've had a significant relationship with. Some would say you have to have loved that person to truly see their spirit. I don't know if that's true, though. I mixed reservoirs with a man once and he started seeing your grandfather everywhere. Scared the daylights out of the poor bloke." Gran chuckled. I wanted to be polite, but in a thousand years, I'd never be able to lighten up enough to talk to my grandmother about her sex life.

I thought of Spirit, wondering if I would ever see her again. Spirit had been more than a friend or lover. She had been a kind of soulmate to me, one that I only recognized after I'd lost her. I loved her, though not in the same way I loved Aaron. Finding Aaron had felt like finding my way home after being lost my whole life and not realizing it, but what I had with Spirit was still love. Ward was the same, in a way. He and I had developed a strong attachment even before I knew he was human.

My heart ached for them, but I shook my head to dispel the feeling of loss.

"How did my grandfather die?" I asked, hoping it wasn't a rude question. There was a whole side of my family that I didn't know about, and I wanted to learn.

"Orion died in battle," she said simply.

"In battle? Which battle?"

Gran eyed me, then leaned forward and pursed her lips. *The Battle of Neesee*, she thought.

I gaped at her mastery of air Connection. I had already known she was an ascendant connector, like my mother, but her skill with the fragment put mine to shame. When she sent me her thoughts, her accent morphed into an American accent, as all thoughts did for me, but her words were accompanied by images, sounds, and smells. I viewed a memory so vivid that it seemed to come from my own mind. Buildings were on fire, filling the air with the acrid smell of smoke that burned the nose and lungs. In the distance, people screamed, and crimson battle dragons screeched over the booming sound of heavy artillery.

"Modern artillery?" I asked aloud, noting the vibration and deafening noise. "Why was there a battle in Neesee?" Gran nodded at my unspoken request. I wanted a story, and she had a good one to tell.

"About seven hundred years ago," she began, switching to spoken words so that anyone could listen, "Anick started projecting himself onto the people of Neesee. He was very gifted and did it so subtly that people would seem normal, living their lives as usual. They were fiercely loyal to him, though. He could cause wives to kill their husbands and children to kill their parents. That is how his cult began."

As Gran spoke, she continued sending images to my mind, a technique I hadn't even thought to try. I closed my eyes, listening as if she were a voice-over narration in a movie.

"The planet had been a mecca of innovation, drawing people from both Hartha and Earth, but Anick rejected advances in technology, claiming that they would lead to disaster. He also outlawed the use of any fragments that might help people oppose him. He banned books that taught things he didn't want people to know and killed or imprisoned anyone he couldn't control. There was an organized resistance that helped some people escape, but most did not.

"And so, over time, Anick took over the entire planet of Monash, but around the beginning of Earth's nineteenth century, he decided that Monash wasn't enough. He wanted to conquer all the worlds. He started with Hartha because we're a peaceful land of connectors, and he thought that made us weak. He didn't understand that connecting to others is what makes you strong. He failed, of course, and he and his thralls retreated back to Neesee.

"After that, the Harthan Rhoyals kept an eye on things on Monash. Your grandfather was assigned to Neesee as a spy and worked as a craftsman in the Woodworkers Guild. During our time there, Orion came up with a plan to assassinate Anick, but he needed a distraction to get past the company of enthralled soldiers stationed around the palace.

"The Rhoyals agreed to be that distraction. They attacked Neesee, pulling Anick's defenses away and leaving only a few bodyguards with Anick while he prepared to take the field. Orion slipped in and killed him before he ever got the chance, at the expense of his own life."

"How did he do it?" I asked, opening my eyes again. Aaron and the crew had all stopped their conversations to listen to her story.

"He had a unique combination of reservoirs, like you. He was a transformer, but he also had Connection and Reflection, which he got from me, and Evocation, which I got from him."

Ah, Aaron was right, I thought.

THE WISDOM OF DISHONOR

Yes, Gran responded, reverting to Connection, *and when Orion received permission from the Rhoyal Chamber—the queen's council—to ascend his Transformation, he raised all three of his lesser reservoirs, making him one of the most powerful fragmentors alive.*

But wouldn't someone in Neesee notice that he resonated with so many reservoirs? I asked, wondering why she didn't want the rest of the room to hear the end of the story.

When he first started, perhaps, but reflectors can learn to make themselves invisible in every way, including sight, sound, smell, and resonance. It takes years to master, but by the time our two daughters were adults, Orion had learned to silence himself and become undetectable. So, he made himself invisible, sneaked into the palace, and burned Anick alive with his bare hands.

He killed him with Evocation? I asked, my eyes flicking to Aaron, who met my gaze. Though he hadn't heard the end of Gran's story, I had a feeling he was thinking the same thing I was. If the Ministry succeeded in bringing back Anick, then Aaron was probably the only one who could kill him again. He had just become the most important weapon we had.

As far as we can tell, yes. You see, Anick was protected, but Evocation complements Protection and can burn through it. It's the only thing that can get through a shield, and the only thing that can kill an ascended protector. Anick thought he knew everything, but he didn't know that; probably because, aside from Conjuration, it was the only reservoir he didn't have. Evokers are rare. You only see a native-born evoker once every few hundred years or so, and, unlike Protection, it runs strongly in families. Actually, just one family, to be precise.

That can't be true, I thought. *Aaron said Evocation runs in his family too.* My gaze was still locked with Aaron's.

I know, dear, Gran thought.

You know? How could you . . . My attention snapped to my grandmother. She was giving me a sad little smile. "No, don't tell me that," I said aloud. "Don't you dare." Aaron had once told me that his grandfather was a master craftsman in the Woodworkers Guild. *No,* I thought, my stomach churning. The coffee I'd been enjoying threatened to make a reappearance.

My two daughters are your mother, Giana, and Violet—Aaron's mother.

"No!" I shrieked. "No, no, no, no, no!"

117

Aaron stood from the table, clearly alarmed. He scanned our surroundings for something to rescue me from, but there was nothing. Our eyes locked and time slowed as all my hopes and dreams for the future came crashing down, landing in a chaotic heap at my feet.

He was my cousin. My goddamned cousin.

And with that, the only piece of me I had left shattered. My center was gone. My home. That little place on my parent's property that I'd daydreamed about, the tree house he was going to build, the years of cooking together, laughing together, being together in every way—gone in the blink of an eye.

I experienced a frozen moment of horror before I laid my forehead down on the table. "No," I whispered one last time. I was hyperventilating now. *This can't be happening.*

Gran giggled like a schoolgirl, her high voice sending a deep cringe through my entire body. *Calm down. It's fine,* Gran thought to me. *That's how the Rhoyal line keeps the rare reservoirs safely within the family. It's how we've done it for thousands of years and we've never had a problem. It's common on your planet, as well, you know. It's only you American Earthlings who are prejudiced against it.*

Lifting my head to stare at Gran in disbelief, I opened my mouth to respond, then closed it again, speechless. I repeated that worthless exercise a few more times before I gave up on responding to her bizarre opinion.

My mother swept into the room, sitting across the table from us. "You told her, huh?"

"You knew about this?" I hissed, glaring up at her. Having acquired a suitable target for my wrath, I suddenly knew exactly what to say. "Of course, you did. You and Marti planned this whole thing from the beginning." I gasped as the pieces crashed into place. "You're the one who named Rogue because you knew he was Ward the whole time!"

I turned my accusing stare on my grandmother, a memory unexpectedly flooding my brain that made me realize why she was so familiar. It wasn't just the family resemblance. "And you! You were in my hospital room the day I woke up. You were my fragging doctor! I can't trust anyone in this family."

Gran pressed her mouth into a line, then rolled her eyes as if I were the one being unreasonable.

I shot to my feet, livid and ready to bolt. Aaron stepped back from the table, ready to follow, but I had nowhere to go. There was no way to run from this. I just stared back at him, horrified at the realization I had been tricked into an arranged marriage with my own cousin. I had agreed to marry him after only two months, knowing almost nothing about him. How could I have been so foolish?

Doesn't matter how it happened, I thought, tears welling in my eyes. I sagged down to the table again, my mind desperately searching through any way to make this okay, to make this "fine," as Gran had said.

I couldn't. This thing that I thought would save me from my collapsing reality was suddenly an impossibility, no matter what my family said. Spirit's face flitted across my thoughts. She had warned me to be careful, but was this what she meant? *They waited for me to fall in love with him before they told me. And now I'm pregnant.*

My mother and grandmother both sucked in a breath. Oops. I hadn't meant to send them that thought. I studied each of them, in turn. They had identical expressions of dismay as they stared at each other, obviously communicating telepathically and cutting me out. After a second, my mother nodded, then fled the room.

"What's wrong?" I asked angrily. "Isn't this what you wanted?"

Gran stared up at me, a deep wrinkle splitting her brows. *It's nothing. It's just that a baby wasn't in our plans.*

Yeah, no kidding. Mine either.

A door slammed somewhere, a sound that made me irrationally furious. I was the one who'd been wronged here. I should be the one slamming doors. My mother had stolen my thunder by rushing away before I could storm off myself.

"Where is she going?" I asked. "What the hell is happening?"

"Don't worry about it, dear." My grandmother got up from the table, picked up a few dishes, and hurried into the kitchen.

I stared after her, speechless. *Don't worry about it? Is she serious?* I was starting to feel like a child playing a game against grown-ups.

I don't know what I was expecting. An apology? Congratulations? I don't know. Something. Not this gaslighting nightmare followed by complete abandonment. *After everything, isn't someone going to at least explain to me what the hell is going on?*

Delya scuttled in from the kitchen, saw my livid expression, blanched, then quickly averted her eyes. She released a long-suffering sigh, then attempted to retrieve every dish at once. "I'll get these," she said. "You all go on and get ready for your big day." She made it sound like I was going to a party and leaving her with all the work. I wanted to smack her stupid cherubic face, deserved or not.

L.E. BROOKS

Aaron and I made eye contact, but, following Delya's example, I quickly averted my gaze, picked up a few plates, and fled into the kitchen. The dishes rattled together as I carried them to the sink. When I'd deposited them next to the others, I spun around. Gran was nowhere to be found.

These people act like I'm the one who has done something wrong, I thought, shaking my head. I had a rotten feeling in the pit of my stomach as I walked to the back door and opened it, peering out.

"What's going on?" Aaron grumbled from behind me.

I glanced back to see a genuine expression of concern. I needed to tell him. I gestured outside, then walked out to the backyard. He followed me, ducking through the doorway and closing the door behind him. The air outside smelled fragrant, like lilac.

Stupid air. It should smell like week-old garbage with all the flies they have on this godforsaken planet. That's what these people deserve.

I turned to see that the entire back of the house was lined with lilac bushes. They were a lot like the potted lilac my mother had grown in my childhood. Had it started from one of these? There was so much that I didn't know about my own family.

Who cares? I don't want any part of this.

Aaron approached from behind and wrapped his arms around me, enveloping me in that scent that I loved so much. I trembled a little, knowing this might be the last time he hugged me like this. I turned to face him and hugged him back, trying to memorize how it felt. My forehead came up to his sternum as he bent down to rest his chin on top of my head. He always hugged with his whole body, making me feel like his arms were the safest place in the universe.

"I have something to tell you," I said, barely managing to get the words out as a tear rolled down my cheek. I pushed away from him so I could see his face. He had the same long nose as my grandmother. I cringed, squeezing my eyes closed. *Oh god.*

"What is it?" he asked.

"I just found out how our mothers know each other," I said.

"Oh? How?"

I opened my eyes again. I didn't want to look at him when I said this, but I owed it to him. I was essentially breaking up with him, and I didn't want him to feel abandoned the way I did. I had promised him that I wouldn't disappear. I might be a terrible person, but I would keep that one promise, at the very least.

"They're sisters."

Aaron stared at me for a minute, his brow furrowed, then he said, "Oh, wow. That's unexpected. You're certain?"

I nodded.

Aaron shrugged. "All right. That's it?"

Hold the phone. "What do you mean *that's it*?" I said, my eyes widening. "That's . . ." My breath caught in my throat. "This is not okay, Aaron. It is very, very, *very* much not okay. It's *super* not okay! It's weird and gross."

Aaron shook his head, his eyebrows pinched together in confusion. "Not really. On Monash, most women prefer to bond their cousins. They're less likely to die unexpectedly like Falon's mother. It also keeps property and reservoirs in the family. That's even more important if your family has one of the Unspeakables."

I was dumbfounded, and I'm sure I had the *look* on my face, but he just laughed. "It's perfectly normal," he said. "Is that all? It sounded like you were having a serious argument. Your mother stormed off."

Is that all?

Apparently, he had already moved on from the incest conversation. I stepped back from him, trying to figure out how to adequately explain to him what this news meant to me while getting over my shock that it didn't mean the same thing to him. This was going to be so much harder now that I knew he didn't think of consanguinity as a barrier. To him, it wasn't going to be a tragic circumstance keeping us apart. It was just going to be me, breaking up with him for no good reason.

Jesus, could this get any worse?

Here's a bit of advice, in case you didn't already know. When things are going wrong, never *ever* ask yourself if things could get any worse. Because the answer is always yes. They can get so much worse.

"I told them about"—I patted my belly, glancing at the door to see if anyone was listening—"and they all ran away." I struggled to come up with a way to break the news to him that it was over. It didn't matter that I was pregnant already. It didn't matter that everyone thought it was fine and perfectly normal. This wasn't rural Pakistan or a fragging HBO series. I couldn't marry my goddamned cousin.

Panic had taken over, and I couldn't reason out what to do. So, I did the only thing I could think of.

Stall.

I took Aaron's hand, connecting, then switched to internal communication to recount the parts of my conversation with Gran that he hadn't already heard.

Fascinating, Aaron thought after I'd finished. *That must be how Eve got my grandfather's staff. And why my family has so many banned books. You were right, I do come from a family of rebels. Orion was a spy, and he killed Anick!*

He got a distant look in his eyes and a silly grin. As adorable as it was, I was about to wipe that grin off his face. *The Battle of Neesee was more than a hundred years ago,* he thought. *Didn't your grandmother say our mothers were already adults by then?*

Huh, I thought. *I didn't even think about that. That would make them at least a hundred. Another lie, or at least an omission.*

Aaron nodded. *Your father is likely a native-born protector who gave it to your mother, so it's certainly possible, but I don't know about my mother or your grandmother.*

Our *grandmother*, I corrected.

Aaron chuckled again. *Relax. It's fine.*

There's that word again.

He pulled me close to him and tried to kiss me, but I turned my head to the side, resting it on his chest instead. He slipped his hand into my hair, then slid his hand down my back, making me shiver.

Stop worrying, he thought. *This changes nothing. I love you. Come with me right now and I'll show you how much.*

For a brief moment, I considered relenting. Everyone except me seemed to think I was overreacting. Was I? I could let Aaron pick me up right now and take me to our room. One touch from him and I'd be ready to let him do whatever he wanted to me and like it. *It doesn't* feel *weird at all,* I thought. *He doesn't* feel *like my cousin.*

"Aaron," I said, disconnecting as I pushed back from him. "I need space to process this. I'm just . . ." I shook my head. *Priorities,* I thought, leaning back on my go-to strategy to get through difficult emotions. *Defeat Anick first, then break Aaron's heart and destroy my center. That's all. No big deal.*

"It's all right," he said, pulling me back for a sweeter, more chaste hug. "Take all the time you need. We can put off the bonding, if you want. The Harvest Festival isn't the only place to get a cuff." He kissed me gently on the forehead. "I have to go back inside and finish planning with the crew anyway."

He released me and backed up slowly toward the door, keeping his eyes on me. "You're going to keep your promise, aren't you?" he asked, though it wasn't really a question.

I nodded. "Of course."

He smiled and then headed inside, taking my home with him. The porch door slapped behind him with a finality that I felt in my bones. I stood there, staring after him with nothing left but lilacs and too many flies. My outrage had cooled to numb shock that left me disconnected not only from him, but from my situation.

Perhaps I was being dramatic, but it felt like my life was over. I had spent so much time trying to get back to Earth, and now I didn't care if I ever got there. I felt utterly lost and alone, like a balloon accidentally released to the sky, drifting on whatever current happened to catch me next. I didn't even know who I was anymore.

Movement through the kitchen window caught my attention, and I glanced up to see Falon staring out at me. The idea of dealing with him made me tired, but I knew it was my fault. He'd made his interest obvious, and not only had I not deterred him, but I'd sort of encouraged him in order to enlist his help. It wasn't my best moment, I realized now.

His gaze was laser-focused, like he knew exactly what was happening between me and Aaron and was waiting on the edge of his seat, ready to swoop in before he missed his chance. As a matter of fact, that's exactly what he was doing.

Chapter Twelve

Linorra glanced back at the shock den as she flew away upon Otterhai's shoulders. She regretted the deception but knew that Syndeth would not agree to take her into danger to find the key. She feared that it was already too late to save her mother from the mysterious illness that had left her bedridden. Even as that dark thought passed through her mind, she felt the same illness take root in her own body, causing her to feel heavy and bleak.

It was early evening before we were ready to return to Neesee. I changed back into my magic Zig dress, which had been miraculously restored to pristine cleanliness overnight. My mother had not yet returned from her mysterious mission, and my grandmother had also disappeared. I wanted to speak to my mother before we left, but Aaron didn't think we should wait any longer.

We met in the dining room, once again, to go over the plan. Aaron's intention was to purchase the bonding cuff anyway, even if I wasn't ready, then check on Jorin's contingent. Falon and I were to return to the boat while Aaron and the manly men scoped out the ceremony site. I was obviously too fragile for anything as dangerous as that, and Falon was more than happy to keep me company.

I promptly threw that plan right out the window. Instead, we would do the most important thing first, which was to scout the ceremony site. We needed to plan where to stand in order to have a balance of cover and sight lines while planning for our retreat if it came to that. I wanted to see if Zig's suggestion of a rooftop perch was feasible. Then we would check on Jorin's group if there was time. The men didn't back down easily, though. So much for counting on Aaron's support.

"This is what you call letting me work?" I asked the group. "You all saw me regrow my head, for frag's sake. What exactly do you think you're protecting me from?"

"There are fates worse than death," Ellis said, dropping his gaze.

"You mean Projection?" I asked. "I am less vulnerable to that than anyone in this room."

"Projection can overcome Protection if you're not careful," Aaron said. "It happened to me, if you recall."

"Actually, I meant the pit," Ellis corrected.

"Okay, tell me what that is exactly," I said.

"It's a pit," Shane said.

I sighed. "I guessed that, smartass. What's so bad about it?"

"It's a deep, narrow tank," Aaron said. "It's set into the ground with a grate on top so that people can see in. They fill it in with wood that's been soaked with lamp oil. Then they strip you naked, dangle you in there by your ankles, and light it on fire. It is accessed from an underground passageway, and there are holes in the access door so that they can light the fire, then stab you from the side for extra fun."

That did sound terrible. "Fine. I survived the pain of ascension. I can survive that." My hand came to my belly before I could stop myself. *And so can she.*

"Ascension took a few minutes," Ellis said. "This is hours or sometimes days of torture. They don't put enough wood in there to kill you. They put enough in there to torture you for a couple hours, then they pull you out, heal you, and start all over again until they get bored or until they *accidentally* kill you."

"It's a show too," Falon said. "If they really hate someone, then they make everyone visit the top of the pit to drop things on you like it's a sacred pilgrimage."

"And they don't show the healing part," Fitch said, "but I heard if you're a woman, they rape you while they're healing you." The room fell silent at Fitch's blunt comment. Their pitying eyes drilled into me.

"Actually, that happens if you're a man too," Falon said, drawing everyone's attention back to him. He didn't meet their eyes. "My father paid to watch from the tunnel once.

They have a room down there where they do the healing. He took Markus with him, and he told me about it. They didn't know it would be a man. Markus said they were sending our father a message." He closed his eyes and shook his head.

"Well," I said gently, "that certainly casts a new light on our attempts to persuade him. He knew the consequences of moving against Seleca." Poor Falon. I couldn't imagine what it must have been like to grow up in an environment where your father would pay to watch someone be assaulted. I wondered if he would ever tell me what happened to his mother. I didn't have the heart to ask him outright.

"Okay," I said. "I can see why you all might want to protect me from that, and I appreciate it. I'm not as physically strong as you, and I would have a hard time fighting them off if they got past my shield, but that is exactly why I need to go. I need to see the place myself. Otherwise, I'm going in blind."

"You shouldn't go in at all," Aaron said, raising his voice. "You should stay where it's safe. A fight this dangerous is no place for a woman. Especially not a—" He stopped himself before he finished the sentence, but he glanced down at the belly I still cradled. I promptly let go, but not before his face turned red, and his mouth pressed into a flat line. Those fire agate stones would start popping any minute.

No place for a woman? I thought incredulously. My blood boiled at that statement. I wanted to scream all the swear words I knew at him. Even if I hadn't found out Aaron was my cousin, that little slip would have been enough for me to walk out. My grandmother had been right. He would always treat me like a helpless damsel that needed to be saved from a burning pit, no matter how many times he saw me rise from the ashes. It should have made me feel better about leaving him behind, but it just made me even more miserable.

"Sorry to interrupt," Gran said, "but I need to talk to Lina." I turned to see my grandmother standing in the kitchen doorway with my mother behind her. Gran's face was set with grim determination while my mother's eyes were red-rimmed and watery.

"What happened?" I asked flatly, not sure if I actually cared. I hoped my mother was remorseful for what she had done, but somehow, I doubted it.

"We'll talk outside. Come on," Gran said.

I stared at Aaron, but he wouldn't meet my eyes. He was pissed.

Ya know what? So was I.

I threw my hands up in the air and followed the women outside. I didn't know what else to do. None of the men had backed me up. I felt as helpless as they all seemed to think I was.

I should just go without them and leave them all here, I grumbled.

Agreed, my grandmother thought to me.

Oh, here I go again. Thinking too loudly.

You've always done that, my mother thought. *Remember when you smoked marijuana and thought you could hide it from us? That was so funny.* She took out a cloth handkerchief that had a little purple dragon embroidered on the corner and blew her nose.

A twinge of guilt pulled at my heart seeing my mother upset and clearly trying to be brave, but I was far from done being angry with her. Even more than that, though, I felt dangerously apathetic about my entire situation. Nothing was right anymore, and I had no one to talk to about it. My parents were liars, my friends were all gone, my lover was . . . what? A dream that had slipped through my fingers as quickly as he'd fallen into my lap. I could feel my old buddy Depression coming to say "wassup" and maybe hang out for a while.

We walked through the kitchen and out the back door, closing it behind us. The scent of lilac hit me again and I inhaled deeply, soaking up any pleasure I could find. Gran and my mother walked in silence down the mulched path. I followed them, my head hung like a prisoner marching off to the gallows. I didn't know where we were going, and I didn't care.

I turned my face up to the sun as we walked, soaking up the warmth and questioning how I would get through this. Violet had seen a way through, hadn't she? She told Aaron that I'd somehow lead him back to his family, and that's exactly what I did.

I huffed out a bitter laugh. *That sneaky bitch did it again.*

The door closed again behind us, and I glanced back, expecting to see Aaron. Instead, Falon emerged and sat on the steps, watching us walk away.

"Where are we going?" I asked, turning forward again.

Just be patient, granddaughter, Gran thought.

Yeah right, I thought obstinately, but I kept walking anyway.

We came to the field where the crew and I had landed when we arrived the night before. A large flat stone that I hadn't noticed last night occupied the middle of the yard, surrounded by a ring of dead grass. It didn't have the telltale *X* carved into it that would have marked it as a bridgestone, but it was the right shape and size.

"What is that?"

"A bridgestone," Mom said, taking in my expression. "This is one of the only ones that insane German didn't desecrate."

"Oh," I said, feeling silly. I had somehow thought that bridgestones automatically came with an *X*. "But why did I arrive over the bridgestone? I thought I would go back to where I was born."

"You did," my mother said. "On Hartha, women give birth over the closest bridgestone to their home. It creates a stronger and more reliable resonance and acts as a meeting point for travel."

"Oh, that's right," I mumbled absently, eyeing the ring of dead grass around the bridgestone. That wasn't normal. The ring gave me the creeps, like we stood upon a Buffy-style hellmouth or something. *What the hell?*

"Enough about that," Gran said, pulling something out of her pocket. "We don't have much time. Lina, take this." She held out a key-shaped yellow crystal attached to what appeared to be a durrite chain.

The crystal key from Violet's story, I thought. *It's real.*

It was exactly as described in Violet's book, with a number eight carved into the head. Made of yellow crystal, the key would have been lovely by itself, but a rainbow of sparkling gems had been cut into tiny cylinders then threaded around the body of the key like beads on a string. It was a striking piece of artwork with an obvious resonance of its own, though I couldn't distinguish any distinct fragment.

As soon as I touched it, a violent vibration ran through my body, like the key stored fragmental energy which then flooded my own reservoirs, replenishing them.

"Whoa," I said. "What in the hell was that?"

Gran barked a quick laugh, then said, "That's exactly what I asked when I touched it the first time. The key is a resonance article. It attracts and stores fragments. This one is made of yellow diamond, crafted as a skipstone for Teleportation, but the smaller beads each attract a different fragment. If your reservoirs are depleted, it refills them whether you want to or not."

Like the bracelet I gave Aaron, I noted. Come to think of it, Terik and Farrah's bonding cuffs also had stones in them.

"The key is a yellow diamond?" I asked.

"Yes. These types of skipstones are rare, and this particular key is one of a kind. If anyone finds out that you have it, you'll become a target for every skipstone thief in the universe. Hang it around your neck and don't show a single person *ever*, not even Aaron."

"That won't be a problem," I said.

Gran gave my mother a meaningful look. "I'm going to teach you how to use the key by taking you to Darion-Ájar," she said.

"We're really leaving without them?"

"Yes," Gran answered. "We must."

I glanced back at the house, uncertain. "Where is Darion-Ájar? We have to go to Monash, and I don't have a lot of time."

"Baby," Mom said. "This is the only way for you to do what you have to do. Just trust your grandmother. We are on your side. Please."

I rolled my eyes. *Trust? Who does she think she's kidding?*

Standing at the threshold of the unknown, it was now painfully obvious that my previous threat to leave Hartha without Aaron had been empty. I'd never intended to actually do it. I'd been angry that Aaron and the crew didn't take my superspecial immortality into account. Now, here I was balking at going somewhere without them, even in the company of experts.

I sighed. "Fine. What do I do?"

"This key is the most powerful skipstone in the universe," said Gran. "It lets you travel anywhere without a bridgestone, even outside our triad, which normally only ascendant teleporters can do."

I examined the key, my eyebrows lifting. *And they're giving it to me? I can see why someone might want to steal this thing.*

"Take the head of the key in your right hand and a beaded gem in your left. Whatever you hold in your left hand directs the bridge, helping you control where it lands. When you go to Monash, you'll take the amber bead in your left hand, which is this gold-colored one." She pointed to the fifth bead. "To go to Darion-Ájar, you'll use the fourth bead, which is made of yellow diamond just like the key."

"Which one is the Earth bead?" I asked.

"This one," Gran said, pointing to the first bead, an aquamarine gem.

"Well, that should be easy to remember, at least."

"There's a mnemonic we can teach you," Mom offered, "but only the first six are inhabited by humans, so it's not as much to remember as you might expect."

"Yes," Gran said, rolling her eyes at my mother. "It's all very fascinating. What a pity we don't have time for another political debate on the definition of *human*. The fourth bead, please, granddaughter."

My eyes bounced between the two women for a moment before I decided not to ask them what the hell they were talking about. I did as requested, taking the top of the key in my right hand and the fourth bead in my left. Gran grasped my right wrist tightly, as if I might take off like a rocket and carry her with me. My mother came over to my other side and took hold of my left wrist in the same way.

"Now, point the bottom of the key toward the center of your body just there," Gran said, pointing to my solar plexus, the same area from which I had pulled the Teleportation reservoir from Axel. "Pull your Teleportation fragment from your body into the key with your left hand, and it will flow through whichever skipstone you hold, then out through the head of the key in your right hand, opening a bridge right on top of you."

"Hurry," Mom added, "you have a secret admirer who also thinks very loudly."

Having no time to analyze what Mom meant, I pulled Teleportation out of my reservoir. Compared to my first attempt at Teleportation, it was easy. Too easy, actually. It was a bit like bracing yourself to lift something heavy and then falling backward when it turned out to be stage foam.

Just before the bridge opened on top of us, sucking the three of us up, footsteps stomped toward us from behind. I was too focused on my task to reach out with Connection. If I had, I would have discovered that I had not, in fact, killed Falon's crush.

Gran and my mother were knocked loose as Falon's surprisingly heavy body slammed into me. They instantly disappeared from view, but I wasn't too worried. I knew that unless I was physically touching them, their path through space might separate from mine but they'd end up in roughly the same place. At least, I hoped that would hold true.

As we flew along the bridge path, Falon pulled me to his body and wrapped his lanky arms around me from behind. He clasped his hands together in front of me and buried his face in my neck as if he were trying to hide. That was when I remembered that the Monashi people are wicked strong. I had once seen Aaron, only half Monashi on his father's side, casually sling a half-ton dragon over his shoulder and carry it for miles. As it turns out, a full-blooded Monashi man is strong enough to accidentally crush a Harthan woman with a friendly hug.

I cried out only to remember that on a bridge, sound waves also vanish the moment they separate from your body. Panicking, I seized Falon's hands and pushed Connection.

Falon, are you crazy? I can't breathe!

Falon jerked, surprised at the internal communication. *Sorry,* he thought, then he loosened his grip. He did not take his face out of my neck, though.

Goddess, she smells good, he thought, then he imagined himself gently biting the back of my neck the way he'd seen Aaron do. I felt him getting an erection behind me and was reminded of the uncomfortable vision his brother had forced upon me. He felt me noticing and pulled his pelvis away. *Sorry,* he thought again.

Falon is not his brother, that's for damned sure. His immediate response quelled some of my anger, but I was still confused.

Why did you ambush me? I asked.

Well, someone *had to. Why did you leave without us? Aaron was already livid that you didn't immediately obey his command. Now that you've disappeared without anyone to protect you, he's gonna go on a rampage.* Falon's telepathic words were scolding, but his attitude was more amused than upset. He was enjoying my spat with Aaron a little too much.

I'm a grown woman. No one commands me. You all need to come to terms with that, trust my judgment, and stop treating me like a child to be taken care of.

I would never do that to you, Falon thought. *I trust you and I . . . I care for you. I'm sorry I didn't speak up, but Aaron scares the spit out of all of us. He's got a reputation, you know. Well-deserved, from what I can tell.*

Okay, that's fair, but you're, what, eighteen? It's never going to happen, Falon.

I'm twenty-seven, actually, he responded hotly. I'd touched a nerve. *Older than you, I'd bet. It's interesting that you just stated age as an excuse instead of the fact that you're with Aaron. Maybe that's because all the two of you ever do is fight and have sex.*

That is not *true and . . . really, twenty-seven?*

Yes, regular healing keeps you young. Transmuters age too quickly if we don't stay on top of it. Markus and I have been regulars at the Rhoyal Healers Guild since we were fourteen. Markus was actually only a year behind Aaron in school. Why do you think he holds him in such contempt? He said Aaron went crazy because they kicked him out. He killed one of those golden guards on his way out, you know. And you're interested in me now. I can feel it. You can't lie to me.

The fact that Aaron had killed a guard was news to me. I wondered if the guard had been a thrall, an unsettling thought. Why hadn't Aaron told me about it?

I didn't respond right away, but I twisted back when Falon lifted his head from my neck to gaze at me. The flecks of green in his irises seemed to almost spark out in the overwhelming green light of the Harthan bridge. He stared into my eyes, then down at my mouth, and back up into my eyes.

Falon, I thought to him, shaking my head. *This is so not what I need right now. I'm pregnant.*

Falon's regard faltered, and he let his eyes fall. His grip on me loosened so that he barely had a hold of me. *There are ways to fix that,* he thought. *People do it all the time when they find out they're having a girl with no greater reservoir. That's partially why Markus can't find anyone to bond. There just aren't that many women like you around. There aren't that many women around at all.*

That sentiment made me think of the day I met Aaron. I remembered thinking that he probably only wanted me because there was no one else. I was there and convenient. I'm not bad looking and I'm in great shape, but if I'd met Aaron on Earth, I would have considered him to be out of my league, a better match for someone like Farrah, not me.

I cringed again, turning forward, away from Falon, and squeezed my eyes closed. The thought of marrying my cousin was like a poisonous gas I couldn't stop breathing. I didn't want to think about it, but it was everywhere. It was so hard for me to believe that Aaron still wanted to bond me, that everyone was just *okay* with it. That my own *mother* was okay with it. It made me angry all over again.

Gently, Falon turned me around so that we faced each other, but I couldn't meet his gaze. *Do you know what bonding is, Lina? It's a sale. And it's finalized the moment you put on the bonding cuff. You can't usually stop it, and you can never take it back. If you ever try to leave, you are hunted down and dragged back or worse. Once you put on the cuff, you are property. Why do you think my father was so surprised that you were bonding to Aaron? There's no way he could pay to bond a fragmentor. And to* volunteer *yourself is like . . . like . . .*

A memory flashed across his mind. A brief glimpse of his mother, a greater producer. She had been the one to create the hanging gardens and the beautiful landscape. Falon had transmuted the front gate in her memory after she died. The flowers shaped into the gate were *dramsigas*, her favorite flower, and the ones that still swathed the Eboros estate in brilliant orange. The gate was his tribute to her.

My mother was bonded to my father when she was sixteen. She was a lot like Farrah, actually. So beautiful, and she radiated love. I waited as Falon struggled to lock down his deep sorrow. It made my own eyes tear up.

She was the first person that Magister Axel tried to bond, years before Farrah. My father said everyone wanted her, but no one was brave enough to challenge Axel. She didn't have anyone to turn to for help like Farrah did, so she went to my father because she knew he could afford it. They'd never met, but she'd seen him at Ministry gatherings. He ... wasn't kind to her, but anyone is better than Axel.

Falon paused, his eyes distant. I let the silence sit, knowing he'd continue when he was ready. *After my brother and I were born, she kept getting pregnant with girls, and none with greater reservoirs. My father kept sending her to the healers to end the pregnancies. Finally, when I was around ten, she got pregnant with twin boys, both with rare greater reservoirs. One was predicted to be a teleporter, which my father had been trying unsuccessfully for years to secure in hired help. I had never seen him so excited.*

Something wasn't right with the pregnancy, though. She was always in pain, but my father wouldn't let her see the healers. I used to sneak into her room to sleep next to her sometimes. I found her ...

I saw his memory of the event and felt helpless to comfort him. It was too horrific. He'd been a child when he found his mother's lifeless body in a blood-soaked bed. He'd been haunted by it ever since, growing more and more angry and reckless. He blamed his father, and the experience had led him to question everything about how his world worked. His brother thought he was crazy, and his father didn't trust him to even transmute for the business. He was alone.

I'm so sorry, Falon, I thought, my heart breaking for that little boy from his past.

Falon shook his head, freeing himself from the memory, then he took a deep breath in and out, his focus returning to my face. His hands tightened on my arms. *If my mother had owned herself instead of bonding to my father, she'd be alive right now.* Had he been speaking aloud, Falon would have been growling. *Aaron knew you didn't understand bonding, Lina. He knew and he still pushed you into it. He still pushes you even though he knows you don't want to bond to your cousin.*

Falon paused for effect. I gawked, unable to mask my surprise. Had he been listening to our conversation? Stupid Monashi super hearing!

Yes. I heard. Please don't be angry. He reached one hand up to cup my chin, running his thumb along my jawline. *I just want you to understand because I care about you.*

I wanted to turn away and deny what he said about Aaron, but he was right. If what Falon said about bonding was true, which seemed likely, then Aaron would have known. He'd dismissed my reservations regarding our blood relation as silly, just like he'd dismissed my objections to being hidden away while the big strong men did all the dangerous work. He wanted to control me, just like he'd tried to do when he kicked Ward out of the house even though I'd promised him that Ward was just a friend. He hadn't listened then either.

Falon watched my face with laser focus, nodding as I moved through the logic in my head, acknowledging the red flags I had previously ignored. I could see hope kindling in his eyes as he stared at me. His persuasion was working, and he knew it.

I would never bond you, Lina. I would only walk beside you. You're only trapped if you want to be. Just think about it. He gazed at me for another moment and then sighed, finally relenting, and let go. Instantly, he vanished into the light to progress along his own path toward the receiving bridgestone.

It wasn't until that moment that I realized I should be ascending Connection and wasn't.

Chapter Thirteen

"*A fear of dragons is common in this land,*" said Otterhai. "*It is difficult, sometimes, for humans to judge not with their eyes but with their minds.*"

I was thoroughly confused now. It was a good thing we landed on Darion-Ájar right at that moment, because if I hadn't been distracted, I probably would have had an anxiety attack.

I had not yet mastered the art of exiting a bridge, so when I landed, my knees hit the bridgestone with a *crack* and lightning shot down to my feet. Falon landed flat on his back an instant later, his head snapping against the bridgestone. He groaned, but he must not have hit his head too hard because he recovered quickly, leaping up to help me to my feet.

The first thing I noticed after the painful landing was that it was cold, and I hadn't thought to bring my jacket. I shivered as I glanced around, crossing my arms over my chest. We had landed in an organized arrival bay that was outside but covered by a high canopy and lit by artificial lighting. It looked like customs at an international airport, except without the maddening line.

Small buildings, painted neon yellow, lined the perimeter just inside a fence topped by razor wire. Beyond the arrival bay, a strip of clear night sky showed between the fence and canopy. The continuous drone of unseen machines or possibly vehicles beyond the fence set my teeth on edge, or maybe that was the temperature.

Falon, ever the opportunist, draped one long arm around me, rubbing my shoulder for warmth and, against my better judgment, I let him. I *hate* to be cold.

My mother waited a few yards away, dusting herself off and scowling at Falon. I suppressed a wave of vindictive satisfaction that swept over me at her displeasure. He'd knocked her loose on the bridge, sure, but she was fine and had arrived all the same.

Falon shrugged, grinning at her sheepishly as he pulled me closer to him. Mom sighed heavily, then she turned to walk toward Gran, who spoke to a dark-skinned man behind the service counter.

I found myself smirking at the wordless interaction between Falon and my mother until I realized another possible reason she might be annoyed. Falon wasn't the person they'd set me up with. Was his presence another unanticipated change of plans? That idea certainly appealed to Evilina, who spitefully wanted to catch everyone's hopes and dreams for me and rip them apart like wet paper.

As we approached the counter, Gran traded a look with my mother, then switched to internal communication, speaking telepathically with the man, whom she seemed to know. He stared warmly into Gran's eyes, nodding occasionally. His hair was long, streaked with silver, and braided with yellow strips of cloth. He wore a faded yellow robe and a belt that resembled my grandmother's, beaded with aqua, green, and yellow.

Gran handed him a blue passport-sized booklet, which he scanned in a little machine set atop the counter, then he laughed at something Gran thought to him as he handed it back. She took the booklet and reached back across the counter toward the man. He took her hand in his, holding it loosely while they communed.

It occurred to me that this might be the man who'd seen my grandfather hanging around. Before I could stop myself, I snort-laughed, then quickly turned toward Falon to hide my expression. If the man and my grandmother used to be lovers, this conversation could take a while. I might as well stay warm.

"Where are we?" Falon asked, taking the opportunity once again to bring me closer. He wrapped both arms around me, holding the cold air at bay. I turned my head to the side and rested it on his upper belly, as that's as far as my head reached. He was so fragging tall.

I brought my arms into my chest, letting him envelop me without returning his hug. He smelled like the soap from Gran's house. It was pleasant, but I couldn't help but compare it to Aaron's natural scent, which I loved so much that I wanted to lick it off him. The thought made me flush, then immediately cringe again.

"Darion-Ájar," I said. "Gran said she brought me here to . . ." I snapped my mouth shut, realizing I wasn't supposed to talk about the key.

"Learn how to use the bridge key?" Falon guessed.

I raised my eyes to his, stunned, but I didn't answer.

He chuckled. "You are all terrible at subterfuge. Don't worry, I know what a big secret that is. My father has been trying to acquire one for years. They can't be purchased at any price. I won't tell a soul, especially not my father."

"Thanks," I said, but I narrowed my eyes, assessing. Falon had said exactly the right thing, but I wasn't convinced I could trust it. What exactly would it cost me to keep this secret? If I told him I wasn't interested in him romantically, would he turn right around and break his promise? Or worse, would he try to take the key from me? If he did, I doubted I'd be able to stop him. I didn't think it would come to that, but I hadn't known him that long. If he wanted to, he could overpower me as easily as Zig had. Getting my shield up in time would be a dubious prospect at best.

I didn't realize it then, but Falon had a knack for timing. It would serve him well later in life, especially after his father died and he and his brother took over the family business. That's how he knew this was the exact right moment to call in his favor.

"Could you take me to Wishmere before we go back?"

"Wishmere? Where's that?" I asked. *That's a weird name for a planet. It sounds like a place where unicorns and leprechauns might live.*

"That's the Transmutation world. Nearly the whole planet is one big city, or so I've read. I've never been there, obviously, but if it's true, nobody will notice that we've come and gone. You owe me an ascension, remember? Let's do it before we go back. That reservoir fills the quickest of any. It will literally take five minutes, and I will be much more help to you in Neesee."

"How?" I asked.

"An ascendant of Transmutation can change anything, even people. I could turn our enemies to stone. I could turn the ground behind us to ice if we're running away. I could do so much more. Please, Lina. I want to help."

It made sense, and it was true that I'd promised him, but I hesitated. It would be good to have someone powerful on my side. *Especially someone who's in love with you*, Evilina added. But Aaron and the crew were waiting.

"Please, Lina," he whispered, sensing my hesitation. His black hair and hazel eyes were lovely against his pale skin, and he had an earnestness about him that was irresistible. "I won't tell anyone about your key, I swear, but use it to help me, please." And there it was. The price. I should have anticipated his request. It was the obvious choice.

I closed my eyes, weighing my options. I had picked that habit up from Aaron. It truly wasn't that much to ask, given how big of a secret he was keeping for me. He would not only ascend his Transmutation reservoir, but he'd also raise his Teleportation reservoir, letting him open bridges. That could be incredibly useful in an ally, not to mention that it would make him an important member of his family. His father wouldn't be able to resist that unique ability, which might encourage Regalinius to help us, despite the risk.

The advantages were too many to ignore. I'm sure procrastinating to return to Aaron's temper wasn't a factor in any way.

"Five minutes?" I asked.

Falon grinned, nodding. "Including travel time," he added exuberantly.

"It hurts, you know," I said.

He nodded. "I remember how Ellis looked after he ascended, but you'll heal me, right?"

"I will," I said. "But I'm going to ascend Teleportation on the way there, so you may have to wait for me to recover or maybe even defend me if we arrive somewhere dangerous."

He nodded, an expression of pure elation taking over his features. "I'll protect you. I won't let go of you unless you want me to."

I shivered. That was exactly what Aaron had said to me just yesterday.

You're the only one I can trust.

Guilt stabbed at me. I pulled away from Falon casually and turned back around to face the counter, then I waited awkwardly, shivering. Falon, perhaps sensing my discomfort, stepped up next to me but did not place his arm back around me, though he was as close as a person could be without touching. While we waited, I let my mind wander to the conversation we'd had on the bridge.

I would never bond you, Lina, he'd thought to me. Bonding was not marriage. Bonding was just bondage. And not the fun kind either. No wonder Regalinius had been confused. For a woman, bonding wasn't something to celebrate or enjoy. I'd had no idea what I was saying yes to. I hadn't even known that bonding happened when you put on the bracelet. I had just assumed that it was like an engagement ring, a precursor to a beautiful ceremony. I had thought I had time to change my mind if I needed to.

I knew that Aaron's love was real, and now that my flash of indignant fury had waned, I could once again remind myself of what he'd done for me. When he'd thought I was dying in the water, he'd jumped in twice. He'd been beside himself. I'd awakened to him sobbing when we'd reached Hartha and he thought I was dead. He definitely loved me, but I also knew that he was a hothead with control issues, and he had been completely ready to purchase me like a horse. A cheap one at that. A freebie, actually. Fantasma had been nearly thirty thousand dollars. I was worth less than her.

What do I do now? I wondered. *I'm pregnant and alone. Yes, I could get an abortion, but is that what I want?*

I didn't think so. I support every woman's right to choose, but faced with that choice myself, it didn't feel like the right one for me. The thought made me clench my fists, then clutch my own belly protectively. I could feel her resonating in there like a tiny badass.

Wait a second . . . with her particular reservoirs, is an abortion even possible? She's immortal.

The whole thing made my head hurt. With my uninterrupted access to birth control, I'd never imagined myself in this situation. *On the other hand, I never imagined myself getting stuck on a distant planet with an alien baby daddy, but here we are.*

I sighed. This was no time for ill-advised jokes. I needed to clear my head and not accept the advances of another man the moment things got tough with my future owner.

Stop it. Stop it. Stop it, I thought, smacking my forehead. *You always make a joke out of everything.* Another thing Aaron had said to me more than once over the last couple of months, whenever he thought I was glossing over uncomfortable emotions. *Jesus . . . I need to talk to him. Except . . . I abandoned him on Hartha and ran away with Falon.*

That's when it really hit me. I had disappeared. I had broken my promise. Guilt speared my heart, making it forget a few beats. *Aaron.*

Focus, Lina, my mother thought.

Focus on what? I snapped. *Where is Dad, anyway?*

He's in the holding area. We are only here for a short time, but they are exceedingly stringent on their visitation rules. You must be accepted prior to arrival. We can't even leave the bridge pavilion without clearance, and we're *visiting dignitaries.*

Why are we even here? I asked. *Also, why didn't I ascend on the Harthan bridge? I was expecting a little more pain, not that I'm complaining.*

You already ascended your Connection reservoir when you were a toddler. We're here so that you can ascend your Teleportation before we go back to Monash, but we have to wait for the key to refill with fragment, so your grandmother is stalling for time, distracting her . . . uh . . . friend.

I snickered. *She's a devious one, isn't she?*

Where do you think Violet learned it?

Before my earlier conversation with Falon, I'd never thought about reservoirs needing to be filled, but it made sense. *If I'm a Connection ascendant, then why can't I connect through the air?*

My mother sighed. I couldn't see her eyes, but I knew she was rolling them. *You're literally doing it right now, Lina.*

Oh, I responded. I should have realized that I would have ascended Connection when my mother brought me from Hartha to Earth. I imagined myself ascending Connection at such a young age. It seemed like a cruel thing to do to a child. I was glad I didn't remember it. *I thought I could only send thoughts because* you *were an ascendant.*

No, it doesn't work like that, she thought. *If your target isn't an ascendant, you can push your thoughts out through the air, but you can't receive a response back or sense emotion without touching.*

THE WISDOM OF DISHONOR

Target, I thought. The word made it sound like an attack. It could be, now that I thought about it. The Connection fragment was turning out to be much more powerful than I had originally thought.

The man behind the counter finally looked up from my grandmother and eyed us. He took his hand back from her, his gaze sliding past me to my companion. Falon might have seemed like a scrawny beanpole, but he was deceptively strong. I would assume someone working at an interplanetary arrival bay would be familiar with the different types of travelers that might appear, especially those from planets with humans known for their considerable height and strength. You might as well disregard someone from the planet Krypton.

Falon withstood the man's scrutiny with a neutral expression, then raised a hand and waved. "Greetings," he said robotically.

I snort-laughed again, drawing the attendant's hard eyes to me.

Here we go, Lina, my grandmother thought to me, stepping aside. *Qadeem will ask you questions, and you will answer as truthfully as possible. If you pass his inspection, then we will be admitted to the holding area.*

Okay, I answered. *No pressure.*

Qadeem approached, looking me up and down, then thought, *Are you an ascendant connector?*

Apparently, I answered.

He nodded. *Good. Do you have any weapons on your person?*

I thought for a minute. *Yes, actually*, I thought. *A dagger.*

Take it out and give it to me, handle facing out, please.

I slipped Ellis's dagger out of the sheath in my magic pocket and handed it to Qadeem as instructed. He took it and stepped back to stare at my dress, his expression unreadable. His nearly black eyes slid to mine, then narrowed.

"What?" I asked out loud.

"Where you have dress?" he asked, pointing down. He had a thick accent that he hadn't had when communicating telepathically. It took me a second to even understand his question.

"A friend made it for me," I responded.

"Who friend?" he asked.

I paused, wanting to be truthful but also *not* wanting to give out Zig's name. "Gerhelm Meriweather," I answered slowly.

Everyone gasped except Falon.

"Jesus. What now?" I asked, exasperated. This conversation was going to a place I hadn't expected. How did these people know about Zig? How the hell did Qadeem recognize his work in the dress? Are dress pockets really that fragging rare in the entire universe? What a sad statement on our collective humanoid existence.

When and where did you last see him? Qadeem asked, his accent disappearing again in the Connection link.

I looked up, trying to remember. Was that only yesterday? Sheesh. *Yesterday, Monash, Neesee docks.*

I was getting impatient. I needed to get back, and this was taking forever. *Except we don't need to get to Neesee before the bonding vendors close because I won't be doing that. Ever. With anyone.* I was surprised at my own firm decision. *It's better this way, but he deserves a chance to explain why he tried to bond me without telling me what it was. And I can still make good on my promise. It's not too late.*

Qadeem went back to communicating with my grandmother. He appeared upset now and shook his head at her, probably thinking to her, *No fragging way she's coming in here.* Gran appeared to be trying to calm him down, then let out her own exasperated sigh. She pointed at me and communicated something else, stomping her foot like a child. Qadeem stopped and turned to me, staring.

"Wait," Qadeem commanded, holding up one broad palm. He motioned to the man standing at the other end of the counter, who I now realized was armed with some variety of firearm, possibly a blaster that he'd borrowed from a Stormtrooper. The man turned to us but didn't come closer. I assumed he was assigned to stand guard.

"He's going to consult with his superiors," Mom said out loud.

"Why?" Falon asked.

"Because Lina is friends with an interplanetary criminal," Gran said, eyeing me. "Why didn't you mention this before?"

"I didn't know he was a criminal," I said. I couldn't help myself. I laughed. *Zig* would be an interplanetary criminal. *What is it with me and attracting difficult men?*

THE WISDOM OF DISHONOR

They're fascinating, Gran thought, then she looked up and to the side, clearly addressing someone I couldn't see. *And a man would have to be tenacious to handle you, granddaughter.* She did not, I noticed, acknowledge Falon's existence when she said that.

"This isn't a joke," Mom spat. If I didn't know better, I would have said she was defending me.

"It's fine," Gran said, holding up a hand placatingly. "It's only another five minutes before they can depart. That will be enough."

"Is he here?" I asked, knowing she would understand that I meant Orion.

Gran smirked, giving me side-eye, then nodded.

"Could you please ask him to go check on Aaron and the crew? I feel bad about how we left."

I knew Falon would be disappointed in my request, and I felt a bit like a coward. He shifted his weight away from me.

Gran gave me a flat stare, as if I had just asked something very rude, then nodded. We waited another minute, and then Gran narrowed her eyes.

"What is it?" I asked.

"Aaron is interrogating Delya. Apparently, she has already threatened to smack him."

I groaned.

"I told you," Falon whispered in my ear. His warm breath against the side of my face sent an unexpected shiver down my spine.

"Thanks for that," I muttered.

"You and Falon will go to my house and collect your crew, then proceed as planned," Gran said pinning me with a look that brooked no argument. "Go straight to the ceremony site. No side quests. Is that understood?"

"What about you?" I asked, annoyed. Did she really think I was going to do what I was told? Didn't anyone in this family know me at all?

"We will stay here with your father. We are welcome here, even if you are not. The Elder Circle of Darion-Ájar won't risk offending the Harthan Council. It pays to be a queen's cousin sometimes. We'll straighten out your visa."

The Elder Circle, I thought, tucking the information away for later. That must be the leadership here.

"It's time," Gran said. "Orion says he thinks the reservoir is full. Just a warning, though. I am told that Teleportation is, by far, the most painful ascension of them all. Keep your mind centered and breathe through it." I nodded, dread building in my gut. *And Lina,* Gran thought, *one last thing. The diamond bridge key is powerful. After you ascend, you may use it to its fullest capacity.*

What do you mean? I asked, but our Connection link snapped, zapping me like static shock.

"Mother!" Mom barked aloud. I stepped back, slightly disoriented from the sudden sensation. Not only did the sound of her voice startle me, but she had also used Connection to reach out and sever Gran's link to me. I didn't even know that was possible.

Gran flinched back as if slapped, reminding me of a time when Aaron had done a similar thing to me using Protection. His Connection spike had felt like a punch to the chest and had also given me a bloody nose. Gran didn't seem to be having that drastic of a response, but she glared at my mother while Mom huffed out a frustrated breath and shook her head.

Gran closed her eyes, took a breath in and out, then turned to walk away. "Good luck, granddaughter," she muttered, privately adding, *and don't let that weasel see the key.*

Gran claimed a chair next to the door Qadeem had gone through, leaving my mother to say goodbye.

"I love you," she said.

"I love you, too, I guess."

Mom let out a little sob-laugh. "Better than nothing, I guess."

I smiled a little. "Can someone get that dagger back, please? It's not mine."

She nodded. "I'll see to it, and I'll see you on the other side. Make good choices, baby."

Her face was strained as if she doubted I *could* make good choices. Though I was angry with her, I still wanted to make her proud. I nodded awkwardly, embarrassed, then stepped forward to embrace her. She hugged me back fiercely, another little sob escaping her chest.

I knew then that I would eventually forgive her. Falon's story about his own mother's death had reminded me of how fleeting this relationship was. No matter what happened, I would live forever, and Mom wouldn't. Even if she had a closet full of skeletons and other secrets, she was still my mother.

Wasn't she?

I froze, the thought finally crystalizing in my brain. It took a moment for the suspicion to penetrate my consciousness, but when it did, it instantly dissolved the goodwill I had just convinced myself to extend.

My parents had lied to me my whole life about who they were. Zig said Protection doesn't run in families, yet my father was also born with it. My father once called me a genetic anomaly because I looked nothing like them. Aaron resembles my family more than I do.

I slowly pushed back from my mother to stare her in the face, and what I saw was pure anguish. I do, indeed, think very loudly.

"Lina," she breathed, but her words failed her.

I held up a palm to her, but it did nothing to stop my heart palpitations or the spinning that had overtaken my vision. It was too much. Too much revelation. Too many secrets. I opened my mouth, but nothing came out.

"Lina," she said again.

Aaron's not really my cousin, is he? I thought to her. That question was easier to ask than what I really wanted to know.

She paused, clearly conflicted, then shook her head.

Protection doesn't run in families. You're not my biological mother.

She didn't answer right away but just stared at me with that tormented expression. Finally, she took a breath and thought, *It's not that Protection doesn't run in families. It's just that Protection makes it nearly impossible to conceive. Unless...*

Unless your partner has Evocation, I guessed, my hand drifting to my belly in a now-familiar gesture.

Yes.

I squeezed my eyes shut, then I opened them and blinked a few times, almost like my mind needed to catch its breath. "I have to go," I said, backing away.

I think I had suspected that I might be adopted for a long time because I looked nothing like them—at least, nothing like my mother—but I had trusted my parents so much that I figured they'd tell me. I wasn't angry, exactly. As Aaron said, my parents obviously loved me. It's just that I was shocked. And suspicious. I couldn't come up with a reason why they wouldn't have told me that didn't involve an interplanetary conspiracy.

Lina, please, my mother thought to me. She didn't have to say what she meant. It was a plea for forgiveness, perhaps for not telling me, or maybe for something far worse.

My eyes widened at all the possibilities as to why a powerful family of fragmentors might adopt a child with rare reservoirs. Had the adoption been legal? Had my biological parents consented to it? Whatever the history there was, I couldn't handle it at the moment.

I have to go, I repeated, before I turned on my heel and fled toward the bridgestone. I didn't even care about the Monash ceremony anymore. Anick would have to be somebody else's problem, and since Ward was supposedly in hiding, what was the rush to get back there? Suddenly, Spirit's warning not to run away at the first sign of trouble between me and Aaron rushed back to haunt me. I hadn't listened.

I never listen.

Falon trailed me to the bridgestone, ignorant of the silent conversation I'd just had with my mother. I glanced back to see Qadeem gently leading my grandmother through a doorway. My mother remained behind, watching us go, her face ashen.

"Ready?" Falon asked, pulling me out of my daze. I'd had too many shocks, too close together, and my brain felt like it had used up whatever rest it had gotten overnight. I had to stop and think about what he was asking me.

That's right. Wishmere first, then head back. And tell Aaron that I'm not his cousin, after all, not that he cared in the first place.

I was nervous about returning to an irate Aaron, especially about what he might do to Falon when he discovered that he'd gone with me. Would he suspect that Falon had tried to come between us? My grandmother probably had, which was why she'd called him a weasel. It was unfair, in my opinion, but it would be the obvious conclusion for anyone who hadn't been on the bridge with me and heard what he had to say.

I also feared that Aaron would yell at me in front of everyone, like he did earlier. Just the memory of it elicited that same livid powerlessness as when I'd experienced it in person. I felt my face flush with it. I needed time to cool off before I faced him. If I had to withstand that right now, I might have blood on my hands.

"Ready," I said. I pulled out the key, staring at it. The thing seemed needlessly complicated.

"It will be the sixth one," Falon said, pointing to the orange bead. "Every human fears death more when he is knocking at death's door."

"Excuse me?"

"It's an old mnemonic," he clarified. "They don't teach it anymore, but I read it in one my father's antique books." He pointed to the beads as he named them. "Earth, Hartha, Feldákin, Darion-Ájar, Monash, Wishmere, Heckleez, Intaru, Killmount, Atu-Intele, Deesha, Delorian. Just think of the key as a magnifier for a bunch of skipstones. Exceptionally convenient, priceless skipstones," he added wistfully.

I nodded, my spirit lifted a bit by his enthusiasm, and took the orange ring into my left hand, grasping the head of the key with my right. Falon positioned himself behind me as before and wrapped his arms around my waist.

I took a deep breath, bracing for agony, and opened the bridge.

Chapter Fourteen

*A*n *everlasting nightmare it was, an omen, and a fitting punishment for her deceit.*

Of all the things my so-called family did to me, sending me onto that bridge without properly preparing me was the worst. I will not, for the rest of my immortal life, ever forgive Gran for the flippant way she advised me to "breathe through it." If I think about it too hard, I start to hate her even more than I hated Seleca. Honestly, it's enough to make a person switch sides.

I can't talk about what happened during my Teleportation ascension. Every time I try, I feel the walls closing in on me, as if by merely thinking about it, I might be forced back into that prison for another thousand years. As very few people have survived the ordeal, I'll write about it here for the historical value this text might someday represent. It's the most I can do.

Teleportation ascension is like being caught in one of those nightmares where nothing makes sense. Time essentially stops, and you're fixed in an endless moment where all your hair is ripped out by the roots just as you're dropped into a vat of liquid nitrogen.

Agony isn't quite the right word. Terror or despair would be closer, but it still isn't enough. Hellacious torment maybe, except instead of the fires of Hell, I remember being profoundly cold, colder than I ever thought possible. I was trapped in Dante's ninth circle of Hell, except I didn't even have Satan to talk to. And it lasted for literal centuries from my perspective.

Pretty early on in my ascension imprisonment, my eyeballs burst like pipes in winter. First one, then, after what felt like a few years, the other. The juices from the eruption flowed down my face like glaciers down a mountain, eventually dripping into my mouth. I couldn't avoid that disturbing meal because, by then, my lips had cracked and peeled away from my face. My skin shriveled and detached, leaving the subcutaneous tissue exposed. When that sloughed off an eternity later, the frozen muscles and tendons snapped and broke apart, allowing some of my bones to drift away like icebergs.

All the while, I was awake but paralyzed, waiting for the pain to release me. I proceeded through all the stages of grief, at first in total denial that I had somehow bound myself in everlasting torture. Anger followed closely behind, mostly at Gran, as I said, for failing to warn me about the possibility of becoming stuck there indefinitely.

I skipped right over bargaining, as the existence of a benevolent deity and that place could only be mutually exclusive, and I fell into a dark depression that made me long for death. Even if my only weapon, Ellis's dagger, hadn't been confiscated, I couldn't have moved enough to end my own suffering. Eventually, I no longer had eyes to cry, a mouth to scream, or ears to hear even if I could, so I waited, frozen in time.

It took many years to reach the acceptance stage, but I eventually found it. I forgot how I'd gotten to Hell and why. I forgot my family and my life. I forgot my beloved trees. I forgot Aaron. I forgot my own name. Nothing mattered anymore outside of endless suffering. I became the pain, and the pain became the only thing preventing all of creation from collapsing into an endless abyss, into the Oneness.

I began to wonder if it hadn't all been a mistake. My own existence and that of everything else in the universe, living or otherwise. To be separated from the Oneness, from wholeness, was the ultimate punishment. For, in the Oneness, there is no pain. There's no joy, either, but you don't miss it because in its place, you reunite with parts of yourself you didn't realize were lost. In the Oneness, you come back to yourself, back home, and you're at peace in absolute stillness.

It took me a subjective millennium to finally ask myself, *Why are any of us here? Shouldn't we just go back to the Oneness?*

At that question, I felt the universe sigh, as if it had been waiting all this time for me to ask. A presence settled upon me that was not a sentient being but rather a state of awareness and union with all creation, which made the whole universe feel like it was me but also not me. For the briefest instant, I drowned in profound comprehension.

It was just like my Connection link to Aaron, when I'd felt like I had been him and he had been me, except this time I was everything in existence. The crushing weight and vastness of it threatened to destroy what little sanity I had left.

This is too much, I cried. *We are too small for this. We are nothing here in this fragmented universe. Shouldn't we go back to being everything? That is what we are in the Oneness.*

And you, the voiceless presence said, *are the one who will answer that question for all.*

With that, the presence retreated. The feeling of profound Connection slipped through my fingers, leaving only an incomprehensible residue. What was left of my body began to gently vibrate, a sensation that unexpectedly replaced the pain that had become my whole world.

Finally, *finally*, I lost consciousness. I had suffered an eternity of torment for one fleeting moment of clarity, and I couldn't even hold on to it. I had understood Violet's and Anick's plans, but that knowledge escaped my matter-dependent awareness, and flew away beyond my reach. I passed through the time bubble and came out the other side as a new, much more twisted creature, one that didn't give a shit whether the world ended or not.

That antihero's journey was all in my mind, however. Falon later told me the whole thing took less than a minute from his point of view. For him, that was the easy part.

He reported that I went rigid once we entered the bridge, and I shook so violently that he had a difficult time hanging on to me. When we arrived, I fell limp to the ground, still shaking, my skin as cold as ice. My body hadn't actually broken apart, but my eyes gushed blood. When Falon opened my eyelids, he saw a mangled mess that made him shriek and yank his hand back. To make matters worse, I glowed a bright yellow color that was the only thing illuminating the space around us.

There was an ominous rhythmic thumping coming from every direction. Terrified, he covered my body with his, trying to warm me, but also preparing to grab me and run away if needed. That's when he noticed there were insects everywhere, scuttling about. Black, with too many legs, they crawled over us, tickling exposed skin and sneaking into our clothing. Falon frantically batted them away, but there were too many.

He was relieved when I warmed up after a few seconds, but then I quickly grew alarmingly hot. He decided to stand, picking me up to get me away from the bugs and to allow air to flow around me. When he did so, he smacked his head so hard on the ceiling that he almost dropped me.

By the time he recovered from his second head trauma of the day, he realized we were in a musty room with broken furniture scattered about. A faint red light emanated from the top of stairs on the other side of the room. He couldn't decide if we should stay with the bridgestone, hoping I would wake up and get us the hell out of there, or if he should try to find me some help.

I was soon covered in sweat and giving off a kind of heat that people don't usually make. That was undoubtedly my Evocation expanding into a greater reservoir due to my Teleportation ascension, but he thought I was dying. He had read that Wishmere was populated by humans, so there had to be someone around. Whether they would be friendly or not was another matter entirely.

The incessant thumping slowed, then shifted into a more sensuous and syncopated rhythm. The sound scared him more than the persistent scampering of insects around his feet.

When I finally began to stir, he called my name several times before I responded. Then, I'd opened my eyes and asked him who he was. He was relieved to see that my eyes had reshaped themselves into something less grotesque, but they were still red with streaks of blood trailing down my face like tears.

Falon, confident now that I was repairing myself, stayed with me until the yellow glow of my skin subsided and the room dimmed. When I asked for water, I seemed desperate, so he carried me, hunched over to accommodate the low ceiling, up the stairs. It was locked, but as we know, the Monashi people are freakishly strong. With me still hanging nearly limp in his arms, he kicked the door open, tearing a metal bolt from the frame and leaving the door askew.

Luckily, deafening music covered the sound of the door breaking apart, and the humans populating the room were too busy to notice our sudden intrusion. The rhythmic thumping had been drums of some sort, but he couldn't tell where they were coming from. The music had no discernable melody but was instead a jumble of sounds that Falon found hard to process. Smoky air seemed to carry red light across the room just below the low ceiling. There were couches everywhere with people on them. They were all naked, or nearly so, and completely preoccupied with each other's bodies.

Falon was so shocked that he dropped me on the floor. That might have been what woke me from my stupor, but I didn't recall anything before the moment I saw Falon's enraptured face gazing upon that room. That and the desert in my mouth. My whole body felt like a desiccated corpse.

"Rhoya! I'm so sorry, Lina. Are you all right?"

I heard his words, but I couldn't focus on their meaning amid our overwhelming surroundings. Everything was red light, smoke, pulsing music, and the discomfort of intense dehydration. I had no idea where I was, how I'd gotten there, or who this absurdly tall man next to me was.

Water, I thought, but I didn't get the word out. My brain was like a drawer full of discarded and tangled power cords, the neurons neglected for so long that I was unable to recall where they plugged in. I couldn't even guarantee that "water" was the correct word.

When I didn't answer him, the strangely familiar man reached down and picked me up again, but he remained hunched over due to the low ceiling.

I coughed weakly, gasping, before I looked up to study his concerned face. Blinking a few times, my mind finally cleared enough to recognize him. *Falon*, I thought. *This is my friend, right? Yes.*

"I'm okay," I rasped, finally finding my voice. It was a lie. I would never be okay again. "Put me down."

I didn't know exactly what damage had been done to my body, but I was convinced that the combination of ascendant Protection and Absorption was the only thing that had kept me alive. My body was healing itself, but sluggishly, like it had forgotten how to heal at normal speeds. My skull felt like it was full of sand, and every movement—the turn of my head or the clench of my fist—felt creaky and stiff, like my joints had all rusted shut. My heart beat in time to the base drum.

Falon let my legs go so I could slide down his body. My knees nearly buckled when I landed, but he steadied me, holding me against him. His jaw ticked as he stared down at me, his expression a lot like a vague memory I had of his father and brother. After a long moment of foggy analysis, I realized his anatomy was pressing against my chest.

Transmutation is a bitch. A horny bitch, apparently, and we had landed on a planet saturated with that ravenous energy. Although we weren't connected, I got the impression that he actively resisted rubbing himself against me. I steeled myself, then stepped back, wobbling only a little.

"What happened? Are we—"

Before I could finish my sentence, something tickled my arm. I glanced down to find a cockroach peeking out from beneath my sleeve. I jumped a foot in the air and squealed, brushing it away frantically. Apparently, even the ninth circle of Hell couldn't erase my all-consuming fear of cockroaches.

The jolt of adrenaline jump-started my brain, but the abrupt movement was too much and Falon had to catch me again to keep me from falling. He chuckled at my reaction. "Think that's bad? We landed in a pile of them downstairs. They don't seem poisonous, luckily."

"Of course not. They're cockroaches," I said. *How does this guy not know what cockroaches are?* Before I could explore that further, a subtle pulsing resonance from somewhere in the room drew my attention. It was Protection, but probably not a greater reservoir. I squinted into the dim, pulsing room, but the resonance was too faint for me to pinpoint its direction.

I heard them before I saw them, two women with high-pitched voices like the lovely tinkling of wind chimes. Clothed only in miles of tattoos and long, slightly mussed hair down to their thighs, they were both of typical adult proportions but only about four and a half feet tall. Their arms wrapped around each other, and neither one seemed at all embarrassed by their nudity.

The one on the right, a woman with glossy black hair reminiscent of an anime character, spoke again, but I couldn't understand what she said. I thought it was just the loud music at first, or maybe my lingering drowsiness. Only after she made a third attempt did I realize she wasn't speaking English.

"Water," I croaked, but neither responded until their eyes drifted from my face to Falon's, then widened, dropping to Falon's protruding anatomy. As if pulled in by a tractor beam, they inched toward us. I expected the Protection resonance to grow, but it didn't. Neither of these women had Protection.

When they got within striking distance, the tiny anime woman—who was immediately nicknamed Animaiden—said something to Falon. Her head reached just to his waist, and she gazed up at him, a slow smile spreading across her face. He shook his head at her unintelligible sentence, his eyebrows drawn together.

My thoughts were still sluggish, and I couldn't quite grasp what was happening. All I could think was how, when I returned home, everyone I knew might be elderly or even deceased. Never mind that Falon hadn't aged a day. I was still foggy and confused, and therefore hadn't successfully processed the details of our situation. But when Animaiden's hand floated out toward Falon, it finally dawned on me that if I let this tiny woman's hand reach its destination, we'd never fragging get out of here.

I snatched her hand out of the air like a poisoned dart. *No, thanks, Animaiden. We don't have time for hentai cosplay right now.*

The woman's head whipped to me as she pulled away, but I held her firmly. Even in my weakened state, she was no match for me. I towered over her like a pissed-off ogre, clenching my teeth.

Stop, I commanded, pushing Connection. She froze momentarily, staring at me in terror before frantically renewing her effort to escape. In the dim red light, she hadn't noticed the streaks of blood on my face until that very moment, and she shrieked as if I were the incarnation of her worst nightmare. Indeed, I caught flashes of a giant puppet with paper-white skin and hair made of red snakes—perhaps a frightening play from her childhood?

I rolled my eyes and groaned in frustration. *I'm not going to hurt you, tiny woman. I just need water, then we'll leave.*

Oh Hecate. She's in my head. The woman's light, melodic voice rang through my mind in perfect English; a translation, I now realized. She considered my hand, which was still holding hers, loosely now. Her eyes narrowed, then she studied Falon with a new level of scrutiny. *You're fragmentors? What are you doing on this side? Are you runners? Why are your eyes bleeding?*

I'm nobody, I thought to her. *And I'll be fine if I just get some water.*

You're feverish, she thought nervously. *Even a minor illness could be deadly here.* Her thoughts turned to an elderly woman, comatose in a bed nearby. *We don't have clean water. I can get you mushroom wine. That's the closest we have.*

As disgusting as that sounded, I almost said yes, but then I shook my head. *I can't have wine.* I didn't send the thought purposely, but my mind went to the baby girl I'd been carrying.

Had been? Or am I still? There was no doubt in my mind that years had passed, but the baby had been immortal, too, hadn't she? I took a deep breath, mentally preparing myself for either outcome, then rested my free hand on my belly.

Christine's Protection resonance hit me first, vibrating much stronger than I remembered, before her other reservoirs bled through the noise. I exhaled, relief flooding my body. Connection told me she was fine, and evidently *healing* herself.

That's my girl, I thought, a smile tugging at the corners of my mouth. It was only then that it hit me. Christine was still a baby. Not even a baby, really. More like a shrimp cocktail. If it had been years, then wouldn't she be grown up?

Yes, I know. How could I have been so slow, right? Come talk to me after you've ascended *your* Teleportation reservoir. If you can do that and tie your shoes afterward, I'll eat Zig's pirate hat, feather and all.

Animaiden looked down at my belly, then over at Falon again. *Sorry*, she thought with genuine regret. *They cut water rations again. You know how it is.*

I blinked, trying to wrap my clouded mind around her words. I was on the planet Wishmere. They had to ration water here and had apparently run out. She thought having Connection made me something called a runner, which sounded ominous. There were cockroaches everywhere, apparently so ubiquitous that people were willing to have an orgy with a giant nest of them in the next room. This world was starting to sound more and more like a dystopian nightmare. Time for Christine and me to GTFO.

It's fine. Thanks anyway. I let go of her hand and turned to Falon. "How long were we on the bridge?"

"What do you mean?" Falon asked. He was still staring at the live sex show, which stared back at him with interest. A man strode over to us with the same woman who had scampered away a few moments before.

He was taller than the women, maybe five feet, and all wiry muscle, and spoke to Animaiden in that same melodious language. She answered back immediately, dipping her head to him in deference. Sporting the same style of tattoos as the others, he was naked except for a leather cord strung around his neck with four beads and a small metal disc displaying a symbol I didn't recognize. On the center of his chest, directly beneath where the disc sat, the tattoo of an eagle in flight caught my attention. A quick survey of the two women confirmed the thought. All three had the same exact tattoo in the same place.

Naked Necklace Guy glared at us like he was trying to decide whether or not to let us live. He was definitely unarmed, but I doubted I could overpower him as easily as I had Animaiden. I pretended to ignore him but kept him in my peripheral vision and brought my hand to my chest, preparing to raise a shield if I had to. I was pretty sure that the Protection resonance I felt was coming from his direction.

"The bridge from Darion-Ájar to here," I snapped impatiently, finally drawing Falon's full attention to me. "How long did it take?"

"A minute maybe?" Then he told me what he'd experienced from the moment I'd opened the bridge to the moment I came to. I listened, dumbfounded, as he recounted his story about our landing, my weird changes in body temperature, how it worried him enough to bring me upstairs despite the unsettling music—he promised it had nothing to do with the giant mound of insects—and lastly, how he finally dumped me on the floor.

The Teleportation ascension had warped my sense of time to the extent that I couldn't fathom how Falon was telling the truth. Had time slowed down for me? Had it stopped at one point? As my thoughts cleared, I realized that I needed to push that experience out of my mind if I wanted to function with any normalcy. My memories were returning, and I had a job to do.

"Then we have time," I said. "Let's go back."

"Um, right now?" he asked.

"Yes, Falon. Let's go."

"But I think we probably have time for . . ." He pointed at one of the couches.

"Falon! Are you serious right now? I brought you here to help you ascend. You promised me five minutes. I already feel like it's been ten lifetimes. Now you want to stay?" *And also*, I thought to myself, *weren't you just hitting on me less than an hour ago? Now you want me to watch you have group sex. Good to know what happens when you have choices.*

"I'm sorry, Lina. It's just that I've never seen so many women at once. SONA didn't have this many at the entire school."

"Why? Girls aren't supposed to learn anything?"

"No, that's not it."

"Ya know what? I don't care. I'm leaving now. Stay if you want." My anger piqued, I glared back at Naked Necklace Guy, who was now staring at us with a bemused expression. I wondered if Animaiden told him I was pregnant. Our argument probably sounded like a lovers' spat.

"What?" I demanded.

Naked Necklace Guy raised his eyebrows and then stepped forward a little too abruptly, reaching out like he wanted to grab me. As he did, I felt his Protection resonance surge like a puff of air shot toward my face. Startled, I stepped back and threw up my shield, just barely seizing Falon's hand in time to pull him into it. Naked Necklace Guy bumped into the shield, then gasped as he stepped away.

A shield isn't fully visible from the outside, but it distorts light enough to know something is happening. If Naked Necklace Guy knew about the existence of shields, which he should if he was protected, then he must have realized what it was the moment he bumped into it. So why was he so astounded? He said another word I didn't understand, his eyes wide, then started yelling instructions to the people around us.

"This whole thing is falling apart. Should we run back to the bridgestone?" I asked.

Two more men, both clothed and armed with truncheons, appeared out of nowhere to flank us, blocking our exit back down the stairs. The pounding music stopped abruptly, and the room flooded with light. People on couches jumped up and started running for the exit, except a few who charged toward us, surrounding our shield. The more they gathered, the more I realized we had crashed a private party. Every single person had the same eagle tattoo on their chest, and I was starting to get major gang vibes.

"It's all right," Falon said, squeezing my hand. "We don't need the bridgestone to get back if you use the key. In fact, I think you could call the bridge right here from within your shield."

"Right," I said, shaking my head. I still wasn't completely back from my unplanned excursion to Tartarus. The key was such a powerful skipstone that it didn't require a bridgestone.

I'd rather not show it to anyone in this room, I thought to him. *Maybe we can talk our way out of this. And you shouldn't mention the key aloud. We don't know whether anyone here speaks English.*

Right, Falon thought. And so, Falon and I were on the same team again and holding hands. My memories of him had fully returned, and while I was nervous about being cornered, I realized that I did trust Falon enough to want him beside me for this. His hand felt natural in mine, and there was something about his touch that made me want to pull him closer. A sort of spark. Or was that just the influence of the planet's Transmutation matrix?

I sneaked a peek in his direction and found him staring at me, one corner of his mouth tugged up. He squeezed my hand a few times in pulses, like he knew what I was thinking. I felt my face flush, and I turned away again. *No time to psychoanalyze. Only time to focus.*

A female voice, high-toned like Animaiden, but with pronounced vocal fry that didn't mesh with the pitch, cut through the drama. A tiny, white-haired woman in a blue threadbare robe appeared in front of us. Just like the other two clothed people, she seemed to come out of nowhere.

Reflector, Falon thought. *She was veiling herself and the two men behind us, unless they're reflectors, too, which seems unlikely.*

The white-haired woman spoke in that same incomprehensible language, directing her words to me. She had one hand up, palm out, like my mother used to do when she tried to calm me down. In her other hand, she held a staff topped with a baseball-sized blue stone that matched the color of her robe. The staff was carved with symbols I couldn't read but which were familiar.

Where have I seen that staff before?

I studied the woman, noting the eagle tattoo and another necklace, similar to the man's, but with six beads instead of four. I didn't know her. Why would I recognize her staff but not her?

Then I had it. The staff looked just like one from my grandmother's memory, a twin to my grandfather's staff, the one Aaron had mentioned that was stolen and now resided somewhere in *Fucking* Seleca's palace. The stone was different, blue instead of reddish orange, but the carvings were the same. I took a shot in the dark.

"Orion? Orion Dragonrider?" The woman shook her head, clearly not understanding. I'd hoped he'd crafted the staff, since he was a master woodworker, but White Hair didn't recognize the name. It must have been made by or given to her by someone else.

Naked Necklace Guy wrapped a rough muslin cloth around his waist while he spoke to her. I would have to downgrade his nickname to just "Necklace Guy"—or maybe that was an upgrade. His abs contracted as he wrapped the cloth around himself, displaying a lean but obvious six-pack. *No, the towel is definitely a downgrade.*

THE WISDOM OF DISHONOR

He caught me checking him out, and he returned the favor with a scan of my body. His flat expression told me he didn't think much of what he saw. What can I say? Some people just aren't into women who cry blood. To each his own.

White Hair lowered her palm and used it to shoo Necklace Guy away, shushing him. She tried to say something else, then she furrowed her brow in frustration. This wasn't working. I'd have to take down the shield to communicate.

What do you think? I asked Falon.

It's risky to take the shield down. Tiny Necklace Man is all worked up. I laughed at the similar nickname he'd come up with. Falon grinned at me boyishly. *But the old woman appears to be reasonable. And now that it comes down to it, I'm not exactly eager to start my ascension. It's too late to back out, right?*

I nodded. *Way too late unless you want to live here. Wait, is that why you wanted to stay earlier?*

Falon hesitated, then shrugged. *After seeing what you just went through, how you were completely helpless when we arrived, I'm not convinced it'll be worth it. What if something went wrong and we landed somewhere even more dangerous than this? If you use the key, there's no guarantee that you'll send us to your grandmother's bridgestone. We only know it will be somewhere on Hartha and that it could be anywhere on the planet. You'd have to take care of me while dealing with that danger. Even if we were able to get down to the bridgestone and use you as the skipstone to go straight there, we don't necessarily know what we'll find when we get to your grandmother's house. What if my selfish request puts you in danger? I didn't think about that before we decided to come here.*

Oh, Falon. The sentiment was so sweet, even though he was still treating me like someone who needed to be taken care of. The orgy undoubtedly played a factor in his desire to hang out, but I could sense through our Connection link that his concern for me was genuine. *Well, you're right about one thing. If we get down to the bridgestone and can get back to Gran's house, Aaron probably* will *try to kill you, but I think I can handle him. And there's always my shield.*

White Hair watched us as we silently conversed. At that point, everyone in the group had likely recognized that I was a connector. She said something else, to no avail, then pointed toward the broken door, asking a question. I glanced at the door, then back at her, still not getting it. More emphatically, she pointed at me, then made a walking motion with her fingers, then pointed at the door.

I nodded. "Yes, we came out of that door."

She raised her eyebrows, then peered back at Necklace Guy. He sighed, then nodded, saying something else. White Hair smiled triumphantly and beckoned us to follow her as Necklace Guy shouted out more instructions. The two guards flanking our position shoved at our shield from behind, tossing us forward. Falon, being the colossus he is, stuck the landing and held it, preventing the guards from moving us another inch. He snort-laughed at them as they struggled.

"They aren't the strongest little people, are they?" he commented.

"Actually, Monashi people are just absurdly strong. If you came to Earth, you'd find the same thing. People would start calling you Superman and asking if you could fly."

"Never heard of the man, but he reminds me of myself, so I think I'll allow it. And actually, after I ascend, I might be able to fly, or float at least."

"Nuh-uh. Really?"

Falon wagged his eyebrows up and down, then surprised me by pulling me close to him and leaning down to whisper in my ear. "And if you're very nice, I might be willing to trade some of mine for some of yours." I blinked, not understanding what he meant, then realized he was talking about mixing reservoirs, which he undoubtedly thought required sex.

On Monash, the Ministry controlled who was allowed to bond for exactly that reason. They wanted to control who had access to fragmental power, which can be transferred from one person to another during intimate moments. Falon was offering to illegally share Transmutation with me through sex, or at least he was teasing me about it. I hadn't yet told him that Aaron wasn't really my cousin, so he didn't know that I was no longer questioning my relationship with him.

And yet . . .

For a moment, I wondered what it would be like to choose Falon instead. He was playful and fun. His childhood trauma rivaled Aaron's, yet there was a lightness about him that Aaron lacked. At least Aaron's parents were both alive. Falon's father had let his mother die, then rejected him outright for caring too much. He had every reason to be angry and damaged, yet he smiled and joked around because that was his nature. Aaron was a warrior and a frightening one at that. Falon was a lover. I'd probably like being with him.

You're engaged to Aaron and carrying his child, remember? I shook my head at my own flakiness. *Yes, I remember. I may have forgotten for a few minutes due to my Teleportation ascension, but it's all coming back. I love Aaron. Yes, he's a warrior, but he's a warrior poet, an intellectual, and he loves me. Nothing has changed.*

I opened my mouth to respond, but Falon leaned quickly away, grinning down at me as he tugged me forward to follow White Hair. The group parted for us to follow her toward another set of stairs on the opposite side of the smoky room. I let Falon lead me, taking one last baleful look at the broken door leading to the bridgestone and contemplating how much time we really had.

I pressed the button on my watch to check the time. It had been set to Eureka's time zone, which had worked well enough for the farm, so I'd left it as is. Now it just blinked a few times, then froze on a screen that had a picture of the Earth underneath four zeros.

That can't be right.

I pushed the button a couple more times, but the screen scrambled and then went dark. The watch wasn't just dead. It was broken.

Chapter Fifteen

*L*inorra *awoke to darkness, dread heavy in her heart. Though Otterhai's body curled around her protectively, she could not dismiss the feeling that if she did not return to Syndeth soon, she would die. Her mother's mysterious illness had settled within her faster than she thought possible.*

"Oh, Syndeth, what have I done?"

The upstairs room of the smoky club was crowded. Almost everyone from below who hadn't run away had followed us up the stairs. They stood so close to our shield that we were wedged in place, and the smell of all those sweaty, still-naked bodies was less than pleasant.

We peered over their heads at an ancient woman lying on a thin mattress on the floor. Shriveled and balding, she was covered in piles of worn and patched blankets pulled up to her chin.

In contrast to the energy in the room below, there was now an air of solemnity, like everyone expected this woman to soon die but were afraid to speak it aloud. She was asleep, breathing in shallow, ragged wheezes. A dirty window was propped open with a stick, letting in the sounds of a busy city street. Voices shouted in the distance. A squealing rang out that sounded like metal grating on metal, perhaps from a train or subway. Yet the silence in the room was deafening.

White Hair took in a long breath and released it, then she knelt by the ailing woman and patted her gently. "Ama," she whispered.

Ama? Do you think that means mother? I made quick eye contact with Falon. He shrugged. The elderly woman didn't move.

White Hair glanced up at me from where she knelt and beckoned us forward. She said something to the crowd of people, who let us through reluctantly. White Hair pointed at me, said a few words, then held her hand out insistently.

She wants me to connect with her, I thought to Falon. I eyed Necklace Guy, who was standing in the front of the group, watching me with sharp concentration, then I glanced back at White Hair skeptically. She smiled, then said something else to the group. They shuffled out, one by one, until only White Hair and Necklace Guy were left. He crossed his arms stubbornly, refusing to leave.

My guess is that Old Sick Lady is White Hair's mother, I thought to Falon, *and Necklace Guy is her son. I doubt we'll be able to get him to leave. I think we'll be safe to take down the shield, don't you? He can't do any permanent damage to me, and you're Superman.*

Falon shrugged again. *You're probably right. The greatest risk would be to the key, but it's up to you. I trust your judgment.*

That comment made me smile. I suspected that he was deliberately setting himself apart from Aaron by letting me do whatever dangerous thing I wanted. Which I truly appreciated.

I mimed to White Hair that I was going to release the shield, then I turned my attention to Necklace Guy, narrowing my eyes in a semi-playful, overly dramatic way. Surprisingly, his mouth twitched ever so slightly, then he backed up against one wall and relaxed against it, never taking his eyes off me.

Keeping Falon's hand in mine, I released the shield, and I was immediately hit by a Protection resonance again, this time from Old Sick Lady. Necklace Guy had lesser Protection, but she was definitely a greater protector. I had assumed that they wanted me to heal the elderly woman, but why would I need to heal a protector who should be able to heal herself? It didn't make any sense. Not to mention that Zig had told me that Protection was the only reservoir that didn't run in families. Did that mean they weren't related after all?

White Hair held her hand out to me, waiting. I eyed Necklace Guy again, who had frozen when I took down the shield. His only movement was a slow blink and the flaring of his nostrils. I wondered what he thought of my ascendant resonance, then decided that I better break eye contact before I found out. I refocused on White Hair, taking her hand.

Thank you, she said. As always, her thoughts were translated into an American dialect of English that matched my own. *Your skin is hot. Are you well?*

I nodded. *Fine. That's my normal temperature.*

She pursed her lips, then shrugged, but I could tell through the link that she was excited. *Please be at ease. We mean you no harm. You came from the bridgestone in the basement?*

I nodded.

Ama, she thought, pointing to Old Sick Lady, *used to tell a story, passed down in the family, of a giant using that stone, but I didn't believe it until I saw the door, broken from the inside.* She looked up at Falon, who appeared a bit uncomfortable crouching under the low ceiling.

We're in a bit of a hurry, I thought. *We need to get back.*

White Hair nodded. *I see. Well, I don't want to keep you. Our family agreed to guard that bridgestone for the giant generations ago, and we will keep our promise. You may come and go, but I warn you that we may not be here the next time you visit.*

Why not? I asked.

Ama is the last protector in the family. When she dies, this territory will be given to another family, and we will be—she paused midsentence, then swallowed, staring down at the elderly woman.

Through Connection, I gathered that White Hair used the word "family" to mean something like clan while the name Ama meant "matriarch." But people often don't understand when they let you in how much information they're giving away. When she uttered the sick woman's name, I sensed that the word meant something more to her. This person who lay helpless at her feet, who'd been like the gravity keeping the community together for years, was also her actual mother. The true bond they shared rested like scaffolding beneath the honorific. The question was . . . who was her father? If her mother was a protector, then her father had to be an evoker, didn't he?

My eyes drifted to the eagle tattoo on White Hair, whose golden head peered just over the top of her thin robe.

We are the only family left that keeps the old ways. Whoever takes our place will undoubtedly dig up the stone and sell it. My son wants to sell it before that can happen. They are quite valuable and would buy us extra water for many years.

That bridgestone connected to the one on Darion-Ájar, where my family was waiting, and I didn't relish the thought of placing them at risk. White Hair couldn't have known that, but she probably at least assumed that I would want to keep the stone safe so I could continue to use it.

I don't have time for negotiations, White Hair. Just tell me what you want.

White Hair blinked, then exhaled slowly. She hadn't expected me to grasp her intentions so quickly and she wasn't sure whether to be relieved or alarmed. She withdrew her hand from me to discuss their asking price with Necklace Guy.

"They're discussing payment," I said, turning back to Falon.

"Payment for what?" he asked, his brows drawn together.

"Oh, just your stereotypical mobster Protection contract," I said. "Not sure I believe it, but they claim to be guarding that bridgestone downstairs."

"Let me guess. Some misfortune has befallen them and they're uncertain if they can do it anymore?"

"You're a genius."

Falon smirked. "What do you think the original payment was?"

"That's a good question," I replied. "Which I didn't think to ask. Maybe I should keep you around after all, Falon. God knows I'm not the brains of this operation." Falon's gaze sharpened, boring into me like daggers. I rolled my eyes, realizing my mistake. I'd accidentally implied that I might choose him over Aaron. "Case in point," I said. "That's not what I meant."

Falon laughed softly, then slipped his arm around my back, squeezing the opposite shoulder with his massive hand. "I know," he said, lowering his voice to a more intimate level, "but I'm making progress. You're thinking about it now, so let me paint you a clearer picture. You and me, traveling the universe, seeing everything there is to see. The jungles of Feldákin with their clans of yeti living in flowers as big as a house, the massive dragons of Heckleez riding magma flows down the sides of volcanoes, the abandoned ice cities of Delorian."

He leaned in closer still, inhaled deeply over my head, then brushed his lips against the lobe of my ear as he spoke. My whole body erupted in goose bumps. "I've read about these places and have dreamed of them, Lina. Let's just go. No rules, no restrictions, nobody telling you that you can't do things because you're a woman. Just freedom. Experiencing everything. *Tasting* everything."

White Hair cleared her throat, and I looked up to see her holding her hand out again. I sat up straight, flushed with embarrassment. Falon had never been this forward with me before, and I didn't know how to respond. I didn't hate it, but every time he touched me, my mind flitted to Aaron, and I was racked with guilt. *I can't run away with Falon, no matter how awesome volcano-surfing dragons sound*, I reminded myself.

I took White Hair's hand. *Well?*

Water, she thought. *We need water. And you will attempt to heal Ama, though I don't think it's possible. Most of our family don't see forty years, and she is more than two centuries old. It seems even Protection can't heal her now. Before she fell asleep this time, she said her reservoir couldn't fill fast enough. And last*, she thought, pointing to her son, *you will mix reservoirs with Rei.*

I laughed out loud. "Um, no," I said. *If you mean "have sex with," then I decline. I'm not some mare to be bred to your stallion.*

White Hair frowned. That last sentence wouldn't translate if they didn't have horses on this planet. Falon looked at me quizzically, and I relayed the demands.

"Why not?" he asked, his expression serious. "Seems like an easy enough thing to do. He obviously wants you."

"What? No, he doesn't. Even if I wanted to do that, which I don't, this isn't Monash where any female with a pulse will do. He's got a whole crowd of playmates downstairs, and he's been giving me the evil eye since we met."

"Actually, he's been giving you the alpha stare down."

"What's that?"

Necklace Guy, or Rei, I supposed, was indeed staring at me, but he appeared more murderous than turned on.

"It's the expression a powerful man gives you when he wants to see you naked. If he didn't, he'd ignore you."

This was the most confusing conversation I'd ever had. A second ago, Falon was smelling my hair. Now he was pushing me into stranger danger. By "no rules, no restrictions," he clearly meant "no monogamy." The whole thing felt gross.

I turned back to White Hair. *I'm not having sex with your son. And that is final.*

THE WISDOM OF DISHONOR

White Hair chuckled. *He's not my son. He's my daughter's mate, but I will tell him.* She thought the word "mate" like they were emperor penguins or something. Rei had absolutely no reaction to my answer except to say two words, which I couldn't understand.

We cannot continue here without a greater protector, White Hair insisted. *This is our final offer.*

And what were you paid to protect it until now? I asked.

White Hair squirmed. *We were not paid,* she thought defensively. *We are the descendants of the giant. It has been our duty and honor to protect the stone, but we cannot continue without a protector.*

I regarded White Hair skeptically. She was the smallest among those I'd seen, maybe four feet tall at best, and she was the descendant of a giant? Likely story.

Then, inspiration struck. *And where did you get your staff?*

The question took White Hair by surprise. Her lips parted as she attempted to formulate a response. Her eyes darted to Rei, then she tried to pull her hand away, but I clutched it tightly.

It was his, wasn't it? I asked. *The giant's. The same one whose eagle tattoo resides on your chest. You probably don't even have eagles in this world. That's an Earth animal. And I've seen that symbol claimed by another person. A man named Anick Aetos.*

White Hair went very still. *She knows his name,* she thought, not necessarily to me. White Hair's family had been involved with Anick somehow, and they were still marked with his symbol. She hadn't, I realized, believed until now that they would even need to keep any bargain that they made with me. White Hair thought I would just heal her mother, boink her daughter's "mate," hopefully giving him full Protection, then go on my merry way none the wiser. But now that I knew about Anick, she was nervous. Anick had not been a man with whom you made idle bargains that you later broke. She had no way of knowing how I was affiliated with him, if at all.

I don't have time for this game, I thought to White Hair, then I released her hand and stepped back, turning to go. Falon fell into step beside me, taking my hand to walk out, but Rei glided into our path. He held his palm up, repeating one word several times. The hand he held up extended to me.

I hesitated, knowing I wouldn't be able to shield against him if he got a hold of me. I also knew that he could have just grabbed me, like he tried to do earlier. I was fairly certain that Falon would be able to overpower him, but it still meant something that he was voluntarily giving me the choice now.

Reluctantly, I took his hand, connecting, and Rei's voice slipped into my mind like silk. I hadn't noticed when he spoke a language I couldn't understand, but when he entered my mind, I understood why he was the leader of this gang. He was smooth, capable, and stubborn as hell.

You're smarter than she thought you'd be. I told her that would happen. And you're right to refuse the offer. But, please, heal Ama. I know you can make her last moments more pleasant than this.

He peered down at the woman, who struggled to breathe. She seemed like she was suffocating, one ragged breath at a time. He pulled me gently toward him, then kissed the back of my hand. *I can pay.*

Through our link, I saw that he was committed to taking care of his clan, and he would do anything to make that happen. Literally anything, including taking a rather ugly outsider into his bed in hopes of growing his reservoir. Additionally, he'd never seen anyone except Ama make a shield and was desperate to acquire the ability himself, along with the associated long life.

The offer was serious, but it was more about protecting his community than getting me naked. In his world, when it came to women, the smaller the better, and I was a giant Amazon woman with boats for feet and a nose that took up way too much of my face. He had plenty more desirable options if sex was his goal, and one in particular he preferred above all others. His mate, Animaiden.

As fond as I am of being the one that gets taken for the team, it didn't seem like an optimal use of time. I laughed under my breath because, like his mate's mother, he hadn't understood how much of his thoughts I would glean from our link. Seeing his own negative opinion of me in my mind, his face flushed.

Apologies, he thought, but he locked my hand in a tight grip, determined not to let this rare opportunity slip away so easily. *What do you want for the healing?*

I looked him dead in the eye. *Nothing. I don't charge to heal people.* I yanked my hand from his grip before turning to Falon, an idea springing to mind that I should have already considered because it was stupid obvious.

"Can you turn wine into water?"

It might seem backward, but I was still so dehydrated that my body rejoiced at the notion.

Falon nodded. "It's one of the trickier uses of Transmutation, but lucky for you, I've had a lot of practice. I used to do it to all my father's illegal imports when I was a kid just to make him angry."

I smirked at his revelation. Falon *would* do something like that. I turned back to Rei, offering my hand again. He took it hastily, his eyebrows raised. *I will try to heal Ama, but I make no promises that it will work. And my friend here will make water for you. Bring me any liquids you have.*

Rei eyed Falon, alarm overshadowing his previous determination. He hadn't realized Falon was a greater transmuter. In this world, at least in the capital city of Brightin, greater transmuters were sequestered into their own elite neighborhoods behind a high wall, along with most other greater fragmentors. They didn't have to fight for anything. Only those on this side of the wall had to worry about water rations.

Those thoughts flew through Rei's head in a half second, and as I gained insight into what it took to survive here, I developed a new level of respect for the man. He fought to keep his people fed, watered, and safe. It wasn't easy.

My chest tightened thinking about it, realizing that when I was finished saving Monash from the Ministry, I might have a second world to save.

We'll do this for free, I continued. *But there is something else I can do for you, too, and it won't be free. I will give you some of my Protection reservoir and teach you to make a shield. In exchange, you will owe me a favor, payable at a later date.*

Rei's expression didn't change at all, but his eyes flashed as he thought, very seriously, *You will be the one who owes* me *a favor after we mix reservoirs.*

I groaned. This freaking guy. *Without sex, Rei.*

Without?

I tried not to be offended by the relief that kindled in his chocolate brown eyes. Even in this world seated in a Transmutation matrix, avoiding sexing me up was still a bright spot in his day. Alpha stare down my gigantic Harthan ass. Maybe Falon wasn't such a genius after all.

#

An hour later, I glowered down into a dark basement. We'd accomplished our goals, having turned all liquids in the building into water, some of which I'd downed so greedily that our hosts balked.

When the wine ran out, people brought buckets of urine for Falon to turn. He refused. I guess no future favor was worth dipping his hand into a stranger's pee. Couldn't really blame him. I told Rei that I'd send water through the portal when I got a chance. And maybe an exterminator.

I healed Ama more successfully than I thought I could. She was still old as dirt, but no longer sick with pneumonia, and her vision, hearing, and memory all improved. In the end, this was what finally gained Rei's respect. I gave him just enough Protection reservoir to heal and make a shield, then we said our goodbyes as tentative allies.

"Are you coming?" I asked, finally convincing myself to go down the stairs into what might as well have been a tomb. But when I glanced back, Falon stood at the top of the stairs in silhouette, facing the room. It had turned red again and resumed its important business.

"I wish." He sighed, then followed me down the stairs. Even the little bit of light coming from the door was enough for his Monashi super eyes, which was a blessing since I trembled like a leaf. No matter how old you get, a dark, moldy basement is still scary. Even a well-timed ejaculation joke can't fix that.

"I've got you," he said, wrapping an arm around my shoulders. "You can do this."

Placing my right hand to my heart, I pushed Protection. The shield sphere sprang up in my chest, as always, but I didn't force it outward to engulf us. I only pushed enough so that my body would react to the fragment and cast a light blue glow.

Cockroaches scattered, and I shrieked, practically jumping into Falon's arms. He laughed outright, but I was too scared to admonish him. I've seen a lot of terrifying things in my life, and cockroaches are still the creepiest thing in the universe. How anyone could find that place sexy was beyond me.

"That glow is handy," he commented, stepping onto the bridgestone with me hanging off him.

"It's an ascension thing," I said. "You may be able to do something like this in a few minutes too."

"I don't know about that," he said. "Transmutation is not something you want to push into yourself. I wish I had Protection, like you."

"I don't know why I couldn't give it to you. I gave Rei Protection just now, and I also gave it to Ward, I think."

"I thought you had to . . . ah—"

"Have sex to do that? No," I said.

"Not that I would mind," he said quickly. "But I always got the impression that Ward definitely *would* mind something like that."

I looked up at Falon, curious. He knew Ward was gay? If Falon really was twenty-seven, then he and Ward were probably at SONA together. "What do you think of Ward?" I asked.

Falon shrugged. "People used to call him a dog, but I don't really think there's anything wrong with him. In my opinion, it's hypocritical to hate him and at the same time enjoy being with two women at once. I know for a fact that Markus does that on a regular basis."

"He does?" I asked.

"Yes, at the Rhoyal Healers Guild. Markus treats them well, though. I've never seen him hurt anyone."

"Wow. That is a very low bar," I said. "You do realize that the healers are all slaves, don't you? They're not there by choice."

Falon didn't answer. He knew, or at least suspected. I had wondered why the Eboros brothers had seemed so much more comfortable with the topic of sex than Aaron. I guess if you're rich enough to afford enslaved prostitutes on a regular basis, you're held to a different standard.

"We're getting sidetracked," I said. "Are you ready for this? Each reservoir has a slightly different ascension process, so I don't exactly know what will happen, but I think they're all pretty terrible. This is going to hurt like a motherfragger, Falon."

"A motherfragger? What is that?"

I smirked. "Never mind. This is going to hurt a lot."

"It didn't seem that bad," he said.

"It never does from the outside."

Falon gazed down at me, his brow furrowed. "I'm on your side, Lina."

I exhaled, cocking my head a little. "I know. That's why I'm still here." I turned away from him, lifting my right hand into the space in front of me and touching my solar plexus with my left. I took a deep breath in and out as he wrapped himself around me. "Whatever you do, don't let go."

Chapter Sixteen

*I*t seemed that every village was more desolate than the last, and Mullberg was no exception. Linorra hoped that she only imagined the glares Otterhai received from the few harried citizens they encountered.

I've always been a good student. That's probably because I like sitting down with a textbook and knowing, with complete confidence, that what I'm reading came from years of research and meticulous recordkeeping by smart people.

Ya know, unless it's history.

It's not that I don't think history is important. It is. It's of the utmost importance. And I'm not disparaging *all* historians. Believe me. I even have a favorite historian, if you must know. It's just that experience has taught me to take history books with a grain of salt. They're filled with cultural and political bias and tend to leave out important details like, ya know, the existence of women. Just ask Rosalind Franklin. Or Jocelyn Bell Burnell. Or Alice Ball. Never heard of them? Gee, I wonder why?

For this reason, it should come as no surprise that my post-Anick era Teleportation textbook failed to mention the Queen's Wicket, or what Violet simply called "the crystal key." If it had done its freaking job, then it would have informed me that this particular resonance article was not only the most powerful skipstone ever created, but that it overwhelms the resonance of any other nearby skipstones. If you try to have the key on your person and use a different skipstone instead, such as your own body, the key will co-opt your efforts and send you to whichever random hellscape it cooks up for you.

In retrospect, I probably could have used the key at that point. No one had followed us to the basement, so no one would have been likely to see us use it. But I already had it planned in my mind that I was going to talk my way out of our predicament, then go down to the bridgestone and use my own body as the skipstone to avoid showing the key to anyone. Like I said, I'm not the brains of the operation.

I knew when I didn't see a bridge sphere that something had gone terribly wrong. Instead of appearing in front of us as a normal bridge sphere would, allowing us to then step on, the key opened the bridge right on top of us. The room disappeared before my eyes, instantly replaced by a sea of pure fragment so brightly orange that I had to clamp my eyes shut to avoid blindness.

Falon jerked, then squeezed me hard enough to crack several ribs. I cried out to a bridge that stole my voice. Panicked, I opened one eye, trying to see what was happening, and grabbed one of Falon's hands just before he convulsed. He let go of me, but I managed to hang on to him, turning around and getting a hold of his tunic on either side. This move undoubtedly prevented his death, which would have occurred had we been separated on that bridge.

I pulled myself toward him, desperately maneuvering to avoid his flailing arms, then I wrapped my legs around him securely. Eyes wide, he arched his back and went rigid, tossing his head back in a silent scream.

He didn't see me. I doubt he remembered I was there. I watched in horror as his skin cracked and split, releasing rivulets of blood that quickly soaked his clothes or vanished into the air like my useless voice.

The fragment we floated in was a physical thing that seeped in and out of those cracks like orange smoke. After a while, his skin hardened and turned black like lava cooling into rock, then it went white and gritty, like sand, the grains of which slipped away into the air before it melted into a glassy surface. His face turned translucent, showing me the muscle and other tissues beneath, until they turned clear as well, revealing bone. Layer by layer, his body took on the appearance of stained glass until orange light shone all the way through his head from the other side.

Suddenly, my legs squished together, like I had them wrapped around a giant gummy bear instead of a person. He went flaccid, then his minor quivering grew to shudders, and his skin wibble-wobbled like gelatin. It would have been comical if it hadn't been so disturbing.

Finally, pieces of him slipped off and disappeared. His ear went first, then his entire left arm.

Holy shit. This is bad. As gently as I could, I wrapped myself around him, cradling his head so it wouldn't fly off. I secured his head, his right arm, and his torso, but his legs still flew freely. He lost both of his feet, then his legs below the knee. I didn't want to send Protection into him in case that would somehow interfere with his ascension. Other than Connection, I had never tried to use my reservoirs on a bridge before. My gut told me it was a bad idea. I was confident that I could heal him once we arrived, even to the point of helping him regrow limbs. I had regrown my head, after all.

Finally, Falon's skin faded to something like its normal color. He stared straight ahead with no sign that he saw me, soundlessly hyperventilating. Then he closed his eyes and went limp, unconscious.

Seconds later, we smacked into a bridgestone. I grunted, the wind knocked out of me, then anxiously looked around, afraid of what I might find.

Black mountains stood in the distance like desert guardians, holding endless sand dunes apart from a blood-red sky. The air, unbearably hot, smelled of sulfur and waved all around us as if the entire planet were on fire. But it was dead silent. There was no wind, no rustle of trees, no signs of life at all. Yet somehow, I knew we weren't alone. Perhaps it was my Connection reservoir pinging, or some other kind of sixth sense, but a feeling of dread crept over me as I took in the black and red landscape.

This isn't Hartha, I thought. *This is Hell*. I ground my teeth. *Figures*.

A whimper from Falon refocused my attention on the task at hand. His eyes were still closed, but he was alive, hyperventilating between grunts of pain. All the body parts that had detached lay around us in bloody pieces, sizzling on the heated bridgestone like slabs of raw meat. He gushed blood from dozens of open wounds. The tangy, coppery scent of it was so potent I could nearly taste it.

Jesus. There was no time to figure out where we were. I was in a race against time to heal him before he bled out.

As soon as I had that thought, the key vibrated against my skin, and I had the odd sensation of floating. My whole body felt like it buzzed with the energy of a thousand cups of coffee. Falon's breathing slowed down, as did everything else. Or maybe I sped up. The light in the sky turned pale green, the temperature dropped, and a low vibrational hum emanated from somewhere beneath my feet.

What the—no. No time.

I searched for Falon's left arm. It was within arm's reach.

Stop it. No time for stupid dad jokes, either, as great as they are.

The limb itself felt dense and heavy, like it had been transmuted into lead, and it was slippery with blood, which didn't bother me nearly as much as it should have. The shoulder was intact, and I tried to force that little ball into the socket, but I couldn't get it to fit. With a growl of frustration, I shoved Protection into him. To my shock, I could *see* the fragment with my eyes as it fluttered from me to him like blue-green glitter. It was beautiful and mesmerizing. Distracting.

After a moment, the shoulder sucked the arm into the socket, accepting it like an old friend. The ragged edges, where the skin had already peeled away after abruptly detaching, seemed to reach out for other shreds of skin, then weave together of their own accord. Droplets of blood puckered out of his wounds but didn't drip.

I found the lower legs, still inside his leather loafers, flung to one side of us, and spent a minute pulling the gory feet out of their shoes. I wanted to ensure that I had all the pieces in the right place before I put Humpty Dumpty back together again.

The feet were easy to arrange, but the lower legs were a bit trickier. I figured it out, though, based on how the feet fit into the ankle sockets. Having successfully reattached his lower limbs, I breathed a sigh of relief. Falon would not be dead or dismembered.

All that was left was the ear. Or was it? I groaned at what I had to do, then I lifted his tunic to check for any other missing extremities. Everything between his legs seemed to still be intact. And damn. Land of giants indeed.

I stood, then turned in a circle to search the ground around me. The ear was nowhere to be found. It was the search for my stupid phone all over again.

He's out of danger, at least, I thought, sighing, then noticed a dull warmth against my chest. The key was heating up, I realized, presumably from the vibration. It quickly went from mildly hot to me frantically yanking it out of my dress so that it didn't scald my skin. *How do I turn this damned thing off?*

At that thought, the sky shifted to red again and the air temperature jumped to sweltering. Somewhere behind me a high-pitched shriek cut across the previously silent desert like an arrow, striking me like a physical blow. My stomach leapt into my throat as I spun around, but I saw nothing except the sand and mountains. A flash caught my eye, beaming out of the wavy desert—a distant reflection.

"Lina," Falon mumbled. I turned back to see him pressing a trembling hand to the side of his head where the ear had been. He was still bleeding there, and though he was now mostly intact, his face was deathly pale with blue-tinged lips. He'd lost too much blood already, and we were running out of time.

"We need to get the hell out of here," I said. "I did my best, but I can't find your ear." My anxiety flared, and I slipped over top of him and sat down, straddling his belly so that I could grab him with my legs in the portal. I took his hand and pushed Protection into him again to make his ear stop bleeding.

Falon moaned with pleasure. "Oh goddess," he said. He grasped my hips and pulled me against him, then he slid one hand under my dress, squeezing my calf.

I felt the brush of his fingers before I felt the subtle buzzing warmth of his fragment, followed by a jolt of lust. It was the weirdest thing. I hadn't been feeling anything like that at all. I had been filled with fear that something was coming for us. We needed to flee back to Hartha as fast as humanly possible. But now all I wanted to do was rip Falon's tunic off and see if the giant could fit.

I clenched my jaw, fighting his hypnotic influence. I was probably making the same face that Falon had made when we came upon that orgy on Wishmere. He was doing this to me, and I wasn't sure if he even realized it.

I reached down and grabbed his hand, yanking it off me.

"Keep your goddamn hands to yourself," I snapped. "Especially right now, because I have a feeling I'm about to ascend again, and I won't be capable of fighting you off."

That shrieking noise hit us again, making me jump. It sounded much closer now and was accompanied by a low rumbling. This time, when I looked over my shoulder to pinpoint the source of the noise, I saw something that my stupid brain couldn't even process.

A horde of red humanoids surged toward us, dust billowing up in their wake. Thousands of them had appeared out of nowhere, red sunlight glinting off asymmetrical metal weapons. It was like they had crawled up out of the sand. My vision narrowed, and I suddenly felt like I might pass out.

"What in the hell are those things?"

"Rojii demons," Falon mumbled, lifting his head up to get a glimpse. "I've always wanted to see them."

"You're an idiot," I snapped, clutching at the key. I searched desperately for the correct bead to use as a skipstone, my heart hammering in my chest. But in the red light of Intaru, the Absorption planet, I couldn't tell which bead was truly green. I stared, paralyzed by fear that I would pick the wrong one and send us to some other nightmare realm.

I glanced back again. The red demon-men were a hundred yards away now, and the sound of their war cry was getting louder and louder, causing my bladder to spontaneously contract. They wore only ragged loincloths and sharp, forward-pointing horns like a minotaur. And they looked really freaking pissed. The ground beneath me vibrated from their stampede.

I focused on the key again, shaking with the weight of the decision.

"It's the second one," Falon croaked. "Hurry, this rock is hotter than Rhoya."

I hadn't even considered the second bead to be a choice. "Are you sure? It isn't remotely green."

"Positive. 'Every human fears death more when he is knocking at death's door.' Remember? Just trust me!"

And I did. I grabbed the second bead, holding it in my left hand. "Hecate help us!" I screamed and opened a bridge.

Chapter Seventeen

"**W**hat has happened?" Linorra asked nervously when she entered the inn. "Why, the streets are nearly deserted."

"Did you not hear?" the innkeeper asked with dismay. "Queen Mortier decreed that all dragons are to be imprisoned or else she will curse the land, killing all our crops and poisoning the water. And here you are traipsing through our town with none other than Lord Otterhai himself!"

Before he became an interplanetary criminal, Gerhelm Meriweather, a.k.a. Zig, spent years collecting subjective data on the topic of ascension. He interviewed people who had ascended and used that information and his own experience to rank them from least painful to most.

Teleportation is by far the worst. It blows all the others out of the water. Historically, it is recommended to avoid that ascension altogether, as only three humans are known to have survived it, those three being Zig, Anick, and myself. It is no coincidence that we were also the only known humans to have both Protection and Absorption reservoirs. All I can say is that I don't, for one minute, blame Anick for losing his sanity in there. Or Zig, for that matter. In some ways, Zig is even worse than Anick, he just hides it better. He's my friend and I love him, but that dude is certifiable.

THE WISDOM OF DISHONOR

At the other end of the spectrum is Production, which doesn't hurt at all and feels almost good, like when you're obscenely hungover and have finally finished vomiting. Just above Production is Absorption. To me, that ascension was the equivalent of a guilty pleasure, emphasis on guilt. It involved no physical pain, per se, but I had to relive every sin or crime I had ever committed from beginning to end with the supreme awareness that I deserved to rot on Intaru with the Rojii demons for each and every one of them. That wasn't the worst part, though. The worst part was having to listen to Evilina's hysterical laugh.

My evil twin is me. We've established this. What I hadn't recognized, though, was that there's a very real part of me that enjoys doing bad things. If you think about it, it makes perfect sense that Absorption is the opposite of Protection. Whereas those with a Protection reservoir tend to protect people who are in trouble, people with an Absorption reservoir are the opposite. They're not evil, exactly. They just don't give a crap if the people around them suffer. That's other people's problem, right? It's not up to me to save every delicate snowflake from melting. That is the nature of snowflakes. It's not my fault they're that way.

When everyone started calling my elementary school bully Mousehead, I didn't tell them to stop. I didn't *want* them to stop. I secretly smiled inside every time I heard it. I laughed out loud about it more than once.

When my family moved out of Eureka to get away from the growing crime and drug scene, I wondered if she'd become one of those shady bicycle people who were always riding around the Eureka historic district making the tourists clutch their pearls. I said things like, "It would serve her right." I didn't even hate her, so I'm not sure why I did that. There was no reason for it except for the pure pleasure of meanness.

In the beginning, most of my sins were of the schadenfreude variety. I imagine my father knew this about me, which was why he encouraged me to just let people dig their own graves rather than actively trying to bury them. I think he was worried I would be a little too good at the latter—that I would enjoy it too much. Like how, while I ascended Absorption, I thought about all the ways I could hurt Seleca. I speculated upon which of the ways would be the most ruthless and satisfying, and I listened to Evilina cackle at all our delightful options. My father had used my Absorption reservoir against me to suppress that urge for revenge. *Just let them hang themselves*, he had said. And so I did.

Charming man, my father. Everyone thought so.

As I ascended, Falon said that I slipped into a light sleep but looked as peaceful as he'd ever seen me, and that we just floated there, weightless in that river of blood-red Absorption fragment. Transmutation, for the record, is the third most painful ascension, just behind Precognition, and is exceptionally dangerous if you're not already an ascendant protector. It is, in fact, a fantastic way to kill someone accidentally on purpose. Just ask Falon's father, Regalinius.

"Oh wait. You can't."

It was raining lightly when we arrived on Hartha. Unlike the cold, biting rain to which I was accustomed, this rain was as warm as bathwater with drops so fine that it was almost a mist. A breeze carried the smell of grass and damp earth into my nose, calming me and prompting me to breathe deeply. My pulse pounded in my temples, quickly at first, then slowing until I could no longer sense it.

I'd landed on top of Falon and rested there, prone and wrapped in his arms, letting the warm water spray us as a balm against the searing heat that had bombarded us on Intaru. I knew I should get up, but I was comfortable for the first time in forever. It was nighttime, and I seriously considered just letting sleep take me right there, saturated with water, weariness, and Humpty Dumpty's yolk.

"I love that smell," said Falon after a moment, his voice barely audible over the rain.

I smiled, surprised he had enough energy to converse. "Me too," I said, rolling off him to sit up. He sat up next to me as I raised a shield to block the rain, creating what felt like a reverse fishbowl. The bubble of Protection in the dark felt safe, but it reminded me too much of a moment like this I'd had with Aaron.

Air crosses a shield, but water doesn't. I should have remembered when I was pulled into the sea.

The rain pattered softly on the top of the shield, and Falon pulled me in close to him so we could hear each other. "I'm sorry I doubted you," he said, his expression serious.

"When?"

"When you talked about the pain you endured. I see now why the pit didn't scare you. The pit is nothing compared to what I just went through." The rain had washed the blood from our faces, but our clothes were stained a reddish brown. My beautiful, formerly cream-colored dress with pockets was a tragic mess.

I reached over and touched the spot where his left ear used to be. "You're still missing an ear. I don't know if I can regrow it, but I could try."

Falon stared at me for a moment, then he laid his hand over mine and shook his head. A shiver ran through me. It could've been the rain or his strangely seductive touch, or both.

"Later," he said. "Right now, I need to ask you something." He leaned his face closer, his fervent gaze capturing mine. "Is it over between you and Aaron?"

I stared at Falon, lost for words. I knew he wanted me, but his direct question left me floundering. When I thought about it, Falon really was a better match for me. He was a free spirit, like me, with a similar wanderlust. We had the same sense of humor and open-minded attitude about sex. Even in a world as repressed as Monash, Falon had concluded that variations on sexuality were fine. I knew I would never see the shocked expression on his face that I had seen on Aaron's when I told him I was bisexual. Hell, I probably could have gotten Falon on board with polyamory if that were my thing. If I were being honest, it very well might have been given my commitment phobia.

Aaron, on the other hand, had proven beyond a shadow of a doubt that he would never share me, not that I would either. He'd called me "his," a sentiment I hadn't openly agreed with, but hadn't denied. I found his possessiveness both annoying and comforting. I'd felt irresistibly drawn to Aaron from the first time he touched my arm and his feelings rushed into me as if traveling an already well-worn path straight to my heart.

I hadn't had the same immediate, blazing attraction to Falon, but he had certainly grown on me. I could indeed imagine myself with him, traveling the universe. No bonding required.

But that hadn't been Falon's question.

"No, it's not over," I said, then averted my gaze. "We should head back to the house." I moved to get up, but Falon took hold of my shoulders, keeping me in place.

"Lina, please. This might be our last chance. Just let me kiss you one time. If you go back to Aaron afterward, I won't interfere. I'll accept your choice but let me show you what you're missing. Now, before his presence makes it impossible."

As I stared into his eyes, I considered his offer. He leaned in slowly to kiss me, and if I didn't turn away right now, it was going to happen. It would be wrong, but I knew I'd like it. It all came down to what kind of person I wanted to be. What did I value more, love or freedom?

The promise, my conscience said. *You promised Aaron you wouldn't just disappear. He said it would kill him if you did.*

Even if, by some egregious twist of fate, Aaron turned out to be my cousin, I was still beholden to that promise. It didn't necessarily preclude an eventual relationship with Falon, but I couldn't do it now without admitting I was someone who did whatever the hell I wanted without regard for who it might hurt.

The memory of what I'd felt on Intaru when Falon had touched my leg burned brightly in my mind. The sudden, overpowering, and inexplicable desire for him had been a wicked invitation that I could scarcely refuse, an addiction waiting to happen. I wanted to fall into that reckless abandon and see if I cracked when I hit the ground. I wanted to kiss him, and I wanted to do it in secret. It was exciting *because* it was wrong.

I admit that it was a close call. My eyes were already closing in anticipation of the kiss, my lips parting. A barely audible whimper escaped my throat, and I saw the look of triumph in Falon's eyes as he wrapped his large hand behind my nape.

Then, Evilina laughed. Out loud. It wasn't quiet either. Her lurid cackle vibrated around me like she'd appear any moment, a separate entity like Spirit. I jerked back in confusion.

I'm hallucinating. It's not real.

"Oh, I'm real all right," Evilina taunted. "And I'm coming for you." Every hair on my body stood on end at the sound of her voice, an overlay of multiple people speaking at once. I heard myself somewhere in there, but also Axel and a few others. I could understand Axel, since I'd absorbed a piece of his soul, but why would there be any others?

The bridge, I thought. *Maybe the Absorption ascension strengthened Evilina.*

It didn't explain the multiple voices, but it had a ring of truth to it. That's when it occurred to me that Seleca was an absorber. That was her original greater reservoir. Maybe the voices came from her. Had she started out like this? As sane as I used to be, but enjoying doing little bad things like I do? Bad things that escalated into terrible things before she knew it or had the strength of will to care? I could easily become one of those people that my father called an evildoer. Part of me would enjoy that.

Falon's warm breath brushed my lips, causing me to refocus on him. He was pressed against me now, his nose touching mine. I lifted my hand and rested it on his lips. "Not like this," I whispered. "It's hard enough for me to continue being a good person without this constant temptation. I like you, Falon, but I can't do it like this. Please..."

Falon laid his hand over mine, shutting his eyes.

"Your skin is so hot," he said.

"I raised my Evocation reservoir." *Aaron. I have to get to Aaron.*

"If you don't want to kiss him, now's the time to pull away," Spirit said.

Once again, I jerked in surprise. "Spirit? Are you there?" My heart burst with joy to hear her voice as my eyes darted around hastily in a vain attempt to locate her. Falon looked, too, though I knew that was due to my reaction since he didn't have the ability to hear her as I did.

"I'm here, Lina, but not for long. This is probably the last time I'll be able to talk to you, and I'd rather not spend it watching you kiss some weasel named not-Aaron."

Damn, I'm glad he can't hear you. And I wasn't going to kiss him, I grumbled, more to convince myself. "What happened, Spirit? Where have you been? Why can't I see you?"

"I'm not a hundred percent sure, but I feel stretched, like something is pulling me away from here. I had to sort of save up to even talk to you. Listen, there's no time. You have to get to Neesee right now." Her voice faded out like a radio station.

"Why, Spirit? What's wrong?" I waited, but she didn't come back right away.

All was silent for a moment, then Spirit said something else, but it was garbled. It sounded like, "It might already be too late."

My eyes widened at her words, and I swallowed a shriek. "Spirit! What did you say? Spirit!" I jumped up, and Falon hopped up beside me.

"What's happening?" he asked.

"Spirit says we're out of time. We need to get back to Neesee." I moved to walk toward the house so we could grab the crew before we went, but Falon held on to my hand.

"Wait," he said, pulling me back toward him, but I tugged my hand away and dropped the shield.

"The time for waiting is over. Spirit has never led me astray. Ignoring her advice is always a bad idea. We need to hurry."

Maybe it was time to stop expecting Aaron to be my perfect Prince Charming and accept that I loved him anyway, warts and all. As hard as it was to believe that Aaron could do the same for me, he seemed committed to it. Even the possibility of consanguinity hadn't stopped him from wanting to be with me. Whatever petty disagreement we'd had about plans and roles could be worked out. It had to be.

Evilina's cold laughter echoed in my mind again. *You and I both know it's already too late for that. You broke your promise and left him. All that remains is to sit back and enjoy the carnage.*

Chapter Eighteen

*L*inorra *slid down Otterhai's scaly spine toward the ground in a panic. "Syndeth! Oh, Syndeth! Are you here?" There was no answer from the shock den. It was eerily silent, but from somewhere far away, she felt her friend's pain as if it were her own.*

Why is it always raining when everything goes to shit?

We jogged down the mulched path toward Gran's house, the mud squelching beneath the saturated bits of wood. We were halfway down the path when I saw that the back door was open, but as I drew nearer, it dawned on me that the door wasn't so much open as ripped off its hinges. It hung askew, making it look like someone had punched my grandmother's house in the face and knocked its teeth out.

Aaron! I thought, my heart pounding. I dug my toes into the ground, flying down the path as fast as I could. I didn't even know I could run that fast. Falon called my name. I ignored him, but it only took seconds for his long legs to catch me. He yanked me back by my wrist, nearly wrenching my arm out of its socket.

"Lina, wait! This was exactly what I was afraid of. We can't just run in there. We don't know what we'll find."

"I don't have time to be careful. The crew could be in there under attack as we speak!"

"Wait, let's just think through a strategy first. Why don't we circle the house and see if there's a more discreet way in?"

I know I've derided myself in the past for not listening to good advice, but in that moment, my experience on the Teleportation bridge made itself blatantly obvious. I forgot who I was on that bridge. My soul had dispersed like hot breath into frigid air, and the person I used to be disappeared. What emerged upon my dubious return was a broken creature, imperfectly pieced back together.

I think my previous incarnation might have taken Falon's advice, but that would have been due to fear. Fear now seemed a moot point. I had been subjected to the most horrific pain imaginable and had returned to spit in the eye of any enemy that dared cross me. I truly felt my immortality now. I felt, if not immune to misery and pain, then immune to giving a crap about it. I had experienced the worst that life had to offer, and unless Gran's house was filled to the brim with cockroaches, whatever I found in that house should fear *me*.

"I have a strategy for you," I said coldly. "How about I burn the house down and you circle around and turn anyone who comes out to stone?"

Falon hissed, pulling his hand back. His palm was seared red where he'd been holding my wrist. An expression settled over his face that I hadn't seen before, one that I hadn't realized until that moment he was even capable of.

When I first met him, Falon reminded me of a younger version of Aaron, like he was trying to emulate him to a degree. Aaron had a dark side, of course. He was fully capable of murder, but I always got the sense that it needed to be for the right reasons, for a noble cause. In other words, he acquiesced to the need for violence but didn't enjoy it. He was cautious, by nature.

Falon, it seemed, was more like me, reckless and wild. He fought his darker inclinations mainly because his mother wouldn't have approved. But like me, a part of him enjoyed doing bad things. The idea of turning the enemy to stone must have agreed with him because instead of horror, the look he gave me was nothing short of bloodlust.

"You think I'm gonna let you go in there alone and have all the fun?"

We locked eyes, sharing what could only be described as an evil smirk. I brought my awareness to the base of my spine, where Evocation resides, and prepared to burn my enemies to the ground. Then, as one, Falon and I strode into the house.

The first thing I noticed upon entering Gran's kitchen was the sound of buzzing insects. I had noticed previously that the yard had a fly problem, and we all know that those little assholes are called house flies for a reason. They always want in, and with the door broken open, they'd swarmed inside.

The second thing I noticed was exactly where the sound was coming from. On the ground near the sink lay a mass of undulating black, set in a sticky, dark red puddle.

I halted, stunned by the sight of what was undoubtedly a dead person, covered head to toe in flies.

Falon cursed, then pushed past me. "Delya," he concluded, "if the red hair is any indicator. We'll have to turn her over to be sure." With the toe of his shoe, he lifted the body at the hip and shoved it onto its back, sending the flies up into the air like a living cloud and confirming his guess.

Ya know, there are heroes and there are heroes. Falon is the sort that will help you flip over a fly-covered corpse so you don't have to.

Who cares about her? Evilina thought. *Just find Aaron.*

I ignored the suggestion and gingerly hovered over her, swatting flies away from my face with one hand while the other felt for a pulse. She was warm, but pulseless, which made sense given the ragged hole in her forehead. The coppery odor reminded me that I had a strange predilection for the smell of blood. I stepped hastily away from Delya's corpse, disturbed by my body's objectionable reaction to the smell.

It's Absorption, I've since realized. When I say that absorbers are vampires, I mean that quite literally. Instead of a feeling of disgust, the smell of blood informed me that I hadn't eaten since morning, and I was starving. I was supposed to be eating for two, after all.

I know someone you can bite, Evilina commented. *Ya know who likes to shoot people in the head, don't you?*

"Shut up," I whispered through clenched teeth.

"I didn't say anything," Falon said.

"I wasn't talking to you."

Falon looked around the room, perhaps thinking I had spoken to Spirit again, but I didn't explain further.

I stood, still as a statue, listening for sounds in the rest of the house. Hearing none, I reached out through the air with Connection, stretching my mind for stray thoughts the same way I listened for noises. There was nothing but an unsettling hollowness in the house, set against a dull ringing in my ears and the thudding of my own heart.

After a moment, I strode through the kitchen toward the dining area. Several chairs were toppled over. One had been thrown against a window, shattering both the glass and breaking the chair to kindling. Food was still on plates, half-eaten and now covered with flies. The aroma of seared meat and onions still hung in the air, causing my stomach to growl audibly over the sound of buzzing wings.

I grabbed bread from a basket in the middle of the table that had been covered with a cloth. Still warm, like Delya. We had just missed them. Scarfing the bread down, I stalked the rest of the house, searching from room to room in vain. They were all gone.

"We have to get back to Neesee," I said, shuffling back into the dining room. Falon was already there, eating another piece of bread. I guess he wasn't bothered by the corpse in the other room either. Next to him sat a plate of steak, neatly cut into perfect cubes. Classic Aaron.

"The key interfered with the bridge last time," I said, "and if we use it, I don't know exactly where on Monash it will take us. But I can't leave it here either."

"It's all right," Falon replied. "I think I can call a bridge now. I'll use my own body as the skipstone. Maybe it will work if you stand far enough away. Hopefully it will take us directly to my family's estate. My father hides a bridgestone in a maze there. He made my mother give birth over it. Nasty place to have a baby, if you ask me."

"Your father has his own bridgestone?" I asked.

"Yes. So does yours, Lina."

"Oh, yeah. Actually, we own two, technically. Hmm, maybe next week we should take the yacht out to Saint Tropez, drink some champagne, and count our money."

"I have no idea what you're talking about, but I'm in," he responded, walking toward the kitchen door. "In the meantime, I'll try that bridge to Neesee. Meet me outside in a one minute."

Falon's bridge worked perfectly except that it dumped us out several feet higher than normal. I fell face down onto the bridgestone and felt my right wrist snap as Falon landed on top of me. I grimaced, remembering my first broken wrist from what seemed like centuries ago.

"You all right, little goat?" Falon asked, suppressing a laugh. Thankfully, he rolled off me, letting me clutch my throbbing limb to my chest.

"Shut up," I grumbled, pushing Protection into the injury to heal it. "Where are we?" We were surrounded by tall, manicured boxwoods. There was a little opening in the bushes, just barely wide enough to slip through. It wasn't raining anymore, but it was dark and cold, and the air was thick with fog.

"In the maze. We made it." He stood, holding out his hand. I took it with the uninjured side and got to my feet, bracing my newly broken wrist against my chest. Electric pain shot up my forearm to my elbow, and I clenched my teeth against it, tears gushing out the corners of my eyes.

I pushed Protection from my heart, through my chest, and into my wrist, but as the bone knit back together, I didn't get the same rush of pleasure that I would have if someone else had forced Protection into me. It felt more like a numbing pressure, followed by a release, then nothing.

"That's handy," I said, shaking my literal hand out.

Falon shook his head at my stupid joke, then walked to the opening in the bushes, looking out. "Come on," he said. "There's a shortcut to the pit. We have to go out the back gate."

I followed him, stepping through the opening in the bushes. Falon led me through the maze, easily navigating around the house and its gardens without coming across a single guard. We came upon the back gate, also hidden in the boxwoods, and peered out between the bars.

"Nobody," he said. "I wouldn't expect anyone to be behind the house anyway. Only the estates have access to this area, but when we get to the next gate, we'll have to be more careful."

I nodded and followed him into a wooded area. He closed the gate behind us, then led me down another paved path. It reminded me of a park I used to visit near my childhood home in Eureka that butted up against the zoo. They'd built an aerial boardwalk out into the park and through the redwoods. I would sometimes walk around beneath the boardwalk, listening to the tourists and hoping they didn't spit on me.

The memory made me smile. I hadn't been back to Earth since I'd come to Monash more than two months prior. I had thought I'd head straight back there the moment I acquired Teleportation, but when it came to it, it hadn't seemed as important as helping Monash. In my post-Teleportation ascendant state, I wondered if I shouldn't just tell this planet to shove it. So what if Anick was back? What did that have to do with me? If he ever came to Earth and tried to start something, we could just fragging nuke the guy. Let this planet handle its own problems.

That's the Absorption fragment talking, I thought. *What you're doing is important. Stay the course.*

Evilina released a snort of derision. *Yeah, let's get into a fight with a maniac who can bench press a Fiat and play* Invasion of the Body Snatchers *with your favorite people. Good move. It's not like you have anything better to do, like travel the universe with a guy who makes you laugh and is hung like a—*

"Shut. Up." I snarled.

"Who are you talking to?" Falon asked.

"The biggest bitch I've ever met. Don't worry about it."

Our walk through the cold, dark woods took about twenty minutes, and we didn't see a single person. That seemed like a good thing rather than being cause for alarm. The Rhoya towered over us, sheltering us from the light rain. When we got to the park gate, Falon scanned the empty streets.

"There's no one around," he said, his eyebrows drawn together.

"The ceremony was mandatory, wasn't it? Maybe there's a preshow," I said, thinking of the pit.

"Goddess, I hope not," he said.

We came out, closing the gate behind us. The streets appeared as if they'd been full of vendors and that it had been busy very recently. The path was lined with tables that still had merchandise or food on them.

"Aren't people afraid that someone might steal their stuff?" I asked.

"Absolutely," Falon said. "This is very strange."

We walked through the dim streets for another twenty minutes, ducking down alleyways that Falon thought might keep us hidden. It didn't matter. We didn't see a single soul anywhere. Cafés which had previously been full of music and the raucous laughter of men were now abandoned.

We heard something, though. It was a man's voice, deep and resonant. It sounded like Aaron's voice. My heart quickened at the sound. Falon led me down another alleyway, and we stopped at the back entrance to a shop, the door hanging wide open.

"This is Beltran Cole's shop," Falon whispered. "The greater producer who works for my father. If we go up to his roof, we'll see the dais and the pit. I used to watch from here when I was a kid. The front of the shop faces out on the main courtyard."

"Is there a chance someone on that side will see us?" I asked.

"I don't think so. No one should notice we're here unless they're in the storeroom."

I nodded, and we filed into the shop, closing the door behind us. An oil lantern on the counter was still lit, revealing a green storeroom empty of people, but with plants everywhere on the counters. Small, narrow windows in the top of the outer wall and more on the inner wall were propped open, creating a draft, and the flame in the oil lantern flickered. The shadows in the room danced around in eerie silence.

Someone had dropped their coat on the floor and hadn't bothered to pick it up. "Beltran's coat?" I whispered.

Falon nodded, scooping it up and slipping it on. "Sort of. It's mine now." He picked up the lantern and led me to a doorway in the corner of the storeroom, then opened it, revealing a staircase. At the top of the stairs was a large room, empty and unfinished except for rows and rows of plants. The front had large windows and a door that opened to a balcony.

"Careful," Falon said. "They'll be able to see us through those windows if we walk too close. The shop is up on a hill overlooking Aetos Plaza, which sits in a bowl, of sorts. There's a dais in the center, and you can stand around the raised sides and hear everything that is said."

Like a Greek or Roman amphitheater. The surname Aetos sounded Greek. I wondered if that was a coincidence. Was Anick from Earth?

"We should be fine if we stay back," Falon said. "Come on."

Falon ducked around the corner and to the left to go up another flight of stairs, this one alarmingly rickety, like it might fall apart at any moment. The door at the top opened to reveal a cloudless night sky. The fog had mysteriously cleared around the plaza, and since Neesee wasn't a city full of electric lights, millions of stars lit up the sky in a way that I had rarely seen before. The air had turned bitterly cold, and the wind gusted over the roof of the plant shop.

Falon stepped into the nighttime air and shivered. "Rhoya!" he said, his teeth chattering, even with the borrowed jacket. I braced myself and followed him out onto a rooftop terrace. The wind swirled around me, and I felt that it was cold, but it felt nice, like a fan blowing on a hot day. A blazing fire burned at the base of my spine that could use some cooling off.

"Huh. I guess I'm fine," I said. "Stand close to me." Falon sidled up to me, and I could feel him sucking heat out of my body like I was his own personal radiator.

"Oh, that's not fair," he groaned, positioning himself flush behind me so that I blocked the wind to his lower half.

I smirked, remembering I'd thought the same exact thing when I snuggled with Aaron. Was he down there somewhere? I peeked over the wooden railing of the terrace to see thousands of Neesians in the plaza below, kneeling in absolute silence.

That's not creepy or anything.

As Falon had described, a low dais was positioned in the middle of the plaza. It was empty except for four men kneeling near the back. I couldn't tell for sure because their heads were bowed as well, but it looked like Fitch, Shane, Ellis and Jorin.

I sucked in a breath at the same time as Falon, who squeezed my upper arms. My eyes darted around, but I didn't see Aaron or Terik. My first instinct was to run down there and search for them, but—my hand came to my belly—this was not the time for rash decisions.

The packed plaza was a barrier to anyone entering by stealth, not to mention a freaking fire hazard. Nobody could get through the crowd unnoticed, even if they had Reflection and could pull a full veil.

"There's the pit," Falon whispered, pointing to a small, circular grate in the ground just to the side of the dais. "And over there"—he gestured to a small outbuilding beyond the pit—"is the entrance. That door leads to stairs that go below the street level."

From the space beneath the pit's grate, soft voices echoed out, the only sound among a sea of silent worshippers. I couldn't tell from my vantage point if there was someone hanging down there, but a thin curl of smoke rose through the grate like a warning to all.

Please don't let that be Aaron, I thought, fists clenched.

That's when I felt the resonance. It was just like when I had encountered Zig for the first time, except *more*. I now had three greater reservoirs and four ascendants. I couldn't tell if it was coming from one person or a group, but whoever was down there cumulatively had every single one of the reservoirs I had, including Evocation.

Aaron? I thought, my heart racing. *Unless...* Gran had said that Evocation was the only reservoir Anick didn't have, but if they'd captured Aaron... My heart jumped up into my throat. *No. Please don't let it be true.*

I called to Aaron's spirit. *Aaron! If you're there, answer me!* Nothing happened. I called again, as hard as I could. *Aaron Atticus!*

Like before, a whisper floated past, but I couldn't tell who it was. It could have been Spirit again, for all I knew.

I searched for the source of the resonance but did not find anything obvious until the door to the outbuilding squeaked open and four men and a woman emerged, one by one. I recognized the man at the head of the line immediately. Dark brown hair and a wide frame clothed in a rugged tunic with dark red boots.

Aaron.

I almost shouted his name as he strutted to the middle of the dais, his chin held high, but then I noticed that he carried a severed head tucked under his arm like a basketball and my nausea flared.

I squinted my weak Earth eyes down at him, trying to make out his face more clearly. He looked like Aaron, but I had never seen Aaron walk like that. That sick feeling in my gut intensified as I studied the tall, slender people following him. Regalinius, Markinius, Axel, and *Fucking* Seleca, in all her stupid yellow pants glory.

That's not Aaron, I thought, choking as my heart forgot a few beats. *It's Anick. I'm too late.*

Chapter Nineteen

"Tomorrow night, the red moon, Ishkar, will meet the white moon, Heshia, in the sky. When this happens, there is a great storm that drowns the land and everything on it. Humans and dragons alike seek higher ground, as anyone who doesn't could be washed away. But don't fret, my dear," Otterhai said when he saw Linorra's frightened expression. "You have at your disposal the only known water dragon."

Sound, like fragmental energy, has its own kind of magic. A mustard plant, for example, can learn what a caterpillar feeding sounds like, and respond by producing mustard oil to drive the invader away. For humans, sound is tied to memory and emotion, which is why we have long used music and rhymes to commit oral histories to memory. Our brains literally evolved to do this.

Even as our species spread across the universe into extraordinarily diverse cultures, we all retained the spoken word as a central element of our lives. The voices of people we know and love embed themselves in our psyche to the point that, even when two voices sound very similar, we can usually tell them apart.

The tone, depth, resonance, and power of each voice makes it as unique as a fingerprint, not to mention the rhythm of how we speak, the words we tend to use, and the types of messages we are likely to convey.

For me, the voices of those I've loved hold a spiritual significance, taking me back in time. Though I have since made a habit of recording voices and entering them into the sacred archives I've devoted my immortal life to keeping, I don't really need those recordings for the people I was the closest to.

I still remember my mother's and father's voices, and I can hear the voices of Spirit, Ward, and all those I counted as beloved friends who have since had the great fortune to cross the death bridge.

Aaron had an exquisite voice, astonishingly deep and powerful without being gravelly or overbearing. It could be so soft, with a vibrational frequency that matched the rhythm of my body such that he could turn me into a wanton animal with a mere word. I still remember the first time I heard him sing. It was a freaking mystical experience. His voice was my home, a place of peace and belonging.

That is why, when I heard Anick for the first time with Aaron's voice, I recognized it for the *abomination* it was.

"Well, friends," Anick said, looking directly at me. "Our guest of honor has finally arrived."

The words sent goose bumps across my body, and every iota of coherent thought came to a screeching halt as my attention was captured and held prisoner. It was Aaron, but not. It was sharper, with an accent that sounded like maybe English wasn't his first language.

It was *wrong*, the way an unfamiliar voice sounds wrong coming from outside your bedroom door in the middle of the night. The sound of it, the idea of it, filled my entire mind and body with rage.

No.

Avelina, don't be afraid. I'm thrilled to finally be here with you in the flesh. Come to me, please. I've been waiting for you for longer than you can imagine. You have nothing to fear from me.

Once again, my mind stopped, this time in confusion. The outrage I'd felt only moments ago abandoned me, replaced by an unjustified tranquility. The voice in my head didn't match the one I'd heard with my ears. Anick's true voice, which slipped into my mind uninvited, was a shade higher, a rich and earthy baritone to Aaron's deadly bass. It was unreasonably beautiful and full of authority but also startling in its kindness.

This was the voice of a man who would make everything okay. I could go down there and forget about doing anything painful or difficult. I could forget about my family's betrayal and secrets and instead find love and acceptance. *Freedom.*

My shoulders felt so heavy, and I knew, beyond a shadow of a doubt, that Anick would help me carry that burden. I could stop fighting and just *be*.

Nick.

Yes, he thought to me. "Yes" is such a small word, yet it was heavily laden with a sense of satisfaction and something wholly unexpected. Relief.

I had no clue where the nickname came from, but it was intimately familiar, as if I'd known this man for a long time and had just forgotten. I had no actual conscious memory of him, but it felt wrong that I didn't, like if I listened closely enough, his voice alone could pry loose a whole slew of memories that were stuck in long-term storage.

I was flooded with déjà vu and stood there, perplexed, profound guilt creeping over me that I'd been working against him, that only moments ago I had wanted to murder him.

Wait a second. This is illogical. This feeling must be Projection. I need to block him.

I squeezed my eyes closed, trying to fortify my mental Protection. He called to me, and I longed to go, aching for the safety that call promised.

You know me, Avelina. You know you do. I could never hurt you. We need each other, you and I. Come to me. Come home.

Home? "You're not Aaron, you bastard," I muttered through clenched teeth, trying to shout but failing. I resisted Anick's pull, though it felt like trying to resist drinking a glass of water after days in the desert.

I imagined a shield around my thoughts, evoking the impenetrable wall I'd encountered around Aaron's mind the first time we'd formed a Connection link. I visualized pushing Protection into that shield as I exhaled, straining with the effort of blocking him. I didn't even know if I was doing it right, but Anick's voice wavered and then fell silent.

I glanced down at my feet. I had walked all the way to the stairs without realizing it. Anick was a gifted projector, they'd said, but how had he gotten past my Protection? He'd projected through the air using ascendant Connection as a carrier. He must have kept all his reservoirs despite his death.

I can't believe they did it, I thought. *They actually brought him back.*

I couldn't help but wonder, if Anick was in Aaron's body, then where was Aaron? Was his disembodied spirit floating around somewhere? Or was he imprisoned in his own body? If he were floating around, wouldn't I see him? Or would he be "stretched" like Spirit, unable to appear to me?

I needed an answer to these questions if I was going to kick Anick out of there and put things back the way they should be. If that was possible. Even if I could get down to the main square and somehow avoid being mobbed by Anick's minions, was I strong enough to rip Anick's soul out and replace it with Aaron's?

I laid my hand against the door to the stairs to steady myself. All of a sudden, the idea of me and Falon coming here on our own seemed like a silly, naive notion. When my grandfather killed Anick, he'd needed a whole army to back him up. How had I thought I could do this with only two people? I needed to get back to Darion-Ájar, to my parents and grandmother.

"Falondeitric, son of Regalinius," called Anick, his voice carrying up to us like a siren song. "You are a friend to the Ministry. Come, join your father at my side."

I spun to face Falon. "We need to get out of here."

"No," Falon said calmly. He rested his hands against the wall on either side of me, boxing me in. He'd been right behind me the whole time, following me to the door.

"You have to run, Falon. Anick can't hurt me, but he can hurt you. You have to go. Open a bridge and go home."

"I wish you would have just kissed me, Lina," Falon murmured. A fervent glint in his eyes sent a shiver down my spine. "It would have been so much easier."

"That isn't important right now," I insisted.

"Oh, but it is. Can't you hear his voice? We were wrong about him, Lina. He is great. If we would have just come to him together, we could have had anything we wanted. Maybe it's not too late. Come with me."

He's trapped in Projection, I thought. *They all are. That's why they just got up and left all their belongings. He's enslaved the entire city, just like before.*

I tried to pull away, but I was cornered against the closed door to the stairs. "He's projecting on you," I said. "Fight it, Falon."

"I don't want to fight anymore," Falon said, his voice cracking with emotion. "It's a miracle, Lina. Can't you see? He didn't even have to wait until the moment of equinox. He's more powerful than time. Come with me, and we'll go bear witness together. We'll be so happy. I'll *make* you happy."

Falon didn't wait for me to agree. He stepped in close, pinning me against the door with his body. One of his hands slid up to my nape and the direct contact sent a jolt straight to my core. That ferocious lust that had almost consumed me on Intaru hit me right as Falon's mouth crashed into mine.

He kissed me hard, coaxing my lips apart with his tongue, and I instinctively opened to him, extending a deep Connection link. His wild desire surged across the link, flooding my senses, and reaching out for my own craving. I'd been committed to resisting, but my whole body buzzed with a visceral need that overwhelmed ethics or reason. I didn't think at all, I only *wanted*.

Yes, Falon thought. *Yes, yes, yes. I knew it.* His hands were everywhere, tangling in my hair, then sliding down my back to my butt. He squeezed, a groan rumbling from deep in his throat. I wrapped my legs around his waist as he picked me up and held me against the door, pushing his growing erection against my core.

Lee, a voice whispered, though I couldn't tell if it was real or my imagination.

I need to stop right now.

My mind continued to resist, but my body screamed at me to welcome Falon in. I managed to yank my face away and tried to yell, but it came out as a wholly unconvincing whine. "Put me down, Falon."

From down in the plaza, Anick chuckled, though it was surprisingly gentle. Then the crowd began to laugh with him; thousands of people, mostly men, all laughing at my precarious position. That, more than anything else, was what pissed me off enough to fight.

I was already connected to Falon, so I pushed Protection into him as hard and fast as I could. It should not have surprised me that he had a higher tolerance for Protection than most since he'd frequented the Rhoyal Healers Guild. To my frustration, he retained his grip on my arms as he fell to his knees, his eyes rolling back in his head. His breath swept across my face from his deep moan, but he held on to me, his firm grip bringing me down with him to the ground.

Lina, please, Falon implored me through our Connection link. *It's time to stop fighting. I know you want me. It's all right. Anick won't mind.*

"I mind!" I insisted.

Falon ignored my rebuttal, pulling me against him and kissing me again. My resistance buckled under the weight of my physical desire, and I gave in, letting him roll on top of me.

Falon felt it the moment I relinquished control and his kiss intensified. He sucked my bottom lip into his mouth and bit down as he yanked my dress up enough to settle comfortably between my legs.

Isn't this amazing? he thought to me. *Doesn't this feel good? We're perfect for each other, Lina. You know that. We're the same. Just let go of the guilt and let me claim you.*

"Go get her!" Anick roared, anger vibrating in his voice now.

Falon was right about one thing. It did feel good. To Evilina, anyway. The question was, which me did I want to be?

The quiet voice whispered again, but it was distant and muffled, and I was too distracted by the growing heat between my legs to listen. My heart pounded as Falon eagerly worked my skirt up to my waist, then ran his hands up my thighs. The wooden floor of the terrace had no give at all, allowing him ample leverage to grind his hips into me. Though he was much taller than Aaron, he wasn't as heavy, and his weight felt almost light on top of me.

I considered very seriously just letting it happen. What harm could it do? Anick's minions would get here in a moment and break it up anyway. For the moment, I couldn't remember why I had been denying myself this pleasure.

"So hot," Falon whispered, then he unbuttoned the top few buttons of my dress and pressed his cool lips to the heated skin of my neck. I gasped for air, wanting the sensation of his mouth to fill my awareness, but the stomping of feet one level below rattled the door in its frame.

"They're coming," I breathed. I was perplexed as to whether I felt annoyed, relieved, or just scared.

"I'll turn the door into a durrite wall." He jumped up, beaming, and placed his hand on the door to the stairs.

The second his touch left my skin, I snapped back to myself. When he touched me, it was like I turned into a different person. I couldn't think clearly, and now I'd woken up from a trance even more insidious than Anick's Projection because I had to fight my own stupid lizard brain.

I have since learned that Transmutation doesn't create attraction, it only magnifies emotions that are already there. If, instead of attraction, I had disliked Falon, then his touch might have turned that dislike into a burning hatred, but I *was* attracted to him. I had kept it at bay out of loyalty to Aaron, but Falon's touch intensified my desire for him to the degree that my fidelity was simply overwhelmed.

As soon as he touches me again, I'll just do whatever my body wants until our reservoirs are so mixed, they might as well be one big ocean.

Falon had the doorway sealed in just a few seconds and turned to me, an expression of hunger transforming his face. I scrambled back to avoid letting him touch me again.

"I thought you were on Anick's side now?" I asked. "Shouldn't we let those men in?"

Falon laughed darkly. "We will. Just not yet." Keeping his wolfish gaze on me, he squatted down to touch the ground.

I jumped up to flee, my left hand coming to my chest to pull up a shield. I hated to do it, but I had no choice. This wasn't my friend Falon but enthralled Falon, the one that appeared when restraint and morals took a vacation. Even if I had decided to give up on Aaron and give Falon a chance, this was not the way it should be. There was no consent here for either of us.

I had the initial shield sphere started in my chest when the ground shifted beneath my feet, and I stumbled, landing on a soft surface. Falon had turned the ground into some kind of cushion. He was immediately on top of me again, pinning both of my arms above my head and taking my mouth with his.

A thrill of excitement shot through me, and I relaxed back, dropping the shield, my mind instantly empty of everything except his weight on me, his tongue probing my mouth. I wondered where else it might explore.

The men who'd been about to reach us banged uselessly on the other side of the new wall, and I couldn't convince myself to care. I opened myself to Falon, wrapping my legs around his waist again. He groaned and then rocked his hips forward, pressing against me through his fine black tunic.

"I told you I was coming for you," a familiar voice whispered. "This is who you are, now. You can't belong to Aaron. You're immortal. You can't *belong* to anyone at all. You were made to do what you want, when you want, taking whatever you crave. No rules. No restrictions. No guilt. Just you and your desire, until you've taken everything and everyone, and there's nothing left but to rip down the walls of creation and collapse back into the Oneness."

What the hell does this have to do with the Oneness? My thoughts flashed to another voice I'd heard recently, in a nightmare. This voice sounded suspiciously like that one. *You're not Evilina. Or Spirit. Who are you?*

Falon released one of my wrists and slid his hand to my shoulder, then down to my breast. He pinched my peaked nipple through the fabric of my dress, making me suck in a breath, then reached under the hem.

"Let us through!" a man's voice bellowed. The banging on the wall increased to an unbearable volume.

Falon had just gotten his fingers hooked into my underwear when the memory of Aaron's true voice came back to me from that moment on the boat. *I need you to fight a little harder to stay with me, Lee. I can only save you so many times.*

The last thing Mom had said to me before I left Darion-Ájar was to "make good choices." I had dismissed it as a cliché, but had she been uncertain as to whether I'd be able to? I couldn't just blame Falon's seductive touch for my behavior. This was my own weakness, and just as Aaron had warned, he couldn't save me this time.

I'd have to do it myself.

"Falon, stop," I said with as much conviction as I could manage. His eyes met mine, a look of incredulity taking over his features. "Stop," I repeated, then I used my free hand to push away the hand that was trying to pull down my underwear.

"You don't want me to stop. You want this as much as I do."

"Part of me does, yes, but that part of me is a sociopath and can go straight to Hell. Get off me. I don't have time for this!"

It was almost as if the key could hear me. It vibrated against my skin, just like it had on Intaru when Falon's body was in pieces on a scorching-hot slab of stone. The colors around me upshifted, and the dim light appeared brighter. Falon was frozen in time and glowing ever so slightly with a beautiful indigo light.

I get it now, I thought. *Falon is still moving, but at a glacial speed. That's what I did when I ascended my Teleportation. I was accustomed to being a time-locked mortal, but now I'm like Spirit. She moved through time like this, so swiftly that she could do things in the blink of an eye.*

"Lee," a deep voice said. Aaron and Spirit stood on either side of me, peering down. They were both ghosts now.

No, I thought. *No!* I had already known that Anick was in Aaron's body, but to see his evicted spirit here in front of me brought home the stark reality of the situation. He was the same except for his eyes, which were still blue but had lost their distinctive shine. Everything about him appeared dull, like he was an old photograph rather than the man in person.

I whimpered, denial filling my mind and body. *Aaron*. I thrashed, trying to push Falon off me, but something about the slow movement of time had magnified his weight times a thousand. I couldn't budge him.

Aaron scowled down at my compromising position. "He really is a weasel," he muttered as my cheeks burned with humiliation and shock.

"I can see the appeal," Spirit commented judiciously. "He is charming. And to be fair, Falon did hold back until he was enthralled. I blame Anick for this."

"Aaron," I cried. I wanted to say I'm sorry, but even my apologies sounded empty to me now.

"It's all right, Lee. You made the right choice in the end."

Aaron sounded like he meant it, but something about his voice didn't sound right. His manner of speaking was different somehow. Not colder, per se, but different. He sounded like a stranger.

"I broke my promise," I said, my voice cracking. "I didn't mean to. I wish I could take it back."

"It's not too late," Aaron responded, his bizarre voice sad but resolute. "You have time."

Aaron had a glow around him, except it was light blue with occasional sparks of other colors. His Protection reservoir was still bright, but his Evocation reservoir was gone, or at least mostly gone. Someone had ripped it out of him, then ripped his soul out of his body.

He was effectively dead. Or was he? Could I get his body back? Is that what he meant by still having time?

Aaron nodded, hearing my thoughts now that he was a ghost. "Use the key," he said.

"Use it how?" I asked. "I can slow down time so that it almost stops, but even if I could get out from under this big oaf, I can't leave him here."

"You don't need to," Spirit said. "Use the key to send him away."

Of course, I thought. *I could just point the key at him and make him vanish.* That would be tricky since he was still pinning down one of my arms. If I was touching him, I might get sucked up with him, and who knows where we would end up? Just because he was a weasel didn't mean he deserved to die. He was still my friend.

Now that I had time to stop and think, I knew what to do. I renewed my effort to push a blended Connection link with Protection, Conjuration, and Transformation. Together, these fragments would connect to his spirit, heal it, and break it free.

It was odd to see the fragments at work in this alternate reality, like clouds of shimmering rainbow steam puffing into Falon's face. They drifted lazily through me and then the air, flowing into my enthralled friend.

"Lee," Aaron said, "Farrah is in the pit."

I stared at Aaron with wide eyes. *That's Farrah down there? How could they? She has three freaking babies inside of her. I'm going to kill every one of those bastards.* "Where's Terik?"

"He's dead," Aaron said. "Beheaded, of all things."

My hands flew to my face and squeezed my eyes closed. *That's Terik's head down there.* Tears stung my eyes, remorse overwhelming me. If I hadn't gone with Gran and my mother, none of this would have happened. This was all my fault.

A million questions flew through my head as Aaron and I locked eyes. I couldn't quite decipher the emotion on his face. It was something like confusion or maybe astonishment. Was it because of Terik and Farrah? Or me? He'd said it was all right and that I had eventually made the right choice, but was it enough? Would he forever have the image of me kissing Falon, my legs wrapped around his waist? Did it even matter anymore?

Spirit traded a glance with Aaron, her uncertain expression mirroring his. It made sense for Aaron to make that face if the woman he loved was pinned beneath another man, but why would Spirit be confused? She had known from the start what Falon's intentions were.

"What's going on with you two? Why do you both look like you're trying to translate hieroglyphics?"

"It's . . ." Aaron said, his face contorting. "Just go help Farrah. Be careful, though. The crew are all down there, but they're in a Projection trance. They won't help you and may even try to stop you."

"Except Ward," Spirit said. "They never caught him."

I sighed in relief. At least one good thing had happened. They might have stolen Ward's whole life from him, but he was free now.

"Why is Anick doing this?" I asked. "None of it makes sense. Is he just crazy?"

Aaron eyed me. He appeared calm, but a profound sadness poured out of him like an invisible fragment. "Yes," he said. "But have you noticed anything strange about this world?"

"You mean the lack of women? Nobody wants to have a baby girl because they have no value unless they have a greater reservoir," I said, my thoughts drifting to the one I carried.

Christine.

"That's true," Aaron said, gazing down at my belly with an unreadable expression, "and now no one can find a woman to bond. All the mothers have gotten too old or have been murdered, and there are no daughters to replace them."

"Is that why every man we've met here is so desperate to bond Lina?" Spirit asked.

I blinked, then my eyes shifted to the man lying on top of me. "Because there's no one else?" I felt a little knot forming in my stomach. "That's the only reason? Is that why *you* wanted to bond me, Aaron? Because it was me or nobody?"

Aaron frowned, his attention shifting back up to my face. "That's not what I meant. You know perfectly well that I had other options."

"I guess that's true, but you obviously made the wrong choice. If Farrah had been with you in that cabin, you and I would've never connected, and you'd still be alive."

Aaron's expression was abruptly stricken. His eyes flicked down to my belly one last time, then into my eyes. The intensity of his gaze was muted, like the bottomless depths his eyes once held were now filled with murky water and I could no longer see through to his soul. Yet I *felt* his pain. Whatever bond allowed me to see his spirit let me feel in my bones what I once saw with my eyes. He had lost me, but he had regained something critical as well.

"I wouldn't change a thing," he whispered.

His words shattered something inside me, and the mental block I had been using to push away my grief crumbled into dust. My eyes filled with tears and my throat tightened. I couldn't hold it in. It was my fault Aaron was dead. I hadn't been fast enough, smart enough, good enough. I hadn't been enough of anything.

"Lee," Aaron said, getting down on his knees, close to me. If he had been in a body, I would have felt his minty breath on my face. "What I'm trying to say is that it's not too late."

"What do you mean, Aaron? Of course, it's too late. I can't fight Anick on my own. It's too late for you. It's too late for *us*!"

"But it's not too late for you," Aaron whispered. "You've been given this chance to be the best version of yourself. To rise up and shine like a beacon instead of falling into darkness as I did." The slight quiver in his voice held a deep pain that I felt in every cell of my body. He shook his head, perhaps as in denial as I was, then sighed.

"Anick wants you for a reason," he said. "Go see for yourself. Eve isn't down there."

"Did he kill her?"

Aaron swallowed, that expression of bewilderment back on his face. He was trying to tell me something, but he didn't want to say it outright. "Nobody's *ever* seen her."

"Are you saying Eve isn't real? Because Ward said he heard her once while he was in that cage. And if there's no Eve, then who is Seleca's mother? That doesn't make sense."

"Did Ward *see* her?" Spirit asked.

I shrugged. "I don't think so, but so what? Even if Eve is a ruse, and Anick is desperate for someone to bond like the others, then why doesn't he just go to Earth and find someone, or to the Rhoyal Healers Guild and pick a slave?"

"Why pick a slave when he could have the immortal Avelina of the Rhoyal Dragonrider line?" Spirit commented. "All he has to do is kill the women in line ahead of you and he'll have bonded the queen of Hartha."

Aaron's face darkened at that, as if the event were a foregone conclusion.

"That's right," I said. I'd forgotten that I was technically a princess. "And the bond would last forever because Anick is immortal, like me."

Aaron nodded. "Forever isn't as permanent as people think. Remember, our grandfather killed him."

"*Your* grandfather," I corrected, which made Aaron's face lift a little, a wry smile breaking through. Then, my eyes widened as his point struck home. "Conjuration," I whispered. "Gran has it, so Orion must have gotten it from mixing reservoirs with her."

"Or vice versa," Spirit suggested.

"True," I admitted, "and Gran said that Orion used Evocation to kill Anick, but maybe it was actually Conjuration because the combination of Protection and Absorption would have saved him, even from burning alive."

"Yes," Aaron confirmed. "It would seem that Conjuration is the most powerful of all reservoirs. A conjurer holds the power of life and death in the palm of their hand."

"A rare combination of reservoirs," I breathed. "Anick wanted Conjuration. He must have *let* Orion kill him so that he could acquire it. For that plan to work, he would have had to prepare a path for coming back to life. He never crossed the death bridge, which is why he didn't have to wait until the autumnal equinox. He must have foreseen my future self through Precognition and knew that I was the key to bringing him back."

Seleca's plan wasn't Seleca's plan at all. It was Anick's plan all along. He must have been helping Seleca this whole time—as a ghost. He probably even enthralled her to make her carry out the plan and then followed her around the same way Spirit had followed us. The Machiavellian scope of it was breathtaking.

And impressive, Evilina noted. I pushed her away along with my grudging respect.

"Couldn't he have just absorbed it from Seleca?" Spirit asked.

"No," Aaron replied. "Conjuration is like Protection in that it can't be absorbed from others. It can only be given freely through Connection, and only then if there is a strong bond of affection. If Seleca was enthralled, then she was only compelled to help Anick, she didn't love him."

"Then Seleca must have died to get it," I concluded.

"Or someone we don't know about gave it to her," Spirit commented. "Although it's hard to believe anyone could love Seleca enough to do that, especially if they had Connection and could see inside her."

A light bulb clicked on in my brain. "Gran is an ascendant connector who also has Conjuration, and she was in the hospital with me the day I supposedly died. I'd been set up to believe that I'd gotten it from dying and coming back to life, but if I can't die, then that's impossible. Gran must have given me Conjuration."

"Unless she ripped your soul out of your body," Aaron said.

I shrugged. Either she loved me, or she hated me. Regardless, she gave me Conjuration, but Aaron's comment jogged my brain into action. "That's it. That's the only way to kill him. I have to rip his soul out of his body, but I don't know how to do that, or if I'm even strong enough."

"Actually, that's not the only way," Spirit said.

Aaron turned to give Spirit a withering glare. "It's the best way," he insisted.

"Not for me, it isn't," Spirit countered.

"Don't," Aaron warned, his voice low and deadly.

The two ghosts stared each other down. I looked back and forth between them, confused.

"There it is again," I said. "You two are keeping something important from me, and I want to know what it is. Tell me right now."

Aaron turned his head to me, giving me that expression of confusion again, but this time I recognized it for what it really was. He was conflicted. His face, so similar in color and structure to my grandmother's, had the exact expression as Gran when she'd made that comment about the key's powers, the same comment my mother had reprimanded her for making.

My mother. Is she even my mother anymore? I immediately chastised myself for that thought. Of course she was. She loved me as her daughter. That much was obvious. The mystery of how that came to be was intriguing, but at this juncture, it amounted to irrelevant white noise. But what about Gran? I barely knew her. Why would she trust me with a rare and valuable artifact like the key? She must have had a good reason. Something I was supposed to do.

"Is this about the key?" I guessed.

"Ha!" Spirit exclaimed, not bothering to hide her triumph. "You see? I told you."

Aaron pressed his lips into a line, flicking his eyes to Spirit, then back to me. Neither ghost was fessing up to whatever secret they had. "This wasn't our agreement," he murmured.

"What agreement? Aaron, what's going on? Why can't you tell me?" My anxiety rose up into my throat as my eyes bounded between the two loves of my life. I sensed that, whatever they were keeping from me, I wouldn't like it.

"She deserves to know, Aaron. And quite frankly, *you* deserve for her to know. You know you don't feel the same way you used to. Admit it. Things have changed. *You* have changed."

Suddenly, Falon's "light" weight on top of me felt like a ton of bricks and I couldn't breathe. *Aaron doesn't feel the same way. Things have changed.*

He doesn't love me anymore.

My gaze turned to Falon and then back to Aaron. He didn't deny Spirit's words. I had ruined what we had with my weakness. Even if I could somehow get him back in his body, he was done with me. And I really couldn't blame him. Who could want me after what I'd done? I was literally still underneath another man.

My heart ached to touch him, but I never would again because I broke my promise. *I love you*, I thought, a tear escaping one eye.

"I know," he said aloud. "I can feel it."

Aaron and I locked eyes, but I noticed the crystal key starting to feel hot where it pressed against my skin. My time with Aaron was almost at an end. "Will I see you again?" I asked urgently, pulling the key out so that it wouldn't burn me. I tried to ignore the fact that he hadn't said he loved me back.

Aaron considered me, that expression of uncertainty creeping back over his features. "Yes, I believe you will. Just do me a favor, would you?"

"Anything."

"Forgive me."

I shook my head, another traitorous tear sliding down my face. I was straight-up sobbing now, though I did my best to swallow the sound. "There's nothing to forgive. This is all my fault. I deserve whatever I get."

Aaron didn't respond right away but just frowned at me as if uncertain of what to say, or maybe how to feel. His eyes drifted down to my belly, then away from me, unfocused, then darted back to meet mine as one corner of his mouth ticked up.

"Sometimes it's wiser to break a vow than to keep it," he said, "no matter how dishonorable it might seem. You taught me that. It's not too late, Lee. Go fight. You're the only one who can."

Without warning, the pause in time ended, the light dimmed, and Aaron and Spirit disappeared. Whatever was happening to Spirit clearly had an effect on Aaron too.

Falon lurched back into motion, the sparkly fragments I'd pushed into him disappearing from my sight. Forcing Transformation into another person is painful, and unlike the last time I'd freed someone's mind from a Projection trance, I now had a full and powerful Transformation reservoir.

Falon let go of me and yelped, rolling away.

I hoped his mind was free, but I didn't have time to make sure. I grabbed the head of the key with my right hand and in my left hand clutched the Earth bead, which was the only one I could identify in my haste.

I scrambled after Falon and pushed Teleportation into him, making him instantly disappear from my sight. I didn't see the fragmental glow that usually accompanied the entrance to a bridge—just *poof*, and he was gone. Hopefully, wherever he landed on Earth would be relatively safe and not the middle of a war zone or something.

Well, that's a nifty trick. Maybe I'll send Anick to that planet where dragons surf down volcanoes. That sounds like a well-earned vacation.

I took a breath, slipping the crystal key into the neck of my dress, then I searched for anything that might help me. I had a lantern. That was it.

If only I had a gun. Or a wheelbarrow.

My impeccable movie reference humor is unstoppable.

I rose from the ground with a grunt of effort and picked up the lantern, then I peeked over the edge of the roof. Señor Body Snatcher was talking to *Fucking* Seleca, who was staring up in my direction, smirking.

On second thought, maybe Seleca is the one who might enjoy a little lava luge. Unless she's been enthralled by Anick? The thought made my head hurt. What if she was a victim this whole time?

Seleca and I locked eyes, and I ground my teeth. Upon seeing her look at me, so smug, so triumphant, I felt my anger and hatred give birth to overwhelming despair. The town was officially enslaved. Anick had returned and taken Aaron's body, which had only been possible because his relationship with me had given him Conjuration. I was so focused on getting Ward back that I hadn't even considered that possibility. Seleca's Projection skills must have overcome Aaron's Protection, something Aaron had warned me about. Why do I never listen?

Even if I were able to get him back in his body, it was over. I had failed. I was completely alone and deserved to be. I might have flung myself off that roof right then if I had thought it would work. Except that I couldn't think like that anymore now that I had a child to protect.

Just use the key and get out of here, Evilina thought. *Falon still wants you. Go find him and escape. Run away on an adventure like Peter Pan and Wendy.*

No, I thought. *Peter Pan was an immature dickhead. Not to mention that Jorin and the rest of my crew are still down there. Farrah is in the pit. I have to save them.*

That's why they're down there, to draw you in, Evilina thought. Or was it Axelina now? I'd absorbed a part of his poisonous soul, hadn't I? From now on, I'd always question if my thoughts were my own or if they were some Axel-colored version of me, but did it really matter? I'd had a dark side prior to that event anyway, and lord knows I'd been changed by my Teleportation ascension. This was who I was now; might as well make the best of it.

It's not your job to save the world, Evilina continued, unfazed by my identity crisis. *You probably can't do anything anyway. It's not your fault that these people are in trouble. You're not even from this godforsaken planet. Just go back to Darion-Ájar and tell your family that you failed. Let the grown-ups handle it.*

Don't be a hypocrite, I answered myself. *You can't complain that people treat you like a child, then go run home to Mommy when things get hard. You promised Farrah that you would be there when she needed you. Are you really going to break* another *promise?*

I sighed. *Okay. Apparently, we're going down there.* And this, dear children, is why Zig and I both consider ourselves crazy. The lesson here is simple. Don't absorb people's reservoirs, don't ascend Teleportation, and don't do drugs. It just isn't worth it. Unless it's *porfinkaramendi* mushroom from the planet Feldákin and you're in the company of the Forest Clan of Yeti. That one is well worth the trouble. Trust me on this.

I studied the street below. People were packed in, and they all stared up at me. If I jumped, Christine and I would heal, but I might kill somebody if I landed on them. I'd have to go down the rickety stairs.

"Avelina, stop fretting," Anick's deceptively soothing voice came to me from the square. "Let my followers bring you here. There's nothing to be afraid of."

"I'm not afraid, Nick," I said. "I'm pissed!"

From somewhere far away, Spirit laughed.

Chapter Twenty

*L*inorra watched in horror as Queen Mortier was pulled into her own spell like a wayward boat into a whirlpool. She had intended to rid herself of the evil queen, but she had not meant to banish her to the outer realms, for that was a fate worse than death. Linorra was convinced that Mortier's screamed curse would be forever burned into her memory, along with the woman's look of pure hatred. She knew that she would fear it for the rest of her days.

The crowd of überzombies dumped me on the central pavilion's dais like a sack of potatoes. After breaking through the wooden wall *next* to Falon's durrite fortification, Anick's thralls had carried me all the way down the stairs, still surrounded by my shield, like a princess in her palanquin chair. Then the mob had shifted me hand to hand to where Anick awaited. The shield did little to block the uninvited warmth of their hands on my body as they scooted me along with no more control than a crowd-surfing beach ball.

I scrambled to my feet on the dais, ready to fight or run, whichever came first. Anick, who wore an upsettingly pale and exhausted version of Aaron's face, followed me with his eyes but didn't approach. Instead, he motioned to Markus and Regalinius, who hefted an ornate wooden chair onto the dais and set it down behind him. They placed another smaller seat to his left, after which Regalinius appeared as if he might drop dead from a stroke, with sweat streaming down his pink face.

Anick tossed Terik's head to Regalinius and sat on the larger of the two chairs, casually crossing one knee over the other. Bright red blood still dripped from Anick's hands and clothing, and splattered Regalinius's face and tunic when he caught the head, causing him to flinch. The whole thing made my stomach turn, and I clamped my teeth together to keep down what little I had eaten.

Anick smirked, then dusted his hands as if he'd just finished an immensely satisfying project. The blood disappeared from his skin and clothing. I glanced down at my ruined dress and sighed. It had been a really long day.

His seat looked every bit the throne it was intended to be. It had been transformed from a piece of redwood and was intricately detailed to depict symbols of the Ministry. Visible just behind Anick's head, a golden *V* was set into the throne's seatback, which then fanned to display its gold-dipped branches. The seat and arms were cushioned and covered with a deep purple velvet that twisted up, intertwining with those branches to create a braid.

Perched atop the throne was the statue of a golden eagle identical to the tattoo I'd seen on the people of Wishmere.

"Avelina Silva," Regalinius said, still holding the dripping corpse head, "it is my honor to introduce Anick Aetos, the Ascended Father, Supreme Ruler of the twelve realms, Noble Protector of the People, Seer of All Things, and your lord and master. You may approach and bow before him."

I went ahead and didn't do that.

Regalinius returned to where Markus, Seleca, and Axel stood behind Anick's throne. He tossed Terik's head behind him, then bowed his head like a good little minion. Shane,

THE WISDOM OF DISHONOR

Fitch, Ellis and Jorin still knelt behind them, at the very back of the dais, likely recaptured in a Projection trance. My heart went out to them, especially Ellis, but there was nothing I could do at the moment.

No one dared look up except Markus, who frowned at me, narrowing his eyes.

Interesting. Is he not enthralled like the others?

"No introduction for me, Reggie?" I asked.

Regalinius glanced up, surprised that I had addressed him. He cleared his throat, then coughed, wiping his bulbous nose with the back of his hand. Sweat dripped down his round face, which appeared more reddened than when I met him only a day ago.

"Go ahead, Reggie," Anick said, his tone amused.

"M-my lord," Regalinius stammered, "may I present Avelina Giana Dragona Silva, daughter of Giana Dragona Silva . . . uh . . ." My gaze flicked back to Markus. His shrewd attention bounced between me and his father, his brow furrowing further.

"Granddaughter of Linorra Dragona," Regalinius continued, "of the Rhoyal Dragonrider line, grandniece of Queen Harthar-a-Dragona, and"—he discretely counted his fingers—"th-third in line to the throne of Harthar-a-Minh of the Ascended Father's second realm." Regalinius exhaled, his pop quiz complete.

Markus's eyebrows shot up as Regalinius listed the last association, clearly as surprised as I was.

Third in line? I masked my own astonishment and suppressed the image I had of my mother's stricken face as I stalked away from her. Was that why it was such a secret that I'm adopted?

"I think he forgot a few," I said to Anick. Regalinius's eyes snapped to me, panic written all over his face. "Beloved of Aaron Atticus, who this so-called 'Ascended Father' is now impersonating. Badly." *Former beloved, I should say.* "Friend to Terik O'Feld, whose head you tossed to that sweaty jackass over there, and soulmate to Spirit Desinot. All dead because of you."

But not Falon.

I sent that last thought to Markus through the air, knowing that he wouldn't be able to respond since he didn't have Connection. *Nod if you understand, Markus. Falon is fine. I sent him to Earth.*

Markus blinked, then relaxed a little, nodding discreetly.

At least he cares about his brother, I thought.

"Beloved?" Anick asked, scowling. "Don't be ridiculous. You overestimate that man's ability to love anyone, let alone someone he just met two months ago."

I eyed Anick, analyzing his tight expression. *Is that jealousy?*

"I guess I'm just more lovable than most," I suggested.

"I've always thought so," Anick conceded, his eyes raking over me from head to toe. I still couldn't identify his accent. Greek, maybe? Like his name? I realized as I glared at him that I didn't actually know anything about him, though he acted like he knew me well.

"I'm always impressed when anyone resists me. Very few manage it. Of course, the last one who did was your grandmother. How is she, by the way? Still enjoying Darion-Ájar with your mother and father?"

I paused for a breath. How did he know that? "I'm not sure," I hedged. "Perhaps I should ask my grandfather. You remember him, don't you?"

Anick laughed, his face filled with sincere pleasure. Unlike Aaron's laugh, which was always suppressed, this was a jolly, hearty laugh. It was unsettling to hear that uninhibited sound come out of Aaron's mouth.

"This is a fun game," he said, "but I know perfectly well that you can't see Orion's spirit. Or at least, I sincerely hope you can't. I've always been open-minded, but even I draw the line at incestuous necrophilia."

Huh? I'd never had much of a poker face, so I couldn't completely hide my confusion.

Anick chuckled. "I see you haven't ferreted out every secret. You can't see a person's ghost unless you mixed reservoirs with them while they had a body. That's how the bond is formed—it's a literal mixing of souls. Since Orion died before you were born, and is technically your grandfather, seeing his spirit would be rather disturbing, don't you think?"

I scoffed. "You've possessed a man's body and you're lecturing me on what is and is not disturbing? Please. And in any case, Orion isn't really my grandfather."

Anick's eyes narrowed, then darted around as if to see who might have heard my revelation. As far as I could tell, everyone in the plaza had their eyes downcast except Markus, who quickly averted his gaze when his master turned toward him.

Anick sighed, then he stood, evidently abandoning his attempt to get me to sit with him. He casually closed the distance between us and leaned toward me. I would have backed away, but I didn't have anywhere to go. I was right at the edge of the dais with a mob of thralls to catch me if I fell.

"They told you then," he murmured. "I wondered what happened after you left the Dragona estate. But did they tell you why you were taken in by the Silva family, or why they didn't tell you sooner?"

I blinked. I had, in fact, just contemplated why my adoption had been a secret. One side of Anick's mouth lifted when I didn't respond, like he knew he had me.

"Why not sit with me so I can answer your questions?" he suggested. "Take your shield down so we can have a productive conversation. I have no intention of harming you. In any case, if I wanted to, that shield wouldn't stop me. I think you know that."

"You can't kill me regardless, and I think *you* know that," I countered weakly, still thrown off by the unsettling knowledge gap that clearly existed between us, not to mention the fact that he'd somehow manipulated me into listening to him in the first place. "I don't want anything from you except that body you stole, so why don't you just release the woman and go back into the light where you belong."

Anick leaned forward, his face alight with keen interest. "Ah, but the death bridge is for regular people, not for immortals like us."

I pressed my lips together. Anick had just confirmed that he'd never crossed the death bridge. Had he been following me as a ghost? If he had, then wouldn't Spirit have noticed him? At the very least, my suspicion that he'd been helping if not directing Seleca had been correct. It was all a part of his plan.

"You *let* Orion kill you, didn't you?" I asked. "So that you could absorb Conjuration, but you knew I would come along before too long and give you the chance to come back."

Anick smiled warmly at me. "You see? You and I have always thought alike, Avelina. Or should I say Evilina? That was always my favorite part of you, the part that I fell in love with so many years ago."

What in the hell is he talking about? Anick acted like we were old friends or maybe lovers, like he *knew* me. It was possible that he'd been following me as a ghost for so long that he *did* know me, perhaps better than anyone. The strangest part was that, now that I stood in front of him, I wasn't afraid. I should have been shaking in my boots, but instead of brainstorming ways to rid the world of him, I was focused on lecturing him about how rude it was to steal a man's body.

Anick dropped his eyes, scratching the beard on that stolen face I'd come to love, and turned to his line of minions. An instant later, Axel glanced up like someone had called his name. He appeared unwell, with pocked, grayish skin and wild hair only half pulled into a tail at the nape of his neck. Perhaps he had been dead a little too long before Seleca brought him back, or maybe it was because a piece of his soul was missing.

He nodded to Anick, a manic grin spreading across his face, then he jumped off the dais and made his way to a small shed that stood a little way off from the pit. Pulling a key from his pocket, he unlocked and opened the door, but before going through it, he turned his evil grin on me.

When he saw that I was watching him, his smile widened unnaturally like he was the Grinch getting a wonderful, awful idea. A chill ran through me that even my Evocation reservoir couldn't quell. Axel laughed softly, then slithered through the door, closing it behind him.

"My nephew didn't make the transition well," Anick commented, turning back to me.

"Your nephew?" I asked.

"Axel," he said. "Of course, I wouldn't expect him to do it as well as I did, but I'm disappointed all the same."

My eyes widened at the revelation. I'd heard that Seleca was Anick's daughter, but I hadn't known about Axel's familial relationship. Did that make Axel Seleca's cousin?

"It might surprise you that I care very much about my family," Anick commented, his eyes tracking me as I inched to one side to avoid being left without anywhere to run.

"So, you have a sibling?" I asked casually. This might be the only time I could gather information on this lunatic.

"I do," he confirmed, his focus lowering to my belly. I wasn't showing yet, but if he was paying attention, then he might be able to sense Christine's faint resonances.

Though he had Aaron's features, seeing that covetous expression turned him into a truly distinct individual. His was a fierce gaze that promised to excavate my darkest secrets. There would be no mistaking this person for the man I loved.

"What do you want, *Anick*?"

Anick took a moment to breathe in and out, perhaps considering his next words. "Is it his face that's bothering you? If I showed you my true face, it might help you remember."

"Remember what? This is the first time I've ever met you. All I know about you is that you plan centuries in advance how to kill people and steal bodies."

"Actually, I'm not that good of a planner. You are, though. You're as good as Violet Atticus. Better in some ways because you've always been able to see both the good and bad in people, to see what they could have been under different circumstances. Who would have guessed that you'd be right about the Dragon?"

The Dragon . . . Aaron?

Anick studied my face. "The Dragon of Minh, Aaron Atticus, the traitor who led an unprovoked attack on Neesee, killing thousands of people."

There was no hiding my befuddlement. Even if I'd heard of a recent major attack on the city—which I hadn't—Aaron had gone from SONA straight into the woods. When could he possibly have done that? And the Dragon of *Minh*? To my knowledge, our visit to Gran's house was the first time he'd ever been to Minh.

"You're insane," I whispered. I continued inching away, moving ever so slowly toward the pit side of the dais.

My words seemed to ignite Anick. His voice sharpened, becoming clipped as he continued. "The man who deemed you a mortal enemy and vowed to kill you over and over again, no matter how many times it took, whom *you* pledged to destroy at all costs so that we could save our people."

Our people?

Anick sighed out his frustration, his face reddening as he slowly pursued me. "Try to remember," he insisted. Then, as a golden glow spilled from his skin, he transformed.

His body shortened an inch or so, and his skin lightened a few shades. His hair also changed, becoming a chestnut brown very close to my own hair color, and his eyes darkened to a more cobalt blue, taking on a familiar, rounder shape. Aaron's long nose shortened and straightened out as Anick took on a leaner, narrower build.

He did, in fact, look vaguely familiar. Then he said, in a voice entirely different than Aaron's, "I know there's still a spark of that memory somewhere inside you, Eve."

I stilled, my entire body tensing as déjà vu struck me again.

Eve?

The nickname, directed at me, and spoken with that voice, triggered something buried deep within my unconscious mind. I had thought his Projection had put the uncomfortable feeling there before, but now I was surrounded by my shield, so it couldn't be.

Eve—it's short for Evilina.

"Aaron was right," I murmured. "Eve was never real."

"Eve was always real," Anick said. "You just couldn't remember."

I stared at him, my brain struggling to dislodge the memory from wherever it was stuck. *I had called him* . . . "Nick," I said.

"Yes, love," Anick whispered, his eyes burning with hope.

"No," I said, pointing an accusing finger at his chest. "No! You don't get to call me that. You don't even know me."

"You don't remember me because you lost your Precognition, but I do know you. I understand you better than anyone because I have been with you longer than you can imagine. I have seen you try and fail to be like the common people around you. I stood by you when your body was burned to ash, then I watched you rise like a phoenix to tear your enemies apart. I have loved you in both our lives, my Eve."

"Lives? There is no such thing as reincarnation. So just stop. This won't work on me." My voice sounded firm, but my mind was far from it. I had a terrible feeling that he was sincere, but I would have done anything to make it not true.

I flinched as Anick took the last step toward me, nearly falling backward off the dais. He leaned his stolen body toward mine as if going in for a kiss. "Not reincarnation," he insisted, peering down at me through half-lidded eyes. He practically rested on my shield. I could smell him through it, like blood and smoke and something else that surprised me even more than his earnest expression of yearning. He smelled like my redwoods—like home.

I froze, my eyes widening. I could not help but inhale deeply of that dearest scent. It shook something loose in me that had been trying to curl up and die. A vision of him—a memory—flashed through my mind. His lips on mine as he pulled me toward him in a brief, desperate embrace. We had been in a hurry to get somewhere. Where, I had no idea, but he had been in a panic, scared of something or someone.

"How?" is all I could croak out.

"My father created a powerful skipstone, a diamond bridge key marked with an hourglass that calls a bridge to take you anywhere. And for those who have ascended Teleportation, it can take you back in time. The queen of Hartha stole it from us, but it belongs to my family."

I resisted the urge to place my hand on the spot where the key rested beneath the collar of my dress. That's what my grandmother meant when she said that I'd be able to use it to its fullest capacity after I ascended. I had thought the key was marked with a number eight, but it was an hourglass.

"We used it to undo the damage the Dragon inflicted after he destroyed everything we built together. The only ones who remember other lives are those with Precognition and the one who activates the key."

"What about ghosts?"

"Ghosts, too, now that you mention it." He smiled at that. "They aren't time-locked, so they see everything. I suppose the Dragon was livid at what we'd done to him once he'd been kicked out of his body and remembered how much he used to hate you. You can take credit for that because this whole plan . . . it was *yours*, Eve, with my expert advice, of course. But the goal was never to defeat me. It was to defeat the Dragon. And it worked. We got him."

Not Anick's plan. Mine. Ours.

"I was there with you that day in the forest when you relearned how to use a shield and used it to ruin Seleca's plans. I never told her you were protected because *you* asked me not to. That was the day I knew your plan had worked, the day the great Dragon of Minh finally succumbed to your will."

If what Anick said was true, and Aaron's spirit remembered that he used to hate me, that might explain why he'd been so confused. My brain ran through the conversation I'd had with Aaron and Spirit during the time pause, reanalyzing.

You know you don't feel the same way you used to, Spirit had said. *You have changed.*

Spirit wasn't saying he didn't love me anymore but that he didn't *hate* me anymore, like he did in other timelines.

Sometimes it's wiser to break a vow than to keep it, no matter how dishonorable it might seem. Was Aaron saying that we should both break that vow to destroy each other?

"It wasn't as perfect as you'd hoped," Anick continued, unaware that I'd retreated into my own thoughts. "Seleca's always been a little . . . overzealous. Her hunger for power developed faster than last time, and now here we are in a world of almost no women. But, in fairness, I think we both underestimated her ability to take perfectly good plans and coax them into an unmitigated disaster."

He took a deep breath in, then out, releasing a soft, frustrated growl. "And now Violet's underhanded deviation from the plan has, once again, created a dark future."

My brain seized, then stumbled to a halt at that. *Violet's deviation from the plan? She had been* in *on the plan? That can't be.*

"Of course, *I* suspected she would," Anick continued. "She's the Dragon's mother, after all. But that is why I need your help to clean up this mess. Just let me give you back your Precognition, and you will see that I'm telling the truth."

My mind was sluggish and fuzzy, like I'd woken up from a deep sleep. I had the irrational urge to lie down, but a woman's screaming cut through the fog.

Farrah.

"Let Farrah go so we can talk about this calmly," I said, shaking off the feeling. "She's done nothing wrong."

Anick glanced toward the pit, then back at me. "In exchange for what?"

I had no answer for that. Was I really going to give myself to this man who thought he knew me, yet still thought I'd watch him torture a pregnant woman and then just go with him like nothing was wrong? Especially when I was pregnant myself? That was insane. Yet, he seemed confident. Perhaps the Dragon had been right about us. Maybe his hatred toward me had been justified. The thought was like a stone in my gut.

Anick breathed in and out, his eyes trained on my face, then reached into his coat and pulled out a durrite bonding cuff. It was large enough that it would cover my entire forearm, and on the wrist was emblazoned the symbol of the golden eagle. Above the eagle, twelve crystals were embedded, each a different color, much like the crystal key. It was impressive and far too extravagant for someone like me, the girl who doesn't wear jewelry. It was strangely familiar, but I could never imagine myself choosing to wear such a gaudy piece of jewelry. That thing belonged on a queen, not me.

"You remember this, don't you, Eve? You always loved this cuff." To my shock, Anick got down on one knee in front of me so that his eyes were just below mine. "There is only one woman in the twelve realms who could wear it. Come with me, and you'll never have to fear being who you truly are. Bond to me again, and from this point forward you will be celebrated as the goddess, Eve Aetos. Take down your shield and give me your arm. Then, I will release the girl and the rest of your crew. You will need them when you are ruling this planet with me."

"What?" Seleca protested.

Anick's face shifted to a scowl in a split second. He twisted to look at Seleca and flicked his hand at her. She released a brief cry, falling to the ground. Her hand clamped over her right eye, which now dripped with blood. Anick motioned to a wide-eyed Markus, who then scampered over to Seleca, picked her up like a baby, and carried her off the dais. I scanned the faces of the rest of my crew, but no one raised their heads from a bowed position.

Anick turned back to me, his face once again a mask of calm confidence. "My love, for the last one hundred years, I've waited for you to be reborn. I stayed away, as you requested, until the time came. It was torture, but I did it because I love you, Eve. Together, we have finally saved the twelve realms from the Dragon and his vicious family, and now it's time for you to come home, as you vowed to do. I've waited for you long enough. It's time. Give me your left hand."

"My left hand?" I asked.

"Yes," he said, impatience creeping into his voice. "The right gives. The left receives. Take down your shield and let me give to you. Come home to your family, Eve, your true family."

There was that expression again, so sincere. He said I'd vowed to return to him. Had I really lived another lifetime at his side as his wife? His queen?

I pondered these questions a moment before an even worse question jumped out and slapped me. Did Aaron deserve this fate?

Spirit had hinted that there was another way to get Aaron back into his body, one that would also help her. She must have been referring to the key, but Aaron hadn't thought that was a good idea. Maybe that was because, now that he remembered what he had done, he knew he didn't deserve to be brought back.

I loved Aaron, but if he really had murdered thousands of people, then who was I to unleash that back upon the world? On the other hand, whose word did I trust more, Aaron's or Anick's? After everything I'd been through, it didn't seem possible that I had been on the wrong side.

But it is possible, Evilina, Axelina, and I all agreed. *And there's really only one way to find out, isn't there?*

"Precognition first," I said. "Then we'll see."

Anick released a breath, then nodded. His eyes had reddened to the point that I thought he might cry. He wiped one eye quickly, as if he feared the same thing, then held out a hand to me, a look of pleading on his face.

I stared at his hand, fully aware that this could either be a huge mistake or the only way to do the right thing, and there was no way to tell which it would be. "All right," he said.

"All right," I echoed, then after one more moment of hesitation, I dropped the shield.

Chapter Twenty-One

Linorra hadn't thought herself capable of such a monstrous act against another human, but she was quite capable, it would seem. Quite capable indeed. She laid her cheek against Syndeth's warm snout.

"I would do far worse for you, my dearest friend," she whispered.

The roar that erupted when I took Anick's hand was deafening. I had assumed that Anick's followers were in a silent trance, and that they couldn't react even if they wanted to. That was far from the case. Jorin and the crew sprang to their feet in excitement, embracing one another like their team had just won Olympic gold. The sudden clapping and joyful exuberance from the crowd surprised the hell out of me such that I literally jumped into Anick's waiting arms.

I stiffened as he hugged me tightly, burying his face in my neck. He inhaled my scent, then he groaned against my skin. The strangest thing about it was that it didn't feel weird. It felt familiar. Safe, even.

"Forgive me, love, but it's been too long. I missed you so much." He laughed, relief spilling out of him. "The Eboros boy is lucky you sent him away. I trusted you to handle it, but he was in serious danger of losing his head like that O'Feld demon."

Oh, right. He'd murdered Terik and stolen Aaron's body and Evocation. He'd also tried to capture me in Projection and had successfully enthralled an entire city. This universal excitement over my decision to drop my shield was far from normal. As jovial as he seemed, I couldn't let myself forget who Anick was. Still, it felt damn good to have a crowd of people clap for me, especially after I'd spent years wondering why people thought I was so odd.

"Put me down, please, and let Farrah go. She's pregnant for Christ's sake."

"I already did that. I sent Axel down there to release her. I didn't invent the pit, I'll have you know. In truth, I find it distasteful. Luckily, there's no need for it now that I've returned."

"But you let them hang her by her ankles," I accused.

Anick's smile dropped from his face. "Of course I didn't. She's just sitting down there in a chair. She's in no danger whatsoever."

"I heard her scream," I insisted.

Anick pursed his lips. "Ah, sorry. That was just Reflection. The danger was never real." His amused expression told me that he wasn't sorry at all but very proud of himself.

My mouth dropped open for a second before I snapped it shut. I still had so much to learn.

"First of all, you tricked me. Not cool. And second, if she's down there with Axel, then the danger *is* real. You called Terik a demon, but Axel is far worse. And now he's a zombie—a literal monster—and you sent him down into the pit to handle a pregnant woman he used to covet like a prized Christmas turkey."

Anick smiled, showing perfectly straight white teeth. He was conventionally handsome, which I'm sure he knew well.

"Same old Eve," he said, utterly untroubled by my concerns. He turned to Regalinius, who still stood frozen next to Jorin and the crew, his eyes on the ground.

Regalinius was not among those who had joined in the celebration. I wondered if he regretted not helping me now that he knew who I was. That would explain why he'd been so nervous while introducing me. His face jerked up to peer at Anick, who gestured at the pit without speaking aloud. Regalinius nodded, having received his instructions telepathically, I assumed, then he hurried off to intervene in what would likely be an unpleasant encounter.

THE WISDOM OF DISHONOR

"There. Reggie will take care of it. No harm will come to the fair Farrah. Now, let's get started, shall we?"

Anick instructed his followers to go forth in peace while we completed the reservoir transfer. It was after midnight, but most of the people of Neesee would likely be up until dawn celebrating. Not only because it was Harvest, but also because the Ascended Mother, Eve, had finally been relieved from her period of mourning. She'd emerged from seclusion to join with the newly risen Ascended Father, Anick. It was a time of great miracles the likes of which promised to usher in a golden age of peace and prosperity. Or something like that. Anick was a hell of a public speaker. Even I got chills, and I wasn't even enthralled.

My guess was that he mostly just didn't want anyone to see him fail at giving me Precognition since he'd never done it before. Passive transfer of a reservoir during intimacy is one thing, but intentional transfer is quite another. It requires a blended link of Connection plus Conjuration, which he'd only just acquired. Anick was a lot like me in that regard. He craved approval and would go to extreme lengths to avoid revealing himself as imperfect.

As I sank into my smaller but surprisingly comfortable throne, we waited for the crowd to disperse. I kept checking the outbuilding, expecting Regalinius to escort Farrah out, but they never appeared. The longer I waited, the more nervous I became. When the pavilion was finally empty of everyone except us, Jorin, and the crew, we began.

Anick stood before me for a moment, taking in the sight of me lounging on my throne with a tender expression on his elegant face before he knelt at the foot of my chair. He held my hand, then extended a Connection link. Even the superficial link that allowed thoughts to flow through felt like a cozy blanket that I wanted to snuggle into.

Ready?

I nodded. Doubt nagged at me, but I ignored it. If what Anick said about Aaron was true, then it might be just as dangerous to choose him. Aaron had asked me to forgive him, but I didn't know if that would be possible once I knew the truth.

I'm sorry, Aaron, I thought, wondering if he'd watched this whole interaction, *but I have to know.*

I closed my eyes, then opened the door to my mental Protection just a crack, letting Anick in. His Connection fragment rushed in, filling my mind with his warm presence, a feeling that should have been awkward and foreign but was instead as familiar as inhaling the aroma of my morning coffee.

I missed this, Anick thought, his accent disappearing entirely. *I missed you.*

His voice was a caress, gliding through my mind as smoothly as if he stroked my cheek. I almost made a joke about him giving good head but stopped myself when I remembered where I was. He heard anyway and laughed in my mind and out loud.

You've made that joke before, love, he thought, *and then I proved how right you were.* He showed me his memory of the event through a rapid-fire sequence of images. It had been a night of bisexual group sex where Anick and I were both with men and women.

He's bi, like me, I thought with awe. My body reacted like it remembered that night, too, and I squeezed my thighs together against the heat building in my core. I took a deep breath in and out, willing it to go away. Anick's concentrated attention was a powerful aphrodisiac—one I had a hard time resisting.

He squeezed my hand, rubbing his thumb in circles on the inside of my wrist, another habit that felt familiar. *You are so cute when you're nervous*, he thought, *but there will be plenty of time for that and more. I am going to give you everything, my Eve.* He took his own steadying breath and then reached for Conjuration, but it floated through his grasp like smoke.

It likes to hide, I thought. *You have to call to it and command it to come to you as if it were a living thing.*

I felt Anick suppress his annoyance that I knew something he didn't, then he tried again, following my instructions. With a grunt of effort, he pushed Conjuration through our Connection link. For an instant, his immense satisfaction that he was able to accomplish his goal rushed through me, but that sensation was quickly wiped out by a nauseating tremor that overtook my body.

Conjuration is unlike any other fragment. It's there, but it's also not there, like a ghost. I think that's why you can't just grab onto it with your mind but have to coax it to you. When Conjuration fragment enters your body from someone else's reservoir, it feels cold in the same way that nothingness feels cold, almost like the fragment itself is a bridge trying to suck you into deep space, only to deposit you into a black hole. Like it is, itself, a death bridge. It's fragging creepy as hell.

Anick was startled by my reaction to the Conjuration fragment, but he quickly moved to push in Precognition, which, if you can believe this, is even worse than Conjuration. Or at least, the combination of the two is. Conjuration and Precognition are two fragments that have a strong affinity because they both affect the spirit. Where Conjuration works outwardly, giving you access to and, to a degree, control over the spirit of others, Precognition works inwardly by giving you access to everything your own spirit knows, whether your brain retains it or not. That's why people with Precognition remember previous timelines.

In retrospect, we should have been more careful about combining fragments we knew little about, but Anick and I were always arrogant and reckless, especially as a team. I know that now. I think, for that reason, it's sometimes better to be with a partner who is different from you rather than one who magnifies all your worst traits by adding their own. It's good to be with someone who complements you, like Protection does with Evocation. Combining Conjuration with Precognition is more like combining vinegar and baking soda.

My head exploded with pain before I passed out. I don't think it actually erupted in real life, but I can tell you that when I woke up, I was covered in fresh blood, an indication of my second eyeball-related injury of the day.

Anick's face, too, was splattered with my blood, and he was healing me. Ellis stood over me, holding a lantern to shine light on my injuries. Fitch and Shane stood just behind him, silently watching. I stared into their worried faces, baffled as to how their minds could have justified their sudden change of allegiance. And what about Cobb? The plight of my crew was just as much my fault as Aaron's death.

"Well, that was a good first try," Anick said matter-of-factly.

My head pounded, and there was a ringing in my ears so loud that I could barely hear what he said. He had his hands on both sides of my face, pushing Protection. I felt the tingling sensation of the actual healing tissues, but I didn't feel the pleasure of the fragment.

"Why can't I feel you healing me?"

"Protection healing is highly addictive," he answered. "I'm blocking the sensation with Connection and Reflection." Anick lowered his eyes, then dropped his hands. Setting them on top of mine, he added, "You taught me how to do it."

Cool.

Having finished his task, he glanced at Ellis, who hurried to wipe my face with his own shirt. These men had been my friends. Now they were servants who didn't speak unless spoken to.

I waved Ellis away, then averted my eyes. I could easily imagine myself as a queen, ruling from a throne. I had pretended as much as a girl, but that vision had never included a retinue of überzombies, and especially not these men. The loyalty of men like this should be earned, not stolen.

"Did it work?" I asked, my voice subdued.

Anick paused, narrowing his eyes as if listening for something. I hoped he didn't detect how unsettled I was. "I feel the resonance, but it's faint, definitely lesser. I doubt it will be enough. Do you remember anything?"

I stared at him, waiting for a glimmer of added recognition, but there was nothing. "No," I said, masking my relief.

"Well, perhaps if you ascended another reservoir—"

A scream interrupted him. I shot to my feet as a thin tendril of smoke rose from the pit in curling wisps, nearly invisible under the night sky.

"Is that Reflection again?" I asked hopefully.

Anick stood up beside me, utterly undisturbed by the sound, but he didn't answer. On impulse, I raised my shield and stepped away from him. Something was wrong here, and I'd bet Jorin's boat that I was the only one who didn't know what it was.

"Your shield isn't necessary," Anick said through clenched teeth.

"We'll see." I jogged over to the edge of the dais and jumped off, running over to the grate at the top of the pit. Contrary to what Anick had claimed, Farrah hung there from her ankles, swinging upside down over a fire.

Beside the fire, in a bloody heap, lay Regalinius's mangled corpse, the flickering light of the fire reflecting off a growing pool of blood beneath him.

"No!" a male voice shouted from a narrow doorway within the pit. Barely noticeable in the shadows, stood Markus. His distraught expression only became visible in the light of the fire as he rushed up to his father's body, a grinning Axel just behind him. Markus didn't appear to notice Axel as the crazed man raised a wooden spear, his intentions clear.

"Markus! Behind you!" I screamed. But it was too late. Axel brought the spear down on Markus just as he turned around, plunging it into his chest and out the other side.

I gasped as Markus was shoved down and pinned to his father's body. Blood soaked his tunic, spilling out and adding to the pool he landed in. Axel stared at his work, one arm still holding the spear while the other stretched out toward the dying man like he wanted to caress him.

I can still save him, I thought desperately. I'd have to take my shield down to heal him through the air, if I could even do that. I'd never tried it before. The shed where Axel had entered the pit wasn't too far. If I could just—

"It's locked," Anick said calmly. I turned to see him peering down into the pit with an irritated expression. "And in any case, it's too late. The boy is already dead. A shame. I liked him."

"I can bring him back," I insisted.

"Ah, I suppose so, but can you deal with Axel in time to save the boy? I think not. Not to mention that you now have another problem. Look."

I followed Anick's line of sight back down into the pit. Beside Axel, Seleca now stood, talking to him in hushed tones. When her eyes landed on me, her right eye still bloodshot, she smirked, then she held a hand out to the firepit. Toward Farrah.

No.

A stream of fire erupted from her fingers, spreading not only to the logs, but also to Farrah herself. She screamed as her raven hair caught on fire, then coughed uncontrollably, rattling her chains as she thrashed.

"Seleca, stop!" I roared. *She has Evocation? But she didn't before, so she must have been the one to take it from Aaron. Did Anick have Evocation the whole time?* My shocked expression only made her smile widen while Axel cackled like a madman. I sucked in a breath as he yanked his spear free of Markus, then raised it again, aiming it right at Farrah's belly.

Fuck.

Beside me, Anick groaned like a man who'd forgotten to bring his lunch to work. He'd looked angrier when I lifted my shield again.

"Do something," I pleaded.

"Take down your shield," he countered, "and put on your cuff. Then, you'll be a queen, and you can have anything you like, just like you've always wanted."

I stared at him, open-mouthed. *No, it isn't. Is it?* My mind raced. *Is that who I was the last time he was alive?*

Mostly, in that moment, I felt stupid. Anick claimed to love me and fancied himself a hero who would save the world from a "dark future," as he put it, but only a monster could watch a pregnant woman being tortured and use it to negotiate. Hello, red flag, terrible to see you again. To make matters worse, he'd supposedly spent years with me and still didn't understand me at all. I racked my brain trying to figure out what I had ever seen in this man.

Gran's voice came to me then. *Never assume that you can change a man. Assume instead that you can't change a damned thing and decide whether you can live with him the way he is.*

Once upon a time, I might have been someone who could live with careless cruelty, but that timeline was dead and gone. I didn't need to see the past to know what I wanted for my future.

It's not too late for you, Aaron had said. *You've been given this chance to be the best version of yourself. To rise up and shine like a beacon instead of falling into darkness as I did.* I closed my eyes, a pang of grief eating away at me.

Maybe it's not too late for either of us, Aaron.

I placed my hand over my belly, contemplating my choices. I wasn't showing yet. I felt no different at all. If I went far enough back in time, it could be like my pregnancy never happened. This was why my mother and grandmother were so upset when they found out that I was pregnant. They knew it would make this choice that much harder. My mother had implied that being a protector made it difficult to conceive.

This could be my only chance. That's why Mom was crying. God, I was such a bitch to her.

I closed my eyes, my mind cluttered with all the downstream repercussions. If I went back, I could save Aaron *and* Spirit. Terik and Delya too. Now Markus, Farrah, and her litter were added to the list as well. If I stayed, I could *maybe* figure out how to put Aaron back in his own body, but that wasn't a given, and it wouldn't help the others. It all came down to who I wanted to save more: Aaron and my friends, or this unexpected but not entirely unwanted baby girl.

Not entirely unwanted. Wanted, in fact. Even if I got pregnant again, would it be Christine? Who knows when the pregnancy happened? For all I knew, it could have been as little as a few days ago. Or a month. When it came down to it, going back in time would risk her life no matter what.

My hand still rested on my nonexistent bump. Even if Aaron agreed to it, which wasn't a given, trying to get pregnant with the same baby over again would be like trying to breathe exactly the same air I did last time. Only a miracle could make that happen. It would be like . . . *chasing life. I was supposed to remember something about that, wasn't I?*

You know what makes things easier to remember? Putting them into stupid, annoying little riddles.

"Did you read Violet's book?" I asked.

Anick blinked at the sudden change of subject. "Her book? I skimmed it. The girl uses the dragon to find her lost love. Viktor, wasn't it?"

"Yes," I said, "but her lost love turns out to be a double-crosser. He tricks her and locks her in a dungeon that her dragon saves her from."

"Atticus's mother wrote it," he countered, glowering. "Of course, she would make the dragon the hero."

"Perhaps," I murmured, peering down into the pit, where Farrah sobbed uncontrollably. The sound shattered me.

I could potentially pause time and run down there; except, I wouldn't be able to open the door while time was paused just like I couldn't push Falon off me before. There was just no way. If this was Anick's plan, then he'd maneuvered me into a perfect, no-win situation. The fact that everyone seemed to be waiting for me to come to a decision lent credence to that theory.

Poor planner my ass.

This must have been his backup plan in case the reservoir transfer didn't work, but maybe I didn't need to win, at least not yet. I only needed time, and that was exactly what Violet had given to me.

And so, my dragon, use the key; and in time, I'll have with me the only thing I'll ever need, my husband, son, and daughter.

Why would Violet make a plan that would lead to her own son's death? Anick himself said that she'd written that book to make the dragon the hero. That didn't make any sense.

Wait a second. The poem didn't say that Linorra uses the key. It was the dragon that uses the key to get back to his family. Because he was lost. What if Violet shoved me into Aaron's life because I was the only one who could save him from himself? And vice versa.

My heart hammered in my chest. That was it. I knew it. *That sneaky bitch.* I gave in to the urge to lay my hand on the key, feeling it beneath the dress collar.

Once she knew, time split in two.

"Farrah, are you still with me?" I called.

"Lina!" Farrah whimpered, her agonized sobs barely audible. Seleca fanned the flames to make them burn higher up Farrah's body.

One path left, straight toward death.

"You only have one choice, Eve," Anick said. He was anxious now, likely because I had ignored his well-planned proposal. "I've already seen how this chapter ends. Take down your shield and give me your left hand."

One path right, chasing life.

"I can't do that," I said, half to myself. "You see, there's something that you don't understand."

Anick clenched his fists as his face reddened. "I am the immortal Anick Aetos, Seer of All Things," he spat. "There is nothing I don't understand."

I sensed Anick's nice-guy routine was coming to an end, and it evoked memories of Aaron losing his shit as the beads on his bracelet popped. I wondered if this was the real Anick, or his Evocation fragment taking over. Did it even matter? I might have bonded to Anick in a past life. I could admit that much, but he wasn't the one I loved, at least not anymore.

"But there *is*, Nick," I said, "because I might have finally gotten Aaron, as you said, but he got me too. I'm sorry. I love him." As corny as it was, Spirit had called it. Aaron was Mr. Right.

"You love me, too, Eve. I have felt your love as our bodies intertwined countless times. As soon as you get your Precognition back, you'll remember it. You'll remember that you're bonded to me already. And you'll bond to me again because I can give you what no one else can—the universe and everything in it. Now, take down your shield or I will kill every single member of your pathetic crew, including your friend down there in the pit. I command you, Eve."

Though both are true, right's up to you.

"My name isn't Eve," I cried, my face heating. "I am Avelina Dragona Silva of the Rhoyal Dragonrider line. And ya know what? Two wrongs don't make a fragging right. So, I think I'm gonna just let the ball bounce another way this time. Because I'm a grown-ass woman, and no one commands me, not even the immortal Anick Aetos."

THE WISDOM OF DISHONOR

Anick's nostrils flared, then he turned to my crew and made a quick gesture of his hand. Jorin cried out and fell to the ground before his body transmuted into a pile of red dust like one of those black snake fireworks on the Fourth of July. With a swiping motion of Anick's hand, the dust was kicked up by a gust of wind, flying into the faces of the rest of the crew.

They appeared confused but didn't move to save themselves, not even when the wind intensified and became a gale that blew them all down. Not even when it became a funnel cloud that threatened to drop from the sky and rip us all to shreds.

Farrah screamed again, this time longer and more sustained. Heat vented from the pit, punctuated by a grotesque, wet grunt, then the screaming stopped. I was out of time. The key vibrated so powerfully that it caused my entire body to shake.

For right to be, use the key.

Anick was right. Somewhere in me, there was a spark of memory. I knew exactly what to do. I pulled the key out and held it in reverse order, taking the end of the key in my left hand and pointing the head of the key at the middle of my body like I had done to Falon.

Anick saw the key and gasped. "Eve, no!" In the blink of an eye, he slammed me down on top of the pit grate, knocking the wind out of me. I grunted and almost dropped the key, but I'd been expecting the blow and hung on. The shield held his body away from me just enough, but I felt the heat rising from the pit below.

Before the fire burns any higher.

"Stop, Eve! You don't understand what you're doing. Christine won't get another chance like this."

Christine? How does he know that name? Did he pull that out of my mind? No, it couldn't be. I'm in a shield.

The funnel cloud descended, and Fitch and Shane were swept away, crashing into the surrounding buildings and each other. The sound of roaring wind was deafening as the dais vibrated, threatening to blow apart. The sky itself pressed down upon us like a charred and blackened pinwheel.

"Give me the key!" Anick's shouted, his voice panicked. I had no time to ponder my last question before his eyes went wild and he harnessed Evocation to push fire through my shield and toward my head. It seared my face as if my shield weren't even there.

I turned my face to the right reflexively in a futile effort to escape the agony. The skin on my left cheek burned first, blistering painfully, then my left eyebrow caught fire. I turned my body away from Anick within the shield, but the effort was awkward and useless. My eyes felt like they would boil in my skull while the hair on the back of my head caught fire. I felt the heat all through my body now, scorching me, disintegrating me.

I didn't scream, for once in my life. By that point, thanks to my Teleportation ascension, I was damned good at enduring pain. Instead, I gritted my teeth through Anick's Evocation assault, closed my eyes, and pictured the last time I had felt truly safe and happy. I saw Spirit, not as a ghost, but the last time I saw her alive, sitting on the couch across from me on my parents' porch and gazing at me with those hopeful eyes.

I wouldn't need one of the key's skipstone beads for this because my destination wasn't about where I was going so much as to when and whom. I pictured exactly what I wanted, holding it as solidly in my mind as I could under the circumstances. Then, agnostic or not, I said a little prayer.

God, if you exist, please let this work. If not for me, then for the people I've hurt with my stupidity and weakness, so that I can make it right. In the back of my mind, I prayed for one more thing, perhaps without realizing it, as I didn't think with words but only felt it with my heart.

Please don't take Christine from me.

I pushed a blend of Teleportation, Transformation, and Conjuration through the key and back into my body. The first fragment was for time, the second for change, and the third for my own spirit. I had a feeling this was going to be a bumpy ride.

The sound of wind intensified when my shield winked out, but for an instant, a high-pitched ringing threatened to rupture my eardrums. I thought I'd failed because nothing happened except that Anick fell on me, his hands enveloping mine to wrench the key from my grip.

"Give me the key, Eve! *Please!* We just got her back!"

We just got her back? Does he mean Christine?

Anick had said this was my second time around. Had I given birth in my last life too? An overwhelming dread that I had just made a terrible mistake crept up my spine and made itself at home in my chest.

Christine.

I stared into Anick's face as it struck me like a bolt of lightning that he wasn't angry. He was terrified. *He knew her,* I realized. *He loved her.*

And so did Aaron, which is why he didn't want me to do this.

THE WISDOM OF DISHONOR

I instantly gave up my struggle at that thought, but it was too late. Under the pressure of Anick's massive strength, the crystal key shattered.

Chapter Twenty-Two

*W*hen Linorra gazed upon Viktor, unconscious on the stone floor, she felt nothing but pity. She remembered her father's callous and cruel ways and could not help but compare him to Queen Mortier.

"I cannot slay him," she said, "because I am him." Syndeth huffed a thin wisp of smoke into the air, a sure sign of a dragon's approval.

***

Aunt Violet later told me her greatest fear was that the remnants of my Precognition reservoir would let me figure out her plan before it was time. Either that momentary déjà vu wasn't the extent of my reservoir, or that moment by the pit was the right time, because I somehow knew exactly what to do.

Anick Aetos, on the other hand, didn't quite understand that time moves in all directions. Not just forward and backward, but side to side, up and down, diagonal, spiraling, and sometimes not at all. He wasn't looking in the right direction, so when he used his Precognition to glimpse possible futures, he only saw me saying yes to his reproposal. He saw the patterns that I'd repeated again and again.

Not this time, Nick. This time I screwed up in a completely new way.

I was sucked up by a tornado like Dorothy's house. Unlike normal bridges, where your physical body becomes immobile and weightless on the bridge, this fragging thing ripped my spirit right out of my body, leaving everything behind, including the ruined crystal key. My spirit was then dragged through a field of cacti and shoved into a jellyfish. That's what it felt like, anyway.

I flopped onto the couch on my parents' porch as if boneless, then I vomited in front of two women who were silently competing for my affection.

"Lina!" Drew cried. "Oh my god!"

"Uuuuugganew," I said. I was trying to say "I'm fine, Drew," but my tongue didn't work. The taste of alcohol mixed with bile and spicy chuck burger filled my mouth and burned my throat. Not to mention that my stupid wrist hurt again. I'd forgotten about that when I chose this moment to return to.

"It's okay," Spirit announced, appearing at my side. "She just drank too much. She'll be fine." She pulled me up, rescuing me from my unfortunate face-down position on the couch. Thankfully, it had only been a little vomit, and it was only on my face and not all over my clothes.

"Thol," I said.

"Towel," Spirit translated in her adorable high-pitched voice. "Bobby, can you run to the bathroom and grab a towel, please?"

Drew, who'd always been squeamish, stumbled out of the way and let Spirit help me. I leaned on my friend heavily. Bobby, the short-haired twin, brought a towel back, handing it to Spirit. She wiped my face, then smiled at me as if she knew my deepest secrets and found them inexplicably endearing.

Spirit had the most brilliant smile I had ever seen, the sight of which made my chest constrict, not only because I had missed her so much, but also because I knew that even though she was alive again, a relationship was not in the cards for us. Too much had happened in the last few months for us to ever be together in that way again. Her eyes twinkled in the dim porch lights, a small detail I hadn't realized until now had been missing when she was a ghost.

"I missed you," I whimpered, then I gingerly wrapped my arms around her. I wanted to weep for joy. She was alive and warm and here in my arms with her twinkly eyes and beating heart and eternally flushed cheeks, smelling like eucalyptus and patchouli and a hint of marijuana. My lovely, perfect, very much *not* dead friend. My Spirit.

"I never left you," she stated matter-of-factly, causing tears to practically jump out of my eyes. She wiped them away with her sleeve.

"No. You didn't," I agreed. I leaned back from her a little, letting my hand fall into hers so that our fingers interlocked.

I wanted to stay here with her all night just to make certain she wouldn't disappear on me again, but I had a promise to keep. Even if I hadn't planned to find Aaron, I'd already let go of my crush.

Spirit was my soulmate in the way that best friends always are, in a way you feel immediately when you first meet someone, but which only reaches its full potential by collecting a shared history. This is especially true when that history includes hard times you've come through by leaning on each other. When a friend has seen you in your worst moments and decides to stand by you anyway, you know it's because they love you.

It made me want to sing the theme song to *The Golden Girls*. If anyone could truthfully sing that tune, it was me and Spirit. She'd make some man or woman very happy someday, someone who didn't watch as much vintage television as I did and who also did not suffer from an acute case of vomit breath.

Spirit laughed softly, like she knew exactly what I was thinking. She probably did. She understood me better than anyone. How could I ever explain to her what she meant to me? This beautiful, brilliant woman was my *person*, a perfect combination of light and shadow who mercilessly broke every social rule while always staying unequivocally good. She had this irreverent mischievousness that made Evilina jump up and do a jig, but she never seemed tempted to dive off that precipice into the dark like I sometimes was.

Like I'd *done*, apparently.

I sighed, then stood. I was a little wobbly, but I managed it. "It's time for everyone to go home," I announced, then glanced at Bobby. "Would you take Spirit someplace safe, please?"

Bobby's eyebrows drew together, but he nodded. "Of course." He turned to his twin, who still sat on the couch, watching the door to Marti and Milo's room.

"Aunt Violet will be just fine," I chirped. The twins' heads both whipped to me. "Uh-huh. I thought so. Listen, I don't have time to explain right now. I need you two knuckleheads to take Spirit and go. Do you understand?" The twins stared for another half second before they both nodded.

"Spirit—" I started.

"I know. I'm going. I'll see you after?"

"Not even death could stop me," I said, and meaning it. The emotion in her eyes wrapped around me like a warm blanket. Spirit was my ride or die. Our relationship might not ever be what we thought or hoped for, but it was love all the same.

"Let's not test that out again," she replied, sniffling.

My eyes widened. "You remember? I thought you lost—"

"No time, Lina," she interrupted, pointing out into the fog. "Look." Rogue stood exactly where I expected him to be, beneath the sign.

"Lina, isn't that your dog?" Drew asked, her words slurred.

I nodded, then turned back to Spirit. "I'm not going anywhere until I know you're safe."

Spirit smiled and nodded, planting her hands on her hips as she turned to the twins. "Bobby and Goldy, let's go. This warrior princess needs room to work."

"Goldy?" I sputtered, doing a double take.

The twin on the left, Goldy, evidently, glanced at me sideways and said, in a distinctly feminine voice, "Yes, cousin. Now, go save my dumbass brother."

I choked a little. "You're Aaron's sister?" I bellowed, remembering how I'd lusted after the so-called twins. I shook myself to dispel the returning cringe, reminding myself that they weren't *actually* my cousins. Probably.

Goldy chuckled. Her face was shifting to something very different than what it had been a moment ago. The two weren't even twins, for Christ's sake. I turned to Bobby. "Are you . . . Goldy's husband?"

Bobby nodded, grinning. "Violet was right about you. You do figure things out too quickly."

A little bubble of warmth erupted in my heart that Violet *definitely* didn't deserve. "Okay. That's enough revelation for one day. I just need to grab one thing before I can go."

"Here," Spirit said. I turned back to see her offering a tube of toothpaste. "I recommend you use this as soon as possible."

As I snatched the tube out of her hand, I couldn't help but snicker at her dig. She mirrored the sentiment, blessing me with her adorable giggle before she handed me one more thing. A box of condoms.

This time I didn't laugh or take what she offered. *Christine.*

"Can someone please tell me what the hell is going on?" Drew asked, eyeing the box in Spirit's hand with consternation.

"Sure, Drew. I'm about to follow a dog to another planet. You are going home. I appreciate your help. I'm really glad we're friends again."

I reluctantly accepted the box from Spirit, jogged over to my bag, pulled out the leash and collar to discard them, then stuffed in the new items. Noticing that I was wearing my watch again, which I had ditched after it broke during my Teleportation ascension, I tapped the button to check the time. Nothing happened. I pressed the button a few more times. Not only did it fail to turn on, but the watch snapped off the silicone band and fell to the floor.

Huh.

My butt unexpectedly vibrated, which made me yelp as I jumped a foot in the air. My phone was in my back pocket, sending me a freaking Instagram notification. I'd forgotten how annoying those were, but . . . *Thank Hecate you're okay, Luigi! We'll never be separated again, my love.* I stuffed him in my sports bra for safekeeping, then yanked the wrist brace off and shook my hand out. My wrist had already stopped hurting.

On impulse, I grasped the brace in my right hand and pushed Evocation into the device. It didn't dramatically burst into flames or anything, but I smelled burning plastic, and a small wisp of smoke pushed its way out of the material. My Evocation reservoir was muted from being on Earth, but it was still there.

I laughed out loud. *Yes! Reservoirs are attached to the spirit.*

Somewhere on Monash, Falon was having a very good day and hearing just fine out of two whole ears. Violet was a fragging genius. Come to think of it, Rei, the small man from Wishmere, was getting his Protection reservoir raised for free after all. So much for favors owed.

Okay, you're back on my shit list, Vi.

I stopped when a wave of melancholy dulled my upbeat mood and, hesitantly, I laid my hand on my stomach. No resonance. No teeny, tiny heartbeat. I closed my eyes, remembering my prayer. *She's gone.*

My throat tightened, but I shook my head, chastising myself. I was entitled to a choice, and I had made it. There was no point in tormenting myself over it now. "Let's go," I muttered.

I led the way off the porch. Spirit and the not-twins helped me coax Drew into her Volvo, letting Goldy drive since Drew was too intoxicated. The others had only been pretending to drink. Jerks.

I leaned toward Spirit through the passenger window of Bobby's, oddly enough, gold-colored Silverado. "Will you be okay?" I asked.

"I think so," she replied. "Come back to my apartment after you find him. We have some things to sort out."

I nodded, holding her eyes for a breath, then I stepped away from the truck. The tires kicked up dust as they disappeared down the gravel drive into the fog. It wasn't the best of driving conditions, but I couldn't risk leaving them there. Violet and her merry band of liars, on the other hand, would have to fend for themselves. I had no doubt that they'd do just fine, the a-holes.

I spotted Rogue, still hovering by the lighted sign. He paced back and forth impatiently now, his pink ears helicoptering backward and forward. I set my pack down, dug for a flashlight, then secured the pack. No need to rush. He'd wait for me, and I was going to do it right this time. I turned my flashlight on and jogged after him.

Just as before, Rogue didn't let me catch him. I was slower and more careful this time, though. I didn't step in any stupid holes. It took us about fifteen minutes to get to the bridgestone. Rogue did what he was supposed to do, leading us to the preappointed spot, then sat and waited.

"Rogue," I said, panting lightly, "I'm tired of chasing you. I feel like I've been doing it for months now."

"Because you have," Seleca said, slinking into the clearing.

"Seleca," I said, turning to face her. She panted a little as she drew nearer, her hair in disarray and her face flushed and sweaty. "You remember our special time together. How nice."

Seleca pressed her mouth into a flat line. "The Ascended Father says you cheated him, but he's still with me. You haven't beaten him."

"To be honest, Seleca," I said, "I don't think I'm even trying to beat him anymore. I'm not sure who's worse, him or me. Or Aaron, I suppose. I just needed time to sort out my priorities."

"Time?" Seleca sneered. "You mean you needed to forget your bondmate, to forget your vows so that you could fall in love with that *traitor*." Seleca snarled the last word, as

L.E. BROOKS

if Aaron had been the bad guy all along. She sounded like a scorned lover. "All the time in the world won't help you, Eve. You betrayed him. He'll see now what I've been trying to tell him for years. You are *not* a goddess."

"Hey, that's my line," I quipped. "Let me ask you a question, Seleca. Did you think that *you* would end up with Aaron? Is that what this was about? Was I supposed to tame the Dragon so you could ride him?"

Seleca's eye twitched. "I have never needed anyone to tame him, Eve. I have always done that just fine on my own. You had your chance, and you chose ambition instead. Aaron eventually saw you for what you were and came to me."

My stomach twisted at the thought of Aaron going to *Fucking* Seleca for comfort. The first time I met Seleca, Aaron and I were in the forest on the way from his cottage to Jorin's farm. Seleca had tracked us, and we fought her, but just beforehand, Seleca had tried to convince him to come with her, telling him about how comfortable her bed was. I had thought at the time that she had been toying with Aaron, that she was trying to lure him away from me to separate us. Maybe it hadn't been as mocking as I'd thought.

"Until now, you mean," I said. "That's the real reason you call him a traitor, isn't it? Because you think he's yours, but it turned out you were his second choice after all." My mind flitted back to what Aaron had said on Jorin's boat.

You will always be my first choice, Lee. Always, whether you choose me or not.

"You were just his first *mistake*, Eve," Seleca spat. Her eyes were a well of fiery rage. "You're everyone's first mistake. Even my brother sees you for what you are now."

"Your brother? Who the hell's your brother?"

Seleca's mouth pressed into a thin line and her face turned red.

"Wait, *Anick* is your brother? I thought he was your father. You know, 'Holy Daughter' and all that?"

Seleca didn't respond, but her sudden tremble made me wonder if she wasn't supposed to tell me that. It abruptly dawned on me that Seleca shouldn't be able to see Anick unless they'd mixed reservoirs at some point. Anick had called it a "mixing of souls," but I thought Anick couldn't get Conjuration from her because there was no real love between them. But they *had* to have mixed reservoirs if Seleca could see him. And they were siblings?

Oh. My. God. Please tell me there's something I'm missing here.

"Ya know what?" I muttered. "I really *really* don't want to hear any more about that. All I know is that if Aaron loved you, you wouldn't have had to steal Evocation from him because you would have gotten it the same way I did."

My precision strike must have hit home because the most unexpected thing happened. A tear slid down her face, and a flicker of uncertainty ran through me as my mind went back to something else Aaron said.

Sometimes it's wiser to break a vow than to keep it, no matter how dishonorable it might seem. You taught me that.

When Seleca absorbed Spirit's Precognition, that would have been the first time she remembered other timelines. She may have actually missed Aaron and maybe had even been in love with him, which meant she wouldn't have tried to kill him unless she'd been forced to do so.

Maybe she really is enthralled. And here I am bickering with her over him like a freaking preteen. It was pure conjecture, but it had the ring of truth to it.

"Freaking Marti," I mumbled, then felt the corners of my mouth trying to pull up as I thought about her stupid poem. The wisdom of dishonor indeed. If I didn't know any better, I'd say this entire time-altering fiasco was just a way for Violet-slash-Marti to break her son up with his psycho girlfriend. That was such a Marti thing to do.

Rogue whined, drawing my attention back to him. He glared at me like I was an idiot. *Perhaps I'm going about this the wrong way.*

"Why don't we sit and have a drink, Seleca?" I said carefully. If she was caught in Projection, then I should have been trying to help her instead of whatever the hell this conversation was. "I've got some disgusting port back at the house. I hear you old people really like that stuff." Okay, so it wasn't my best joke, but they can't all be winners.

Seleca glowered at me. "You think you're so clever, but you still don't understand. Now that the Father knows Violet had the key, it's only a matter of time until he finds it. You've changed nothing."

"That's not true," I said. "None of us are the same people we once were. By the way, how's your eye, Seleca?"

Seleca's hand came up to her right eye, the one that had gushed blood when she'd dared question Anick. She trembled, radiating what had to be suppressed rage, then seemed to realize what she'd unconsciously done because she let her hand fall, wiping it instead on her yellow pants.

I hoped, after tonight, she might opt for a wardrobe change for once in her life, but for now, it was time to end this game.

I took a small, shuffling step toward Seleca, planning my next move. I'd gotten a lot better at blended links since the last time I'd fought her. Before, I had to add the fragments to a Connection link one at a time, but that wasn't going to work on her. She was too powerful. I needed to hit her with a strong first punch. She would see it coming, of course, but if she was fighting the Projection trance, as Ellis had done, maybe she would let me do it.

I took another step toward Seleca, this one a little bigger, but she stepped back. I'd been in this clearing with her once before, and she'd stalked me. Now, she was the one backing away.

Screw it.

I squared my shoulders, then pushed a blend of Protection, Conjuration, and Transformation into a Connection link, sending it out through the air between us. And . . . nothing happened. I'd forgotten that Earth blunted reservoirs. Maybe that was why I couldn't get my link to connect through the air.

Okay, take two. I took a fortifying breath in and out, then sprang at Seleca, just barely grabbing hold of her wrist before she escaped my grasp and pushed the blended link again.

This time, Seleca gasped and fell to her knees, shaking violently. She had tremendous resistance, despite not having Protection. After a moment, she grabbed my forearms and squeezed them like stress balls before burning through my skin using Evocation. I clenched my teeth against the sudden blinding pain, tears gathering in the corners of my eyes, but I pushed harder, using the pain as motivation.

Pain of any kind, I've noticed, is a bit like fire anyway. When it burns you, it creates a charred, hardened surface—a barrier against the world. Some people celebrate that toughened exterior, calling it "strength," but that type of barrier separates humans from one another and can make us think we're enemies. We point fingers at each other's scars and sling labels around—words like "psycho," for example.

We may think we understand one another, arrogantly believing that we are the seers of all and that there couldn't possibly be anything we don't understand. We learn to hate each other.

I'd hated Seleca more than I had ever hated anyone in my life. I had literally wanted to kill her. But there's a solution to that problem, and it isn't love. As much as that idea appeals, this isn't about love. This is about freedom. It's about exalting in the exquisite pain and pleasure of being whoever it is we are and expecting nothing more or less than that from the people who occupy the same space we do. It's about seeing beyond that charred, scarred surface and reaching into the dark and terrifying wilderness of humanity so that we can all be more.

That's what I remembered by forgetting. When Anick took my Precognition, I saw the world with new eyes, more innocent eyes that know how much they don't know.

Ever so gently, I pushed my own Evocation. I didn't want a torrent of fire that would burn her, only a lantern to see by. I couldn't understand everything, of course, but I could perceive what lay just past the hardened surface. It was enough.

A thread of memories, deeply buried and haunting her every day, rushed into my mind. I experienced it all at once, like a lightning bolt, only more painful.

She was eight when he came to get her from the Rhoyal Healers Guild. She was terrified of him. There were many fatherless children like her, running through the guildhalls. The ones with no greater reservoir were the lucky ones. They got to leave and never come back, but at least she wasn't a protector. She had been fortunate enough to be born with Absorption, so she couldn't be infected with that reservoir either. At least, she had thought she was fortunate until *he* came to get her.

"Don't be afraid," he said. It didn't take long for him to push into her mind. She had no defenses. Her mother had sheltered her from the worst of what happened in the healers compound.

Come to me, Seleca. Let us spend time together. I will take you to the eighth realm, and then we will see what you can do. He held out his hand to her.

The eighth realm? There was no such place, and if there was, she didn't want to go there. She knew she had no choice, though. Her mother had warned her that this might happen someday. Her eyes filled with tears. She wanted her mother, but she reached out and took his hand anyway. It was warm, and she knew instantly that she'd been wrong. This was the kindest man in the world.

No, not a man, she thought. *A god.*

Yes, he thought. *You are the one, a Holy Daughter of my father's line. I see his face in yours. You are destined for greatness, just as I am.*

Somewhere in the background, faint and muffled, she heard a scream. It sounded like her mother, but she trusted that it was nothing to worry about. She sniffed, then followed him onto the bridge without a word of protest.

She was twelve, and finally back on Monash after spending forty days in the deserts of Intaru with the Rojii demons.

"You must learn to survive if you want to rule Monash with me," he'd said. "You may return when you find a demon with any greater reservoir, kill it, and absorb your ticket home."

It had taken her days to find the entrance to their caves in the black mountains, then learn how to transform into one of them. She had achieved a passable impression, she thought, but they could always smell her. The demons were attracted to blood. It was intoxicating to them. She could kill them with Transmutation, sure, but it was much easier to live among them. All she had to do to hide her scent was wear a demon's skin.

She was seventeen. They'd spent time on Earth and Wishmere hunting for new reservoirs but hadn't found Teleportation. Anick had let Seleca absorb Production from him as that reservoir resided in the hands and was easy to transfer, but the rest would undoubtedly require the source to be culled during the absorption process. Unless, of course, Seleca could make someone fall in love with her.

A trusted acolyte from Wishmere, Kyuli, who she found to be endlessly irritating, seemed like a good choice for culling. He had Teleportation, but the Father didn't want to lose him, as the "true loyalty" he showed was as rare as his reservoir.

He ordered Kyuli to mix reservoirs with Seleca until she had enough to raise during her next ascension. The man had reluctantly complied, but it hadn't worked. The only thing she'd absorbed from him was a pregnancy. They'd had to kill him to take his reservoir. A shame, but it couldn't be helped.

She was twenty-three. Her mother had escaped again. She found the wretched woman hiding with the caravanners and dragged her back by her hair, but the Ascended Father hadn't been satisfied.

"We need to set an example," he declared. "Take her to the pit."

She did as commanded. The woman obviously deserved it, but something was bothering her. It was a voice, faint and muffled; nothing to worry about, she was confident. She never worried about anything. She let him do that. She instructed a healer to initiate the purification, but Anick stopped her.

"You must do this one yourself," he said. "Do this, and you will be ready."

Her heart quickened. It was time. He would be leaving for a long time, and she would rule Monash in his absence. She was finally good enough. All she had to do was purify this last one. She hurried to the tunnel.

Her mother screamed her name. The sound echoed painfully in her mind, but Seleca ignored it. There was another voice, too, but much quieter.

No, it said. *No, no, no.*

Seleca paused, confused.

"Yes," she said to the voice. "This is the Father's will." She picked up the torch, hesitated for only an instant, then lit the fire.

Seleca's eyes flew open, and she screamed, crumpling my forearms like scorched paper, then she let go and fell backward. I did too. The pain in my forearms was all-consuming, and I could do nothing else until I healed it. If she had squeezed any harder, she might have detached my hands entirely.

I pushed a surge of Protection into them, straight from my heart, and I felt the tissue re-forming itself. After a moment, the pain lessened, and my arms healed. I was getting faster at healing my own injuries.

Sitting up, I peered over at Seleca, panting as if I'd run a marathon. She had stopped screaming and lay on her back with her eyes closed. Rogue walked up beside me. His adorable face, I noticed, did not have the white handprint. He wouldn't remember the last two months because, from his point of view, they hadn't happened. His spirit remembered, though.

I stared him straight in the eye and thought to him, *Ward, stay!* His ears swiveled toward me, turning pink, and the whites showed around his eyes in a far-too-human look of shock. It must have been astonishing that not only did I know his real name, but I was a fragmentor powerful enough to neutralize Seleca. He whined once, then sat at attention.

I used my elbows to get up because my arms still couldn't take the weight. I approached Seleca cautiously, then knelt next to her and patted her down gingerly, searching for my dad's Glock. I found it in the right pocket of her pants and took it back from her.

"Seleca," I said. No response.

I waited, then I shook her a little. Still nothing. I frowned down at the woman I'd spent so much time hating. I had watched her relive her past, and I was confused as to how I should feel about her now. It was all very sad. Anick had trapped her in Projection when she was still a child. Now she lay on her back, her black hair splayed around her head like a squashed spider. Helpless, just like she started.

I nudged her with the gun. "Wake up, Snow White. Don't make me kiss you 'cause I'll do it."

"One hundred sixty-four," Seleca mumbled, her eyes still closed.

I squeezed my eyebrows together. "Huh?"

"Years," she whispered. "A hundred and sixty-four years."

That's how long she was enthralled? Holy shit. And I thought Ellis had it bad. No wonder she's nuts.

Seleca finally opened her eyes and stared at me. "My Conjuration reservoir, you have to take it. I don't want to see him anymore. Take it. Please."

She meant Anick, I surmised.

"Seleca," I said, ignoring her plea. "I need to know what you're going to do now that you're free."

"I won't help you," she said. "It's pointless. I hated him and he still found a way to make me see his ghost—through reservoir absorption, not . . . that other thing."

I sighed in relief, then stopped to wonder why. I mean, obviously I'm vehemently against incest, but that wasn't it. It was more like I wanted Anick to be redeemable.

"You can't beat him," she insisted. "See for yourself. I'll give you Precognition too."

"Hard pass."

"I'll let you *absorb* it," she clarified. "It's useless for seeing the future. I saw two or three outcomes, and none of them came true. Take it. All I want is to stop seeing him." She held out her hand to me. A tear leaked out of her eye and ran sideways across her cheek, toward the ground. "Take all of it. Don't leave anything behind."

I glanced at her hand suspiciously but didn't move to take it. I was at an obvious disadvantage in terms of knowledge. This was the first time I'd heard that you had a choice in how much of a reservoir to absorb. I'd only done it once. That I could remember, anyway.

"Take it," Seleca insisted, reaching for me. "As payment for freeing me, if nothing else."

I didn't know if this was a trick, but I knew that Precognition was hard to come by—and that I would need it to defeat Anick if he found a way to come back again.

I got my mental defenses ready, and then I took her hand.

I immediately felt a pinprick at the edge of my awareness, then I was overwhelmed by anxiety. *I made the wrong choice in coming back*, I thought. *I lost Christine. It's not too late. I could still go back. All I have to do is let her in through my Protection.*

"Seleca," I said, "I've been fighting with my inner bitch my whole life. Do you really think that's going to work on me?"

Seleca blinked, then her jaw tightened. Like a light switch had been flipped, her face morphed into cold rage as she clenched my hand, snapping the bones in the outsides of my palm.

Ow. Fuck! How are these people so freaking strong?

I crammed my eyes shut involuntarily against the pain and released a pathetic whimper. Then she yanked me toward her, grabbing my neck with her other hand. She squeezed again, crushing my throat and choking me to silence.

When my eyes bulged out of my head and my mouth flooded with blood, a random thought flicked through my mind. *You know, the Rojii demons might be onto something. Blood actually doesn't taste that bad.* Dark laughter erupted in the back of my mind as I imagined myself latching on to Seleca's neck.

It was such a shame. For a minute there, I had honestly believed that Seleca could be saved. I had wanted her to be a victim to be rescued, but the innocent girl who had wanted her mother all those years ago was dead. All that was left was a demon wearing Seleca's skin.

"I don't want you to think I'm ungrateful," she said, flipping us over so that she sat on my chest. Her face was a mask of bored indifference. "I've been under that bastard's thumb for so many years that I can't remember what it was like before, even now that I have my Precognition back. Goddess, did you really believe I'd let you take power from me?"

In answer, I gurgled, blood dripping across my face to my ear. Rogue's response was a bit more decisive. He lunged at Seleca, but she saw him coming and batted him away like an annoying gnat, sending him skittering into a tree. His heartbreaking yelp caused a red mist to descend over my vision that I recognized as Evilina taking over the reins.

Fucking. Seleca.

Seleca clicked her tongue like we were unruly children. "So predictable. You know, you should never have let my brother take Precog from you. I was telling the truth when I said it's useless for seeing the future. The future is mutable, after all, but Precog is essential for seeing the past."

She looked up into the sky, blinking her eyes repeatedly as if to clear them, then back down. She sighed and murmured, "If you could remember how you used to be, Eve, you'd know that you deserve to die. I know I'm not perfect, but at least my family still wants me around. Your real family threw you away like the garbage you are."

Her words struck me in the chest, cutting me open and rushing into my veins. My vision blurred as I fumbled for the gun, but my will to fight had taken an enormous blow. Seleca snorted, then let go of my neck, pulling the gun away from me with complacent ease. I pushed Protection into my throat and gasped for air as it cleared, coughing up blood. Specks splattered onto Seleca's face, and she wiped them away with a smirk, then pointed my father's Glock at my head.

Oh good. That never gets old.

"You can't imagine how long I've been waiting for this, how I've longed for the day when I could do as I wished." Her tone was casual, resigned even. There was no crazed gleam in her eye as I was used to, only cold calculation. "I've decided that burying you is the best path forward. I'm going to seal you with cement and bury you like the vampire that you are. You'll probably be in there for a thousand years before someone finds you randomly while digging in the ground. It will be a fitting punishment for you, and I'll be doing the world a favor, especially Aaron."

She leaned close to me and whispered in my ear as she wrapped her fingers around my neck again. "He doesn't remember you, Eve. When I go to him, I'll tell him my sad story, and he'll take pity on me. Then I'll make him happier than you ever could while you're rotting in the ground."

I'd like to say that the thought of her stealing Aaron was more frightening to me than being buried, but the threat hit too close to home. The thought of being imprisoned for another thousand years, helpless and alone—like on that Teleportation bridge—awakened a primal terror within me. My teeth chattered for a moment before I clenched my jaw to make it stop.

"Then again," she added, a grin spreading across her face, "maybe I'll just kill him. I'll decide when I get there."

THE WISDOM OF DISHONOR

As Seleca's hand squeezed my neck again, I laid my hand over hers and pushed Protection. Her grip loosened a little but not much. She closed her eyes and gritted her teeth, groaning through it, then she laughed, quickly renewing her efforts to choke me.

"I've been fighting that sensation my whole life," she said, echoing my earlier sentiments. "Do you really think that's going to work on me?"

With that, she tightened her fist, completely collapsing my windpipe. The world spun as I suffocated, and I could think of nothing but breathing. I pushed Protection into my throat harder than I ever have before, but Seleca held her grip, and I knew that even my ascendant Protection reservoir wouldn't be enough to save me before I passed out. Then I'd be all set for my live burial.

I was almost unconscious when instinct took over, or maybe it was desperation because I did something that I didn't even know was possible. I used Teleportation by accident.

Teleportation is a complicated fragment. It dwells within your solar plexus, which is basically a fistful of nerves that radiates out like a star to the rest of your body. The fragment is complex because, similar to the solar plexus, it affects multiple organs, such as your diaphragm, and some of your body's instinctive responses, like your fight-or-flight response.

I didn't know it then, but that's actually how the crystal key works to slow down time. When you get desperate, your Teleportation reservoir pulses out from your solar plexus to activate the key, which slows down time so you can save yourself. It's ingenious.

Surprisingly, this happens even when you don't have the key, just not to the same degree. If I had been paying attention, I would have noticed Anick doing this very thing when he charged toward me. Because, for those few of us who've had the misfortune to endure Teleportation ascension, the reward is that, when we get upset, we move like lightning.

So, just as Seleca's attention was redirected by something outside my field of vision, I punched her right in her stupid face. At the speed of a locomotive. It might not have been that strong, but it was fast as hell, which is almost as good. Unless you're the bones in my hand, which shattered on impact.

I heard a crunch as Seleca's head whipped back, flinging her off me. My father's gun flew from her hand to land next to Rogue. Freed from her grasp, I pushed Protection up from my heart so I could heal my crushed throat and take a breath.

Despite my newfound speed, I wasn't fast enough. I had just begun to take a breath when my vision narrowed, flickering lights sparking at the periphery, and everything went black.

Chapter Twenty-Three

*L*inorra clung to Syndeth as he crouched before the ruined dragon door. She could not bear to leave him behind.

"Syndeth," she said, feeling bashful for the first time since she'd met the dragon. "We do belong to each other after all, for I am tied to you as surely as the shore is tied to the sea."

"That was well done."

I jolted awake at the sound of Zig's voice, then sat up only to fall back again when my head exploded with pain. "Jesus fucking shitballs."

Zig knelt next to me, grinning widely. "It never ceases to amaze me how ladies in this age swear like seventeenth-century sailors whenever the mood strikes. It's positively delightful."

"Glad I amuse you. What are you doing here?" I squeezed my eyes shut, willing my heart to return to a normal cadence, opened them again to see Zig looking nonplussed.

"You owe me a dinner," he said defensively, then slid one hand behind my back to help me sit up. "I've come to collect."

On the other side of me sat Rogue, a very undoglike frown on his adorable face. His bright amber eyes darted back and forth between me and Zig, clearly following the conversation. *How did I not realize he wasn't really a dog?* Rogue huffed, then repositioned himself behind me so he could lay his head on my shoulder as I scratched behind his ears. He seemed fine.

"What happened to Seleca?" I asked. "I thought she wanted to whack me and bury me under a construction site or whatever."

"I talked her out of it," he said.

"Meaning . . ."

"She took one look at me and ran away screaming. Of course, the screaming could have been because she had a dent in the middle of her face." Zig's expression was oddly smug.

"I see. So that was you distracting her. Thanks for the assist." I sighed. "I just love it when a big, strong man rescues me."

Zig stared at me for a second, his expression sobering. "Lina, you don't need to be rescued. The sooner you learn that the better off you'll be. That woman is bigger, stronger, and more experienced than you, and yet you're here while she ran away."

"Because of you," I said.

"No. Because of *you*. That punch surprised her; although, it shouldn't have." Zig's face lit up again with laughter as he mimicked a punch coming toward his face. "She'll have to go back to Neesee to seek a healer now."

"Does that mean I have time to find some ibuprofen?"

"You don't need that either, just give it a minute. Trust me, we have plenty of time to rescue your big, strong man from Seleca."

I groaned, clutching my head to make the world stop spinning. "You know, I'd like to go just one day without passing out or breaking a bone. Is that too much to ask? I'm shit at fighting bad guys."

Zig chuckled. "Lina, if I know you—and I think I do—you'll be able to do much more than that. You've already made it to this time and place, changing not only your future but everyone else's too. The people you love are alive and well while Old Saint Nick is floating around in purgatory somewhere."

"Old Saint Nick," I repeated, a smile forming despite myself. "I'm totally stealing that."

"You didn't do it alone, but none of us ever do. In fact, if it weren't for you, I'd probably still be drifting mindlessly at the bottom of the sea." He glanced down with a thoughtful expression. "In a way, you're the one rescuing me. And you demonstrated something that I thought was impossible."

"What's that?"

"People can change if they really want to. Do you remember how I said I tried to drown you because I thought you were someone else?"

"Of course. You thought I was Seleca."

"No, Lina. I thought you were Eve."

He thought I was... oh. God, what the hell did I do? Even Zig thought I deserved to perish ... wait a second.

Something wasn't sitting quite right. I narrowed my eyes at Zig, trying to pin down what it was. He'd thought I was Eve, but he knew she couldn't be killed, didn't he? So he couldn't have thought drowning would work. Had I just caught him in a lie? Or was it just that in his animal state, he hadn't been thinking clearly?

I opened my mouth to speak, but something kept me from asking the question. If it was a lie, then it was probably better if he thought I hadn't caught it. He'd been there to help me, sure, but Spirit had mentioned when I met him that he wanted something from me and she didn't know what. If I had learned anything during my time on Monash, it was that the power of fragmentation tended to go to people's heads—it had a corrupting influence just like any form of power. And Zig was the most powerful fragmentor in the universe.

Other than our first encounter, Zig had never done anything except help me and, if I was being honest, flatter me with praise and attention. I wanted to believe that it was because he liked me, but the more I thought about it, the more I realized it would be incredibly naive to assume that was the case. I mean, how great was I really?

Your real family threw you away like the garbage you are.

I swallowed, refusing to shed even one tear over people I couldn't remember, but the truth was that Seleca's words had gotten under my skin. They were a little too similar to things I had said to myself a thousand times, even before I knew I was adopted. I needed to get my Precognition back so I could remember what I used to know, but I wasn't sure I wanted to know who I used to be.

"So, you see," Zig continued, "I kept my promise. I told you I'd help rescue everyone from the evil queen, and it seems to me that Eve is gone forever. Congratulations on defeating her."

"Thanks, Zig," I said, though I didn't mean it. I didn't deserve praise. I had a horrible feeling that I deserved a repeat Teleportation ascension. Rogue whined in my ear, stealing my attention before he licked my face. How did he always know? "And I appreciate your impeccable timing, but I'm gonna have to take a rain check on our dinner date. I've got places to be."

I pushed Protection into my throbbing head, speeding the healing process along, and after a moment, it faded to a dull pressure. Nudging Rogue gently away, I took the underside of one of his paws in my hand to connect.

Hey, Roogy-Roo. I'm gonna get you out of the mess you're in, okay? You just need to trust me.

Rogue stared at me, not bothering to respond in thought while I relayed to him what I had been through over the past couple of months. I explained that if he came onto the Earth bridge with me, he'd ascend the Protection reservoir I'd given him and raise his Transformation reservoir back to the level of greater so he could use it again. I was confident that he had enough left to do so, even though he'd given some to me. Hopefully, he'd be able to transform back into Ward once we arrived on Monash.

"I really do have to get to Aaron now before Seleca does."

"I can help you get there faster, if you like." Zig reached into his shirt and pulled out the crystal key.

"What? Where did you get that?"

Zig dangled the unbroken yellow diamond key from its durrite chain in front of me, a self-satisfied grin on his face. I grabbed the offered key and surged to my feet, then wobbled and had to throw my arms out to both sides to keep myself from falling.

Zig smirked. "I stole it from the queen of Hartha years ago. For that, they call me an interplanetary criminal! Can you believe that? The hypocrisy is astonishing."

I smirked at his indignation. "Yes, Zig. I *can* believe that. But if you had it all along, then how did my grandmother get it?"

"That's a long story, and I heard you have a man to save. Here, let me show you a trick."

He's deflecting, I thought as Zig pulled a small pebble out of his pocket. He placed it into the bottom half of the hourglass-shaped hole in the head of the key. I hadn't noticed before that the key had a little divot there, almost like sand was really supposed to fall from the top and collect in the bottom.

"Gather small rocks from any destinations that you want to revisit. As long as they are native to that region and not transported there, you can set one in that holder, and it will take you directly back to that location when you use the key, like a mini bridgestone. I collected that rock from under a tree behind Aaron's cottage this morning. A word of warning, though, you can only use a rock once. It's not like the beads. Once used, it will turn to—"

"Sand," I guessed.

Zig nodded appreciatively. "Precisely."

I smiled in response, feeling very proud of myself, then moved to bring the key up to my solar plexus, but Zig held out a hand to me.

Wait, he thought. *There's one last thing before we go.*

What is it?

Zig hesitated, his mouth pressed into a thin line, then he blew out a breath in what appeared to be resignation. Since he'd switched to telepathy, I assumed he didn't want Rogue to hear whatever he was about to say. *I know what you gave up to come back here.*

My hand unconsciously went to my belly. Zig glanced at it briefly, then lowered his gaze to the ground. I dropped my hand, frowning at him. That had been nobody's decision but my own and I wasn't about to justify it to Zig. *And?*

And I know you feel guilty about it. But you shouldn't. You did the right thing. That decision will end up saving a lot more people than you realize.

I wasn't sure how to respond. Was he implying that I had saved the world? God, I hoped so. I was *so* ready to be done with this annoying galaxy quest.

But that wasn't the only thing you sacrificed, he thought, a pained expression taking over his face.

Uh-oh. What don't I know?

Zig sighed. *Reservoirs stay with your spirit, as you must know by now, but when you ascend, that's something that happens to your body.*

I stared at him blankly. *What do you . . . oh, no. No, no, no, no, no.*

When I turned back the clock, my spirit left my body behind and found the one I'd had before. The only ascension I'd have kept was Connection since I'd completed that one as a toddler.

Nooo . . . My mind immediately shot back to my Teleportation ascension.

I'm afraid so, Zig thought.

My eyes widened when I grasped my current predicament. *Ward's not the only one who's about to ascend, is he?*

Zig shook his head, a chagrined expression on his face. *I'm sorry, Schatzi.*

I glowered down at the key with new trepidation. The Protection ascension had been nothing compared to Teleportation, but it still hurt like a son of a bitch.

There's nothing for it, I thought, taking a steadying breath. *It has to be done.* I grasped the head of the key with my right hand, holding the little rock into the divot.

I waited for Zig to take hold of my arm, then glanced down at Rogue. "Are you coming?" Rogue chuffed, then nodded his head, an odd gesture that I'd never seen him do before. I took a deep breath in and out, then held the key in position.

I'm going to murder Gran.

Ward and I both ascended Protection on the way back to Monash. I had warned him about the pain, but I don't think he believed me. They never do. I myself had doubted my own memory.

According to Zig's reckoning, Protection ascension is the fourth most painful, just behind Transmutation. However, I think pain is a bit like pleasure. The more you're given, the less you feel. And that first time is always the most intense. If you're not careful, you could find yourself chasing past experiences until you become completely numb.

When the bridge spat us out at the other end, Ward's naked human body flopped down onto a bed of pine needles. I, on the other hand, landed as gracefully as a cat. If cats landed on their feet, then fell over sideways.

"Ward?" I asked, crawling toward him. "Are you okay?"

"Hmf," Ward said.

"I know, I know. Do you need a minute?"

"Mm-hm."

"Okay," I said, digging into my pack. I pulled out the emergency foil blanket that my mother had packed and laid it over top of him, covering his nakedness. I was wrong—that survival kit came in handy after all.

Ward had several resonances coming from him now. When I'd connected deeply with him in Jorin's farmhouse, he'd gotten not only greater Protection from me but also lesser Connection, Conjuration, and even Evocation. Having raised all of them during his

Protection ascension, he was now one of the most powerful fragmentors in the universe. His life had changed forever.

"Just stay here and rest, Ward. We're behind Aaron's cottage. I'll be back, okay? Don't you dare run away again."

"Hmf," Ward repeated. Like mine, his body glowed faintly blue, and I smiled a little at the memory of my own first ascension, one that had also led me here, to this cottage.

"I'll stay with him," Zig whispered. "Holler if you need me. Just because you seduced the Dragon last time doesn't mean it will work this time. Be careful."

"I will," I said. I didn't bother whispering. I was sure that Aaron, with his Superman hearing, had already detected us. "And he's not the Dragon anymore. Now he's just my Bear Guy."

Zig furrowed his brow, then shrugged. "Whatever you say, Schatzi. Just be cautious."

I nodded, mentally noting to ask him what his nickname for me meant, then I snaked around the evergreens that lined the back of the cottage, making my way around the outside of the fallen redwood logs that protected the sides. I thought it best to approach from the front, in full view. This time, I remembered to look up.

Aaron lay flat on the roof of the cottage for his early morning watch, his eyes trained on me. If I hadn't known exactly where to focus my attention, he would have been nearly invisible. My heart leapt for joy when I saw him despite the fact that he was pointing his little crossbow at my head again. I couldn't quite suppress the nostalgic smile that fought to break across my face.

"Aaron Atticus," I called. "My name is Avelina Silva. You might know me as dog girl?"

I waited, but he didn't respond. What if Zig was right? What if that time I had with Aaron was the only time I'd ever get? What if the normal state of things was for him to hate my guts, and our relationship was just a fluke?

"Uh . . ." I said, channeling Regalinius. "I'm here to bring you to your family?" Why that came out as a question, I couldn't say. The whole thing felt incredibly anticlimactic.

Aaron studied me while I stood there, trembling with anticipation. Finally, after a subjective lifetime, he said, "Prove it."

Prove it? How the hell am I supposed to do that?

I took a breath. "Uh. Okay. Well, about an hour ago, your Evocation disappeared, but your Protection increased dramatically. You can make a shield now and heal yourself and others." I paused, thinking. "You only have one bolt left, and you're almost out of oil.

You were planning to go to Jorin's farm. He's not there, though. He's at the Moore farm helping them with their harvest. He didn't plant this year because Farrah is pregnant and there was no point. Her effect on the weather and the crops while pregnant makes it too unpredictable. You're hiding from Seleca out here, which would normally be a great idea because she thinks you belong to her, except that she found out where your cottage is, so this place isn't safe anymore. Not for you alone, anyway, unless you ascend your Protection. But we need to get to Farrah so we can bring her back to Earth. She's having triplets."

I was rambling now. *Get it together, Silva, this is Aaron. Just Aaron. All you have to do is remind him how much he loves you.*

Aaron remained silent for a few moments, processing what I had just said with narrowed eyes, the way he always did. Finally, he stood. "That proves nothing. You could be lying about Seleca, and I doubt that Farrah is pregnant since they can't get a permit."

I groaned at my own clumsy attempt at persuasion. "Aaron, I'm the one your mother told you about. You've been waiting for me since you were fifteen. I still don't fully understand why, but Violet thought it was necessary. Surely it speaks well of me that Rogue trusts me. He's just behind the . . ." *Crap, he doesn't know Rogue is Ward. That's just going to make him more suspicious.*

Aaron glanced over his shoulder toward the trees where Ward and Zig waited, but I doubted he could see them from where he stood. "You can use your new shield if you don't trust me." *Good save.*

Aaron hesitated but lowered the crossbow. After another moment of contemplation, he put a tentative hand to his chest, made a face like someone had just offered him oysters for the first time, and raised a shield.

His eyes darted all around, presumably to follow the sparks of color swirling around him that I couldn't see from the outside. If I didn't know him so well, I probably would've thought he had no emotional response whatsoever to raising his first shield, but I could see from his posture that he was stunned.

We locked eyes, and I knew I had him. I smiled broadly. "You're welcome," I said smugly.

Aaron lowered the shield briefly to climb down the side of the cottage, then he raised it again and approached me. I could tell that he was nervous from the way he held his chin low while he stared at me. I didn't move as he advanced, and I kept my hands where he could see them, giving him the time that I knew he needed to work through his decision.

I smelled him through his shield, too, so I closed my eyes and inhaled deeply, taking his scent in as he drew closer. My throat burned with the unexpected emotion triggered by his scent. I thought I'd never get to smell it again. And just like that, I was in his room, lounging on his too-big bed, listening to the rain tap on the oculus.

"Why should I believe you?" he asked, bringing me back to the present.

I opened my eyes to see him staring at me with that same penetrating gaze I remembered from the day we met. I wanted so badly to wrap my arms around his solid body and feel him lean down to smell my hair. I needed my damned center back.

I pulled my pack off and dug through it for Violet's book, then I held the book open in front of him so he could see the inside of the back cover. His eyes widened when he saw the photograph of his mother.

"I know you, Aaron," I said, my voice cracking. "I know you well. You're brave and kind, but you have a temper and a tendency to be jealous, not that I blame you in this world of no women. You're a serious person but you appreciate irony, like me, and you can be more lighthearted than you let on. You're organized and meticulous in your habits. You like to think things through and not jump to conclusions or make hasty decisions, but you can if you have to. You're good in an emergency and deadly with a crossbow. You're a good cook. You love to read. You don't like sweets. You're a light sleeper and a blanket hog, but at least you don't snore." *Not too loudly, anyway.*

Aaron stared at me like his eyes could extract the information he needed from my face.

"Your mind doesn't remember me," I said, "but your spirit does. That increase in your Protection reservoir—it came from me."

It really hit me, then, that I had a decision to make. Was I really going to restart this whole thing with him? I could go off with Falon or Zig, and he would never know the difference. There was nothing tying me to him anymore. *Except my love for him.*

I placed a hand on my belly, then released a breath.

Christine.

That was one decision I could never take back. Spirit's face flashed through my mind, then I looked back into Aaron's ice-blue eyes. They reflected the light again, a detail that he'd been missing as a ghost.

Tears tried to form in mine, but I lowered my gaze, swallowing the lump in my throat. I couldn't meet those dazzling eyes right now. It had nearly killed me to see Aaron's ghost, knowing that I had failed him so utterly and that my angry escape to Darion-Ájar had led to his death. Coming back had been the right decision. That, I was sure of. But was winning him back best for him, or was I just being selfish?

I heard Falon in my head, saying that all Aaron and I ever did was fight and have sex, and Spirit and Zig both telling me to be careful. Ward had once said that his reservoirs had been a curse. Maybe that's what I was to Aaron . . . a curse upon his life. He'd wanted to kill me at some point in time, hadn't he? Maybe he was better off without me.

"You're wrong," Aaron said.

I glanced back up, startled. He had taken his shield down and I hadn't even noticed. "What do you mean?"

"My Evocation reservoir isn't completely gone," he said, taking another step toward me. "I can feel your resonance and . . . there are other new ones too."

"Connection," I confirmed, "and a couple others." Resonance is harder to distinguish with lesser reservoirs, but I thought I detected Teleportation and Transformation.

Aaron nodded, capturing my gaze and locking it in place, like he was determined not to let me look away again. "I could feel something had changed. It felt like . . ."

"Déjà vu?" I suggested.

His brow furrowed. "It felt like I walked into a room to do something important but couldn't remember what it was. Then I tried to light the oil lantern and couldn't manage it." He shook his head. "What happened to me?"

I paused to consider my answer, then I sighed. I didn't know what was right, but I knew that I would have to do things differently this time. No more holding back. No secrets.

I pulled out the crystal key. "This is—"

"The Queen's Wicket," Aaron blurted, his eyes focusing on the key.

"Gesundheit," I said. I'm not the brains, I'm telling you. Aaron's eyebrows squeezed together. "Sorry, I mean what did you say?"

"The Queen's Wicket," he repeated. When I gave him an uncomprehending stare, he explained further. "I recognize the hourglass in the head of the key. As you said, I love to read. Meriweather has an illustration of it in his book *Ascension: Twelve Worlds, Twelve Bridges* and theorizes about a Conjuration planet . . ." Aaron's voice trailed off.

"Killmount," I said, surprising even myself.

THE WISDOM OF DISHONOR

Aaron searched my face, then glanced down at the key and back up. He must have made the connection between the key and his memory lapse because he took one final step toward me, coming so close that I could feel his minty breath on my face. "I know you," he whispered.

"Yes."

"And you know me."

"Pretty well," I said, taking a ragged breath to steady myself. It didn't work. His proximity was dizzying.

"So it would seem," he mused, "based on your knowledge of my sleeping habits."

Now or never, I thought, then I smiled, remembering the first time I'd thought that in Aaron's presence. He didn't smile back, but he reached up and grasped my jaw with one hand. It was gentle and secure, a hold that said, "I could hurt you if I wanted to, but I won't because you're mine."

"Show me," he said, a soft demand.

I laid my hand on top of his and tentatively quested out with Connection. His mental wall pulsed like a live wire. It had been strong when I met him and had strengthened considerably when his Protection reservoir expanded from mixing reservoirs with me. Now, it seemed, after his very body had been invaded, it had electrified, daring anyone to try that shit again. Something clicked in my brain when I felt it, because I recognized that fortification. It was the twin to my own.

I closed my eyes for a few heartbeats, then reopened them. If I let myself go there again, would I survive when it ended? Yes, of course I would, but all I had to do was observe Zig to see what the consequence would be.

I don't care, I thought. *As much as it may hurt when it's over, I don't care.*

"May I come in?" I asked.

Aaron blinked a few times and then took a deep breath, exhaled, and let the barrier between us come down enough to give me access.

Maybe I should have been surprised that Aaron, of all people, decided to trust me, a complete stranger from his perspective. I wasn't, though. I'd felt our bond before I even touched him, just like I had the last time we had our "first" meeting. We had something that defied time and space, something I'd felt that first time we slept together in his attic bedroom and dozens of times since.

We were like two rivers running downhill. Our paths had twisted and coiled, even doubling back on themselves at times, but eventually, gravity had its way with us, pulling us together to become one. To be with him was to reach my destination, to create something bigger than myself.

I showed him my memories of our time together, the good and the bad. They rushed into him one after the other, filling his mind with instant knowledge that I knew from experience would feel like recovering from amnesia.

I showed him the first time we met, or at least the first time I remembered meeting him. He had seemed to hate me but then later showed me that his attitude had been the result of his conflicting feelings of resentment, grief, and irresistible attraction. Through our Connection link, he confirmed the presence of those same feelings now, pulling me closer so that my chest touched his.

I showed him how I'd healed him after the dragon attack, how we'd connected so deeply that only me passing out had prevented him from picking me up and carrying me straight to his bed. His soul remembered the feeling of me pressed against him, my scent, my lips, and when that memory reached his mind, he recognized it as truth.

He groaned and then slipped his hand behind my neck, running his fingers into my hair and pressing his forehead to mine. We breathed each other's air as all the memories since that moment flooded his awareness. Our walk to the farm, his mother's book, our fight with Seleca in the woods, the revelation of Ward's secret, his stomach-turning jealousy, our first night together.

A drop of rain hit my forehead and I chuckled. I'd asked myself once why it was always raining when things went to hell, but here was proof that I'd been wrong. The world wasn't out to get me. The world didn't even know I existed. I wasn't some "chosen one" slated to save the universe. I was just Lee: one person with hardly enough mass to attract attention, let alone make the universe spin around me.

I felt Aaron shiver in the chilled air. I'd never known him to do that before, and it seemed to surprise him as much as it did me. The rain picked up, and he pulled me flush against him, soaking up my unnatural heat the way I used to do from him.

Almost as a habit, I pulled up a shield to protect us from the rain. The colorful, flickering fragments appeared within the shield, swirling in loops and spirals. I had been expecting seven colors for my seven reservoirs—aqua, green, blood red, magenta, vermilion flame, molten gold, and the neon yellow of Teleportation. What I got was very different. Aaron's eyes widened as he beheld the inside of my shield, which now lit up with all twelve fragments.

What the...

A new chartreuse fragment seemed to stick to the other fragments, gooping them together, then dripping and splashing straight toward the ground. That one was Production. A bright orange color moved against the current of the other swirling fragments—Transmutation. Three cooler colors, purple, cobalt blue, and indigo, now added a depth to a full rainbow. I had the whole set.

Seleca, I thought, my breath catching as I took in the jaw-dropping kaleidoscope. I had pushed Absorption into her while trying to break her Projection trance, hoping that it might result in gathering enough Precognition to remember my past timelines. It hadn't worked—I didn't remember anything new, and I felt no different. But Absorption has a mind of its own, and if you're not careful, you can accidentally suck the life right out of someone. Somehow, during Seleca's little walk down memory lane, I'd absorbed a tiny bit of all her reservoirs. I hoped to hell that it didn't mean I'd absorbed some of her soul too. I was already crazy enough.

"You don't snore, either, Lee," he said. I lifted my eyes to meet Aaron's. He watched me intently, squinting as if to see me more clearly.

"What?" I asked, taken aback by the abrupt non sequitur, then I grasped what he implied. I couldn't have given him a memory of me sleeping.

I froze, my whole attention on his face, and in that stillness, I detected a resonance so faint that I wouldn't have sensed it if I hadn't been searching for it. Precognition. I loved him so much that it only took one touch for us to begin mixing reservoirs. "You remember?" I asked breathlessly.

He paused, then shook his head. "Not exactly. It's more like I *know*." Slowly, he leaned forward until his lips brushed lightly against mine.

I closed my eyes and pressed into him, giving him clear consent to proceed. A near-subsonic rumble arose from his chest before he let go of his restraint, crashing his lips to mine and sinking his tongue into my mouth. I accepted it without hesitation, starving for the kiss that I'd taken for granted and thought I'd lost forever. If a touch alone let us mix reservoirs, then this was like throwing them in a blender and hitting max.

Everything I was surged into him and he into me, creating a Connection link so deep that we were as one person. He knew what I knew and remembered what I remembered.

He recognized it all, those months in the farmhouse, how he showed me his library and taught me how to cook and how to use a crossbow, how he helped me practice fragmentation and told me about his family.

He saw the fight with Axel, Ward's recapture, the crew, Jorin's boat, the encounter with the mountain bear, and his fear that he'd lose me to Zig. He relived my reunion with my parents at Gran's house and knew they were *his* family, a revelation that changed everything I'd believed about myself and my origins. He became aware of my time with Falon—all of it—and what Falon told me about bonding.

Finally, he saw what I'd learned about my past, and about his own past. I had been the bad guy, and maybe so had he. Neither of us were who we thought, but by some miracle, I'd been given the Queen's fragging Wicket, the most idiotically named artifact ever created, and the key to literal time.

So, I made a choice. And my choice was Aaron.

He picked me up in his arms and carried me toward his front door, the memories still pouring in, inundating us both. *You're the only one I can trust,* he remembered saying now, could almost remember feeling. He fumbled with the doorknob, then kneed the door open. *You didn't break your promise,* he thought. *You came back. You saved me from death and came back.*

I'll never leave you again. I swear, I thought, tears spilling onto my cheeks.

Then the memory of feeling Christine's resonance hit Aaron, and his steps faltered. *Oh,* he thought. *Oh.*

She had been unexpected but not unwanted. He set me down on my feet just inside the cottage and pulled away to stare at my face. He looked shocked, tense in a way that I had never seen before.

"I'm sorry," I said. "I'm so sorry. I'm sorry." I was sobbing now.

"Shh," he cooed, brushing my tears away. "I'm sorry too." He pulled me back to him, wrapping his arms around me. I buried my face in his chest, relieved that he felt comfortable enough to embrace me.

"Why are *you* sorry?" I asked.

"I'm sorry I didn't better explain what bonding is. I should have known that you would think it's a purchase. That's what it is for many who live in Neesee, so close to the Ministry's seat of power, but what you must understand is that it wasn't like that for my family. My parents were in love. They still are, from what I've gathered. And though

Jorin and Clare never showed affection in public, it was obvious they were devoted to each other. They were never apart a single day. Wherever Jorin went, Clare followed, be it Neesee or the Moore farm or on seed-buying trips with the caravanners over the Gales. When Clare died, Jorin wanted to follow *her*, but he couldn't because he had to take care of me. Anyway, that's what bonding is to me. It's a partnership."

Even as relief at Aaron's explanation coursed through me, I berated myself for having assumed the worst of him. I, of all people, should have known that Marti would never agree to be anyone's property. What a fool I'd been for giving in to Falon's request when what I should have done was go straight back to Aaron to demand an explanation. It had only taken a few minutes of clear communication for us to work it out. We wouldn't be completely back to where we were without greater Precognition, but he was my Aaron again—my center.

"This was all a lot to process," he said, "but I think I understand how we got to where we ended up. You blame yourself for everything, but you shouldn't. Zig was right. None of us ever do it alone. The good or the bad. There's only one thing that I regret."

Christine. I tensed in anticipation of the difficult conversation and prepared to explain my need to save not only him but also Spirit and the others.

"I can't believe I broke the seal and didn't remember it."

I raised my eyes to his, frowning. "Broke the what?"

One corner of his mouth tugged up. "The seal. You know, my first *time*? It looked incredible, and then it all got erased like it never happened."

Oh.

Yes, it never happened. Thus, no baby. My chest squeezed at the thought, but Aaron wasn't upset about losing a baby he'd never met. I supposed it made sense. But even though I was relieved he wasn't angry with me, it still felt like a knife to the heart. I had never met Christine, either, but it felt like I had. I missed her like I had known and loved her for years—to the point that I could almost remember her face. I knew, somewhere inside me, that I had loved her fiercely in another life.

Christine.

Aaron bent down and brushed his lips to that sensitive spot behind my ear, pulling me out of my reverie. He inhaled my scent and whispered, "I recognized you the moment I saw you, but I didn't know why. I think that probably happened in our last life too. I never want that to happen again, Lee. Let's get it right this time." He took my face in his hands and stared straight into my eyes.

Mine, he thought resolutely, then he kicked the door closed.

Epilogue

*S*yndeth *looked astonishingly different in his new form, but Linorra would have recognized those dragon eyes anywhere. She could see now that they shone only for her.*
"*I would take any part of you,*" *said Syndeth,* "*and I would not regret a minute of it.*"

Aaron

"Well, here we are again," Lee said, glancing around the inside of Uncle Jorin's farmhouse. Zig stood beside her in the entryway. "I've always loved this house," he said.

"You've been here?" I asked.

"Of course! I helped your grandfather build it." Lee looked at Zig quizzically, displaying that small smile she always had when focused on him. "Who do you think gave him that oculus in the attic?" he continued. "That beauty came straight from Rome, I'll have you know, and it's older than I am. Of course, I transformed it to fit the domed glass, but it's otherwise in pristine condition."

Lee's eyebrows lifted practically through her hairline, then she laughed. "Of course, it is. Just like you. May I offer you some port, my geriatric friend?"

Zig wrinkled his nose. "I'm a stout drinker myself, though I once heard a brilliant man say that wine is pleasure reduced to mathematics."

I was relieved to see Lee as confused as I was by Zig's comment. I'd never heard of port or stout, but I guessed them to be another variety of Earth alcohol, like the Harvest Festival wine I used to sneak into my dorm when I was fourteen. In any case, the idea that Zig could have a conversation with Lee that I didn't fully understand was unsettling. I didn't trust him, no matter how much she seemed to.

"Do you think Seleca will come here to attack us?" Lee asked. With Ward a dead weight in my arms, I cut between her and Zig in a not-so-subtle effort to separate them. Despite my renewed anger over Ward's betrayal, I'd helped dress him in one of my tunics and then carried him through the bridge Lee had made with the key, straight to Jorin's personal bridgestone overlooking the sea.

I'd always called that bridgestone the "sight boulder" and used it to get up high to see farther out. I'd recognized the telltale *X* marked into the stone, but no one had ever used it in living memory. Not even Jorin knew it still worked. Axel had always taken a plant or a fresh scoop of dirt from the property to use as a skipstone when teleporting in to harass Terik and Farrah.

Zig shrugged, eyeing me cautiously. "I doubt Seleca will come at all. Even if she were able to find a healer quickly, knew you were here, and happened to have a fresh, usable skipstone to come after you, she knows I've taken an interest now and will think twice about showing up."

"You *are* terrifying." Lee laughed. "Especially in that pirate hat of yours." Zig smirked at her, then leaned in like he might whisper, but he didn't. He just stared at her, wagging his eyebrows up and down.

Ascendant connector, I concluded, a presumption supported by his intense resonance. *He's sending thoughts to her through the air.*

Lee chuckled again, then playfully slapped his arm. No, I didn't like him at all.

"So, what's the plan?" she asked, turning to me. I concealed the immense gratification I felt that she came to me for the plan and not Zig.

I had never believed in love at first sight, but when Lee showed up at my cottage in the woods, I was instantly converted. Her face, as pale and lovely as the goddess moon Heshia, showed so much more than she realized. When she gazed at me, I saw adoration shining in her eyes that I didn't deserve but was too selfish to turn away from.

The openness and vulnerability she'd shown in the first moments of our reunion had stunned me, and it had been all I could do not to leap off that rooftop and run to her. Instead, I'd pretended suspicion, listening with some guilt as she fumbled adorably through her attempt to convince me that we'd already met. I can't explain to you why I trusted her right away, but I did. Against all reason, I'd taken my shield down and reached for her. I'd just met her and already I needed her more than air.

That need surged in me now, sinking through my body on its way to my groin. I plunked Ward down indelicately on the green couch so I could go to her, then I wrapped my arms around her, pulling her close. She was so small and warm, and she smelled like a blend of garden herbs that I couldn't identify.

She made that short little grunting noise she makes when I hug her, and before I could stop myself, I imagined myself plunging deep into that savory heat over and over. *Soon*, I thought, then I glanced up to see Zig watching us closely. The bastard had banged on my cottage door the moment I'd gotten Lee in there and had been cockblocking me ever since.

"We'll stay here one night," I said, clearing my throat. "Then we'll hike down to the Moore farm in the morning since there aren't any bridgestones down there. Should take a half day at most."

"Good," Lee said. "I can't stomach the idea of ascending again right now, and that's what will happen the moment we get on a bridge to Earth. But Farrah should see a doctor as soon as possible for those babies." She smirked at my confused expression. "A healer. We can take them to one on Earth. Then, I suppose, we should go to your parents."

My parents, I thought. I'd dreamed of finding my way back to them in the early days. I'd thought it would be like finding my way back to safety, but that had never been anything more than a child's fantasy. That home I'd depended on for the first fifteen years of my life was gone. My mother had seen to that. Still, I would feel like I'd left an important task unfinished if I didn't go back. That's what seeing my parents was now—an item to check off my list.

Zig watched our interaction like a wolf waiting to pounce. In the flood of memories Lee had shared with me, I saw that we'd had several disagreements about her friendship with Ward. Begrudgingly, I'd resolved not to further press her on the issue, but Zig was another story. I'd have to be careful not to give the impression that I was trying to control her, but I'd lost her once, maybe more than once. I'd only let that happen again on one condition. Over my dead body.

"I'm exhausted," she groaned. "I really need to sleep." She didn't wait for me to agree but pulled away and headed for the stairs toward my bedroom. I'd never seen a woman in pants before, let alone ones so tight. I could see the defined muscles of her perfect backside working as she took the stairs two at a time, hopping with the easy grace of a silken goat. Zig and I both watched her leave, then focused on each other.

"So," Zig said, the smile dropping from his face, "you think it's your turn, eh?"

"My turn to what?" I asked with a sigh. I walked to a wooden chest behind the couch, pulled out an oardoo-feather blanket for Ward, and laid it over him, trying to sort out what had happened in the last few hours. My memories were a jumble of confused bits and pieces, but one thing was clear: I loved her. I think I had loved her for a long time. It just hadn't been sequential time.

Zig gave me a level look. "Your turn to *have* her, to be with her. You may not remember, but it's what you've wanted for a long time, no matter how much you professed to hate her. I can understand why Seleca hates her so much, but not you. Never you."

"Seleca has no reason to hate her," I said, turning away from Zig to fiddle with the chimney flue. It needed to be opened if we were to cook anything. Jorin had the flue rigged to a lever, but it liked to stick when not used for several days, which it hadn't, if the musty smell in the house was any indicator.

"Oh, she does indeed. Your eagerness to fall right back into Lina's arms is reason enough."

I jiggled the flue handle, taking the opportunity to construct my response to Zig. Lee had shown me her own memories of our time together, and I had integrated them so thoroughly that they almost felt like my own experiences, but they really weren't. I didn't know what manner of relationship I'd had with Seleca, if any, but I couldn't imagine that our association had held a candle to the attachment I had to Lee.

"I bet you wish you could remember all the times you had with her, not just the ones that she remembers. Am I right?"

This man never stops talking, I thought, then I glanced back at him. He'd seated himself in one of the cushioned chairs next to a large window, casually hooking his fingers behind his neck and crossing one ankle over the other, a knowing smile on his face.

"Of course," I said disinterestedly, as if his calculating mind didn't unsettle me. I needed to get this snake out of my house before his presence became a more infuriating version of Lee's friendship with Ward. At least Ward had Lee's best interest at heart, and he never directly challenged me in my own house like this smug prick.

"I can help you with that. Let me give you Precognition. That way, you won't have to rely on Lina's memory of what happened. You know that her perspective colors the truth." When I turned to him with a sour expression, he backtracked. "Not that she's purposely deceiving you. It's just that she's human. And a woman. Her recollection of the events isn't going to necessarily match the one you would have with your own memories back. Don't you want to know the truth?"

I schooled my expression. "I thought you needed Conjuration to give someone a reservoir. Unless you're planning to fall in love with me so we can mix reservoirs." *Rhoya forbid.*

Zig pursed his lips, perhaps considering the possibility, then he shrugged. Maybe he thought if I remembered why I'd hated her, those feelings would return. I thought back to what Lee had shown me of myself as a ghost. I had seemed confused, she said. I had told her that sometimes it was better to break a promise than keep it, no matter how dishonorable, like sometimes doing the right thing meant doing the wrong thing.

"Lina told you that it requires Conjuration, but she is a novice. There is always more than one way to do things, and I'm . . . well, let's just say I've been around the block a few times."

"And what do you want in return?"

"Oh, I don't know. Nothing right now. I'm just doing this to help our girl. She's my . . . friend."

I narrowed my eyes at him, the use of "our girl" not lost on me. "I'll consider it. Thank you for the offer. Will you be staying here?" It was as subtle a dismissal as I could manage.

"It would make an effective deterrent against any attack from Seleca or the Ministry, wouldn't you agree?"

Reluctantly, I nodded once. His presence was indeed a threat in and of itself, but a threat to whom? "Take Terik's room," I said. "I'll show you." I'd lock the trap door to the attic, not that it would make a difference with this monster.

"I can find my way. To the left, yes?" he asked, again giving me that troubling feeling that he knew things he shouldn't. I nodded again, then watched him disappear up the stairs. I listened for the sound of Terik's door, which squeaked in a particular way when opened. I heard the *squeak*, then the door softly closing.

"Don't do it," Ward mumbled.

I started, having forgotten he was there, then I peered over the back of the couch to see him stretched out, his eyes still closed. "Don't do what?"

"Anything that guy wants you to do. I wouldn't trust him to screw in a light bulb let alone tinker with my reservoirs."

I sighed, again disturbed by my lack of familiarity with Earth terms. I could only guess that a light bulb was similar to the glass globe of an oil lantern. Nevertheless, I understood his meaning and emphatically agreed with it.

Ward shifted onto his side, bending his knees to get comfortable. "Thanks for the blanket," he murmured, then he quickly fell back into deep, rhythmic breathing.

Ward was right about Zig. That man was a menace, but I needed to get *all* my memories back, and my Precognition reservoir wasn't great enough to remember other timelines.

I remembered my mother dealing with Precognition when I was a child, and the migraines she suffered as a result could be debilitating. It would not be easy, but I'd deal with the pain if gaining that knowledge would give me back the time I'd lost with Lee.

Additionally, it might help protect her from the Ministry. Anick might have had a setback, but he wasn't gone, and neither was Seleca. I didn't know what interest Zig had in "our girl," but I was certain it wasn't a passing one. Men don't look at women like that when they want to be friends. I just hoped that Zig's goal was to simply win Lee out from under me and not something more sinister. The former, I was confident, had become unlikely while the latter remained possible.

It didn't matter that I'd technically just met her. Lee was mine. Even she had finally agreed that was true. I'd had to die, come back to life, then literally forget she existed for her to realize it, but she got it now. If Zig had some nefarious plan in mind for her, he'd have to go through me to do it.

Lee, I thought, heat flushing my face. *What the hell am I doing down here when she's up there? Food can wait.* I turned away from Ward and headed up the stairs toward a future I'd anticipated for more than one lifetime. This time, I'd make it stick, no matter the cost.

THANK YOU FOR READING!

I depend on reviews from readers like you. If you enjoyed this book, it would mean the world to me if you left a review on Amazon, Goodreads, or the platform of your choice. To authors, leaving a review is like leaving a tip. It's what makes all this work worthwhile!

ADVANCED REVIEW COPIES (ARCs)

Readers who leave reviews for previous books are my first choice to receive advance copies of future novels. If you're interested in receiving future ARCs, email lebrooks@brooksbooks.net, or sign up for my newsletter.

LET'S CONNECT!

Sign up for my newsletter and I'll send you the first chapter of *Time Beyond the Trees*, the third book in The Cult of Anick series, due out in 2025. I also like to send out updates on new releases, interviews, and book signings. Unsubscribe at any time. www.brooksbooks.net/newsletter or scan this QR code:

ACKNOWLEDGMENTS

Thank you so much to my dad, Bill, who facilitated the success of my first book in a way I could not have predicted. You know what you did.

Thank you to my friends and beta readers, whose encouragement keeps me going, and especially to my own little book club. You ladies are the only ones who ever see me drunk and yet miraculously still seem to like me. You make my heart happy.

Thanks again to my sister and alpha reader, Jennifer. I really need you to tell me when things don't make sense because if *you* don't understand something, then pretty much no one will. But no, my characters will not stop using foul language. However, you may like Anick's chapter in the next book as he feels the same way about swearing as you.

Thank you to my ducklings, who continue to not kill me even though I spend a *lot* of my free time writing, and who give me great "business" advice. I wouldn't be me without you, kids. I love you so much.

Thanks to my amazing editors, Becky Wallace, Jennifer Cappello, and Laura La Tulipe. I have come to depend on your insight, enthusiasm, and cringe removal services. Avelina and I are so lucky to have you!

Thank you once again to Rebecca Frank for lending me your endless talent in the form of cover art (and for putting up with me—please don't fire me), and to Leo Hartas for your illustrations (and sense of humor).

Also, a big thank you to Heidi Cox-London, who agreed to be my cover model again. Cuz who wouldn't want you on the front of their book? Crazy people, that's what.

ABOUT THE AUTHOR

L. E. Brooks (Lauren) has been writing songs, poetry, and short stories since the days when she still looked like this picture (apparently way back when the "Rachel" was in style). She is the author of two romantasy novels published under the name L. E. Brooks, with another contemporary fiction novel (nonfantasy) forthcoming under the name Lauren Brooks. She lives in the Midwest with her husband, two kids, and a ferocious pack of hell hounds.

Made in the USA
Middletown, DE
09 February 2025